LOVE IN UNLIKELY PLACES

AN AMISH ROMANCE

LINDA BYLER

New York, New York

LOVE IN UNLIKELY PLACES

Good Books books may be purchased in bulk at special discounts for sales promotion, corporate gifts, fund-raising, or educational purposes. Special editions can also be created to specifications. For details, contact the Special Sales Department, Good Books, 307 West 36th Street, 11th Floor, New York, NY 10018 or info@skyhorsepublishing.com.

Good Books is an imprint of Skyhorse Publishing, Inc., a Delaware corporation.

Visit our website at www.goodbooks.com.

10 9 8 7 6 5 4

Library of Congress Cataloging-in-Publication Data is available on file.

ISBN: 978-1-68099-601-2
eBook ISBN: 978-1-68099-637-1

Cover design by Koechel Peterson

Printed in the United States of America

TABLE OF
CONTENTS

CHAPTER 1

SHE SAT AT HER DESK, A WEARY SLUMP TO HER SLIM SHOULDERS, AND brushed back a strand of auburn hair. She stared unseeingly out of the schoolhouse window.

It was over.

It was the last day of her tenth year of teaching school in the one-room schoolhouse nestled in a grove of pines in Hickory Hollow. She had taught there every school year and spent summers working in her father's produce fields.

But last month she had told the schoolboard no, she would not be teaching the following year. Her announcement was met with groans of protest and the promise of a substantial pay raise. One of the men went so far as to say they could not get along without her, wrapping her efficiently into an itchy blanket of guilt.

But she was sick of teaching school. She'd never understood the term "burnt out," till now. All her enthusiasm had slowly leaked away in the past year, and though she felt a small sense of relief in having given her resignation, that was no match for the guilt and indecision that now plagued her. Not only had she disappointed the school board and her students, but she had no clear idea of what she was to do next.

At twenty-six years of age, she had to accept that she may be single for the rest of her life. The best ten years for being chosen by a suitable man were already in the past. The hope of getting to be a wife and mother, every young Amish woman's dream, was quickly evaporating into a dense fog that hung over her whole existence.

"Mysterious," they called her. You couldn't figure out Emma Beiler's intentions. She'd had plenty of chances, more than a few nervous young men asking if she'd begin a friendship with them. "Picky," the women said to each other at quilting parties that Emma didn't attend. She was too picky. She read too many romance novels, building up expectations as high as the clouds and as untrustworthy as sunshine on a March morning.

Emma leaned back in her chair, propped her feet on an open drawer, surveyed the bare walls of her classroom, and sighed. She supposed she'd spend the summer as she always had, the work in the fields interspersed with housework, laundry, and yard and garden maintenance. She had always enjoyed working in the produce fields, the sun hot on her back, her body young and strong and capable, her father's praise and her siblings' camaraderie satisfying and familiar.

But now she wanted more. Something different. She wondered if that made her greedy, selfish. She had always been taught to be content with what she had, to be grateful and not complain.

She leaned forward, her feet hitting the floor with a dull thump that echoed through the empty classroom. Reaching out, she gathered a pile of artwork with blue sticky tack marks on every corner and absentmindedly riffled through them.

Here was Ida's horse, done all in pencil. She was a serious budding artist at ten years of age. The girl was gifted, for sure, but what was the use in furthering her education? She'd never be an artist, in a real sense. After eighth grade she'd attend vocational class, then go through *rumschpringa*, and then, if God wills, she'd become a wife and mother. Oh, she'd draw a horse for her children, and they'd be amazed at her ability, clamor around her and beg for more. If she's lucky, her husband would admire her skill. But she'd never receive professional art training, never exhibit her artwork, sell it to wealthy couples to hang on their walls. Perhaps it was a blessing that Ida didn't know how good she was, that she had the talent to go far. She didn't need to know what she was missing out on.

Emma sighed again, then gathered up the artwork and shoved it into a folder, snapped it shut decidedly, and got to her feet.

It was over, she assured herself for the hundredth time.

She had to be firm with the men on the schoolboard, firm with herself and her long awaited decision. She needed a change. It felt like her life depended on it as much as it depended on the ability to breathe.

But she was crying as she turned the key in the lock for the last time. She wept for the bygone days when her youthful innocence had carried her along on waves of enthusiasm, met challenges like a warrior, knocking down hurdles with the sword of her calling. She'd been convinced she would grow old in the classroom, the intensity of her days never waning.

She picked up a plastic tote stuffed with papers and books and carried it down the steps to the waiting horse and carriage. The white horse shed stood in stark contrast to the dark of the pine woods. The blue skies of May were a lovely benediction that lent beautiful color to the scene.

Hickory Hollow School, smack in the middle of a pine woods; the irony of it always made her smile.

"Whoa, Trixie. Hold still now."

Trixie began prancing the minute he heard her walk toward the carriage, the blinders on her bridle preventing a good look until she turned her head, as if to remind Emma she'd been taking too long, leaving her tied at the hitching rail.

She lifted the hatch on the back, tilted the seat, and placed the tote inside, then returned for more items that had accumulated over the years. She had packed them all into plastic totes that were organized, labeled, and ready to be stored in the attic of the farmhouse at home.

She untied Trixie, fastened the rein to the hook on top, and gathered the driving reins. Then she hopped into the buggy and drew back steadily, watching carefully as Trixie leaned into the leather britchment, backing the carriage away from the hitching rack, turning to the left before tugging eagerly on the bit.

Leaning forward, Emma pulled back on the reins and watched for traffic both ways before allowing Trixie to begin her easy trot on to the macadam road. The last ride home from school brought a fresh wave of emotion that caught her unprepared as the warm breeze wafted through the open window.

Was she ready to embrace change?

She didn't know, so she allowed the tears to course down her tanned, lightly freckled cheeks until she sniffed, blew her nose on a crumpled Kleenex she extracted from the small door built into the oak dash, and took a deep cleansing breath. She inhaled the scent of new growth, moist earth, and huge deciduous trees that flanked the road on either side.

The countryside was sparsely populated, the woods and fields of Crawford County, Pennsylvania, only dotted occasionally with small homes, lots containing mobile homes with older cars and muddy pickup trucks parked in gravel driveways. The Amish had moved into the area in the nineties and established productive farms by building new dairy barns and applying the traditional work ethic taught by their forefathers. When milk prices fell, they added workshops or dog kennels, making ends meet by other methods of profit, and as the years went by, the farms prospered, the fields producing bumper crops of corn and hay, vegetables and soybeans.

They tilled the soil with six horse hitches, keeping the old ways as much as possible and living their lives according to each man's conscience and ability. The small tight-knit community flourished in time, with six different church districts that neatly kept twenty to thirty families in each one, a distance of twenty-five miles containing these designated districts in smaller groups living in a five or six mile radius.

The Crawford County settlement was known as a place to purchase farms well below the exorbitant fee paid in Lancaster County, but there was always the consideration of taking wives away from parents, friends, and siblings. Without their own vehicles, the cost of traveling to and from the homes in Lancaster was considerable, and had to be taken into account.

Emma had been four years old when her parents decided to strike out and help build the budding community, so this was her home. She had only faint memories of her first home in Lancaster and had no reason to want to return the way her mother used to. The oldest in the family, Emma could remember the times her mother cried discreet tears of homesickness that never failed to strike a numbing fear in her little girl's heart. It was especially hard on her mam when there was a new baby, of which there were nine.

Now, two of Emma's sisters had already married and gone off to establish homes of their own with young ambitious husbands. Sam King had started his courtship of her sister Esther when she was barely sixteen years old. He swept her straight off her feet and carried her along on the proverbial whirlwind until she was married with stars in her eyes and a smile that stretched across the width of her face and then some.

It was the story of Emma's life. Though she kept it quiet, she had felt drawn to Sam King the day she met him and hoped he might ask her for a buggy ride. But he hadn't, and instead snatched up her younger sister the moment she entered rumschpringa. But that's how it went. The young men that actually intrigued Emma were the ones who showed interest in someone else. Someone like her sister—quiet, sweet, and without a creditable opinion in her pretty head.

Ruth was a carbon copy of Esther, although she had a few flings with guys who didn't qualify, in Emma's opinion. Ruth was eighteen by the time Emanuel Lapp asked her to go skating one Friday night in January. He twirled and looped his way into her heart with his acrobatic stunts, his gray beanie making him look like a sea turtle with big light brown eyes framed by heavy lashes and roofed by his black unibrow. He was quite dashing, though, and looked the part of a handsome groom on his wedding day, his jet black hair contrasting his snowy white shirt, his black bow tie crisp and straight. It was a perfect wedding. The bouquet of red roses with the wedding gifts was immense and her mother's mouth had loosened as she struggled with her emotions, sniffed, and gave up to extract a lacy handkerchief to blow her nose, in the end.

Emma was happy for Ruth. Those sea turtle eyes didn't appeal to Emma, but she was glad Ruth had accepted him, and they got along swimmingly. No pun intended, of course.

Sam King was another story altogether. He'd returned from Alaska, blown in from the north one winter day to stay with his brother and his brother's wife before going home to Lancaster County. Tall, husky, with rugged good looks and an "English" haircut, a nonchalant, loose-limbed walk, and eyes that were far too experienced and intelligent for an Amish youth. Emma felt the first flutter of attraction within seconds and was quickly blown away by the cruel attack of love. She endured that weekend caught firmly in a grip that rendered her ecstatic one moment and miserable the next. When he left for Lancaster she spent an absentminded week in school hoping he'd return.

And he did return, two weeks later.

The hymn singing on that Sunday evening was still excruciating to think about. She had tried hard, through the years, to place a mental block so she didn't have to think about it.

Why now?

Why did her own thoughts assault her so suddenly in the middle of a bright May morning with the sound of gaily trotting hooves and the crunch of steel wheels on macadam lending wings to her spirit after the goodbye to her schoolhouse?

He was her brother-in-law. Her sister's husband. The pain had long diminished, melted away by the heat of her fiery pride and resolve.

But he had noticed her first. He had smiled his slow, easy smile in his lopsided manner, his eyes kindled by the fire in hers. It had been there, whatever *it* was. She'd been dressed in her lime-green dress, the one that brought out the green in her eyes, produced lights from the waves in her auburn hair. She knew her own attraction. Knew it well, in fact. Confident, unashamed, they both barely sang a chorus, but carried on a full-fledged flirtation that would have been shameful by her mother's standards. She had picked a strategic point to be caught easily, and he found her. He leaned up against the wall of the barn and asked her questions, laughed with her.

Finally, after four years of rumschpringa, she had found her prince. Alaska! What adventure. What daring it took to break away from the traditions expected of him. They would return after they were married. She saw their lives together unfolding in her mind's eye—they would travel, explore, share ideas, fill their days with laughter and intellectual discussions.

When he brought the conversation to a close and wandered off, she felt the smile slide from her face, shivered as the loss extinguished the flame. It was far too long before she found him, deep in conversation with her sister.

He never left Esther's side, and she never left his.

They were married after barely a year. Her mother muttered something about the cradle being robbed, but gamely sewed wedding clothes, hosted quilting bees to finish off the three quilts, and filled the cedar hope chest with bed sheets, towels, and table linens.

And Emma was part of the bridal party, seated with his distant cousin who was dull, overweight, and dating a girl from Bowmansville.

Over time, Emma's heart was mended by a growing patchwork of bitterness that clouded her view of any other potential suitor. She threw all her energy into her school, the merciful days spent in the company of innocent children and the monumental task of instilling wisdom into their bright heads. The years accumulated, and to her surprise, Sam evolved into nothing more than a brother-in-law, one who held no romantic intrigue, so thoroughly was he devoted to her sister Esther. She spent countless weekends at their house playing card games, sleeping in the guest room, making breakfast, caring for their first newborn baby when he arrived.

They remained close, Esther and she. They shared everything, poured out the contents of their hearts for each other's examination, analyzed every given situation before giving it back. And for this, Emma was glad.

Ruth tried her hand at finding a husband for Emma, but was always met with the same flap of dismissal from Emma's slender fingers.

"No, not him. He's much too young. How could I ever think of marrying someone five years younger?"

Every eligible male was too young, too old, too stupid, or too whatever else in Emma's mind. Her sisters gave up, deciding perhaps she was being called to a life of singleness after all.

When Emma reached Rocky Road she tugged lightly on the right rein and applied the brakes for the descent down the winding road across Pebble Ride. Her home was situated just below this picturesque hill in a wide valley called Williams Valley, named after William Penn, the founder of Pennsylvania. At least it made more sense than naming a school Hickory Hollow in a stand of pine trees.

The house was covered in gray siding, and the porch pillars were white, as was the wide trim encasing the windows. It was a remodeled farmhouse, squat and wide and two storied, with the usual array of flowers and shrubs, trees, and a newly tilled garden that showed thin lines of freshly planted onions, carrots, radishes, and peas. The barn was red, and appeared as scenic as a photograph on the calendars at the local feed mill. Squares of white board fence separated the barnyard and horse pasture from the domain of the black and white Holsteins, those pedigreed milk producers whose tongues slashed at the heavy new growth in the sloping pastures that led to the base of the ridge.

Hmm, Emma thought, seeing two buggies parked by the implement shed. *Esther and Ruth?*

It was midmorning, and she was starved. She was thinking of yeast rolls and bacon with scrambled eggs. Maybe biscuits and sausage gravy.

As Trixie drew the carriage past the house, the door was flung open and an arm flapped in her direction. Ruth cupped her hands around her mouth and called out, but Emma could not comprehend a word, so she waved back and hurried to unhitch, water, and feed her horse before carrying the first tote into the side door, where she dropped it onto the washhouse floor.

"Hey Emma! Need help?"

"You can. I have two more."

Both sisters appeared at the door, smiles on their pretty faces, dressed in blue and green with black bib aprons and neat heart-shaped white coverings.

They slid their feet into someone's Crocs and hurried after her, catching her shoulder, saying, "How are you? Haven't seen you in some time. *Vie bisht?*"

Emma laughed. "Fine. I'm fine. Last day of the last year of school teaching. I am so done with it."

"Are you serious? Is this for real?"

Esther's dark eyes were filled with concern, the genuine caring she always displayed for her older sister.

"Yes. I am serious. I'm not going back."

Ruth reached for a tote, yanked, and groaned.

"What do you have in here?"

"Stuff. Ten years of stuff."

"Ten years, Emma? Are you really twenty-six?"

"I am Crawford County's first old maid. Singleton. Single lady, right here."

Her sisters' laughs rang into the clear bright morning and Emma felt a weight lifting from her shoulders. Everything would work out, one way or another.

The totes deposited into the washhouse, the sisters slid off shoes and entered the kitchen, talking and laughing, the room bright and airy with spring sunshine, the chatter of little people, babies fussing on highchairs, her mother's face flushed and happy as she hurried to heat the sausage gravy and break a few eggs into a pan on the stove.

"Hey, Titus!"

Emma bent to pick up her oldest nephew. Sam and Esther's three-year-old, Titus, was a robust, curly-haired boy with a ruddy complexion. He worshipped his Aunt Emma.

"Hey . . . hey . . . look. Watch!"

He wriggled, slammed his feet into her sides till she released him and stood back to watch him execute a cartwheel of sorts, albeit a wobbly, dangerous-looking one.

"Wow!" Emma clapped her hands. "Good job, T."

He closed his eyes slightly, then rushed over and hugged her legs. She bent to pick him up, kissed his round cheek, which he immediately swabbed with the back of his hand, his eyes laughing into hers.

"Hey! No wiping off kisses. I'll have to give you another one."

She bent to greet Emily, Ruth and Emanuel's two-year-old, who stood patiently waiting her turn for her Aunt Emma's attention. A shy, thin child with blond hair pulled into a ponytail on each side of her head, she held up two fingers before Emma grabbed her.

"Look, Aunt Emma. I'm two. Two fingers."

"Yes, you are two. Big girl. Soon you'll be washing dishes, right?"

Emily nodded and placed two small hands on either side of Emma's face, a serious concentrated look in her eyes. Then she placed a kiss on the tip of Emma's nose, giggling with a tinkling sound.

"Aw, Emily you little sweetie. I love you so much."

Emma crushed Emily to her chest until the little girl grunted.

"You must be doing something right, raising these lovable little ones. You wouldn't believe how they brighten my day."

"Here are your eggs."

Her mother placed a Corelle plate with two perfectly fried eggs in the middle, followed by the pan of heated sausage gravy. She brought the reheated toast and a glass of juice, her rounded figure moving with ease from stove to table, the same route she had taken hundreds of thousands of times through the years. Then she returned to the stove to flip the sizzling pancakes.

"Thanks, Mam. I am starved."

Emma spread softened butter on homemade toasted bread, followed by a heaping spoonful of raspberry jam. There was no delicate partaking of food at that point, so she lowered her head and enjoyed large bites for the first few moments before sitting back with a wide grin.

"Mm-mm. Nothing better, Mam. Your sausage gravy should be nationally famous. Better than Bob Evans."

"Oh, now come on."

Her mother's pleasantly wide face was shining with the praise, her green eyes snapping behind her rimless eyeglasses. A compliment was not easily received, but brushed off lest one become *grosfeelich*.

Emma liberally buttered two pancakes, upended the maple syrup and drenched them before cutting a portion with the side of her fork.

"Where's Abram and Steven?" Esther asked, lifting her coffee cup to her lips.

"They're both working for Henry Zook on the construction crew," her mother answered.

"What? When did that happen? I never thought Dat would allow it. Who's going to help with the produce? Emma?"

Oh boy. Here it comes, Emma thought.

She ate bite after bite of her pancake, her eyes downcast, suddenly deciding the business of keeping her eyes at pancake level was best.

"Are you, Emma?" Esther asked.

"Am I what?"

"Going to help with the produce?"

"Probably not."

Her mother's face turned toward her, a shocked expression emerging as Emma's words assaulted her.

"But . . . Emma. Dat is counting on you and Dena."

"I know."

The words were forced from compressed lips.

"Emma, whatever. You're acting strangely. Look at us." Ruth was moving a spoonful of sausage gravy toward fussy little Owen's mouth.

Emma lifted her eyes, sat back against the chair, crossed her arms around her waist and nodded. She took a steadying breath and then launched in to the explanation she knew she'd have to give eventually.

"Okay. This is hard. Mam, I know this will not be easy for you or Dat, but I have come to a decision. I need to expand my horizons, get off the farm, away from the teaching. I know I am no longer the teacher I used to be, mostly on account of being sick and tired of it. I need to go out into the big scary world and get a real job."

"But teaching *is* a real job, Emma!" Esther burst out.

"Do you know how much I was paid, Esther?"

"Well, yeah. Of course. You're single. It doesn't take much. You of all people should know that."

"You know, Esther, this may sound harsh, but you don't know how boring it gets doing the same thing endlessly. Teaching school. Helping Mam. Laundry, cleaning, the produce fields for Dat. Has it ever occurred to anyone that I might want a life of my own?"

"A life?" Ruth shrieked. "What in the world is wrong with you? You go on trips with Anna Mae and Carla, you buy whatever you want, you own a hundred dresses and thirty pairs of shoes and as many coats. You don't have to answer to one other person and you want a *life*?"

Esther gave supporting testimony with a resounding, "Whatever."

As usual, her mother's wisdom kicked in, and she said nothing. But she gave away her agitation by rising to her feet and gathering dishes to carry to the sink.

Fifteen-year-old Dena made an appearance, carrying an empty laundry basket and a telltale comic book with a finger inserted between pages.

"It took you long enough to put away that basket of laundry." Ruth quipped.

Dena ignored her before flopping on the recliner and opening the comic book.

"Mam, why do you let her read those Archie books?" Esther asked, querulous now that her world was off its axis with Emma making a choice she would neither accept nor try to understand.

"Oh, there's nothing wrong with a lighthearted book every once in a while," her mother answered quietly.

"See, that's what happens to big families. The youngest children are spoiled. The parents become soft in the heart. And the head."

A giggle from the sink turned into a full-blown burst of laughing, till her mother turned around, drying her hands on a dish towel.

"That's not the only thing that turns soft. Feel this."

Ruth pinched a sizable portion of her mother's hip, her mouth opened in disbelief, and she howled with glee.

"Mam! Is that all *schpeck*?

"What else would it be? Bacon? Whale blubber?"

The judgment lifted, a lighthearted camaraderie returned, and they shifted to discussing Emma's options away from teaching and the produce fields. Her mother said if she truly was not planning on staying, they could hire someone, even if it meant extra work to train them.

"Emma is an adult. She's well past the age of twenty-one, so no matter what we think she should do, this is her choice."

Grudgingly, the sisters agreed in subdued tones.

"So what do you have in mind, Emma?" her mother inquired, more kindly now.

"I have absolutely no clue."

"Well . . . but . . ." Ruth sputtered.

"I definitely won't apply for a job building skyscrapers in New York City, so you can relax. Perhaps I'll get a market job, or a job as a cook in a restaurant, or start studying to be a midwife."

She was gratified to see the expressions of horror on both her sisters' faces.

CHAPTER 2

HER FATHER RECEIVED THE NEWS OF HER IMPENDING DEPARTURE WITH stoic reserve, stroking his beard methodically as he contemplated her words.

"I can't say I blame you," he said quietly.

Quick tears filled her eyes, her heart softened by his kind understanding.

"It's just that I'm on the wrong side of twenty-five, which is, you know, sort of the tipping point between a young girl and a . . . what do they call old maids?"

Her father's slow smile moved across his face.

"Leftover blessings."

"Yes."

"Which is what you would be if you chose to remain single. A blessing at Hickory Hollow and a blessing to my produce fields. You're a hard worker."

"I'm sorry to do this to you."

"It's perfectly fine, Emma. Don't worry about it. There are always fourteen- and fifteen-year-old boys who would love to be away from their own farm."

"And they will definitely keep Dena in the field."

Her father chuckled softly.

The porch swing creaked with the sound of the chain moving on sturdy cast iron hooks as twilight spread across the farm, turning the ridge into an uneven silhouette, darker than the sloping pasture. To the west, the thin line of clouds dispersed, allowing one last sliver of orange to escape, the grand finale of a perfect spring day. Down by the pond the old bullfrogs gave their deep baritone voices to the hysterical chirping of the many tree frogs.

A cow began a soft lowing, which was followed by the anxious bawling of her calf.

"Hear that?" her father asked, raising a finger.

"What?"

"It's not a fox. Coyote."

"Did I tell you Benuel's Elmer saw five of them in his uncle's back fields on the last day of archery season?"

"I heard about that."

A contented silence ensued, until Emma rubbed her hands up and down her forearms, shivered, and said she was going to bed.

"Goodnight, Emma."

"Goodnight, Dat."

Inside, she found her brothers at the kitchen table, dunking chocolate chip cookies in milk and telling stories from their day setting trusses. Both of them attempted passing it off as nothing, but she could tell by their cheesy grins that the day had been hard for both of them, learning to straddle creaky walls and walk on narrow boards at least twenty feet off the ground.

"Makes produce fields and the cow stable look pretty cozy, huh?" Emma asked.

Abram grinned, ran a hand through his thick, wavy hair the color of a russet autumn leaf.

"Yeah. I mean, try to keep your balance and watch for an incoming truss hanging from the end of a crane. It takes acquired skill and practice, man."

"We're starting, Abe. Just getting started. We'll be authentic truss monkeys in a year or so." Steven puffed out his thin chest with false bravado.

"If we're not flattened by a swinging truss," Abram answered.

"Well, brothers, I myself am about to embark on an unknown quest, seeking my life's calling."

Without so much as a glance in her direction, Abram told her to speak in a language ordinary guys could understand.

"What high-minded thing is that?" Steven snorted.

"Just kidding. I quit school and the produce fields."

"Serious?"

"Yep."

"And?"

"I don't know yet."

"Just don't set trusses."

Dena joined them, lifted the lid of the Tupperware cookie container to find only crumbs, straightened, and said quietly, "Hogs."

"We are hogs," Abram agreed. "I ate at least six."

"We could bake a double batch of these every week and there wouldn't be enough to go around," Emma said.

"I'll buy some at Sheetz tomorrow, okay?"

By now Dena had gone to the pantry and returned with the corn flakes box, got down a bowl and spoon and poured a rounded pile into it.

"What? Corn flakes at this time of night?" Steven said, examining the back of his hand before picking at a blackened scab.

"I happen to like corn flakes. If someone wouldn't inhale cookies like there was no tomorrow, I might have been able to have a couple."

Benjamin and Lloyd, at twelve and nine years old, miniature replicas of their older brothers, padded through the kitchen in stocking feet before solemnly retrieving the corn flakes and disappearing into the living room.

"Hey. No eating in there!" Emma shouted after them.

She heard a murmured assent from the recliner, where her mother was resting her aching foot, an old childhood injury that flared up occasionally.

The box was dutifully returned to the pantry, immediately replaced by a large square box of Tom Sturgis pretzels, followed by a plastic container of *schmear kase* from the refrigerator. Everyone crowded around, dipping the small, salty pretzels into the soft cheese, coming away with globs of it attached.

"Somebody should make a pitcher of tea," Abram said directly to Emma.

"Make your own. You know how."

"Hey, look at this. President Trump isn't getting his wall."

Steven hung over the *Daily Gazette*, his thin shoulders hunched in a way that wrung Emma's heart. He'd had Lyme disease when he was a child, and seemed to be easily tired out, especially on stressful days such as this.

"How do you know?"

Abram joined his brother, reading out loud, snorting after every sentence.

"I don't know what it is about that man qualifying as a conservative Republican, let alone president of the United States."

"He's just trying to protect the country."

A rapid fire political discussion followed, with Emma's strident voice heard above her brothers', opinions flapping like crow's wings across the table. Eventually an argument commenced, till their father put a stop to it, the kitchen was cleaned up and they all headed upstairs except Emma, who flipped through the paper, read a few comics and the weather forecast before sleepily scanning the help wanted section.

Certified Public Accountant needed.

Dr. Dean Sissler seeks a dental hygienist.

Roofing workers needed for a local construction company.

Equine specialist, Bachelor of Science or equivalent experience required.

She was about to fold the paper when an ad in the next column caught her eye.

Live-in nanny needed for two children, aged two and four. Serious inquiries only. Please call. 879-6240.

Were nannies trained and certified, she wondered? What would her parents say? They would surely object to the live-in part. What would they say about her living with an English family?

She closed the paper, folded it, and dropped it into the magazine basket, called out a goodnight, and went to her room.

The night was chilly, so she closed the open window to a few inches above the sill, just enough to catch the scent of fresh new leaves, the dew-laden mown grass. Everything was so beautiful in the world dressed in spring, as if all the growth was flaunting new clothes.

Emma drew in a long, slow breath, savored the beauty of the night, before heading across the hallway to the shower.

She was up early, helping her mother with breakfast, packing huge lunch containers for Abram and Steven. She caught sight of the newspaper with the ad and quickly put it on the top shelf of the bookcase. It wouldn't hurt to call for more information, right? Would it be that different from being a *maud* for an Amish family? No one would think twice about that. Single Amish women were often hired by Amish couples who had just had a baby and needed some extra help around the house until the family settled into life with one more child.

Emma waited till breakfast was over, and then took a few minutes to savor her coffee, to appreciate the fact that she did not need to rush off to school. Sallie and Amanda, the little girls, were on the bench along the wall, their hair loose, tousled in dark waves, wearing flannel pajamas that said "Cuddle Me" in dark letters.

"You know, Mam, you wouldn't have allowed me to wear those cute pajamas when I was growing up," Emma remarked.

"Oh, are you sure?" her mother asked, reaching for someone's uneaten toast, taking a bite, then another.

Sallie made a funny face at Emma, giggled when Emma wagged a warning finger in her direction. Amanda smiled at Emma, then tried to imitate Sallie.

Emma got to her feet, scooped Amanda up in her arms and rained kisses all over her face, with Sallie hopping beside her, squealing for attention.

Her mother shook her head.

"You are so good with the little ones, Emma. You really should continue teaching, if you can't have any of your own."

The perfect opportunity had just presented itself.

In one swift swoop she retrieved yesterday's paper, placed it front of her mam, and jabbed a forefinger to the words she wanted her to read.

"What?"

Squinting, her mother lifted the paper till her bifocals aligned with the print, then said, "Hmm. A nanny. Sounds pretty high up there."

High up there. Her mother's words oozed disapproval.

"Seriously, though. What do you think?" Emma asked eagerly.

"Oh, I don't know."

Emma could sense her cautious attitude, the old traditional suspicion of anything new. The world was fraught with danger—cell phones and televisions, strangers, fashion, fast-moving cars. All of it was a long claw reaching her children, an invisible talon that would curl itself around the minds and hearts of her ten offspring.

"Live-in?"

"Nanny's don't always do that, I don't believe. Perhaps they'd allow me to be there for twelve or fourteen hours and spend the night at home."

"Who would transport you? Besides, you know the danger of men having affairs with the help. Some English men don't think twice about being unfaithful."

"Mother."

When Emma said "Mother" and not "Mam," her mother knew she had overstepped.

"Well," she defended herself.

"Not all of them. We haven't met them yet and already you're predicting the worst."

"Well."

"So what do you think?"

"It's your decision."

"What will Dat say?"

"Oh, you know how he is. Anything you want to take on, he'll support."

Emma's hands flew, clearing the long breakfast table, washing dishes, wiping countertops, grabbing the broom to sweep the kitchen. Then she ran to the shed where the telephone rested on a shelf inside the door.

Amish homes were without the use of a telephone, using public pay phones or a neighbor's phone until the call booths became obsolete, or an English housewife became irate at the Amish neighbor's intrusion, mud or manure caked on to his work boots. Change occurred slowly, but eventually a neighborhood shanty sprang up on the edge of someone's field, a telephone placed on the wall which accommodated four or five families. Even more slowly, but eventually, each family was granted the wish to have their own telephone, as long as it was away from the house. No Amish housewife had the luxury of sitting on a comfortable chair in the warmth of her home to spread gossip throughout the community. Better to be without that. Cell phones brought a whole new set of serious concerns and warnings.

It was another gorgeous day, so lovely in fact that Emma's heart leaped within her at the sheer joy of being alive. She glanced at the fading tulips, their petals dangling among the waxy olive-green leaves that had been displayed in all their glory a month before. She felt real sympathy, knowing they'd be smashed beneath a layer of mulch after the petunias and snapdragons were planted in their place.

Poor things, such a short time in the limelight, she thought.

She felt new appreciation for her health, her youth and anticipation, the God-given ability to thrive.

She placed her call, waited anxiously for the voice of her employer- to-be.

"Hello?"

"Hello. Good morning. I'm calling to answer your newspaper ad about someone to help with your children."

Somehow, she couldn't bring herself to say the word "nanny." She was not trained or certified and really had no idea if one had to be in order to use the term.

"Yes. Yes, of course."

"My name is Emma Beiler. I am an Amish schoolteacher who is, um . . . looking for work . . . for the summer."

"Did you say 'Amish'?" The woman's voice asked. Emma affirmed, and then there was an awkward silence.

"Oh, yes. Well, I'm having quite a time of it here," she said wryly. "I have not found anyone suitable, and it's been months since I started looking online. The ad in the paper was a stab in the dark, I suppose. What kind of experience do you have? You said you're a teacher?"

Emma told her how many years she'd worked at the schoolhouse, then mentioned her younger siblings and nieces and nephews and how she'd helped care for them. And then she paused, waiting for a yay or nay or whatever was to come.

"Hmm, well . . . we're actually spending the summer in North Carolina, where we purchased a beachfront property and are renovating extensively. We're actually renting a house beside it in order to oversee the proceedings. I am a lawyer, actually, and my husband is a surgeon in Harrisburg, so we will be coming and going. You can see the need for a trustworthy applicant."

"Of course."

What? North Carolina? Beachfront? She'd never seen the ocean. Never been allowed to accompany her gaggle of girlfriends to the rented beach house at Rehoboth or Lewes or Chincoteague Island. No way, her mother had said, in that purse-lipped way where Emma knew her mam and dat would stand united and she may as well give in immediately.

"No child of mine will ever be subject to that fearsome place. The ocean has strange currents no one understands except God, so don't even think about it."

That was the end of Emma's proposed ocean going.

But she was an adult now. That evening, she confronted both parents, laid the facts before them without hesitation. She decided not to ask their permission, exactly. She just said, "I think I should give the lady a chance," and then waited for their reply.

Her mother's mouth opened in protest, then snapped shut as her father jumped in and said he couldn't see why not. It might give her a chance to see a part of the world she hadn't seen before. She was twenty-six years old and had a good head on her shoulders.

Emma had ended the call with Kathy Forsythe saying that she would give it some thought, as she hadn't planned to move so far away, but that she'd get back to them that evening. She wanted to yell "yes!" right then and there, but she didn't want to appear too desperate. Plus, it was only fair to at least mention it to her parents before moving ahead. But as soon as she finished speaking with her parents, she practically ran to the shed and called Kathy back. They made arrangements for her and her husband to bring the children the next afternoon so they could all meet and get a feel for each other.

The next day, she asked her family as gently as possible to give her space during the interview, a request that her mother met with raised eyebrows. But she acquiesced. Emma dressed in her best everyday clothes, made sure the kitchen was spotless, the porch swept, and Rover the German shepherd tied in the barn. She sat on the sofa with her perspiring hands knotted tightly in her lap, waiting.

When the white Cadillac SUV came slowly into the drive, Emma wished she would never have answered that ad. This was way out of her league. Who did she think she was, really? But she answered the door, welcomed them into her parents' home, and without a thought, got down to the children's level to greet them warmly, a practice that came as naturally as breathing.

"Hello, little people. And what is your name?" she asked.

She was met with a thin little boy with a dusting of blond hair cut short, his huge blue eyes radiating curiosity and good humor, with a smaller female version of him carrying a tattered elephant with her thumb in her mouth.

"I'm Brent, and this is Annalise."

The boy spoke softly, then looked at his father for reassurance.

"Hello, Brent. How are you, Annalise? I'm Emma. It's so good to meet you. I was looking forward to this."

The thumb popped out and the elephant presented solemnly.

"This is Charlie Brown."

"Well, hello there, Charlie Brown. You are the best-looking elephant I have ever seen. He's very handsome, Annalise."

"He eats peanuts and M and M's."

"Oh good. Does he share?"

"Sometimes."

Kathy shared a look with Roger, her husband, that said, *This is it. This is it!* They went through the formalities, the summer plans presented in detail, with Kathy doing most of the talking. A slight woman with blond hair cut in the latest fashion, with quick intelligent eyes that missed nothing, she presented her case like the negotiator she was. Her husband was also short, thin, and well spoken, with reddish hair and the sharp quick eyes that almost duplicated the color of his wife's.

He spoke with a low, self-assured voice, telling her how much they could offer for pay.

The wages were astronomical. Three times the amount of her schoolteacher's pay!

"I'm . . . I'm a bit uncomfortable with that amount," Emma managed awkwardly.

"Oh," Kathy glanced at Roger, who nodded. "We can do a bit more," she assured her.

"No, no," Emma laughed, ashamed suddenly. "It's just too much. It is money I will never earn, fairly. I am not trained in the sense . . . I mean . . . I am not a real certified nanny."

"You have nine siblings, taught eight grades for ten years. I can think of no better certification," Kathy said, followed by the rumbling assent of her husband.

Emma tried protesting again, but Kathy waved her off, saying they could discuss it later.

"Charlie Brown isn't allowed in the bathtub," Annalise said earnestly.

"Why is that?" Emma asked, her full attention turned to the serious little girl.

"Because."

Brent rolled his eyes in big brother fashion, then told Emma it was on account of being a stuffed animal.

"He goes in the washer," Annalise informed him.

"That's different," Brent said.

The parents smiled indulgent approval from their seats around the kitchen table as Emma assured Annalise if the elephant was put in the bathtub, he might drown, whereas a washer spun him so fast the water couldn't go up his trunk. This was met with Brent's vigorous agreement, while Annalise inserted her thumb and stared at Emma with doubtful eyes.

"So, your most pressing duty will be the children, of course," the mother continued. "Renovating this old house is taking up too much of my time and patience and we've hardly even started."

She threw her hands in the air in an affected manner, which brought another smile from her husband.

"We are taking a two week vacation, of course, but will be flying to and from Harrisburg throughout the season. So there will be occasional nights when you'll be alone. I'm assuming that will not be requiring too much."

"No, no. That should be fine."

"Good."

The date and time of her departure was discussed, and they rose to their feet, thanked her for the interest she showed in the job, herded the children through the front door, and were gone.

Emma watched them go, noticed the careful arrangement of the many belts and closures of the car seats, before they drove slowly away. A mixture of excitement and apprehension made her heart flutter, her breathing accelerate, as if she'd been running from the house to the barn.

Should she do this? Was she capable?

The two children appeared well trained, with caring parents. It was not exactly a recipe for disaster, but still. She knew a lot could go wrong.

Well, she'd ask the Lord to go with her, keep her in His care, as well as the little ones and their parents. She believed God loved them all the same, and therefore had no reason to count herself more than her prospective employers.

Her family appeared as if by magic, stepping out of the wood-work with a hundred questions, especially her mother with all her newfound imaginary catastrophes. She had seen that the family was (gasp!) *rich*.

"Oh my, Emma, do you have any idea how worldly you could turn out to be? What an influence? You are old already and have no boy-friend. You already seem to think there's no Amish man good enough for you. I mean, think of it. You'll get used to the life of convenience. Electric lights, television. Soon you'll think of driving that big car. Get your license. Just say no, Emma. It's that simple."

Emma frowned, and told her mother she was exactly like the story in the old reader where the bride-to-be sat and cried herself into a miserable state as she stared at an axe stuck in a ceiling post and all the dangerous things that could happen to her beloved bridegroom if it fell out.

Her mother narrowed her eyes, laughed with a short barking sound and said cheerily, "Ach. Whatever."

"I want to do this, Mam. It's quite an opportunity."

"But . . . what about your rumschpringa?"

"What about it?"

"Well, at the end of summer you'll be almost twenty-seven. And . . ."

Her mother turned to the stove, lifted the corner of her apron, and swiped at a spattering of grease she had missed.

"And . . . you're terrified of me becoming an old maid, aren't you?" Emma asked, trying to keep the laughter at bay.

"No no. That's not true. I'd be happy to have you here till you're thirty years old. For always, actually."

"Admit it, Mam. It would be awful hard on your pride."

"Stop it, Emma."

But both were smiling, and both knew the truth.

Dena threw a bag of Henry's hard pretzels on the table, then opened the door of the refrigerator to pull out the *schmear kase*.

"Why are you so worried about Emma being an old maid? She already is one." She dunked a pretzel and held it aloft, a glob of cheese like icing. She plopped the plastic container on the table, then fell into a chair, propping the sole of her foot on the seat.

"Dena, *net so govverich*."

Down came her foot, with eyebrows lowered in rebellion.

"No one can see me."

"I can," said her mother.

"I'm going to the ocean with you," Dena announced.

"Wish you could."

"Why can't I?"

"They don't want you. Besides, who would help Mam?" Emma asked, suddenly feeling a wave of guilt. Would Dena really rise to the challenge? Would she help with the gardens, the canning, the wash, the little kids? Currently she seemed to be determined to do as little work as possible.

"Well, rest assured, Emma," said Dena. "There will be no available men in North Carolina. No Amish settlement for miles around."

"Why are we even discussing my love life? Maybe I like being single."

This sent her mother scuttling straight into nervous breakdown mode, with eyebrows that shot above the tops of her glasses, her mouth compressed into a tight line of disapproval.

"Let me tell you something, young lady. All this independence is not good for the young generation, and I mean it. You would be blessed to have a husband and children."

"Of course I would, mother dear. But that doesn't seem to be in the Lord's will right now, does it? I have not had one man ask me for as much as a buggy ride—or at least not one who comes close to being suitable."

"See? That's your entire life, right there."

A lecture of mammoth proportion followed, with Emma and Dena exchanging winks behind their mother's back, then throwing an arm across her shoulders after she had worked herself into a fine dither, berating herself for not having taught Emma to be a virtuous woman. When they kissed her cheek, she laughed aloud in spite of herself.

CHAPTER 3

SHE SIGNED A CONTRACT OF SORTS. SHE WAS BOUND TO THESE CHILDREN and their parents for the summer. After that, they'd reassess.

She packed her clothes in the largest piece of luggage she owned, going down the list she had made for herself. Seven or eight dresses in various colors, all made with the same pattern, cut and sewn according to traditional *ordnung*, plus four black bib aprons, the typical everyday wear for young girls. She added two clean white head coverings and a small stack of *dichlin*, the cotton fabric cut and hemmed into triangles and wound around the head to be tied in the back. There were sneakers for walking, and the sandals and flip-flops she had purchased at the Shoe Department, footgear that was frowned on by most ministers and the elderly, but accepted by many families. Any change was always slow to be allowed, but each individual home followed their own consciences in some matters, too.

Mam took one look at a pair of sandals she brought home, and told her flatly those things were going in the trash. Of course, Dena loved them, begged Emma to give them to her. Emma apologized to her mother, but packed them along with everything else, much to Dena's glee.

"Dena, I'm twenty-six. I'm going to the beach. I don't mean to be a poor example, but . . ."

"But you are."

"But I am."

Dena sat cross-legged on Emma's bed. Did she ever sit in a lady-like position? She peered into her luggage and sighed regularly to let Emma know this was the hardest thing she had ever gone through in her life.

"I mean, it wouldn't be so bad, but you know the battle I'm going to have just to get her to let me go with my friends."

"I never went out with friends at your age."

"You are now."

"As an employee, Dena."

"Still. It's not fair."

Emma clucked a sympathetic sound. "Poor baby."

"Well, I'd be scared out of my wits to go with those people. What if you can't handle those rich kids? I guarantee they're nothing like Amish children."

"But you don't know."

"Neither do you."

"*Ach*, Dena. I wish I could take you with me. I'll miss you so much."

"I'll miss you, too. But Emma, how can you possibly enjoy yourself sitting on a beautiful beach, knowing I, your own flesh and blood sister, will be slogging away in the produce fields?"

In Dena's dramatic fashion, she leaned forward and slapped the lid of the suitcase with the palms of her hands.

"I know, Dena, I know. And I do feel bad. But you know how many summers I have labored in those fields, side by side with Dat and our brothers?"

"All you did was throw tomatoes."

Emma grinned. "It was fun. I'll miss Abram and Steven. You know, Dena, working together builds character. It creates a . . . you know, a bond."

Dena rolled her eyes, and then a silence fell between them.

Emma stopped packing and sat down next to Dena. "I'm nervous."

"I'm surprised you admit it."

"I'm really scared, actually. But excited, too."

She thought of everything that could go wrong. What if one of the children got hurt or went missing while they were in her care? She thought about how there would be no other Amish people, no weekends of rumschpringa or evening singings. She would miss a few of the girls, but she couldn't think of any boys she'd think much about while she was gone.

There was Eli, twenty-eight, with a receding hairline and an arrogance that bordered on rudeness. She knew he wanted her, but . . . well, perhaps someday. She did feel a fondness, a sort of friendship. But there was no spark of romance.

It was just that she couldn't forget the way she felt when she fell so hard and so fast for Sam King. It wasn't that she wanted Sam at this point—she had long since accepted that he and her sister were meant for each other. But she wanted to feel like that again about someone—and to have that person feel the same for her. What was the point of settling for anything less?

There was Paul. Slight of build, he was kind, but so bland. His eyes held an obvious longing for her, so she avoided meeting his gaze whenever she could. Besides, her friend—tall, gangly Annie Riehl—was waiting for the day when Paul would finally come to his senses and realize what a fantastic wife she would be.

John was too young, too wild and immature, although she admitted to herself he held a certain fascination with that long dark hair, the way he went to Colorado every year and came home with some trophy elk or sheep. He'd asked her to accompany him once, and she asked him if he was crazy. Girls didn't go on a hunting trip with a group of guys.

"*You* could," he said, with emphasis on the "you." His eyes left no doubt about his feelings for her, and as always, she slipped away, made some excuse to extract herself from the conversation.

The thing was, her circle was so small. There was no way to meet other young men, unless she were to travel to a distant Amish community, but then everyone would see her as desperate. Most girls just stayed put and waited for the Lord to provide a man, something

Emma found deplorable as she grew older. She would not settle for someone she did not love, and never would, just to save herself the humiliation of staying single.

Occasionally, there would be a girl who seemed happy with nary a man in their life, ever. Emma was starting to think this was, indeed, who she was. She was happy enough, wasn't she?

She did not have to get married. Even the Bible said it was okay. So, she'd venture away from home, sit by the seaside, and allow her heart and mind to be cleansed of all the clutter that came with years of rumschpringa. All those years of spending weekends with friends, playing volleyball or ping pong, eating popcorn and cookies, and wondering if romance were around the next corner. Which it never was.

In the morning, she wet and combed her thick auburn hair, sprayed a liberal cloud of hairspray, chose a mint green dress and black bib apron, applied sunscreen in the form of a foundation that matched her skin, and surveyed the result. She had never found anything that successfully covered freckles, but the tanned skin on her face had already faded their appearance. Wide green eyes, fringed with black lashes, the tips receding to a reddish brown that matched her hair. Her nose and mouth were completely satisfactory. She had wide, full lips that had the perfect bow, like her mother's. A mouth that was attractive when she was serious, enhanced by a wide smile that flashed easily.

She set the white head covering evenly, inserted two straight pins in the *fettadale*, and turned around to hold a small mirror to her face to check the back part of the covering.

Everything in place, she put the mirror in the pocket of her suitcase, threw her journal and pen on top, and zipped it shut. She gave one last look around her lovely bedroom, all the things she'd acquired from the many years of teaching school. A part of the attic was stacked with plastic totes from Wal-Mart or Dollar General, filled with sheet sets and towels, cookware and dozens of mugs and plaques with kind verses about good teachers. She had enough artwork from the children to fill the whole attic, but had burned some of it in the burn barrel.

She heaved the suitcase off her bed, set it on end, and straightened the quilt, adjusting the pillow shams before thumping down the stairs.

It was a bright May morning, the sun's rays already stealing through the sides of the drawn shades in the living room.

"What a racket," her mother observed.

"This thing is heavy."

"I wouldn't be surprised. So you're ready?"

"I think so."

"We'll miss you, Emma."

Her mother's eyes filled with tears, something that occurred regularly. Dena said her mother could form tears on demand, anytime she wanted to make anyone feel bad, which made Emma laugh, thinking of her own secret rebellion at fifteen.

"I will miss home, Mam. All of you. Especially you, though. You know how much I like being your daughter."

Her mother swiped at her streaming eyes, her mouth already taking on that loose wobbliness that meant a tearful deluge was imminent.

Small wonder Dena was dramatic.

"I like being your mother, you know that," she said, turning her back to reach for Kleenex from the box on the counter.

"I'm so afraid for you, this summer. The ocean is so powerful and you are so daring. I know you can swim, but a pond or a lake is completely different from the ocean. Do you have to go swimming?"

"Mam, of course I do."

"Oh, yes. I know. I know. But promise me you'll be very careful. Did you pack your Bible? And you do realize that the man could become attracted to you, and for English people, that's not *verboten*."

Emma retained a snort of outrage, counted to ten, and said quietly, "I think this couple is completely devoted, Mam."

"Well, you never know. And you're going to be living in the same house . . ."

She left her dire predictions dangling at the end of her sentence, like a sticky fly hanger that attracted all sorts of dark and fearful thoughts.

"You be careful how you walk or handle yourself around him. *Ach* Emma, the world is so full of danger for a young woman, and you are so innocent yet."

Emma hid her grin, the sparkle in her eyes.

Ah, mother dear, you may go on thinking that, she thought. Mothers simply did not know everything, now did they?

Breakfast was the usual happy clatter of dishes passed, forks and spoons scraped against plates, conversation flowing easily around the table, the children chiming in with their own plans for the day.

Sallie said she was going to wash her doll clothes, that Ada's sleepers were looking gray around the collar, to which her mother said of course she should do that. It looked as if it would be a good wash day.

Abram and Steven rose from the table when their work driver pulled up to the end of the sidewalk. They turned to Emma, and with an awkward pat on her shoulder, said, "See you. Behave yourself," and grabbed their lunch containers and thermos jugs.

"Have a good summer, guys," she called after them.

"You too," was flung out without a backward glance.

"Brothers," Emma said, trying to laugh, but she found a quick lump of emotion had already formed in her throat.

Dena was silent, a sour expression written all over her face. She played the martyr well, but then, Emma knew this really would be hard for her. She'd have more responsibility around the house, plus Emma was her confidant, the one person Dena could safely share all her teenage feelings with.

Extracting herself from the ties of a close-knit family was much harder than she had imagined, so when the Forsythes arrived, it was a relief, really. She hugged and kissed the little girls and tried hugging Benjamin and Lloyd, who wriggled expertly out of her grasp and stood watching from the sidelines as she hugged the reminder of the family, promised to call or write, and picked up the heavy suitcase.

"Goodbye, Mam, Dat. See you, Dena."

Dena waved silently, her hands clenching the back of a kitchen chair, her face a mixture of sorrow and self-pity.

"Goodbye," they called, as she let herself out the door and into the brilliance of the May sunshine.

She found her parents and all her siblings trailing behind her and was vaguely embarrassed until she saw the Forsythes step out of the vehicle with welcoming smiles of appreciation, greeting the entire family warmly.

Her father's manners were impeccable, looking tall and bushy with his Amish hair and beard, her mother with her rounded figure and homemade clothes and her eyes clouded with apprehension.

The meeting of two worlds, Emma thought, but was gratified to find the conversation flowed freely, with genuine interest from her employers, before the fond goodbyes started all over again.

"Remember your upbringing," her mother whispered, inserting the final word of caution in her prolonged embrace.

"Bring us seashells," Amanda said, looking to Sallie for confirmation.

"Starfish. And jellyfish. Some sand," Sallie ordered.

Everyone was laughing as Emma climbed into the backseat beside the two children who were strapped into their car seats.

"Is that enough room?" Kathy asked. "Or would you prefer the seat in the back?"

"No, this is fine."

"Okay, then we're off."

Roger got behind the wheel with Kathy beside him, and with many waves and goodbyes, the car moved slowly away.

"Oh my," Emma said softly.

Kathy laughed. "That's quite a family, isn't it?"

"It took up most of the morning, all those goodbyes."

She turned to the children.

"How do you do? How do you do? How do you do again?" she quipped, a favorite greeting for small children she had used often for first graders as they entered the strange new world of the classroom.

Annalise giggled. Brent laughed outright.

"I am fine," he said.

"Charlie Brown does not want to go to North Carolina," Annalise said soberly.

"Oh, I know. Elephants don't like to travel. They never do."

Annalise nodded solemnly before taking refuge in her thumb. Emma took notice of the elephant's ears being slipped between a thumb and forefinger when the thumb was inserted. She couldn't help wondering about that, given that thumb sucking was discouraged among pediatricians. Or at least it used to be. She'd have to remember to write Ruth and Esther to ask—they always knew the latest parenting trends.

Roger drove through heavy traffic on 518, campers taking advantage of the sights before the summer influx began. Horses hitched to gray and black carriages traveled on the wide berm, allowing vehicles to pass at normal speed.

"Is this small town of Beaver Falls always like this?" Roger inquired, his dark glasses in the mirror giving away nothing.

"When school lets out, there are always the campers and RVs on their way to Beaver Lake. Everyone stakes out their spot before the rush."

"I'm surprised. This far north."

"Well, the main road through this area leads to the Pennsylvania Turnpike, so, yes, it can become congested."

"Horses are okay with it?"

"Not all of them, no. From time to time, there are accidents."

There was a brief comfortable silence.

"I have a question," Emma said.

"Okay?"

"Why did you run an ad in a newspaper so far from Harrisburg?"

"Oh, we work in the city, both of us. But we live about halfway between your farm and where we work," Kathy answered.

"I see."

But Emma didn't really see. Why would a person commute fifty miles to work every day if there were plenty of homes in and around the capital? What about the cost of fuel, their time? Wouldn't it be more economical to live closer to their work?

"We bought a farm in State College, and my work is there, mostly. Roger drives to and from his work in Harrisburg. Sometimes I have to do the same, but not every day. We placed the ad in many different papers, all over the internet as well."

"I see."

But she didn't see that, either. Miles must not be important. Going ten miles was a considerable distance for the Amish. She began to grasp the very small space that contained her existence.

Perhaps I do live a very secluded lifestyle, she mused.

They reached the well-traveled interstate highway, and as the vehicle hummed along, both children began to whine.

"Mommy, I'm thirsty."

"Emma, in the insulated backpack below her seat, there is a box of juice."

"I don't want juice."

"What do you want, honey?"

"Chocolate milk."

Roger turned his head to stare at his wife, whose face had taken on a look of disbelief.

"What should we do?" she mouthed silently.

Roger glanced in the rearview mirror, drew himself to his utmost height from the seat in order to see his daughter's face.

"Annalise, Mommy forgot to pack chocolate milk, okay? You can have some juice."

Annalise flung both feet out, her legs as stiff as pokers. Charlie Brown went flying across the front seat and a howl erupted from Annalise's small, wide open mouth.

"Anna honey. Baby, listen. Mommy packed your favorite. Grape juice."

"No! I don't want it."

"Roger, we're going to have to stop at the next exit."

"She won't drink the grape juice?"

"No. She won't do it, I'm pretty sure."

"Baby. Daddy is getting off soon, okay? We'll get your chocolate milk."

"I want Charlie Brown back."

Quickly, the gray and white elephant was handed over and was crushed into Annalise's clutches, followed by the thumb.

Brent reached into a pouch fastened to the side of his car seat and extracted a handheld Game Boy device of some kind, snapped it on, and in seconds was engrossed in a colorful display on the lit screen.

Emma felt her good humor dissipate like steam from a teakettle. What was this? Seriously. She felt a clenching, clawing lurch in her stomach. Did parents actually do this? Why were they giving in to their child's unreasonable demand so quickly, and at the inconvenience of the rest of the family? Well, perhaps this was only on account of traveling. Perhaps they were just being a little indulgent because of how long they knew she'd be stuck in that car seat. They had a long ride ahead of them.

Relax. Go with the flow. Observe and learn, she told herself.

"McDonald's?" Roger asked, maneuvering the car down the ramp.

Kathy shook her head.

"You know what will happen, Roger," she said quietly.

He nodded and turned right into a Sheetz parking lot.

"Plastic bottle with a straw, if you can get it. Emma, would you like something to drink? Use the ladies' room?"

"No, thanks. I'm fine."

"You're sure? Brent, chocolate milk?"

"I want a Coke."

"Honey, chocolate milk would be better in the morning. Don't you want a chocolate milk?"

Emma gritted her teeth.

"I want Coke."

Roger got out of the vehicle and returned in short time, bearing a Coke and a chocolate milk. He opened the back door and handed them both to Emma, with two straws in cellophane wrappers.

"There you go, kids."

Emma opened the drinks, inserted straws, and handed them over as they pulled out of the parking lot.

"Thank you," Brent said quietly.

"You're welcome," Emma replied.

Annalise threw a fit, saying it was not real chocolate milk. The bottle was not the kind Charlie Brown liked to drink.

Kathy became agitated, her voice rising quickly to a near hysterical pitch as she began pleading with her daughter.

"Annalise, it is good chocolate milk. Honey, don't cry. It's okay. Please stop. Baby. Roger, pull over. This isn't working. Honey, look. See the brown cow? That cow is so awesome. Look, Anna."

By this time, she had loosened her seatbelt and was on her knees, turned backward and leaning over the seat and begging Annalise to calm down. Annalise was slamming her head from side to side, her feet thumping the edge of the seat, her stomach thrust forward in a defiant arc.

"I don't like that chocolate milk. I don't want it!" she screamed.

Roger entered the fray with interjections of his own, saying the brown cow was good friends with Charlie Brown, which brought emphatic nods from his wife.

The chocolate milk went untouched.

Emma reached into the insulated bag and produced a purple juice box, unwrapped it, and calmly inserted the bendable plastic straw. She reached over and took the chocolate milk and put the grape juice in its place.

"Charlie Brown said he wants purple juice," she said calmly and with total confidence.

Everything stopped. Slowly, Annalise looked from the elephant to Emma and back again. She thought for a moment the little girl would refuse, but she took the juice and began to drink it.

"It's good," she announced to Emma. "Charlie Brown loves grape juice."

Both parents turned, sank into their seats, and sighed with collective relief. Seat belts were clicked into place and they drove away, Annalise drinking the grape juice she would have had in the first place.

For some time, Emma was very quiet. She felt her blood pressure rise and had to restrain herself from making an unkind remark. For one wild moment, she wanted to ask Roger to take the closest exit, to turn this car around and take her back to her family. Back to the safety of a culture she understood.

What kind of parenting was this? How could this teach children the importance of obedience?

Well, Lord, you'll have to see me through. She'd accepted this job, so it was up to her to see it to the finish.

A few hours later, both children had nodded off, after many different snacks, books, and video games. Emma found Annalise to be completely endearing after the display at Sheetz, and Brent quite an amusing little boy. She allowed herself to relax again, and even felt a prick of guilt for being so judgmental.

Brent would be five in November. On the sixth, he told her. He pronounced "November" with a long O, very properly, his English so much better than Emma's first graders who had learned most of their words in Pennsylvania Dutch, the language learned from babyhood. English was the children's second language, so by the time they completed first or second grade they were bilingual. But these children spoke the language very well, surely mimicking their highly intelligent parents.

At lunchtime, they all agreed to picnic at a rest stop. When they rolled to a stop somewhere in Virginia, the day could not have been more delightful. Warm spring sunshine, lush grass that had been mowed quite recently, clean restrooms and plenty of picnic tables dotting the landscape.

Kathy spread a plastic tablecloth while both children raced across the grass, eager to run. Roger brought a Yeti cooler and flipped the lid, taking out a jar of what appeared to be dark brown and purple olives floating in oil. There were saltine crackers, peanut butter, and apricot preserves. She saw several cups of yogurt and a bag of pita chips, plus one bar of dark chocolate with almonds, wrapped in colorful paper.

"We're ready, kids!" Roger shouted.

Emma held back, unsure how to proceed. Kathy handed her a Chinet plate and a plastic fork and knife. She thanked her and watched Roger dig in, following his lead. First, they ate the yogurt, with a handful of golden raisins, followed by the saltines with both spreads, then the pita chips and olives, which turned out to be delicious. Kathy and Roger each took one tiny square of the chocolate bar, so Emma followed suit, turning her face away to hide the shock she felt at the bitterness. But it was good to be in the open air, surrounded by colorful scenery, the scent of lilacs and mountain laurel, both parents keeping up a lively conversation.

She was not satisfied at the end of the meal, but far too polite to eat more, noticing their birdlike appetites, the small bites and frequent blotting of napkins.

Oh dear. She longed for a toasted cheese sandwich with tomato and mayonnaise on homemade bread, with fresh chicken corn soup and a tall glass of iced tea. She imagined a big slice of chocolate layer cake with caramel–cream cheese frosting and felt a stab of homesickness, but brushed it away. She would make the most of this new experience. And it probably wouldn't kill her to eat a little more healthfully for one summer.

CHAPTER 4

S HE HAD NEVER BEEN TO THE OCEAN, BUT SHE COULD FEEL A DIFFERENCE IN the atmosphere as they approached, a humidity with a scent that could only be described as briny. Salty.

They were, in fact, very close, Roger informed her. In less than an hour she should be able to see the bay on the right, although the actual ocean would be to her left. He rambled on about the Wright Brothers, Kitty Hawk, the launch of the first airplane, so primitive, but the right idea.

Emma was well versed in history, this subject especially, having read more than a few books on the subject, which had always intrigued her. Roger had a few of his facts wrong, but she didn't correct him. She was the help, and would always keep that fact in mind. She was also weak with starvation by that point. How did these people survive on so few calories?

The children snacked on Fruit Loops and cheese popcorn, orange segments, and grapes that were sliced in half. At least they fed their children. She sneaked a few Fruit Loops when she didn't think anyone would notice. She drank water and listened to the rumbling of her intestines.

She had many conversations with Charlie Brown, which was entertaining as long as the food-induced high spirits remained, but after hours of traveling with nothing to eat, Charlie Brown turned into an annoying stuffed animal she would gladly have thrown out the window.

Finally, they entered a small town called Point Harbor and pulled into the parking lot of a little restaurant where Emma was introduced to fresh seafood with locally grown vegetables cooked to perfection. She had eaten plenty of shrimp in her time—Christmas was not complete without them, her father cooking them outside on the two-burner canner her mother used in summer. But scallops and crabs, clam and oysters? She found them all delicious, along with the fresh lettuce salad, green beans, and some fried balls of corn flour called hush puppies.

This meal was eaten with abandon, all calories and dainty manners aside. The table was spread with brown paper, galvanized buckets for shells, and wooden mallets to crack crabs, with the most delicious sweet tea she had ever tasted.

The meal would always be etched in her memory as a true culinary experience, followed by her first sight of the bay. It was breathtaking, this large body of salt water, with seagulls weaving their flight patterns in a perfectly blue sky, the black wing tips and saucy gray heads swiveling from side to side.

"Rats of the ocean, seagulls," Roger informed her.

"Beautiful birds," Emma answered.

"They're bandits. Absolute bandits. They'll steal a snack from a child's hand," Kathy said, finishing with a light laugh.

To say Emma was in awe was not adequate. The sand, the vast open water of the bay, dotted with sailboats like tiny triangular handkerchiefs flitting across the water, the occupants like miniature figures. How could one describe the diamond sparkle on restless water, the magical trail that traveled to the sun, the horizon, and far beyond? Seagulls cavorting like disobedient children, cackling their mischief to the far-flung clouds. Dull brown pelicans gliding over the water, the pouches below their outsized bills filled with fish.

And who could know what teemed and undulated, slithered and waved below the surface, in that deep briny world?

"See the fish crane?" Kathy called out, pointing with a forefinger.

"Great blue heron," Brent informed his mother.

Emma smiled her approval.

Brent shrugged his shoulders. "We come every year," he said, clearly proud of his knowledge.

Kitty Hawk. Kill Devil Hill. Bodie Island. Then Nag's Head.

"What names!" Emma commented.

Kathy laughed. "I imagine there's a reason for all of it. I should Google it for you."

And to the right, the ocean. The unimpeded body of water was so huge one could barely comprehend its depth or width or length.

Roger drove to a lookout point surrounded by a guardrail, and they all got out to stand and absorb the setting of the evening sun, hovering over the white capped waves that rose, curled, and broke in a never-ending symphony of sound and movement. The surf at the water's edge produced an incoming maelstrom of water that surged into roils, then washed back in the opposite direction with a swishing sound. The thump of the waves, the constant restless heaving and receding, was amazing to behold.

What caused this cycle of turbulence? Why couldn't the water be calm like the bay? She knew from a book she'd read that the waves of the ocean, kicked up by a wind thousands of miles away, created troubled waters that washed against undersea mountains, which sent ripples, the ebb and flow she was watching now, spellbound.

This was the true version of "awesome," the world flung in her circle of friends as regularly as breathing. This was beyond adequate description.

A shiver of tiny birds like a nervous rash spread across the sand. She allowed herself to get lost in the unceasing cry of the wheeling seagulls.

She fell irretrievably in love. She was swept up in an unexplained emotion that immediately bound her to this seacoast, this salt-sprayed sunset that created a path into the unknown. It was like heaven on the edge of the earth.

She didn't care what circumstances she would face now. She was here for three months at least. But perhaps she would never leave.

In that moment, she could not imagine returning to the land-locked cornfields and mountains, which seemed achingly dull and uninspired. How could she have lived for twenty-six years without catching a glimpse of this world, which was less than a day's drive away?

She turned, suddenly eager to feel the sand, to walk along those seething restless waters.

"I'm ready."

"You sure? We can stay longer," Roger offered.

"No. It is amazing, but I'm anxious to see the rest of it now."

She barely remembered the remainder of the journey, trying to take in all the sights of towns, seaside villages, fishing boats, shops, restaurants, everything she had only seen in magazines or books. Glimpses of the bay, inlets, the surf crashing only on occasion, and always the many seabirds.

They drove through Rodanthe, Waves, Salvo, and finally, after darkness was spreading across the unfamiliar territory, Roger turned the steering wheel to the left and the tires crunched on the white oyster shells that made up the driveway. The headlights shone on a house set on massive piles, like telephone poles except even wider in circumference. A wide staircase led to French doors on the second story and a wraparound porch with many windows. That was all she could see, with the veil of night descending swiftly.

But the smell. That smell was here, too. Emma felt as if she could taste the deep salty flavor of black muck, tall grasses waving in the ceaseless ocean breeze, the smell of fish and shells and salted water.

She breathed deeply again and again, filled her lungs with all the moisture, the air containing droplets of magic that invigorated her entire body.

Kathy went ahead, opened doors, flipped light switches, rectangles of cozy yellow light welcoming them all. Roger heaved totes and luggage and set the children on the sandy grass at the bottom of the steps, where Annalise set up a mournful wail of fear and desertion.

Emma remembered the children were her first concern, so she scooped her up and took Brent's hand before making her way up the stairs.

"Oh, there you are," Kathy said, squinting at the thermostat on the wall. "It's too cold in here."

She turned, punched a few switches, then clapped her hands.

"Alright, guys. Emma is your new nanny, so she'll be unpacking and bathing both of you. Come this way, Emma."

Another flight of stairs led to a wide hallway with four heavy doors ajar, all painted white, like ghostly soldiers standing at attention. Again, Kathy flipped switches, revealing bedrooms, a bathroom large enough to contain three of the ones in the farmhouse back home.

Everything was white. Walls, furnishings, pillows, bedcovers, rugs on hardwood floors that gleamed with the dull luster of money.

"This is your room, Emma."

Emma nodded, restraining the urge to fling out her arms and run in circles, the way Dena did when she was excited about something.

"Roger will lug your suitcase up the stairs."

Emma did not take time to part curtains to look at the view, but instead took charge of the weary children, herding them into the bathroom, finding soap and towels, turning the heavy spigots to create a cascade of water.

Annalise was yawning, rubbing the back of her hands into her eyes, following up with an artificial sob or hiccup, Emma wasn't sure.

"Alright, duckies. Into the pond."

Brent smiled, pulled his own T-shirt over his head, then shucked his jeans and boxer shorts in one downward tug. He sat on the bath rug and peeled off his socks before stepping into the bathtub. He grabbed a washcloth and set to work washing behind his ears with a calculated concentration.

Annalise yelled and yelled, protesting everything, until Kathy came pounding up the stairs.

"Baby girl, whatever is wrong, honeybunch?"

Emma stood aside, expressionless, saying nothing. Annalise's mother knew the moods of her difficult daughter, so Emma would observe, try to learn the ways she dealt with the unreasonable fits.

"I don't want her to bathe me."

"She's your new nanny. This is her job. Come on, Annalise. It's late and I'm tired, just like you. Please? Please will you get in?"

"No!" Annalise shrieked.

Emma stepped forward. "Look what I brought."

She knelt, producing a small Rubbermaid container filled with yellow rubber ducks, tiny pink sponges, and small bottle of bubble soap.

"One duck is for you. Her name is Marlena. She misses the water."

Annalise watched Emma with narrowed eyes. The thumb entered the pouting mouth, then was released when she said, "I hate Marlena. Her name is Duck."

"Okay. I'm sure she's pleased to be called Duck."

With that, Emma set them both afloat, and handed Brent the sponges. She was ready to hand over the bubble bath when Kathy stopped her with a hand on her arm.

"You'll think I'm crazy, but I don't allow bubbles unless they're organic." Emma had guessed as much, and proudly displayed the Melaleuca label.

"Perfect. Emma, you're a godsend. I knew this would work."

Once Annalise decided to join Duck in the water, Brent was allowed to upend the bubble soap, which produced at least thirty minutes of happiness for both.

Emma unpacked the children's luggage in the room containing two full beds with a nightstand in between, two dressers with rattan mirrors hung on the wall behind them, and turquoise rugs with orange starfish lines through the middle.

She filled drawers with adorable "English" clothes—shorts, T-shirts, sweaters, underwear, and socks. She hung up sweet dresses with stripes and floral patterns and set row after row of sandals and sneakers on the floor of the closet. Finally, she brought toothbrushes, toothpaste, hair brushes, and first aid supplies into the bathroom.

She watched the children's play, wondering how to cajole Annalise to get out of the bathtub if she wasn't quite ready.

"Alright, time to brush your teeth," she said, hoping to get some results. Much to her surprise, Annalise looked at her and said, "You need to shampoo my hair."

Kneeling, she applied the shampoo liberally, rubbed and washed gently, before holding the child under a half flow of water to rinse while she squeezed her eyes shut. Toweled and dressed in clean pajamas, they brushed their teeth with the whirring battery-operated toothbrushes.

Annalise allowed the brush to be drawn gently through the wet tangles before heading to her room, looking for Charlie Brown.

Emma was unsure if she should tuck them in, or if she was expected to summon their mother, so she asked Brent.

"No," he said. "Mommy is done with us. Her and Daddy are having their drink when Josie put us to bed. So I guess you'll have to learn."

"Okay. I'm sure it's not hard."

"No, it isn't. We just hop in and you help us say our prayers, then you have to read to us. We're not allowed to have the TV on."

"Oh."

Prayers. So there were prayers. That was reassuring.

She lifted Annalise and Charlie Brown into the bed and drew the covers around them both, while Brent climbed into his. They all said the simple child's prayer in English, of course, before Emma looked around for a book.

"Where are your books, Brent?"

"I have no idea. Mommy may have forgotten to pack them."

"I'll just tell you a story, if it's alright. The story is called 'Yoni Wondernose.' It's about a small boy about your age who is very curious."

There was a sigh from Annalise and her eyes drifted shut. Brent blinked and yawned, and Emma had hardly gotten into the story before he, too, fell asleep.

She turned off the light, left the door ajar, and tiptoed to her own room. Was she expected to go back downstairs to unpack? She went to the window, astonished to find the deck below flooded with light.

Emma went closer to the window, drew back the light muslin curtain, and lifted the white Roman shade. Roger and Kathy were seated side by side on a swing, their hands entwined, a wine bottle on the round patio table, a wine glass in Roger's free hand. They were deep in conversation, their bright blond hair radiating a golden pair beneath the porchlight.

Wow, Emma thought. To relax with a bottle of wine, to share their day so intimately, was a testimony to the sturdy foundation of their marriage.

Amish folks did not approve of alcoholic beverages, especially after marriage, but this English couple likely didn't think anything of it. They simply continued a tradition their parents carried on from their own.

So there was her answer. After the children had their bath, they were in her care, the parents taking the opportunity to share their day with each other.

Emma smiled to herself, feeling a stab of jealousy. How that must complete a person, this snug feeling of being with the one you love.

And for the thousandth time, she felt a deep remorse, an intense longing for what she would likely never experience.

It was the ocean, the allure of the restless water coupled with the excitement of being on her own. The combination brought back all the intensity of the attraction she had once experienced, the exhilaration of longing and desire. She allowed herself to feel it wash over her for a moment, and then sucked in a deep, cleansing breath. It wasn't right to wallow in those kinds of feelings.

She took a relaxing bath, but then found herself unable to fall asleep, thinking of the narrow appendage of land the house was built upon, the storms of summer, surrounded by all this water. It was a bit unsettling, wondering how many people had been drowned in a hurricane's wrath.

And the children. Would she be able to handle them? Annalise was hardly manageable, and with both parents going back to their jobs . . . Well, she'd do her best. She'd have to leave it to God to guide her through each day.

In the morning, everything was rosy with promise. She dressed and went downstairs to find the house secluded, the family still asleep. The clock on the stove said 6:30. Back at home, her family would be sitting down to breakfast together.

Coffee. She could hardly wait for a steaming cup to take out on the porch. She found what must be the coffee maker, but had no idea what to do with it. And where was the coffee? She found the little plastic cups that she knew contained coffee grounds, opened one up, plugged the machine in, and then just stared. She could guess which buttons to press, but what if she broke it? And was she to dump the grounds into the top, or what? The French press they used at home sure was simpler. Sometimes electricity just complicated things, she mused.

She gave up, tossed the cup in the trash, ashamed to leave it on the counter, and started to wander around the downstairs. She stopped at the big glass sliding doors that led to the porch, absorbing the beauty around her. Then she went quietly from one window to another, before simply standing silent, gazing with worshipful eyes at the grasses in the sand.

The sun had already begun its ascent into the lavender and cornflower blue hue of the early morning sky, like a dazzling brushstroke of yellow to surprise the soft serenity around it. The ocean was darker, the water calm and glistening as far as Emma could see, which was to the edge of the horizon. She couldn't see the pounding, seething water's edge—it was blocked by the tall grasses that sprouted from the sand like an old man's whiskers. There was a wooden walkway to the right.

Oh, there it was. That must be the house the Forsythe's were renovating. Very quietly, she unlocked the sliding door that led to the deck overlooking the sand, the picturesque walkway, and the tall tufts of grass. She took notice of the color of the grass, muted, a hue that blended with the sand, the sky, and the water.

She thought how God must love creating beauty to delight His people. Here at the ocean, He had poured out a cornucopia of enchantment.

Emma breathed deeply, then stood, her hands at her sides, in awe.

From a distance, she could hear the ocean emptying itself on the sand, then taking it all back in an undercurrent, ambitiously rearranging shells and bars of sand. The ocean was like a busy housewife, going about its duties every day, working to ensure that life went on for its creatures as smoothly as God intended.

She turned to the right and saw an immense house, also on poles, which she had learned were called piles. Driven into the sand by powerful equipment, into the sturdy foundation of earth or rock, they held the entire house away from storm surges. The house was being unclothed, the old siding half torn away. If they were planning on the renovation being complete by September, someone had better get started.

She heard the low hum of a diesel engine, watched as a white double cab pickup truck pulled up to the structure. It was a schrina truck, one of the construction vehicles common in Amish settlements. Driven by an English person, they were how contractors got to and from work. As farming became more difficult, with low milk prices and the inability to compete on account of horse-drawn, old-fashioned, steel-wheeled equipment, the younger men took to construction work. It was an acquired skill, but the traditional Amish work ethic was in high demand.

She thought how this schrina truck was not filled with Amish men, the way many of them were at home.

She flattened herself against the side of the house, not wanting to appear curious like the proverbial nosy neighbor. *Bid she was*, she thought with a low chuckle.

The driver wore loose shorts, a T-shirt and a cap. He was an older man, his beard graying along the sides. A second man emerged, younger, wearing a straw wide-brimmed hat . . .

What?

It surely couldn't be. Not an Amish man. Not here by the ocean!

Both back doors of the cab were flung open, disgorging three young men that stretched and yawned, held coffee cups, those essential insulated travel mugs that were like a growth from a construction worker's hands.

Emma's heart was pounding now. She sidled back, away from their scrutiny. She did not want to be seen. She was embarrassed to be spying on them, but her curiosity was intense.

Two of the workers were barely old enough to be on the job, legally, she bet. Skinny, with their hair cut short, they were dressed in the broadfall pants of the Amish, but were wearing T-shirts. They were soon chasing one another through the sand, rolling and tumbling like half-grown puppies, the older Amish man turning to watch, laughing.

And then . . .

He came around from the other side of the truck, opened the door of the truck cap, began to retrieve tools of some kind. All she remembered later was that he was tall, sturdy, with blond hair, disheveled, long. No beard, although he was easily old enough.

An older single man. An *Amish* single man.

Oh great, she thought. And went inside, opening the sliding glass door too quickly, her uneasiness sending it back against the frame with a dull thud.

"You're up!"

Roger stood at the counter, the strange black bulk of some electric device gurgling coffee into a single mug. The smell was so wonderful, Emma had to restrain herself from grabbing it.

"Good morning, Emma."

"Good morning."

"I hope you slept well."

"Of course. The bed is very comfortable."

A lie, in a white sort of way, but still . . . She had slept well once she finally dozed off.

"Coffee?"

"Please. It smells wonderful."

She watched as he took the little cup (without opening it, she noted), lifted the black lid, inserted the cup, punched a button after setting the mug in place, and turned to smile at her.

"K-Cups. The greatest."

Emma smiled back. "I've noticed them at grocery stores. I wondered what they were."

"Seriously?"

Emma smiled. "I'm Amish." Shrugged her shoulders.

"You don't actually have electricity in your house?"

"No. Although we have battery-powered lamps. Actually, battery-powered almost everything if we want. Some things change from time to time."

Roger smiled.

Emma's eyes kept wandering to the east windows.

"Your construction crew arrived."

"Oh. Already?"

"Looks like it."

Roger went to the master bedroom to talk to Kathy, then pushed his feet into the brown sandals by the door and let himself out, saying, "Help yourself to a bagel there on the counter."

Emma thought Kathy might make an appearance after her husband's visit, but everything remained quiet. Unsure whether to open the refrigerator door to look for creamer, she sipped the black coffee, her eyes going to the east window.

Roger and the older man stood on the back deck, deep in conversation.

An orange and yellow lift with wide tires set far apart was crawling over the sand, the arm extended to allow one of the youthful workers to climb in.

The whole apparatus was driven by . . . *him*.

As the lift advanced, she had a fairly good view of his profile. She turned away.

She felt the cloud of desolation, of discouragement settle around her, the sight of that tanned face with the short wide nose, the perfect mouth like forbidden territory, but one that beckoned with all the allure of an unexplored landscape.

What if it happened again?

She found herself weak-kneed, having to sit down. She knew what she had experienced at the window, knew the perils it held. Only once she had been in love, an attraction that turned her world upside down with its cruelty.

Never again, she vowed.

She sipped her coffee, got up, and went to the window. She was unable to stop herself from one more look, one more curious glance to cement the fact that he was heart-stoppingly attractive.

He was standing beside the lift, looking directly at the window where she stood, a quizzical expression on his face. Their eyes met, and Emma turned away, vanished behind the white curtain, hoping he had not seen enough to recognize her as an Amish girl.

When Kathy made a sleepy appearance at the door of her bedroom, Emma was trying hard to regain her usual calm. She actually stood toward the middle of the living room so Kathy wouldn't guess at her curiosity at the window.

Another K-Cup was inserted, another steaming cup produced, and together they stood looking out the sliding glass door to the now waving grasses and the glistening light on the restless water.

"Lovely, isn't it?" Kathy remarked.

"It's quite unreal. I have never been here, of course, but I find it hard to comprehend. The vast area of water is hard to imagine."

Kathy smiled contentedly, sipped her coffee, and said that was the reason they were putting everything into the renovation next door. She and Roger would grow old by the ocean, together.

CHAPTER 5

BREAKFAST WITH THE CHILDREN WAS A LESSON IN PATIENCE. BRENT ATE A bowl of cereal, drank his juice, and went to the living room to watch cartoons, while Emma tried every tactic, everything she had ever learned as a teacher, to get Annalise to eat or drink.

Kathy was over at the house, having left clear instructions about the children's breakfast, their vitamins and juice.

But Annalise wanted none of it. Not that cereal. Or this one. No oatmeal. She hated bagels. She wanted potato chips and candy canes.

Candy canes? In May?

Emma decided to be firm. She poured milk on a bowl of Rice Krispies and placed it in front of her, along with a cup of juice and the gummy vitamin, then sat beside her and stayed there.

It made no difference what Emma tried, Annalise would not eat. Emma told her to listen for the snap, crackle, and pop, she tried telling her a story about a child who never ate, she tried asking her sweetly and then asking her firmly to take a bite. Annalise simply sat in in the booster seat, kicking her feet and refusing to eat.

Emma felt a moment's panic. These people had been so sure she was a good choice, and here she was, helpless in the face of one strong-willed little two-year-old.

"Anna, look. If you don't want the Rice Krispies, can we go on the porch and give them to the seagulls?"

"No." She shook her head vehemently.

"Then you'll have to hurry up and eat them."

"I don't want to."

Which meant she wouldn't do it.

Emma glanced at the window, afraid Kathy would return to find her incompetence in full display, her daughter without breakfast.

No bagel, no toast, no cereal.

Which left eggs. She remembered her mother's treat when they were sick. An egg in a nest. It was worth a try.

"Why don't we try making an egg in a nest?" Emma asked. "You can sit here on the countertop and watch while I make it."

Without asking, she helped the child from the booster seat, settled her a good distance away from the stove, and proceeded to show her the first step, which was to cut a hole in the middle of a slice of whole wheat bread.

"What are you doing?" she asked, sliding closer.

She showed her how the remaining toast was buttered on both sides, placed on a pan, and an egg broken carefully into the hollowed out center, the heat turned low until everything was cooked to a golden brown. A sprinkle of salt, and it was set before her with a child's knife and fork.

Annalise said the egg was for Charlie Brown, but she'd eat the toast, which is what she did, cutting miniature bites with the dull knife and spearing it with her fork.

She was eating, which left Emma sighing with relief, and tackling the bowl of soupy Rice Krispies herself.

"You're eating the seagull's breakfast," Annalise said, but laughed amiably.

"They can have the rest of my bagel," Emma answered.

Annalise nodded, smiled, steadily eating her way through most of the egg in a nest. She brought Charlie Brown to her plate and bent her head low to ask in a confidential tone whether he was hungry this morning.

"He will eat this, but he needs more salt."

Emma obeyed, sprinkling a bit of salt on the egg, and was gratified to see it disappear in very small but consistent bites.

Brent returned to the kitchen to ask what he could smell.

"An egg in a nest," Annalise informed him airily.

"What is that?" he asked.

So Emma was making one for Brent when the parents reappeared, both tanned, slight, dressed in shorts and T-shirts, their hair disheveled, but somehow exuding an air of being well dressed, comfortable in their own skin. It was a sense of knowing they had accomplished much in their young lives and were about to tackle another worthy project.

"Mm!" Kathy said, sniffing the air.

"Someone is cooking breakfast," Roger said, rubbing his stomach.

This is how Emma was introduced to her role as a cook, along with keeping the beach house spotless. There was a grocery list to keep up, the laundry, and the child care, so Emma's forenoon was taken up by instructions, then the job of carrying them out.

She hadn't bargained for the cooking. Nothing had ever been said on the subject, and she'd imagined their taste in food would be too gourmet, too classy for her, but this was not the case. She had found many food items from Aldi or Costco or the Great Value brand from Wal-Mart as she unpacked the boxes and bags of grocery items.

Well, everyone had their own way of budgeting money, no matter how much or how little they had available, and it was certainly none of her business.

So there would be meals to plan with a limited amount of resources. She longed for her mother's cookbooks, the stained recipe box containing the dog-eared recipes that had been used over and over. She thought wistfully of the basement shelves filled with an array of colorful jars, the freezer filled with beef, chicken, and pork, most of it butchered on the farm in winter.

Grimly, she read labels. Strange grains, pastas, sauces.

What was hummus? Quinoa? Couscous? She was expected to cook this stuff? Seriously?

Well, they'd eaten the eggs and toast, called it grilled instead of toasted, pronounced it delicious, so she was off to a good start.

She tidied the living room, where both children remained, watching their shows, then cleaned the kitchen before the clock showed the arrival of lunchtime, or the hour before when she would have to think of something to serve. What would tempt the picky Annalise, as well as both parents?

Almost, she wished she had not taken the opportunity to be a nanny. They had not mentioned the cooking part until she was safely placed in the center of this white kitchen and all its confusing gadgets. She felt as if each one was glaring at her with a worldly malevolence, daring her to try to figure it all out.

As if on cue, there was an outraged howl from the vicinity of the living room.

"No! I don't want to watch the Minions!" Annalise was shouting at her brother.

Emma decided it was best to stay out of it, which was the very moment Kathy came pounding up the steps to the back deck, her face flushed with animation, ready to spill her morning's plans the minute she opened the back door.

"I don't know how we lucked into this construction crew," she trilled.

"They are wonderful. They say by next weekend the siding and windows should be replaced and they'll be ready to gut the interior."

She placed her hands in the position of prayer.

"I hope and pray Daniel can get along with the architect we hired."

Since Emma knew nothing about this kind of thing, she kept her thoughts to herself while smiling and nodding. When Kathy emerged from the bathroom, she waved a hand and told her not to worry about lunch for her and Roger, they were involved next door, and if she wanted, she could pack a lunch and spend the afternoon on the beach with the children.

"Brent?" she called.

"What?"

His small form appeared at the door, a question in his eyes.

"Do you want to go spend the afternoon on the beach with Emma?"

A leap of pure exuberance was followed by a shriek and a dash to his sister who eyed him with disinterest, a thumb in her mouth and an elephant dangling over one arm.

"Pack a few bottles of water, a few juice boxes. They won't eat sandwiches but they'll eat a few slices of the deli ham. Cheese popcorn and these."

She set a box of granola bars on the counter.

"That will hold them over till dinner."

Dinner? Oh, that was the evening meal. Supper.

"Swimsuits . . . you unpacked them. Sunscreen. Apply it before you go out and every two hours. I know . . ." She waved a hand. "They say you don't have to, but I won't take chances. I don't want my children exposed to the harmful rays. You know, the old hole in the ozone."

Emma thought of days in the produce fields with the heat of the sun beating down, never thinking of sunscreen or harmful rays. Perhaps the sun was different by the ocean, or perhaps there was more of the body exposed to the rays that were potentially harmful.

"So, plenty of sunscreen, and you know the rest. They are not allowed in the water at all unless they hold your hand, and then I want you to stay at the water's edge. Don't let them feed the gulls. Watch for jellyfish or horseshoe crabs washing ashore. And most important. Do *not* let them out of your sight."

Neon letters flashed through her bewilderment. She definitely would not let them out of her sight. But what was this about jellyfish and horseshoe crabs? She had read about both, of course. Had seen pictures. But did they really wash up on the beach?

Her list of frightening experiences was becoming quite lengthy, indeed. Dinner to plan without recipe books or the usual amount of home-canned or frozen food. Weird creatures afloat in that restless water. Sunburn on little bodies. The man next door.

Kathy left with two granola bars and two diet sodas.

Emma had no trouble getting both children into their swimsuits, then donned her own olive green one piece suit. She thought of wearing the white cover up for the walk to the water's edge, but decided against it, with the construction crew next door.

Perhaps she should. It would serve as a disguise, and he would have no idea she was anyone he would want to become interested in. That was a good thought, she decided, and hung her pale blue dress on a hook, pushed her feet into an old pair of flip-flops and went downstairs.

Brent and Annalise took no notice of her change in appearance, merely looked at her without comment and walked or danced, either one appropriate on your way to the beach, evidently.

A large straw hat completed the disguise, so the walk to the water's edge was without discomfort. Swimming had always been a part of the family's life, the farm pond cleaned and disinfected with chemicals each year, the children diving, tubing, and paddle boating their way around it. They had picnics, late-night campfires, races, volleyball, family gatherings down at the pond, so swimming was certainly nothing new.

Many conservative Amish would not swim at all, and certainly not with brothers or fathers, or men in general, but there were others who were more liberal and thought nothing of it. Emma's family was among those who enjoyed many forms of recreation, including the water in the pond, or spending an occasional long weekend at a cabin on the lake in New York.

The sun was like a hot blanket thrown across her shoulders and down her arms. She might have to think twice about sunscreen. The children scampered ahead like young puppies, stopped to hang from the wooden railing, flop back on their feet, and race ahead.

Emma cringed, thinking of splinters.

Here on the grass, the scent of salty mud, black muck, and brine was even thicker. She loved the smell of it, the salt and wet earth repulsive in a good way. Fishy. Sea smells.

She smiled, breathed deeply. Whatever she would have to face would surely be leveled evenly by the sheer pleasure of being in this wonderful place.

The sand was surprisingly hot. A dozen steps and Emma experienced real pain on the soles of her feet. She stopped, reached into her canvas tote, and quickly put the flip-flops back on her feet.

Driftwood and clumps of the yellowish grass gave way to a wide expanse of beach, dotted with an array of bright umbrellas like artificial flowers. Small groups of beachgoers gathered around them, while children raced and shrieked at the water's edge, with doting grandparents that hovered like anxious gulls. Some of the more daring adults swam out so far they bobbed like corks in calmer waters, having dived through the stronger waves closer to shore.

Emma found a spot that did not interfere with other beachgoers, spread the large towels, unfolded her beach chair, and took both hopping children by the hand after serious negotiations about Charlie Brown, who Emma said had to stay on the chair. Emma told Annalise in a firm voice that elephants were not accustomed to salt water and it might melt his trunk.

Annalise looked from Emma to Charlie Brown and back again, before turning to set him on the chair with a tube of sunscreen. "Just in case he might need it," she said seriously.

At these moments, the child could be so winsome, so endearing with her oversized imagination, that disliking her was simply not a possibility.

Through her years of teaching, she had her share of experiences with first graders such as Annalise. Adorable, and absolutely impossible, their mothers distracted or intimidated by the antics of their child, or simply undone by the amount of the daily workload, the remaining children and their needs, or other concerns more important than those of a stubborn little six-year-old.

Every family may have a different reason for producing this kind of child, but the reasons were there, no doubt. The nature handed down by either parent, perhaps difficult themselves, or neglect, even if it was unintentional, or in some cases it was too much attention that made a child act in such a way.

Emma saw Annalise as a fierce little warrior with her mother's lawyer-like skills, coupled with a decided lack of boundaries. The boundaries she so desperately needed at this tender young age.

She was a nanny for the summer, not a psychiatrist, or a counselor, or even a child specialist. She had merely been an Amish teacher in a one-room schoolhouse for ten years.

Ten was nice round number. A goal reached. From here on out, there would be new ideas, new jobs, new attempts to find out what really fulfilled her.

At this moment, it was standing at the water's edge with two children's hands clutched in either one of hers, hopping ridiculously high every time a small ripple appeared, sending the waves up over their ankles.

They would never tire of it, Emma thought, so with promises of a sandcastle, she got them away from the water's edge.

It was very warm, and she longed for a swim, but knew it was not possible with both children in her care, so she moved the towels and chair closer to the water, where the breeze from the water cooled her considerably.

They dug with plastic shovels and bright yellow buckets, tamped the sand down with the palms of their hands, and began all over again, upending the buckets to form the base of the castle. Emma was covered in sand, on her hands and knees, listening to the screech of the gulls, half hearing the chatter of the children, when a larger wave rushed up to the half built structure and washed it away. Brent stood in the sand and rushing water, his feet and ankles disappearing as he sank, and laughed out loud, his mouth open wide. Annalise, on the other hand, was knocked off her feet, landed on her bottom with a squawk of indignation, followed by a storm of weeping and wailing. She accidentally rubbed sand into her eyes, which brought a fresh torrent of outraged howls, until Emma reached her, picked her up, and took her to the water's edge to be rinsed.

They returned to the towels and chair, unpacked the food, and drank thirstily, the children draining their juice boxes and asking for granola bars.

Emma felt the burn on her shoulders, but thought she'd be fine. Her skin was not pale, but a golden hue all year long, so there was no reason to apply the smelly stuff.

They watched hermit crabs burrow deep into holes in the sand, tried capturing a few, but let them go after too much effort was spent.

Emma fell into a half doze as she lay back in her chair, listening to the constant sounds of the incoming waves, the cry of the gulls, the distant chatter of the people surrounding her. It was both peaceful and mindboggling, this oceanside observatory, as she had already labeled her chair.

There was so much to fathom, to see, hear and understand, and no matter how she catalogued her observances, not too much of it was understandable.

What really caused those waves? Where did all the shells begin to form? What did hermit crabs eat? Could they eat anything, or was their life span so short they didn't really need a menu to choose from? What kept the gulls from dying of food poisoning, with all the snacks and plastic wrappers they stole like hooded robbers?

She watched the children, who were mostly engrossed with shrieking and hopping over small ripples, then ate a granola bar, glancing at the wrapper. "Kind." She wondered if they were kind, as in nice to your intestines, or if it was the German word for child. Either way, they were very good for a store-bought granola bar. Her mother made a big batch of homemade ones every week with oatmeal, Rice Krispies, coconut, wheat germ, honey, peanut butter, melted marshmallows, and a few more ingredients. They were the best thing ever.

What would she make for supper? Dinner. She'd have to get used to these new ways of speaking.

They'd better get back, if she was to have dinner on the table by six. She guessed six o'clock. No one had really spoken of the hour.

Brent did not want to go back, but after mildly protesting, he helped her pack up. Annalise was red with irritation. Wait, red? She gasped. She had forgotten to apply sunscreen after two hours. A thudding of her heart was followed by a sickening realization of her oversight.

It was too late now.

She was too sick at heart to notice any surroundings on her return, simply herded the children into the house and their bath, applied a soothing after-sun lotion, settled them in front of the ever-present cartoon shows, and had a quick shower of her own.

She was in the kitchen, reading the label on a jar of spaghetti sauce, when Kathy came tripping up the stairs, laughing back over her shoulder, followed by her husband who was out of breath.

Kathy stood quite still, looking at Emma.

"Wow," she mouthed quietly.

Emma raised an eyebrow.

"What?"

"Your hair! It is so gorgeous."

"I . . . oh, thank you."

She stammered, remembered the proper response to a compliment. In the world of the Amish, a compliment was hard to come by, children raised in fear of a damaging pride in their own looks or accomplishments. Parents were careful to keep their offspring from becoming *grosfeelich*, which left Emma with genuine surprise at this worldly woman's response to her hair freed from its restraints, the small pile of steel hairpins and thin hairnet that held the coil of hair to the back of her head. Dena had often told her she had quite the head of hair, but Dena talked all the time, with half her observances free of sincerity.

"Your hair! I had no idea!" Kathy elaborated. "Roger, go away. We'll have you running off with the nanny."

Roger's face expressed good humor, and he agreed that Emma had a head full of thick wavy hair that was very unusual in its coloring, followed by a resounding, "What's for dinner?"

"You know, Roger, we told them to come for grilled shrimp tonight."

Kathy's tone took on a forceful whine.

"You did."

"I want them to come over. We don't have much social life here. No parties, nothing. So why can't they come over?"

Roger didn't answer, merely walked into the living room to scoop up his son and settle himself into the soft folds of the recliner, the remote in his right hand. Brent settled himself against his father's shoulder, a small smile playing around the corners of his mouth.

Kathy sighed, put her balled fists on her hips and went to the recliner.

"I'm talking to you, darling, and I think I deserve an answer."

Roger's response was unintelligible.

"Oh, for . . ."

Kathy came stalking back to the kitchen, her eyes snapping, then made a quick decision by going into the bedroom with a door flung against its frame.

Roger brooded, his quick blue eyes clouded over, his eyelids half-closed. When Annalise tried to pull herself up, he told her to go lie down, he wanted to watch this show. Charlie Brown was gathered into her arms, the thumb inserted and the slow dejected walk to the couch begun.

Emma breathed in, released it, and turned away.

She reminded herself she was the nanny. She could observe, but that was it.

That first night she made spaghetti and meatballs from the recipe on the generic jar of the tomato sauce from Aldi. She tore romaine lettuce, added croutons, shaved Parmesan cheese, and made her own dressing, winging it completely and hoping for the best.

Roger sat sullenly and Kathy refused to make an appearance, although the children kept up a lively chatter, especially Brent who loved the spaghetti. He told everyone about how Annalise had been upset on her bottom by the water.

The meal was very difficult, with Roger's silence, but she got through it with respectful silence of her own. The children were told about Mommy's headache, which seemed to satisfy them enough to play with their electronics after the food was eaten.

Emma cleared the table, put the leftovers in containers, and was ready to run the hot water when Roger came to help her with the dishwasher.

Blushing, Emma told him she was sorry to be so electric illiterate, which set him to laughing, saying that was a smart phrase, right there.

He said he supposed he was wife illiterate himself, to which Emma raised an eyebrow, and asked softly, "Why?"

He opened the dishwasher, reached under the sink for a green box of soap, measured, and poured.

"Now stack your dishes. Pots on the bottom, like this. Plates, silverware, glasses on top. There you go. Close door, press button. Now how hard is that?"

"Not hard at all," Emma grinned.

Roger leaned against the counter, crossed his arms and threw one ankle over the other, his gaze held steadily on her face.

"Why, you ask. Women are hard to figure out, that's what. One minute she's head over heels for me, the next she's like a . . . well, whatever.

"She took a shine to that Amish guy. I don't care what she says."

Ohhhh, Emma thought.

"So I told her. She's . . ."

He jerked a thumb in the direction of the bedroom door.

"I assume it's part of being married," Emma said honestly, listening to the sound of water coming from the dishwasher.

"Yeah well, I'm getting really sick of it."

Of what? Emma wondered, but didn't say it.

"She's smart, she's wealthy, has the classic blond good looks, and most of the time, I'm okay with her flirting. I mean, I trust her. As much as a man can, I guess. We are married, so I guess that counts for something. But in today's world, it's about as secure as being wrapped in wet toilet tissue."

Emma protested.

"I'm serious. Not one of the colleagues I work with has his first wife. Not one. Some of them are on the third go round."

His earnest blue eyes touched her heart. She was surprised he was confiding in her so quickly, but she felt it her duty to listen.

"I can't imagine."

"Do you guys, like . . . stay married?"

"Divorce is rare, but it happens, I suppose. In isolated instances. Although, we are very normal. Marriages are not perfect, but divorce isn't really an option. Our vows are pretty serious."

"So were ours. Or mine were, anyway. I do love her."

"Of course. Of course you do. You should be telling her this."

"I can't tell her."

"Of course you can. And should."

Emma turned to wipe the counter, but felt his eyes following her.

"You know you're beautiful, don't you?"

Emma bit her lower lip, shook her head. What was the proper procedure here? Were there rules for nanny behavior when the husband acted this way? She kept her eyes downcast.

"You are, you know. I'm not trying to come on to you, Emma. Seriously. I just can't figure out why a girl like you isn't taken. You're the real deal."

Emma gave a small laugh, a nervous sound of acknowledgment. Then she excused herself to collect the children for their nighttime ritual, leaving Roger watching her receding figure, the auburn hair with the glorious ripples like an overlay of gold.

Slowly he walked to the bedroom door, lifted his hand to knock, then lowered it and inserted it self-consciously into a pocket. He turned, poured a glass of wine and let himself out into the warm night and the sound of the pounding surf.

CHAPTER 6

KATHY MADE AN APPEARANCE THE FOLLOWING MORNING, LATER THAN usual, with a freshly washed head of hair, her makeup applied flawlessly. She wore a white pair of shorts and a blue shirt, the same striking shade of blue that played up her eyes. She was short and petite, with perfectly tanned legs, the physique of an athlete.

"Good morning, Emma."

"Good morning."

"Sorry about the headache last night. Look, I'm going into town. I need a day of shopping. The pressure around here has been profound, and I'm definitely not up to one of Anna's moods, so I'm taking a day off."

She inserted the coffee into the coffeemaker, walked to the living room window and watched the men on the lift.

"These guys are amazing."

Emma said nothing.

"I'm starved."

She pulled a bagel from the bag, laid it in the toaster oven, turned a dial, punched a button, and walked away, back to the window that looked out over the renovation.

Emma was washing windows with Windex and paper towels.

"Where's Roger?"

"I haven't seen him this morning."

"Well, where is he?"

Kathy became quite agitated, grabbed her cell phone from the table, swiped and lifted it to her ear, shaking her hair back as she did so. The phone rang four times before she stamped a foot in irritation, held the device in both hands as her thumbs danced across the screen.

"So irritating, that guy. He never answers his phone."

She opened the door of the toaster oven, spread low-fat cream cheese, and went to the refrigerator for a container of yogurt.

Her phone pinged.

She reached for it immediately.

"Oh my word. He's in town. Can you imagine? He wants me to join him for breakfast."

The bagel was tossed in the trash, followed by the almost full container of yogurt.

"Tell the kids where we are."

She grabbed her car keys and phone.

"Oh, and I noticed Annalise was . . . her skin was red. Did you forget the sunscreen?"

"Yes, I did. I'm sorry."

"Try to remember today. They should actually wear a T-shirt."

She let herself out the door.

Emma sighed. Roger had evidently spent the night on the recliner in the living room, his shirt and shoes thrown beside it, a cotton blanket rumpled on the seat. *Well, alrighty then*, she thought. The first few days of being a nanny and here she was, plunked down in the middle of this faceless drama that hovered through the rooms like carbon monoxide, invisible but highly dangerous.

Not yet, she decided. They merely had a quarrel, a lover's quarrel, about the . . . She knew who Roger was talking about. Likely Kathy had merely been attracted and he'd blown it all out of proportion with his petty jealousy.

He'd meant well, giving Emma that honest compliment. She simply wasn't used to anyone noticing her looks, that all. She chalked it up to a cultural difference.

She went ahead with the window washing, her thoughts going to her own sisters and their drama, real or imagined. Married life could not be one smooth, glassy sea of constant perfect love and trust, no matter your religion or your way of life. It was two people who were thrown together by that first attraction, a friendship build over the course of a few years of dating, a wedding, and there you were. Taken away from the security of your own home and parents, to live with a person you thought you knew inside out and upside down, only to discover he was picky with his food, had an annoying habit of leaving one shirtsleeve turned wrong side out in the laundry hamper, he didn't brush his teeth well at all and had bad breath much of the time because of it.

And if you shakily ventured out of your "good wife" shell to tell him this, he pouted for days and days.

Your own personal Romeo, the man of your dreams, suddenly so very human.

Would she have felt the same if her life had turned out differently? If Sam King would have been her husband instead of Esther's?

She never dated him, so how could she tell? He was the perfect man, sprouted to fantastic proportion in her mind's eye, the first heart-stopping palpitations of a fierce love the only thing she could remember.

Marriage was a gamble, she supposed, but that gamble looked pretty appealing after ten years of teaching school and wondering if she'd ever meet a suitable partner. It would be one thing if she could know for certain that she'd be single the rest of her life. Then she could just embrace the role of old maid and make the best of it. But it was emotionally exhausting to wonder, to dabble in longing, to navigate the fragile feelings of unwelcome suitors and hope for the right man to show up.

Here were Kathy and Roger, the perfect couple, having a silly disagreement about absolutely nothing. Or at least it seemed like nothing from her perspective. Just a misunderstanding, at worst.

She was on the outside of the glass doors, wiping with paper towels that were too wet to continue, so she stepped inside to tear off another bunch of dry ones. As she stepped outside, she caught sight of . . .

Oh my.

It was him. Coming up that long flight of stairs.

She felt cornered, panicked.

On he came.

Emma turned slowly to face him, the Windex bottle in one hand, the paper towels in another. The morning light was behind him, the sun already well in the sky.

He was, indeed, very tall, his hair blond and windswept, cut in the Amish style. His cheeks and jaw were clean-shaven, the symbol of an unmarried man. His eyes were not blue, neither were they green or brown. The color was indiscernible, but they were wide and flat and twinkling with happiness.

"There you are."

That was how he greeted her. As if he had found a long-awaited treasure, and it was even more delightful than he'd anticipated. He came up those steps till he towered above her, dwarfed the deck they stood on, and didn't say a word. He looked at her until he was finished, and she looked back at him observing all that in a moment.

He smiled, a genuine warmth reflected in his eyes.

"You didn't know I knew you were here, did you?"

She was so muddled, so taken aback, she couldn't piece that sentence into something she could comprehend, so she nodded, her eyes never leaving the height and breadth and wonder of him.

He extended a hand. She looked down at it as if she was not quite sure what she should do, then held up the Windex and paper towels, before setting them on the patio table.

She took the proffered hand. He held it far too long. It was ridiculous. When he released it, she wanted to be united again, the handshake so comforting and promising, so secure and warm.

"You thought you were safe from other Amish here, I bet."

She smiled. The sun shone on her auburn hair and shot it through with light and waves. Her teeth were very white and a bit crooked in front where one tooth overlapped the other, her skin was gold with flecks of freckles like crumpled copper, and her eyes so green it was like the ocean in winter, except she didn't know any of this.

She was wearing a pale pink dress and nothing on her feet. Her white head covering framed her lovely hair like the angelic halo he imagined she should be wearing.

"Roger and Kathy Forsythe. They told me about you."

She smiled.

"Did they call me their nanny?"

"They did. An honorable title, a nanny."

"Thank you. I taught school before acquiring the title."

"Who are you? As in family lineage?"

"I'm Emma. Abe Beiler's Dan."

He shook his head. "Lancaster?"

"No. Crawford County."

"But originally from there?"

"Aren't we all? The motherland."

He laughed, clearly delighted with her wit.

"I can only stay a minute. And it looks as if your work just woke up."

Emma turned to find Brent and Annalise standing directly inside, Charlie Brown draped unbecomingly over one arm.

"Oh."

Emma turned, ushered them out, and made the proper introductions, including the sagging elephant, her eyes telling him to be serious.

And he was, shaking the elephant's leg just as he had shook the children's hands.

"He is a very nice elephant."

"Thank you," Annalise said, before sharing the information about his frequent washings in the washer, plus being dried to make him fluffy.

"I have to go, guys. I'll see you around, surely. It will be hot today, so maybe I'll see you on the beach."

With that, he was gone, clomping down the steps and hurrying across the sand.

On the beach? *Mercy days*, as her mother would say.

But she found herself with a spring in her step, felt as if she could take the stairs two at a time, or three. She cleaned both bathrooms after making perfect eggs in a nest for Annalise, with orange juice in a sippy cup for her and a small plastic tumbler for Brent. There was bacon, so she fried a few slices for each child and was rewarded with exaggerated eye rolls and tummy rubbings, as the children informed her this was not always allowed.

"Today it is. Today is a great day for bacon," Emma announced, twirling across the kitchen with her skirt billowing.

"Yay! Bacon day!" Brent shouted and Annalise clapped her little hands before reaching for her plate.

She told them the story of the gingerbread man while they ate, and promised to bake gingerbread men some rainy day, which was met with more cheers.

The day on the beach was like the one before, except she was dressed quite properly in her dress, with a black *dichly* (bandana) attached to her head. She would never allow him to meet her on the beach in that green swimsuit. Never. She was raised in a home that practiced modesty, and modest she would be. She sat primly in the boiling hot sun, drank cold water from her water bottle, and tried to stay sitting instead of getting up to rearrange her chair, telling herself it was not to check on the construction worker's whereabouts.

The children were taken to the edge of the water, sandcastles were built, futile attempts at capturing hermit crabs established again, sandpipers chased, dolphins sighted.

The dolphins were seen after a group of children began to hop up and down, wave their arms and point out to sea. Emma got out of her chair, shaded her eyes with her hand and strained to see these beautiful creatures. In spite of herself, she gasped audibly when the graceful arc of a leaping dolphin came into view. Then another, and another. They seemed to leap slowly, without any effort, rising from the water and reemerging with a fluid motion. The sight was beyond anything Emma had ever seen and from that day on, she kept a keen eye out for the frolicking dolphins.

She remembered the sunscreen this time, applying it to her own burning face. She'd be as brown and as wrinkled as an old lady if she wasn't careful in this sun.

For a moment, she felt a keen sense of homesickness, for the days in the fields. She missed Dena. If she were home, she and Dena would be getting up early to help her mother with breakfast, which was no small feat with the ten children, the table spread across the middle of the kitchen, which was the largest room in the house. Then they would wash dishes and tidy the kitchen, followed by hours of working side-by-side with Dena under the same sun that lent its intense rays now. By July, they were tanned, fit, so used to the heat and the hard work, the days flew by with crate after crate of zucchini, cucumbers, green beans, red beets, all of it harvested, cleaned, and packed to send to the produce auction or sold at the roadside stand at the end of the driveway.

She was surprised how much she missed all that action. It was the days of purpose, of knowing there was so much work that sixteen hours of daylight were barely enough. There was the farm mortgage to pay, and Emma knew her father was putting down double monthly payments during the summer. That was when the children were taken to the optometrist in town to have their vision checked. Benjamin had a serious dental problem with overlapping growth, so he was taken to the orthodontist in summer, when the cash flow was available.

It was all a challenge, a goal, the reason for getting out of bed in the morning. She missed it more than she was willing to admit.

She felt the sun's warmth weakening, saw the spread of gray obliterate the blue, then watched the children playing in the sand, unaware of a change in the weather. She'd let them play. She'd not planned supper, since Kathy would be in town and she wasn't sure about Roger. She and the kids could just grab something easy.

Suddenly, there was no more light or heat from the sun. The clouds hung like a blanket of gray and the ocean looked cold, ominous, frothing white caps of the waves taking on a sinister appearance. Currents came and went, the temperature of the ocean water unpredictable with all the tides and underlying ebb and flow. They had talked about the unusually warm water for the end of May, the sun's heat strong, like July, but now perhaps this was about to change.

Already a breeze was tugging at umbrellas, beachgoers struggling to fold them into a more manageable position, calling children away from their play. Emma got up, folded her beach chair and called to the children.

"Brent!"

He looked up from his digging.

"Come. Let's go back. I think it will rain soon, okay?"

As usual, he dumped the water in his small pail, picked up the shovel and plastic colander, then turned to his sister. Emma watched him say something, then more forcefully, spreading both arms and waving to make a point.

Annalise put both feet on the sand and refused to budge.

Oh boy, here we go again, Emma thought, but walked to their play spot, hunkered down and began negotiations. This was why she had been hired, and her she was, failing miserably.

If Annalise were her own child, Emma would have picked her up and carried her firmly to the house where discipline would have been measured out. Children needed boundaries, needed to know what was expected of them, and when. But this stubborn child was being raised by the terms of modernity, the new gentle way that would not harm the child's self-esteem.

The old fashioned way was to break the will of the child, to teach obedience from the time they were old enough to understand, but all the senseless abuse in the world created a new way, with child welfare services ready to pounce on any form of physical discipline.

The gray clouds were churning now. Emma heard the distant rumble of thunder.

"Annalise, come. It will rain soon, okay? Charlie Brown will get wet."

A baleful glance.

"He likes rain."

"Anna, come on." An impatient Brent stamped a foot.

"I want to play in the sand," Annalise said, beginning to dig with her shovel.

"Emma sighed, looked on helplessly as groups were hustled to the walkway, casting covert glances in their direction.

"Anna honey, listen. When we get back to the house, we can make cupcakes."

"I don't like them."

"Charlie Brown does."

"I love cupcakes. Come on, Anna!" Brent shouted.

When she began to cry, Emma decided if she was going to do that, she may as well pick her up and get going, which is what she did. Brent carried the lunch basket, Emma hanging on to the screaming, wriggling Annalise while carrying the chair.

She made it to the boarded walkway before she dropped the chair and lost her grip on Annalise who chose to stiffen her body for a desperate try at freedom. She slid down Emma's side and plunked to the sand, her eyes squeezed shut as the back of her head made contact.

After that, it was all a blur of howls and screams that were completely embarrassing, people arriving with blankets and umbrellas rolled under their arms, casting annoyed or sympathetic glances her way. Emma sank to her knees, tried to cradle her in her arms, soothe and comfort, do anything.

Brent picked up the lunch basket, set it down, and looked toward the house.

What if the parents arrived to find this disaster?

Emma sank to the sand, pleaded with Annalise, to no avail. It seemed as if her very presence only made matters worse.

Then he was there.

Tall, strong, sympathetic, he hunkered down beside her and she looked into his eyes with her own filling up with genuine tears of distress.

"I don't know what to do," she said, soft and low.

"What's her name again?"

His eyes were looking into hers with so much kindness, she grappled with an emotion she could not name. It was a combination of failure at being an honorable nanny and shame that he had found her like this.

"Annalise."

She choked on the word, turned away.

"Annalise. Look. I have something for you." He said, reaching for her. But the child was beyond reasoning, giving herself over to a wild fear of being controlled, and when Brent's face crumpled and he began a soft crying of his own, Emma knew her fate was sealed.

She'd be taken home, replaced with a more competent person. The wind picked up, sending the tall grass into a disheveled dance, the sky darkening overhead as they sat helplessly with the shrieking child.

He shook his head.

Emma turned to Brent.

"Come here," she said gently, and when he did, she pulled him on her lap and held him close, murmured words of comfort.

"I'll carry her," he said decisively, picking her up in his sturdy arms.

He carried her, kicking and sobbing, as Emma followed with Brent, swallowing her distress. When they reached the house, he kept going up the stairs, through the glass door, strode through the kitchen to deposit Annalise on the sofa, before turning to Emma.

"Good luck," he said quietly, and briefly touched her shoulder.

She nodded, watched him leave as another rumble of thunder was heard in the distance.

And she still did not know his name.

That evening she had an honest talk with both parents, knowing there was no alternative.

She laid out her expectations.

Roger listened, wide-eyed, nodding. Kathy's face showed an impassive block, the setting of her mouth as impenetrable as cement.

"Look, this isn't good for anyone," she said. "Especially Annalise. To give in to her every whim is only worsening the situation. She's too young to have such control over her own environment. And it's not fair to Brent, either. He got stuck in the pouring rain today because I couldn't get Annalise to come when I asked her to."

Roger looked at his wife with something akin to pleading.

Kathy sighed.

"We should have known better than to hire an Amish schoolteacher."

Her words were clipped, emphatic.

"I'm sorry." Emma said quietly. "But these are my terms. If I am allowed to deal with her tantrums, I'll stay. If not, I'll go back home."

"There will be no physical punishment in my home," Kathy said tersely.

"I don't expect to do that," Emma answered, facing Kathy's belligerence with the remaining courage she could gather.

"How will you go about getting her to give in to you?" Kathy asked, with the beginning of a sneer on her lips.

"Time out? Ignoring the screaming? There are ways."

"Well, you will *not* leave my child out on the beach by herself," Kathy said.

"Yes. I will, if this happens again. I'll watch from a distance to make sure she's safe, but she needs to learn I mean business."

Emma felt her anger rising, felt it in her eyes as she faced Kathy. That it had come to this so soon was incomprehensible, but she knew there was no turning back. She refused to grovel, to stay here, no matter how beautiful it was, with all the impossibility of dealing with mother and daughter.

Roger spoke up.

"Kathy, you know it's been a rough ride with Annalise. Why not give Emma a chance? She promised not to lay a hand on her."

He was met with a stony silence.

"On one condition," Kathy said finally.

Emma lifted an eyebrow. When she met her employer's eyes, she knew she had the upper hand, the indecision flickering in Kathy's.

"I have a book for you to read. The contents are the protocol I want you to follow. If you are unwilling, then we'll terminate your contract."

Short-lived upper hand, Emma thought.

But she agreed to read the book, wondering if it would prolong what had turned into a skirmish.

And so she was handed a hardcover book with a glossy jacket. She read the description on the flaps, and sighed. Clearly whatever methods were outlined in the book hadn't worked so far, so she had no reason to believe they'd work now.

But she was willing to give it a try. She laid the book aside and went to the window to absorb the sight of a rainstorm, complete with thunder and lightning across a dark sea that was a seething mass of dark waves, the lighter froth appearing as a wave crested, then disappearing to be replaced by another.

Jagged lightning illuminated the turbulence of the water, followed by deep claps of thunder that shook the house. Rain pelted against the doors and windows and wind lashed the sides of the house until Emma thought the whole structure would surely be blown off the piles.

Kathy sat in the living room, holding her daughter who had fallen asleep after wearing herself out earlier. She was stroking her hair, gazing into her small face with so much love, for a moment Emma wished away the whole nasty business that had cropped up on the beach. She knew she had no children of her own, so who was she to judge the bond between a mother and her tiny daughter?

She turned back to the thunderstorm, the wind and the roiling water, the streaks of rain like a veil of water that obscured the horizon.

She had never experienced such dark and terrible beauty. The grasses were whipped into a frenzy, bowed by the weight of the water that clung to each stem. Lighting struck out like forked tongues, so fast and so brilliant it was blinding.

The glow of lamps and recessed lighting was comforting, along with the hum of the refrigerator and the flickering blue light from the televisions, the sturdy windows and doors built into the walls that separated them from the elements. She thought of Jesus and His disciples in the boat on stormy waters, the lifting of His hand when He said, "Be still," and everything, the wind, the waves, obeyed Him. How could anyone truly know this had actually occurred? No one could. That's where faith came in.

And faith seemed precious, real. She could hold it in her heart here on the Outer Banks of North Carolina, where a narrow strip of land jutted out into the Atlantic Ocean for miles, with a road and sturdy beach houses dotting the landscape like houses on a Monopoly board.

CHAPTER 7

THE FOLLOWING DAY, KATHY AND EMMA REACHED AN UNEASY TRUCE, with Annalise displaying her best behavior, dressed in a simple white sundress that made her appear angelic, a poster child depicting sweetness and light.

Roger spent most of the day with the contractors while Kathy was on her computer, telling Emma to keep the children entertained so she could get her work done.

No small feat, she thought, but nodded agreeably.

"Oh, and we're having the contractors in tonight. Roger will buy the seafood and prepare it, but we'll need something for dessert. And sides."

With that, she disappeared up the steps.

Emma swallowed. Her mouth went dry. She had to entertain the unruly Annalise, plus conjure up a few miraculous dishes in an afternoon, plus, he was coming to dinner. She groaned silently.

Well, no use shirking her duty. She'd prepare the food she was used to, and if it didn't pass muster, then so be it.

Both children were watching their morning shows, so she checked the cupboards for supplies before making decisions. She couldn't imagine Kathy wanted to be disturbed, so . . .

Milk. Heavy whipping cream. But no cornstarch or cocoa powder. Apples, flour, butter. Apple pie, perhaps. There was no shortening for pie crust, either. Butter would have to do. She found a small container of brown sugar as hard as a rock on the back shelf of a corner cupboard. If she could cook this lump of hardened sugar, dissolve it with water, she could thicken the sauce with flour.

Lord willing, she thought grimly, and set to work.

Both children drifted into the kitchen, having heard the pots and bowls on the countertop.

Emma turned to smile at them.

"What are you doing?" Brent asked, in his polite way.

"I am making two apple pies," Emma answered. "For tonight."

"What's tonight?"

"We're having company."

She said it brightly, to inspire Annalise.

The child frowned, petulant. "Charlie Brown doesn't want company."

"He doesn't?"

This was thrown out without much thought as Emma poured a mixture of water, beaten egg, and vinegar to wet the pie crust crumbs, thinking how her mother would throw her hands up and shake her head, seeing the butter used as shortening.

Emma had baked pies since she was fifteen, helping her mother replenish the supply at the roadside stand. They made shoofly, apple, raisin, blueberry, cherry, vanilla—too many to think about.

"We want to watch," Brent said.

"Here. I'll move the barstools and you can climb up."

She helped both of them to a seat, then watched as they positioned themselves onto their knees and leaned on their elbows as Emma mixed the pie dough.

She scattered flour on the work surface of the island, the detached appendage to the kitchen cabinets, a wonder that Emma resolved to add to her own kitchen if she ever had the good fortune to have one.

"I want to! I want to!" Annalise shouted, clapping her soft, dimpled hands.

So Emma placed a small amount of the pie dough in each one's hand, scattered some flour, and allowed them to play with a knife and fork to cut the dough into pieces.

They squealed, talked incessantly, clearly delighted to be able to do what Emma was doing.

And Emma assembled the pies, crimped the crusts, brushed the tops with egg wash and sprinkled liberal amounts of sugar on top before carrying them to the preheated oven. Then she mixed a yellow cake, baked it in a fluted pan, and made a cooked caramel glaze with the last of the brown sugar while the children played with the dough. Charlie Brown lay beneath a barstool, completely forgotten.

She peeled potatoes and set them to boil, whole. She watched carefully to remove them as soon as they boiled, and set them aside.

She tore romaine lettuce, boiled eggs, and cooked bacon. When Annalise demanded bacon, she allowed her a small piece and one for Brent, but when she wanted another one for Charlie Brown, Emma said no.

Annalise glared at her, took in two gulps of air, her mouth taking on the projected downturn, a signal for the coming shriek.

Emma stood directly in front of her and glared back without restraint.

"Don't do it, Annalise."

She said it in what she hoped was a non-threatening tone, but one that meant there would be no monkey business.

"Well, Charlie Brown *needs* a piece of bacon," she said in a grownup voice, dipping her head in an elaborate motion.

Emma smiled.

"But if he eats it we won't have enough for the salad."

Annalise eyed Emma, then clambered off the stool and went to find her mother. Quickly, Emma detained her with a scoop of her arm, told her firmly that Mommy was working and she could not go up there.

"But I want to tell her I want bacon."

"You can't tell her, okay? She's working."

The kitchen was being filled with the scent of baking pies, the yellow cake giving off a rich buttery smell that gave Emma a pang of homesickness.

Kathy came down the open stairway, saying she couldn't work with these outrageous smells seeping into her room.

Emma opened the oven door to check on the pies, then closed it again, placing the hot pad on the island countertop.

"It's just apple pie."

"Just!"

She threw her hands up, saying it couldn't be ordinary, everyday apple pie.

"A cake, too."

Kathy lifted lids, smiled, and oohed and aahed her way through the kitchen, then turned and told Emma she was truly a wonder. Any trace of the former animosity was gone.

"Thank you. But I'm afraid it's plain Pennsylvania Dutch cooking."

"It will be perfect. These men are your people, aren't they?" Kathy asked.

"Yes. Except the driver."

"I personally cannot wait to savor every dish."

Kathy patted her shoulder, then said she was going for a run.

"Me come too!" Annalise shouted.

"Do something with her," Kathy mouthed, before kissing the top of Brent's head, tying her running shoes and letting herself out the door without as much as a glance in her daughter's direction, who by now was taking deep breaths with the accompanying downturn of her mouth.

She scrambled off the barstool, threw herself at her mother, her cries gaining volume.

"Honey, oh honey. Don't cry."

"Me go too!" Annalise wailed.

Emma washed her hands at the kitchen faucet, then reached Kathy's side in a few quick strides, gently lifted the howling child, and turned away.

Kathy let herself out, swiftly, leaving Emma to deal with the girl's inability to accept a refusal to her will.

She sat on the sofa and held the small heaving child, who was

crying heartbrokenly this time, without the usual kicking and screaming that accompanied her anger.

"Me go too!" was released between sobs and hiccups.

Emma thought of the food preparation, checked the clock, then
told the children to get their sneakers, they were going for a run.

"Me go with Mommy!" Annalise wailed.

"No, Anna. We are going to do something else special," Emma
told her, putting her on the couch before heading to the bathroom
for a ponytail holder.

The sun was so huge and so bright, the landscape washed clean
by yesterday's shower. Shore birds trilled or warbled or called in their
high-pitched voices and the wind tossed the tall grasses and sent a
fine layer of sand skidding across the oyster-shell driveway. Emma
breathed in deeply, something she did without thinking. Oh how she
loved the brackish smell of the low-lying pockets of salty water surrounded by the thick growth of sea grass.

What an absolutely perfect day!

The sky was so blue it made the ocean appear almost artificial, as
if someone had painted the scene in an amateurish way. The white
haze of humidity had been swept away by the storm, leaving this
clear, gorgeous view, this world she would never want to leave.

"Hey!"

She turned to find him running up to them.

"Hey!" he said warmly, as if they were already old friends. "Do
you want to take a walk tonight? On the beach? After a storm, there
are thousands of shells."

Emma watched his animated face, the way the sun ruffled his
blond hair and revealed the darker copper colors underneath. His
skin was bronzed from the days in the sun, and it was only the end
of May.

"I probably shouldn't consider walking with a stranger, so I guess
you'd better tell me your name."

He lifted his face to the sky and laughed, sobered, and said
solemnly.

"Benjamin Glick, Junior. Ben is sufficient."

"How do you do, Ben?"

They were both laughing when they shook hands.

"So it's Ben. An honest, common Amish name," she remarked. "Actually, I can't go walking with you. You are supper guests at our house. At seven o'clock if I'm right."

His eyes narrowed. "Have they come to an agreement, then?"

She knew nothing about a disagreement, so she said evidently they had.

He clearly did not relish the idea, but shrugged his shoulders in a good-natured way and smiled.

"Well, that takes care of the walk, then. Tomorrow night?"

She nodded.

"We could do that."

"How's everything going?"

"Alright."

He saw the hesitation, the flicker of doubt, and made a mental note to ask her again when he could. He had to get back to work, and anyway they couldn't have a real conversation with Annalise pulling on her hand, begging her to get going.

She lifted a hand, and he was gone.

What was this? So soon. A walk on the beach—the epitome of romance.

She stared across the glittering wavelets on the horizon, the doubts and misgivings crowding her senses.

"Hey, come on, Emma," Brent said, coming back from his digging in the shallow sand by the driveway.

"Alright, here we go," she said, taking off in a pretend fast run.

Annalise giggled, then lowered her head, pumped her arms, and ran on her short little legs, the white dress billowing around her. Brent was soon so far ahead she had to call him back.

When they reached the road, she made them turn around. There were passing motorists that would make it unsafe for small children. Annalise was breathing hard, real or make believe, but Brent was like a skittish young colt, seemingly able to run for hours without becoming winded.

When she heard the crunch of tires on oyster shells, she glanced over her shoulder, herding the children to the side as Roger drove the SUV to a standstill.

"Hello there, Emma. Returning from a walk?"

Roger hung from the window, a thin freckled arm looped across the top of the car door, his blue eyes open and friendly.

"Yes, in fact, we are."

"Daddy! We were running!" Annalise shouted, breathing heavily in exaggeration.

"Good! See you at the house."

She watched him unload shopping bags, then climb the front stairway with them. When they entered the sunny, white kitchen, he had already dumped the oysters, shrimp, and scallops in individual bowls. He opened a brown paper bag and sniffed.

"Mm-mm. The best clams on the eastern shore."

The kitchen smelled as if he'd brought the ocean in with him. She looked forward to his cooking skills, hoped the simple food she had prepared would go well with the seafood.

When Kathy returned, there was a display of hugging and kissing, the children largely ignored, as Kathy tripped up the stairs as gaily as a teenager, trilling something about doing her nails.

Annalise fell asleep on the recliner, and Brent found a show to watch on TV after his father shooed him out of the kitchen. Emma was grateful she had gotten her baking done in the morning so she didn't need to share the workspace with Roger.

"What? What is this?" he shouted. "Apple pie!"

Emma said nothing, dusted the top of the furniture, and pulled out the sweeper.

"Did you make these, Emma?"

"I did."

"Oh my lady! How can this be true?"

He came close to her and bowed from the waist, an expression of worship on his face, until Emma couldn't help herself. She burst out laughing.

"Oh come on," she said, still smiling.

"When we hired you, I had no clue we were getting a pastry chef in the deal. Give the lady a raise!" he yelled.

Kathy was on the stairs, checking on the ruckus from her husband.

She laughed, but it was more like china breaking, a forced sound that held no merriment at all.

"The lady doth bake!" he shouted again.

"Oh come off it, Roger. It's not as if you've never had an apple pie before."

"Oh, but honeybun. These pies will delight the palate, no doubt."

Emma started the vacuum and turned her back to escape Kathy's answer. She stayed intent on her work. By the time the stemware was washed and dried, it was too late for a shower, so she merely ran a comb through her hair and took a washcloth to her face. She changed into an olive-green dress and called it good enough.

Kathy floated down the stairs, a vision in a summery dress of pastel yellow, her arms bare, her hair a beautiful blond halo. Roger had no time to change, with the streamer going, measuring spices and oils, managing to create the biggest mess Emma had ever seen. There were at least half a dozen dishcloths laying in disarray, two tea towels around his neck, and one protruding from the pocket of his apron. The ceramic tile floor was slick with oil and water, the blender splattered with green. She tried to stay out of the way, but had to assemble the salad and make the dressing without getting caught in the hurricane that was Roger in the kitchen.

Precisely at seven, the crew came tromping up the stairs, with Kathy flushed and eager, her manners impeccable, making the five workmen feel at home immediately.

What a beautiful woman, Emma thought. She withdrew to the background, remembering that she was the help, not the hostess or a guest. She served the children's dinner on trays and supervised the meal before taking them upstairs for their bath and bedtime story.

Then she reappeared to fill her own plate and eat at the bar that ran along one side of the patio.

These had been Kathy's instructions, making it clear that after the meal was served it was her duty to look after the children until they fell asleep. They were not to be brought to the table for any reason other than an emergency.

The table was set on the patio with Kathy seated to Ben's right and Roger at the head, presiding over the meal. Daniel sat to his left and the three others next to him. They talked about the renovations, each one trying to impress the others with their knowledge or wit or experience. The workers complimented the seafood, tossing empty shells into big bowls and heaping more potato salad onto their plates.

Emma watched Kathy lean into Ben, touch his arm, and gaze unabashedly into his face. She told herself it was nothing—another cultural difference between the English and the Amish. Ben stayed polite but aloof, which seemed to fuel Kathy's eagerness until it became obvious she was speaking exclusively to him and ignoring the rest of the table, which initiated darts of disapproval from her husband.

Emma served the apple pie with vanilla gelato, which was evidently an Italian ice cream. She had never heard of it, but she found it smoother and even better than ordinary ice cream. The cake brought plenty of praise.

"Who made the desserts?" Ben asked.

"I did, of course!" Kathy quipped, slapping Ben's arm playfully.

"It was Emma, the pastry queen," Roger said levelly.

She was partially hidden by a tall houseplant, so there were no comments in her direction. The meal wore on and on, so Emma began cleanup, her back to the diners who were ready for coffee, which she served properly.

When Ben caught her eye, she looked away immediately. She was still washing dishes when they all trooped over to the house to discuss the ongoing work.

Emma sighed deeply, went to the bathroom, then sat down at the bar with a huge slice of cake. She poured a tall glass of tea over ice and enjoyed the time alone before finishing up the cleaning.

The kitchen was spotless when she went back out onto the deck to enjoy the moonlight path on the water, the dark swaying of the grasses, the absolute charm of this lovely strip of land that lay between the ocean and the bay. She would never tire of breathing in the scent of water and salt. She wished she could bottle it to take back home in September.

The day had gone okay with only a few minor blips. Everyone had enjoyed her potato salad and the desserts. She reflected on the day's preparation, the baking and cooking and cleaning, how different her culinary habits were from Roger's. But she really liked Roger, she decided. He felt almost like a brother or a cousin. He was funny, unpretentious. You would never imagine he was a surgeon at this young age, but perhaps he was older than he appeared, or gifted, sailing through classes in double-quick time.

Staring across to the sandy beach, she tried to imagine what her walk with Ben would be like. Did she want it to be romantic or not? A walk on the beach could easily just be a walk on the beach, as long as you kept your priorities straight. That was the most practical way to view it. Just a simple walk on the beach, nothing more.

She asked Kathy if she could leave at seven and if, perhaps, she and Roger could do bedtime that night.

She was met with lowered brows, a thin line of irritation appearing between them.

"Not really, Emma. We are both extremely pushed."

"What?" Roger's voice drifted from the living room.

"Emma wants off at seven."

"Why can't she?"

"Are you putting the children to bed?"

"Of course. I'm not doing anything."

"Yes you are. The Sheffields are coming over for drinks."

Roger leaned against the doorframe, a slight figure in cargo shorts and an old T-shirt, as if he still attended high school.

"No they aren't. That guy is a bore, I mean, a total . . ."

He spun a forefinger close to his temple.

"Really Roger? A mere 'no' would have sufficed."

"Well no, then."

"Well, okay then."

Kathy smiled at her boyish husband and everything was set straight, although Emma employed every ounce of willpower to keep from laughing at the spinning forefinger.

At 6:30 Emma showered, dressed in her pale pink dress, black apron, and white head covering. She decided to go barefoot—no reason to wear sandals on the beach in the evening, when the sand would no longer be fiery hot. She glanced in the bathroom mirror, pleased to notice the disappearance of quite a few freckles, the deepening tan on her face, the sun streaks in her hair.

The evening was too perfect, like a stage set for a play, with the evening sun painting everything with a pink glow. She peered out of the upstairs window and found the sight almost indescribable, the beauty of a seaside evening on the cusp of summertime.

She watched Ben walk up the road from the house the crew rented, and when he came to the back stairs, she hurried down and slid noiselessly through the sliding door. He watched her ascent, a light in his eyes, a smile on his face.

"Don't you look nice," he said by way of a greeting.

"I'm wearing work clothes, really."

He grinned. "How are you?"

"Doing well. You?"

"Good. I love my job, so time flies."

"When you're having fun."

"Yup."

He looked down at her feet, then into her eyes, raised an eyebrow and pointed.

"No. No shoes, I'll be fine."

"Okay."

They walked down the walkway, turned left, and walked along the water's edge where the sand was wet enough to provide solid footing. Sure enough, what appeared to be wavy lines of dirt turned out to be seashells in a profusion of colors and shapes.

Emma lifted her hands, a small gasp escaped her.

"Oh my word. Seriously."

She bent immediately to select the perfectly scalloped ones, the small black ones, the conch shells that swirled with wide ranges of color.

When her hands were full, she looked at Ben.

"Oh, we don't have anything to put these in."

He drew a plastic grocery bag from his pocket.

"I came prepared."

"Oh great. This is great. I'll get greedy and fill the whole bag."

"I figured you would."

She forgot about Ben and became like a child again, picking up shells, turning the over, exclaiming over the unique designs.

"Look. Look at this one."

She held out a half-formed conch shell with pink and gray spirals.

"It is absolutely beautiful."

She looked up at him for his response and found his eyes had changed into a light that seemed to imprison her own. For one long breathless moment their gazes were locked, united with the silent universal attraction of first love.

"So are you," he whispered.

Emma blinked, blinked again, the only thing she could do to eliminate the spell he cast. She remembered his words then, and shook her head in denial.

"I am not beautiful. You should see my sister."

"Now why would you say that?"

She shrugged, didn't trust being captured by his eyes.

"I asked you a question."

"My sister Esther is a true beauty."

"I would like to meet her."

"She's married."

"As you should be," he said, grinning.

"Twenty-six and growing," Emma quipped.

"You can't be serious."

"I am twenty-six years old."

He whistled soft and low. "You look about eighteen. Maybe nineteen."

Emma smiled. "Thank you."

He took her hand and held it, until she bent to pick up yet another shell. Then another. She was scurrying now, like a sandpiper, her feet and hands moving fast at the edge of the water as he stood watching.

CHAPTER 8

WHEN SHE RETURNED TO HIM AFTER ANOTHER FORAY INTO THE COLD water, holding her skirt up in one hand while she used the other to fish for more shells, he told her he had never seen anyone with skin and hair like hers.

She dumped another handful of shells into the bag.

"Makes sense," she replied. "Last I checked I didn't have a twin."

"You just don't look like anyone I have ever seen." He ignored her clever evasion of his compliment. "You're not really a redhead, you're not blond, and you're definitely not a brunette. I don't know what you are. Do you color your hair?"

"Yeah," she said, with sarcasm.

He laughed. She loved his laugh.

"You really do intrigue me. And it's more than your amazing beauty."

"My what? Oh come on."

"I am serious."

"Why don't we change the subject? Can we talk about you? Like how did you wind up here? I didn't think there were any Amish settlements in this area."

She had abandoned the shell seeking and matched her stride with his. The sun was slipping almost to the expanse of water that met the sky, which was like a jumping-off post, a straight line where the ocean simply quit and the sky came down to meet its parallel line. The sky that had been blue was being painted in brushstrokes of purple, lavender, and a deep gold that surrounded the orange sun, a kaleidoscope of color that seemed to change as they walked.

Tiny sandpipers bustled along at the water's edge, their long, thin beaks probing the sand like knitting needles, finding whatever it was these birds loved to eat. Fat, insolent gulls with bold yellow eyes plodded beside them, the avian garbage trucks who would eat anything they could find, edible or not. They weren't particularly impressed with the two human beings who walked along without resting on beach chairs. It was the ones who packed a basket of food and allowed them the leftovers they cared about.

"I come from Lancaster County. Bowmansville," he answered.

Emma almost choked on her own gasp. What? Bowmansville. That was her sister's husband, Sam King's, hometown. It was an omen. Already, the dark crows of warning flew across her thoughts. She could not endure another monumental love that dropped her into the blackest chasm of loss and despair.

"I came here to be the best builder I can be. I don't have any attachments at home, only married brothers and sisters and aging parents who are still totally self-sufficient. So I'm staying all summer. I'm a partner with Daniel now, learning to go out on jobs by myself, without his crew. I love it. I especially love this job."

"I'm here for the summer too."

He caught her hand and held it close in his own.

"Oh good! Perfect."

He looked at her and smiled, but she refused to look at him.

"Don't you want to stay?"

"I do . . ."

"What?"

"Oh, I don't know."

She tugged at her hand till he released it.

She said softly, "I am simply not good company so you might not want to hang out with me."

He stopped, made a sound of exasperation.

"Now whatever is that supposed to mean?"

She shrugged, looked away.

"Oh come on. You know, finally I have found someone who, you know . . . Alright. I'm getting this all wrong. Look. I'm twenty-eight years old. I'm no spring chicken, more like an old rooster, and I'm just trying . . ."

Here Emma burst out laughing, in spite of wanting to stay aloof.

"No, I'm serious. I'm getting older, and so far in life, I haven't found anyone I want to continue seeing, as in dating seriously, with marriage. Picky, they say. You're too picky. Which I am, I guess. But every girl I ask, or that I have ever dated, is just . . . well, not what I am really looking for."

"Didn't anyone ever break up with you?" Emma broke in.

"No. I didn't date a whole lot."

Emma said nothing.

"Anyway, my sisters have done everything except tie me up and drag me to girls, and now they've actually given up. They tell each other I'm a stubborn old bachelor, spoiled rotten, baby of the family, and blah, blah, blah."

Emma hid her smile. She loved his expressions, his earnest hand movements.

She decided to be honest.

"Well, you're lucky. I have had my heart broken into a thousand irretrievable pieces and I have absolutely no intention of letting it happen again. I don't mind hanging out with you, but if you're looking for more . . ."

She shook her head.

"Oh come on now. Don't tell me I'll have to fight for your affections like a valiant knight." He pretended to pull a sword out of his belt and wave it in front of her.

She didn't allow herself to be amused.

"Of course not. Save all your time and energy, cause it won't happen. I'm not going through it again."

But she knew she would, for him. She would, certainly.

"So how do I go about this if I want to be friends? As in walking for miles along a beach without the thought of romance entering my head? Not to mention the heart, which must remain absent, of course."

She burst out laughing. She couldn't help herself.

He was a delightful conversationalist, besides being one of the best-looking men she had ever seen. And he was so confident. It was a rare trait among her people, who were taught obedience and humility from a young age. How deeply and how often had ministers extolled the virtues of Rebecca of old, who had drawn a veil across her face when she met Isaac.

Breezy, confident, his gait energized, jaunty. He was who he was and not ashamed of it. How many men would have come up those stairs to present himself to her like he had?

Oh, she felt the same tug, the same wonder of him she had felt for Sam King. Was she ready to meet this challenge? Knowing the outcome of the first disastrous try?

"You know, this is getting complicated. If you have never experienced heartbreak, you have no idea."

He stopped and turned toward her. In the fading light, with his blond good looks, his eyes open wide, his eyebrows in arcs of incredulity, he was a powerful force.

"But, Emma, you have to start somewhere. You can't go hiding under a rock, peep out from time to time, and figure a guy will come along with a sign on his shirt that says 'This one is safe,' or 'This one is the right one. He won't break your heart.'"

He was so earnest that in spite of trying to remain serious, she burst out laughing yet again.

"You really are different," she said. "We have known each other for only a few days and here we are, talking about personal issues that would take some men a year."

"What do you mean?"

"Oh, nothing. Just forget it."

It was beyond twilight now, the heaving ocean having swallowed the sun. The sky's vibrant colors were being subdued into submission by the approaching night, the stars appearing one by one, as if there were tiny holes poked into the huge dome overhead.

"It's getting dark," Emma said.

"It is never very dark on the beach," Ben answered. "It seems the starlight and the pale color of the sand sort of lights everything up. I love the ocean at night. Sometime I want to go on a cruise. You know, one of those huge ships that have, like, ten stories, or whatever. They just plow through the waves, totally master of the seas. Wouldn't that be great?"

"Like the Titanic, you mean?"

"Oh, come on. That was over a century ago."

"It can happen."

"But there is all this technology to predict weather."

The night was coming on fast now, and it was, as he said, magical. They needed no light to guide them, with the pristine stars and the pure slice of a brilliant half-moon that seemed to be suspended very close above them. The night was crisp, chilly.

Emma wrapped her arms around her waist, shivered slightly.

They had a long way to walk, in her estimation.

"Getting cold?" he asked.

"Sort of."

"I could put my arm around you, but that would be too much like romance, right?"

"Whatever," she said.

"Now what is that supposed to mean? Whatever, as in, okay, if you want to, or whatever, as in, don't even think about it, you really have a nerve?"

And again, she found herself laughing where she wasn't planning on it.

"Let's run," she said.

"Okay."

She ran beside him, in an easy lope, energized by the chill that crept up around them. She had always been proud of her ability to run with Dena, her legs strong and capable from the hard work in the produce fields. Her breathing accelerated as they ran, her bare feet leaving small indentations in the sand. They didn't speak, simply sliced through the wonders of sand, water, and the ever-increasing light from the stars.

She slowed, and stopped.

"How will you know where we are?" she asked.

"The houses. It isn't far. Let's walk. I hate for this night to be over. I'm afraid you won't do this again."

"We can," she murmured.

"When?"

"It's not easy for me to get away. I am in charge of the two children. If I'm not there for their bedtime, I'm not doing my job. Roger and Kathy are very busy people. She's always working on her computer, and he seems to take his responsibilities as surgeon very seriously."

"They definitely have money," Ben said.

"A powerful work ethic, too."

"You're right. I can't begin to imagine the amount going into this house. They're reinforcing everything to twice the recommendation for hurricanes."

"They're smart."

"They say some of these houses have been completely rebuilt, from one storm or another. I've questioned how wise it is to own a house in an area that can be like a sitting duck for the elements."

"But it's so beautiful. The scenery here is unreal. I love the scent of salt water and sand, and . . . and that swampy, mucky smell."

For a long moment he said nothing, so that she was afraid she'd said something disturbing. When he spoke, his voice was thick with emotion.

"Emma, I believe we are kindred spirits," he said.

She did not know how to respond to this.

"I mean, I love the smell of this place, just like you. I love it. We are both older, with no luck at getting married. We are considered oddities by our families, because Amish people get married. It's what we do."

"Not everyone," she said.

He laughed softly.

"Your Titanic is always going to sink."

"What? Are you saying I'm a pessimist? An old maid pessimist?"

She punched his forearm. He caught her hand and held it.

"No. You are most definitely not destined to be single. Don't you believe in God's ability to plunk us down exactly where He wants us?"

"You mean like a Monopoly board where we roll the dice and go where we're supposed to? One shake of the dice and I land in North Carolina where you have already been parked. But I might get a go-to-jail card and that's where I'll sit. You can't know the outcome of anything."

"This is ridiculous."

He spoke with a note of exasperation, released her hand, and guided her to the faint outline of the walkway with a hand pressed lightly to her back. They stopped at the stairway leading to the back deck, and the glass door that would be slid back to swallow her whole, leaving only disappointment in its wake.

"Goodnight, Emma. I'm sorry if I have offended you. I'll see you around."

"Goodnight."

He moved off through the night, the sound of his shoes creating a soft, sifting note of finality.

She stood very still, listening to the fading footsteps. Why did she do that, she wondered. Why had she purposefully repelled him? She had always done it, ever since Sam King. Held them all away, jabbing at each suitor with her sharp-edged saber, afraid of reliving the pain of heartbreak.

Somehow, she could not bring herself to climb the stairs, so she sat on the bottom step, cupped her hands around her face, allowed her shoulders to fall with despair. There were no tears, only a dull acceptance of her fate.

She sat on the bottom step until the chill of the night became an uncomfortable veil that she shrugged off. She turned and went up the steps, knocking lightly before trying the door. Inserting her fingers in the handle, she tugged, then pulled. There was no doorbell, so she rapped on the aluminum frame, harder.

Putting both hands against the sides of her face, she peered into the kitchen, tilted her head to see the soft yellow glow of a lamp in the living room. There was no one in front of the television, although she could tell it had not been turned off.

What if they had both gone to bed early, locked the doors without a thought for her return? She did not relish a night spent on the deck, neither would she hunker down in the sand below. Turning, she stood at the railing of the deck, taking in the semi dark of the night, the mellow breeze that held the chill of early summer by the sea, pondering her dilemma.

Her employers had a television set in their bedroom, which meant if they were engrossed in a show, or working on their laptops, would they hear a rapping sound or a doorbell? Surely they would hear the bell if there was one.

She made her way down the stairs, around the side of the house, and up the front steps. She saw the small orange glow before reaching the top. Yes. She reached out and held a forefinger to it and was rewarded with the sound of a clear ding-dong inside. She stood back, wrapped her arms around her torso, rubbing the palms of her hands up and down her forearms.

Nothing.

She tried again, and waited.

The third time, she heard footsteps, the sound of a lock being turned. Then another. Kathy's form was in silhouette against the backdrop of a low yellow lamp.

"Oh!" she exclaimed.

"I'm sorry," Emma said.

"Oh! Well, I forgot you were out."

She laughed self-consciously, stepped aside to allow Emma to come through the door.

"I didn't think I'd be this late," Emma answered.

Kathy stepped out to lock the door again, then drew herself up to her full height, and laughed again, a grating sound of condescension.

"So . . . the walk must have been rather engrossing?"

Her voice rose at the end, turning it into a question.

"We . . . I was gathering shells. They're on the back deck."

"It's okay for this one time to be going out like this, but I'd appreciate if it wouldn't happen again. Thank you."

With that, Emma was effectively disposed of by Kathy, who turned her back to enter the hallway that led to the bedroom. Emma stood, staring after the receding figure in the white bathrobe before making her way slowly up the stairs, feeling like a truant schoolgirl.

But what exactly had she done wrong? She fought back the urge to yell at Kathy, tell her she was an adult and capable of making her own decisions, and if she wanted to walk on the beach with Ben, she would.

She did not sleep well, her thoughts unraveling the evening until nothing made much sense. For the first thing, Ben was talking about a relationship far too soon. Yes, she wanted to quit teaching school, and yes, she certainly wanted to get married someday, but she was not quite ready for this.

She needed time. Time for what? Time to push Ben away, the way she had pushed so many of them? No, she wanted him. He was different.

And there was the whole problem.

She was always the first one up, so she quietly made her first cup of coffee and let herself out on the deck to breathe in the smell of the sea, the vast open space that made her feel her insignificance, the power and majesty of God so much bigger. He calmed the wind and the waves, so He would control her destiny as well. The fear and foreboding of the night before had dwindled away as her faith rose and swelled. She whistled softly under her breath, the song she had been taught at school.

"God is bigger than any mountain that I can or cannot see."

She returned to the kitchen to begin mixing waffles, as a treat for the children, hoping to win back Kathy's good graces. When she finished, she set the bowl on the back of the countertop and turned to find Brent coming down the open stairway, his pillow sliding along behind him, a corner of the pillowcase clutched in his hand.

"Good morning, Brent," she whispered, holding a finger to her lips. He mumbled something unintelligible, gave her a small grin, his eyes drooping with sleep.

"Do you want to lie on the couch awhile?" she asked.

He nodded. She helped him to settle comfortably, covered him with a soft white shawl that was draped across a chair, fluffed his hair and smiled into his eyes.

"You okay?" she asked.

He nodded again, rolled on his side and closed his eyes.

Roger was next, rubbing the sleep from his eyes. Emma couldn't help but compare the two, so very much alike. Friendly, unassuming, always thinking of those around them.

"Hey, good morning!" he said. "I smell coffee."

Emma smiled. "Good morning. The only coffee is mine."

He grinned. "I figured."

She was getting sausages from the refrigerator when he tilted the bowl to inspect the waffle batter, then let out a long low whistle.

"You didn't," he said.

"What?"

"Mix waffles from scratch?"

"I did. It's almost like pancake batter. It's easy. I found the electric waffle iron and figured it had to be easier than a waffle iron you heat on a gas burner."

"I wouldn't know. Never tried it. We're just renting here, so I have no idea what you'll find in the cabinets."

"I'll give it a shot."

He got his cup of coffee, sniffed appreciatively, and took a sip. His blue eyes squinted.

"So how'd it go last night?"

"What?"

"You know. The walk with Ben."

Suddenly flustered, she busied herself at the counter.

"Oh, it was alright. I just felt bad, having to go around to the front to ring the doorbell. I guess I forgot to mention that I might be late."

There was no answer, only a clipped voice instructing her to keep the batter for another hour, he was going for a run. She watched in bewilderment as he left his steaming cup of coffee, pushed his feet into running shoes, and let himself out the front door.

Now what had she done?

Shrugging, she turned away, decided there was no way she could understand these people and their mood swings. Perhaps it was the way of highly intelligent people. They simply didn't communicate the way ordinary people did, or manners weren't a necessity, or their brain waves moved along in sequences too quick for her to grasp.

A wail came from upstairs.

Emma hurried up the stairs to the source. Annalise, her hair like a dust mop, her small mouth stretched to capacity, was howling.

Oh boy.

"It's okay, Annalise. I'm here," Emma crooned, rushing to lift her from the bed.

"I can't find Charlie Brown!" she yelled.

He was not in the bed, or underneath it, but stuffed between the mattress and headboard. Once he was safely in the little girl's arms, everything changed, much to Emma's relief.

Together, they went to the bathroom to brush Annalise's hair and teeth, and get her dressed in a clean pair of shorts and a T-shirt with small white socks on her feet.

Such a pretty little thing, Emma thought, but what a firecracker.

"Alright, Anna. We're done here. Can you walk down the steps by yourself while I grab the hamper with clothes to wash?"

"Yes, I can," she said, agreeably nodding her head until her pony-tail bounced. So they were off to a good start, finally.

Once in the kitchen, she gave Annalise a cup of milk, saying they'd have waffles when Daddy returned from his run. She was completely alright with that, smiling and nodding, holding up Charlie Brown to remind Emma that he loved waffles.

She sliced fresh strawberries, allowed Annalise a few, and one for Charlie Brown. When Kathy came to the kitchen in her bathrobe, there was no sign of the previous evening's animosity, or whatever had caused the refusal to allow another evening with Ben. She hugged and kissed her children, cuddled with them on the couch, drank coffee, and told them how much she loved them.

Emma had a smile on her face when Roger returned, dripping sweat and breathing hard. She heated the waffle iron as he entered the bathroom for a shower.

The waffles turned out to be perfect, a deep golden brown, and with butter and maple syrup, fresh strawberries and sliced bananas, they were a rare treat, one both parents raved about.

Especially Roger, who said after the house was finished, how could they bear to part ways with Emma? This brought a tinkling laugh from Kathy, a nod in agreement, saying she already had them terribly spoiled.

Brent waved his fork and announced the need for waffles every morning.

The sun shone into the white kitchen, creating a golden yellow light that suffused everything with warmth and cheer. The windows sparkled, the filmy curtains billowed at their sides, allowing the sea air to permeate the whole interior of the house. Annalise smiled with all her small white teeth showing, her hair a halo of pale yellow around her face, and Emma felt as if there would always be good times, and new beginnings. Nothing was without flaws, nothing could be expected to be pleasing all the time, but this was good.

CHAPTER 9

IN MID-JUNE, ROGER AND KATHY BOTH RETURNED TO THE STATE OF PENN-sylvania, taking care of business for days at a time, leaving the children in her care. The renovations on the house were all limited to interior work now, which meant she only caught glimpses of Ben on some days.

The weather turned increasingly hot and humid, so Emma spent most days on the sand in the water with the children. It was a delightful way of being employed, she thought from time to time, although not without its responsibilities. Annalise continued to buck her rules and throw fits when things were not to her liking, but Emma's days were better without Kathy, who had continued to be especially moody after the night of the beach walk. Emma learned to hold her at arm's length, very carefully.

Kathy had spent all of May with the guys in the house, poring over blueprints, making changes, constantly overseeing, ordering, and choosing. And it was the same on the days she was home in June. She'd arrive home, give the kids quick kisses, and then head straight for next door. There were deliveries daily, sometimes two or three in a day. Trucks containing flooring, insulation. An electrician. A plumber. There were appliances and light fixtures.

The activity was mind boggling.

And never once did Ben make an overture. Emma and the children were forbidden to enter the renovation zone.

Safety measures.

Emma couldn't help but feel a sense of remorse. If only she had not been so cold, so unwilling to welcome his bid for friendship. And now she had to endure Kathy and Ben poring over prints, the laptop, discussing every aspect of the changes, talking, talking, talking.

It was all foolish, she knew, but it could happen. He was single. English people got divorced. Amish men left the faith. Of course it could happen. And no one was ever going to tell Emma that Kathy was not attracted to Ben, because she was. Emma was faced with searing anger, followed by a suffocating remorse. She took to spending time on the back deck, reading a book, or writing letters on the patio table, a glass of tea beside her.

She developed a headache from using her peripheral vision. To sit at a patio table trying to keep up the façade of intense writing or reading while desperately searching for one person was extremely tiring.

Now that she had admitted to her ballooning sense of insecurity, everything was written in black and white. This was her own doing, so she could not blame anyone else.

The day was hot. Brassy hot. The kind of heat that shimmered above driveways and made men and beasts seek shade, and the relief of many cold drinks.

The sky appeared overheated, a white film of humidity effectively putting the blue of the sky in hiding. Air conditioners whirred and clanked on and off along the strip of houses that lined the sandy roadway. The beach was blooming with brilliant umbrellas and squares of blankets and towels, colorful kites dotting the atmosphere like free-flying petals. The water's edge contained a line of shrieking children with various floats, boogie boards, or buckets filled with water and carried away. Farther out, where the waves were large and constant, heads floated and bobbed, shoulders appearing above the water, to disappear into an oncoming wave.

Emma sat immobilized, fried into the low beach chair by the unforgiving rays of the sun. She could not take the swim she longed for, having to stay with the children. The breeze that normally came from the water was blowing from behind, from the overheated sand that brought the green-headed flies out of the low-lying areas, voracious in their quest for blood.

Emma lifted a foot, slapped viciously at a determined fly that flew expertly away from her hand.

"Alright," she muttered. "That does it. Kids!" she yelled. "Come on. We're going."

They both looked up from their play, their skin darkened to a butterscotch hue by the sun's rays, despite the sunscreen, their hair bleached almost white.

Obedient as always, Brent picked up his playthings and walked down to the water's edge. Annalise sat back on her haunches, squinting her blue eyes. Emma had no intention of putting up with another temper tantrum. She reached down to scratch the bite inflicted by the green-headed fly, swatted viciously at another, and told Annalise to hurry up.

"I want to stay," she chirped, standing with her feet planted apart, her toes pointed outward, her red plastic bucket clutched in both hands at her waist.

"Not this time, sweetie. The flies are biting really bad today."

That seemed to do the trick. She rolled her eyes and sighed like her mother, which made Emma smile. She could be so lovable, so old for an almost three-year-old, and at times like this Emma genuinely loved her.

"Okay, Brent, did you wash the sand out?"

He nodded, "So what are we doing the rest of the day?" he asked. "We'll see."

They straggled through the burning sand, the hot wind at their faces. The tall grass bent and swayed, rustling in the gale, whispering the secrets of the sea. The sound of their slapping flip-flops on the weathered boards, the weight of the blanket and cooler, the folded chair, all of it was so familiar now.

Emma loved this place, with an emotion that tugged at her sense, the way she loved her classroom those first years of teaching. Only ten more weeks till the end of August, and she would return to her home in the hills and valleys of Crawford County.

She missed Dena most. They'd talked on the phone, with Dena wailing and complaining about all the work, and how "un-fun" it was without her. She spoke to both of her parents, who said they would be glad to have the summer over with. They were concerned about her becoming used to luxuries, to a vacation spot that would hold her in its grip.

No sign of the builders today. The truck had not been there all day.

She hoped there would be some sign of life. With Roger and Kathy both gone for the week, it was beginning to feel creepy at night.

The wonderful cool interior was a blessing, for sure. Those squares of metal and whatever else was used to construct a central air unit was surely the best invention ever. She herded the children through the door, got them both in the shower, rinsing sand down the drain at an alarming rate.

She supposed the drainage system was made to take care of all that, but still. There was an outside shower to rinse the sand off, but the children despised the shock of cold water, so she no longer bothered with it.

Showered and in fresh clothes, the children both fell asleep in front of the TV, leaving Emma to wander around the house after putting in a load of laundry.

She was restless, unsettled. She wondered what she would do the remainder of the day. She wandered to the sliding glass door, just in time to see the large white pickup truck pull up to the neighboring house. She drew back, but watched as the men got out, climbed the steps to the house. In a few minutes, they retuned. Daniel got into the truck but Ben stopped, looked at the house where the Forsythes stayed, then spoke to Daniel.

Oh no.

He was headed straight in her direction. Whatever.

She moved away from the door in time to see his large form appear on the deck, his hand lifted to knock on the frame.

She slid the door back.

"Hi."

"Hello, Emma. How are you?"

"I'm okay."

"Hey. I hate to be nosy, but I know Roger and Kathy aren't here. I guess you know they're predicting quite a storm later tonight. I was worried about you, being here by yourself."

"It's not hurricane season," she said stiffly.

"No. But I didn't know how you felt about being alone in a storm."

"I'm fine. There are neighbors."

"I'd feel better if you weren't by yourself, though."

"How serious are the predictions?"

She'd seen the forecast, but wasn't about to tell him.

"Bad enough. High winds."

"We don't exactly have a basement to go to if it gets bad."

"You're right."

"We'll be fine," she told him.

"Look. This is ridiculous. You know you'd feel better if I stayed here, right?"

And cause a storm of epic proportions in her heart?

"No. It's okay."

"No, it's not. I'm staying."

With that, he made his way down the stairs, went to talk to the driver of the pickup, then made his way back up the stairs. Emma stood by the dining room table, gripping the back of a chair for support. This couldn't really be happening. He let himself in, filling the light from the door with his presence, at ease, unselfconscious, as if this was something he did every day.

He moved toward the table, pulled out a chair, and sat down.

"So, here we are," he said, with the infectious grin that made her knees go soft and wobbly.

"I guess so," she answered with a weak smile of her own. She knew she should tell him to leave, call the police if she had to. But the fact remained that she was really glad to have his company. And who knew what the storm might be like? She had to admit that if things got bad, she'd have no idea what to do to keep them safe.

He looked around, taking in the kitchen, the sleeping children in the living room.

"So how have you been?"

"Alright. I'm enjoying my summer."

"As long as I stay where I'm supposed to, huh?"

"I didn't say that."

"Oh, it's okay. Sit down. You can relax. I'm just here to be your protector, nothing else."

"I don't really need a protector."

"Probably not. But you'll feel better once the storm hits with me here."

His confidence level was unbelievable. Didn't the man ever have self-doubt?

She thought of Allen Kauffman, the one youth who had asked her for a date, the humility with which he presented himself, the kindness and grace with which he accepted her refusal. Surely he would have been a kind and caring husband, just the opposite of what she supposed this Ben could be.

"Well, you're here now, so I guess I should offer you a drink. We have tea, lemonade."

"Coffee?"

She raised an eyebrow.

"Coffee? In the afternoon?"

"Why not?"

She didn't give him the satisfaction of a reply. Why not, indeed? He had know idea what a hard time she had falling into a deep sleep in this house when the parents were absent, even without caffeine lingering in her system. She wouldn't be telling him how the nights grew long and wearisome, listening to the dull roar of the ocean, the ticking and clanking, the pinging and creaking, keeping her wide-eyed, wondering if the sturdy piles were firmly situated on the ground beneath the unstable sand.

Brent awoke, stretched and yawned, then made his way to the kitchen to lay his head in Emma's lap. Her arms went around him immediately, drawing him up on her lap, where he snuggled contentedly.

"Annalise still sleeping?"

He nodded, watching Ben with a slanted gaze.

"This is Ben, Brent." She said.

"I know."

Ben was watching them with a soft expression on his face.

"I would paint a picture of you two, if I was a painter."

Emma laid her chin on top of Brent's head and drew him close. He was the easiest child to love, like one of those that had stolen her heart in first grade, and kept it till they moved from eighth grade to vocational class. Brent was so sweet, so advanced for his age, always the peacemaker between her and his sister.

Brent sat up. "You could take a picture the way Mommy does."

"Emma might not appreciate that."

He nodded, looking up into Emma's face.

"Let's make those cookies, Emma," he said. "Please?"

She could not have refused him, so she gathered ingredients, made a cup of coffee for Ben but none for herself. There was no baking molasses or ginger, so she mixed a sugar cookie recipe. Halfway through, there was a wail from the living room, the usual sound of Annalise being woken from a deep sleep.

"I'll get her," Ben offered.

Emma opened her mouth to tell him it likely wouldn't work, but watched in disbelief as he reached the sofa in a few long strides and scooped her into his arms.

"Hello, little girl," he said, returning to the barstool, with Annalise staring up into his face, Charlie Brown clutched in her arms. Annalise didn't protest, seemingly enjoying the attention from this unexpected visitor.

The afternoon was spent in the cool, comfortable kitchen, a scene of domestic harmony, the chilled dough rolled out on a floured surface, the children taking turns to cut trees and bells and angels with a set of old tin cookie cutters that had been stored away behind an angel food cake pan, a bundt pan, and a heart-shaped set from Wilson Baking Company.

"Now who would come to the beach to bake?" Emma asked, as she pulled out the dusty pans.

"Evidently you," Ben teased.

Emma's cheeks were flushed, her eyes bright, like an emerald, he thought, her skin deeply tanned and still dotted with an array of copper colored freckles, especially over her nose. Ben had never seen a more attractive girl, he decided then and there, a fact he'd tried to deny, with all her standoffish ways. She was the girl of his dreams, and he could not understand how she could remain single in the Amish world, where most girls were snatched up before they reached the age of eighteen or nineteen.

And so he held Annalise, stole glances at Emma, and fell steadily and irretrievably in love. The recessed lighting in the all-white kitchen was the perfect backdrop for the vibrant colors that made up this girl. Try as he might, he could barely keep his eyes off her as she bent over the children, guiding, helping, and encouraging.

The result was row after row of trees, some of them crooked with far too many sprinkles, some too thin with hardly any at all, a few botched Santa Clauses, and at least ten partially winged angels.

Brent sighed, stretched his shoulders, and said he was really getting tired of this. He allowed Emma to wash his hands and wandered off to the living room to play with his Legos. Annalise was feeding a crumbling bell to Charlie Brown, making a mess all over the floor, but Emma said nothing, just stored the cookies in a plastic container and began to wipe the counter.

The wind was kicking up, bending the grass almost double, the sunshine taking on a dull yellowish look, as if someone had covered the windows with a thin coating. Ben glanced at the sky from the sliding glass door, shoving yet another cookie into his mouth. Emma came to stand beside him, her eyes going to the sky that seemed as if it had taken on a greenish hue.

Ben shook his head.

"I bet the lightning will be awesome," he said. "I've never seen a really hard electrical storm over the water. Have you?"

"No. This is my first time at the ocean, you know."

The sound of the phone ringing made her jump, an unaccustomed jangling that set her teeth on edge.

"Hello?"

"Hi! Hey, it's me, Kathy. I am listening to the news, on my phone, and it sounds bad. Are you okay? I called Daniel, and he said they aren't working. If you'd feel more comfortable, you can get a room in town. I don't want to think of the children being scared."

"I think we'll be alright, Kathy."

"What are you doing?"

"Well, we made cookies this afternoon. Christmas cookies, I'm afraid."

Kathy laughed her polite tinkling sound that held no real mirth.

"Oh. I'm sure the kids loved it."

"They did."

"So you're by yourself, then?"

"No. Ben is here. He insisted. Said the storm might be severe. I told him we'd be fine, but it didn't do any good."

Why did she feel as if she had to make excuses? That none of this was her fault?

There was a silence, a breath suspended.

"Well, whatever. Look. I have to go. I'll call later."

With that the phone line was disconnected. Slowly, Emma's thumb pressed on the off button, and she replaced the handset to its base, keeping her face averted as she busied herself at the sink.

Ben watched her, but kept himself from asking who it was. Figured it was Kathy or Roger.

Emma turned, drying her hands on a dishcloth.

"Kathy's worried."

Ben nodded. "It's good to know they think of the children."

"They are very good parents."

Ben looked at her, said nothing.

"Let me dry those for you."

She handed him a dish towel. He smiled at her. Their eyes met. She told him how glad she was that he was there without saying a word at all, then turned to her dishes as if they were the most important thing in her life.

"You have a dishwasher here. Why don't you use it?" he asked, standing much too close.

"I'm Amish, you know. I love to wash dishes. It's a process that fills a domestic need, I suppose."

"Do all Amish women enjoy washing dishes?" he asked.

"How would I know? I'm only one woman, and I don't hang out with the marrieds."

"No, I guess you wouldn't. I bet there are more than one of your friends who have two or three children."

"Try five."

"What? You're not serious."

"Rachel Ann."

"Who is she?"

"One of my friends. She was married before she was nineteen. She's my age, so in seven years, she's had five children."

Ben shook his head.

"Is that normal? Like, for this day and age?"

Emma shrugged. She did not want to tell him about their deep sense of what was right and what was wrong, choosing to leave the number of babies in the Lord's hands. That was their own personal decision, and a subject she was not willing to broach. Not with him.

"She looks a lot different now."

"You mean . . . ?"

"Well, she's gained quite a bit of weight. And she's, well . . . tired. She's just so worn out. She has her hands so full. I mean, can you even imagine the laundry alone? I don't like to go there, it just seems too overwhelming. Marriage, all that suffering . . . "

Ben's laugh rang out.

"So *there* is the reason you're teetering on the brink of singledom. Finally. I have broken the code. I understand you now."

She swatted him with her dishcloth.

"That is not the reason. How shallow do you think I am?"

"Pretty shallow, in my opinion. Isn't every respectable Christian girl meant to get married and have at least a dozen children? You know, her husband working by the sweat of his brow? Like me, over there in the house we're renovating. I mean, on most days, the sweat just runs off me. So I would definitely keep my side of the bargain as far as being a husband. The rest would be up to you."

"What?"

She stared at him.

"Don't you like where this conversation is going?" he asked, a grin elevated to his eyes, watching her response.

"I don't want to get married if that is all there is," she huffed.

"You pity what's her name? Rebecca?"

"Rachel Ann."

"You pity her."

"Well, no, not really pity her. It's just that it all seems so overwhelming. I mean, that isn't even the right word. There is simply too much expected from a young girl, that's all."

Ben sobered, searched her face.

"I can see you're serious. You're smart, Emma. A girl like you thinks more than many of our people do. You are much more complicated than this Rebecca Ann."

"Rachel."

"Rachel Ann. So perhaps she is genuinely happy. She's fulfilled in her role as wife and mother. Shouldn't she be?"

"Of course. But I'm not convinced it is necessary. In God's eyes, I mean."

"Okay. Dishes done. I wish they weren't. This time with you is better than any time I have ever spent with a girl. Let's get all the dishes out of the cupboard and wash them again."

Emma laughed. "Oh, come on."

"I'm serious. I'd stand here all evening drying dishes, talking to you."

The wind slapped against the north side of the house. A chair went sliding across the back deck, banged into the railing before it stopped, followed by the empty flowerpot beside it. Ominous clouds welled up like dirty sheep's wool, obscuring the light of the late afternoon sun. A clap of thunder brought both children running to the kitchen, their arms outstretched.

They sat in the living room, then, a child on each one's lap, as rain lashed the windows in wind-driven streams. Lightning was like scattered streaks across the sky, the ocean like boiling broth in an overheated kettle. They moved to the glass door to take in the fury of a midsummer thunderstorm, the sight a renewal of faith in a living God whose hand controls the wind and waves.

Emma felt the magnetism of Ben's solid form, inched closer until she felt her sleeve brush the fabric of his. She winced when a blinding flash illuminated the room and everything stopped. The house was eerily silent without the steady rumbling of the central air unit, the sound of the TV in the living room. The house turned gray and shadowy, with all the cozy yellow lights without power.

And still the storm increased, until Emma declared she felt the house shiver in the gale. She felt his hand on her back, then slid around her waist, a very small amount of pressure applied to draw her against him.

She leaned in, gladly, her heart hammering.

"It's dark," Annalise whispered.

"The electricity just went off," Brent told her in his grown-up manner.

"I don't like to be here," Annalise said, drawing in her breath, the first indication of producing one of her famous fits.

Emma wanted to move toward the living room, wanted to sit on the sofa away from the wind and lashing rain, the jagged lightning that illuminated everything in blinding blue flashes, but could not bring herself to step away from the protection that was Ben. When

Annalise cranked up her objection to a full-out howl of indignation, Emma stepped away.

Ben followed her, sat a safe distance away, and sighed.

"You know, Emma. It's pretty dark in here. You think we should light the candles? I saw a couple jar candles on the dining room table. Or would that be too unabashedly romantic?"

She smiled, so clearly delighted with the word he used to describe romantic.

Oh but she loved this man's company. He was smart, funny, unself-conscious, and very easy to know. But who knew in which direction this would go?

"Candles are just candles," she said, and got up to light them.

He stayed, so she brought a candle into the room, lit it, and set it on an end table. They watched the flickering flame in silence until Annalise said she did not like that fire.

"Charlie Brown likes it. Look at him," Ben said, shoving the elephant to the top of the end table, where he sat with his polished black eyes gazing across the top of the small orange flame.

CHAPTER 10

EMMA FOUND HERSELF HOPING THE STORM WOULD LAST LONGER THAN IT did, with the cozy atmosphere in the house. Ben's company helped to keep the children distracted so that they didn't get too frightened. When the lights came back on, the refrigerator's hum seemed intrusive, as did the brightness of the television screen.

At twilight, the earth was soft, washed clean with the sluicing rainwater. The air was moist with salt spray, a sharp pungent aroma that delighted her senses. Puddles of water were everywhere, droplets on the railing, dripping off the patio table, small pools on its surface. The dull roar of the ocean seemed a comforting lullaby now, no longer the unsettling crash of mighty waves.

It seemed as if Ben was settled in for the night, comfortably housed in the living room, a child on either side of him, reading the favorite "Babar" book. She slowly slid the door shut, turned, and wondered what the proper procedure was to have an overnight guest that seemingly was self-invited.

He looked up as she entered the room.

"Storm over?" he asked.

"Looks like it."

"So you were hoping I'd leave, or do you want me to stay over?"

She swallowed, opened her mouth to say, yes, he could leave, but that was not really what she wanted. Her answer was like a piece of food stuck in her throat.

"Yes or no?"

He raised one eyebrow, that lopsided grin playing dangerously with her emotions.

He was impossibly good-looking, impossibly handsome, beguiling her in an unfair way.

When she didn't answer, he said, "It's okay. Another storm could come up, so I better stay. What do you think?"

She did not say yes or no, merely shrugged her shoulders.

He took that as a yes, and said, "Good. I'll be glad to stay."

They made chocolate milk with Nestlé Nesquik and a large bowl of popcorn, sat around the table and played four games of Candy Land with Brent.

She took the children upstairs for their bath and bedtime while he cleaned up downstairs. She tried to take her time, but found herself impatient, reading the story too fast, watching eagerly for the drooping of their eyelids.

He could sleep in Roger and Kathy's bed, but he'd need clean sheets, so she carried a stack of neatly folded ones to the downstairs bedroom. She had taken off the heavy comforter and all the pillows when he came into the bedroom in his stocking feet, making no sound.

"Need help?"

She jumped, a hand going to her chest. "You scared me."

"Didn't mean to."

"I got this," she said.

"Let me get this corner."

He proceeded to help her stretch the fitted sheet, then the flat one, tucking it along the bottom neatly. They put clean pillowcases on the memory foam pillows, before he stopped, looked at Emma, and laughed.

"We seem just like an old married couple, huh?"

Her face felt like a radiator.

"We're not, though," she told him brusquely.

"We should be."

She shook her head. "The things you say. And here I am, painfully blushing my head off."

He laughed a full boisterous laugh that put her immediately at ease.

"Don't worry, Emma. I enjoy teasing you, just to see how long you'll be effective at treating me like a mosquito."

He mimicked spraying insect repellant.

She laughed, "No, it's not that bad."

"Isn't it, Emma?"

She looked up from fluffing the last sham, and went cold.

He was looking at her with an expression she could not decipher. The silence in the bedroom was deafening, the air charged with unspoken feelings.

"Emma."

Then he came around to her side of the bed, his gaze never leaving her face. When he reached her, he lifted both hands to encircle her waist, drawing her slightly, very gently, toward him.

He was so tall, so solid, and so terribly attractive. Here were all the feelings she had ever longed for, and then some. To be carried away like this, given another chance of allowing someone to claim her whole heart, was surely an undeserved blessing. Or another ride down the oiled chute of heartbreak.

Her eyes told him all of this. He read acceptance, desire, attraction, followed by doubt, then real fear.

"It's okay, Emma. I'm not going to speed this up before you are ready. I make all these offhand remarks, but in my own heart, I'm not sure I'm capable of actually pursuing a girl. I have never done that. I'm dead serious. I truly have never met a girl I felt about the way I feel now and it's just as scary for me. I understand you. I do."

A small tug of his hands on her waist, and she was in his arms, her face scrunched into a sob, her mouth turned downward, her eyes squeezed shut as tears poured from them.

"I'm sorry. I'm so sorry," he kept saying, rubbing her back as if she were a small child.

Her face was blotchy with tears and the onslaught of remembered pain. Tears spilled from her eyes as she stepped away to reach for a handful of Kleenex from the nightstand. She pushed past him, out of the bedroom and into safer territory, honking into the tissues she held to her nose.

He switched off the lights and followed her to the back door, the large door that was her window to the adjacent house, the sea, and the sky. The place she had spent too much time watching for him, too much time allowing herself the luxury of attraction.

They stood together, in silence. Finally, with a deep breath, Emma spoke.

"I think we're just a bit over the hill, both of us," she said. "When we're young, we're, I don't know, innocent? Naïve. Whatever you want to call it. We're simple when it comes to attraction. Boy meets girl, they like each other, date, get married and live happily ever after. Something like that."

She would not meet his eyes, but she told him about how she had fallen in love before, how he had married her sister. She spelled it all out, slumping down on a bar stool and staring out the window to avoid his eyes.

He listened, took a deep breath, put his hands in his pockets and looked out of the glass door into the dark night. After a while, she felt his presence behind her before his large hands circled her shoulders.

"Emma. I'm willing to wait, for as long as it takes. I knew from the first day I met you that you were the one."

Slowly and quietly she said, "I . . . would like to be so sure."

He gave a small groan, then turned her around, helped her to her feet.

"Look at me, Emma."

She obeyed, and was swept into oblivion, blinded by the message in his eyes.

Slowly, he bent his head, touched her lips with his, a whisper, the audacity of a new beginning. When she did not pull away, but stayed, his arms went around her and he drew her close. Their hearts beat as one when he touched her lips with his own, again, and this time it was not a whisper, but the full assurance of everything he had told her.

His kiss spoke the language of a powerful love, one that would not be taken lightly. Her arms went around his shoulders and stayed there, as she was held in a crushing embrace.

Tremulous, ashamed, she turned away.

He held her still, a hand brushed lightly across her cheek, to cup her chin, to turn her face to his.

"You're everything I imagined," he said hoarsely. "You are beautiful and sweet and good, and we've only just met."

"This . . . whatever it was, is only a . . . a . . ."

She stopped, confused.

"It's the beginning of a great love, is what it is," he said firmly.

"Then we had better get to know each other immediately," she said, stifling a laugh. "I mean, talk about family, our goals, our past, all the stuff you're supposed to talk about."

"Or we could skip all that and go get married," he said.

But they did settle together on the couch, his arm possessive around her shoulders, and they did talk almost through the night. He told her of his ordinary upbringing in an ordinary Amish household with a loving mother and strict but caring father that set boundaries he respected to this day. She told him about the hard work in the vegetable fields in summer, Dena, her married sisters and their shenanigans.

They shared a love of the outdoors, he promised her a trip to Colorado. She told him about her years of teaching, the good times and the times when she felt as if she would fail at everything, having run the gauntlet of difficult parents with opinions set in stone, children who were underqualified but propelled through eight grades in spite of failing grades.

They made more hot chocolate, sat on barstools to drink it, talked about churches and church leaders. They spoke of the practice of shunning, of excommunication and the amount of young people who no longer gave themselves and their way of thinking to the old traditional way.

"Three of my buddy group left last year for that reason," Ben said. "I mean, it's getting to be quite the controversy, and it won't go away any time soon. So far, I'm okay with staying more conservative, knowing the outcome of so many who have left the church. I'm just glad we live in a country that practices religious freedom, rather than having to serve something we don't believe is right."

"I love our way of life," Emma said, "but I can see how some are upset by shunning. It's an old practice, but sometimes I still view it as a boundary for myself. We all need guidelines, which is the way of human beings everywhere."

"That is interesting, Emma. We all say the Bible is our road map, which it is. But the interpretation of the individual verses will lead one person his way, and another in a completely different direction."

"So in the end, attitude matters."

"It certainly does."

They talked about his job, the love and dedication to his craft, the joy of viewing the completed project, the many homes he had helped to build or renovate, the additions they had added through the years.

When the clock struck three, they laughed together, and he drew her closer until she lay her head on his shoulder and kept it there. She allowed herself this bold move, one he accepted with hope, his heart thumping in his strong chest.

A comfortable silence made all the difference now. The agreement of having begun something, even if he couldn't call it dating, or a relationship—barely a friendship—took away the sharp edge of her denial.

"Why don't we just sleep here on the couch?" he asked. "I hate to think of going to bed."

"We can't sleep together on a couch," she said.

"In the old days it was called bundling," he said, laughing.

"Not just the old days. The here-and-now days," Emma answered.

"Parents and ministers have worked on it for hundreds of years, the practice of bundling, haven't they?" he asked, giving a soft laugh. "But when the heart is young, it feels cuddly at times."

Emma found herself shaking with laughter. He was simply the most outspoken person, the most forthright with his unvarnished view of his surroundings. He was quite simply the most humorous person she had ever met.

"Now what's so funny about that?" he asked.

"Just the way you express yourself."

"So that means you're starting to like me, right?"

"Whatever, Ben," Emma said, pretending exasperation.

"Yes or no?"

"Maybe."

In the morning, he fried bacon while she made eggs in a nest for all of them. The truck had been there for an hour, the dull sound of hammers and skill saws in a distance, and still Ben remained at the bar with his coffee, watching Emma with her hair piled in a loose knot on top of her head, her cheeks flushed, her eyelids drooping from lack of sleep.

When the front door opened, they heard voices before Roger and Kathy made their way into the kitchen. Both children tumbled from their stools, shrieking and running to greet their parents, who caught them up into a warm bear hug, complete with effusive greetings and kisses placed all over their faces. Ben and Emma sat watching with smiles on their faces, both thinking what good parents these people were proving to be.

Roger turned to Emma, said how glad he was to be back, clapped a hand on Ben's shoulder and asked if it wasn't a bit late to get to work.

Ben wasn't intimidated at all, merely said it was, yes, but he hadn't finished his coffee yet. Roger grinned, picked up a slice of bacon, and went to make a cup for himself.

Emma looked up to greet Kathy and was shocked to find her blue eyes cold and calculating, shocked even more when Kathy turned her back to Emma and immediately launched into a conversation with Ben about tile versus concrete for the floor in the kitchen.

Ben was polite, helping her to weigh the pros and cons of each option, but when she placed a hand on his forearm and leaned in as if to whisper something to him, he quickly got up and said he needed to get back to work. "We should really include Daniel in this," he said, by way of taking his leave. "He knows so much about flooring."

He disappeared down the steps, and Roger watched him go, then turned to Emma.

"So, that was a homey scene, you and Ben at the kitchen island," he quipped, grinning widely.

"Yeah, Daddy. He was here all night," Brent shouted. "They were talking in the bedroom. They thought I was asleep but I wasn't."

He laughed at his own sneakiness, lifted his face to the ceiling.

Kathy's eyebrows were raised, her eyes popping from her face. Roger smiled a wide, knowing smile.

"No, Brent, I was changing sheets so Ben would have a clean place to sleep," Emma said, as she felt the color leave her face.

"He was there, too. I heard him."

"Yes. He came to see if he could help."

"Sounds pretty complicated," Roger said, laughing good-naturedly as he added cream to his coffee.

"It's not," Emma assured him.

"Well, we'll see whether it is or not," Kathy said, attacking Emma full force with a level stare of animosity.

Emma swallowed nervously, tried to smile, but failed.

That evening, she was confronted by both parents and accused of sleeping with Ben and neglecting the children. Kathy did all of the talking with Roger silent at her side.

How did a person extricate oneself from this stone cold accusation? Emma felt powerless, trained to be meek and humble, where Kathy was a trained lawyer, with skills honed for this very purpose.

Emma sat at the dining room table, her face pale, composed, her freckles visible, as beautiful as a carving, and as cold.

"No, Kathy. It's not what you think. I'm serious."

"Emma, my disappointment in you is profound. Never in all our weeks together did I imagine you to be like this. Ben is not supposed to be in our house, let alone spending the night. And to lie about it . . ."

"I'm not lying," Emma broke in.

"I have a difficult time believing you made that bed together and stayed out of it. I mean, come on, Emma. I am a woman of the world and this just doesn't happen. I don't know how you can live with yourself."

"But . . . we . . . it didn't happen," Emma said, her lips pale and dry.

"Brent heard you."

"He heard us putting clean sheets on the bed," Emma insisted.

Kathy rolled her eyes, took Roger's hand.

"Sneaky. Sneaky," she said, in a cold, mocking tone, her eyes already claiming victory. There was no hope of winning this sense-less and unfair argument after seeing the light of achievement in those eyes, the gathering of Roger's alliance against her.

Clearly, she wanted Emma gone. She had wanted her out of sight and mind since the fateful walk in the starlight. The only way Emma could win was if she confronted Kathy about her own attraction to Ben. She could make her squirm, make her admit this was precisely why she was being "let go."

Roger spoke, then, of the Christian values they tried to uphold, and the fact they did not want their children to be under the influ-ence of an unmarried couple carrying out a clandestine affair.

Emma nodded, her eyes on the knot of fingers in her lap. She remained steadfast in her view of nonresistance, of turning the other cheek. She would accept her fate rather than fighting back with the weapon of truth. Yes, it would be satisfying to see Kathy confronted with Emma's own accusations, accusations that were actually grounded in reality. The way Kathy spent every free moment over at the house with Ben, the way she positioned herself next to him at din-ner that night and pretended like the rest of the guests didn't exist, the way she took every opportunity to touch his strong arms. But what was the use? She could "win," but in the end it would just create more strife between Roger and Kathy, and Kathy and Emma would never trust each other again either way.

All she wanted was a chance to say goodbye to Ben.

How incongruous. How bizarre was this turn of events. Kind and unassuming Brent, who never caused a moment's disturbance, and here he was, accusing her without even realizing it, the blue eyes devoid of guile, having no idea the consequences of his observations.

And darling Annalise, the hurricane of temper fits, who now threw one of major proportions, kicking and howling because Emma would be leaving.

"We have a driver for you at nine tomorrow morning. Here are your final wages. We are sorry indeed that things turned out this way, but we feel it is for the best. Ben is a necessary component there at the house, whereas, you can be replaced," Kathy informed her.

With leaden steps, Emma went upstairs, sat on her bed, and stared at the opposite wall. There was too much fury, too much self-denial for tears. She felt numb and cold, completely bereft.

To leave this beautiful place, to leave Ben, never knowing if he was told what had occurred. She got to her feet, went to the window, prayed for a glimpse of him. They had kissed, yes. They had not stayed apart the way some couples might have, but they most certainly had not slept together. And she hadn't neglected the children!

Still, was this God's answer for her? Perhaps this was God's way of saying no, Ben is not for you. She went hot, then cold, her body reacting to the fever in her brain. So many unanswered questions, so much blatant unfairness.

And yet, she held some guilt, perhaps. She had let him stay, had kissed and carried on. Was being banished from this beautiful place the consequence of her sin?

She slept fitfully that night, despite being exhausted from so little sleep the night before. In the morning, after glancing at the red numbers on her electric alarm clock, she tugged her luggage off the shelf and began to pack, dashing to the window for a glimpse of Ben. There was none, so she carried everything downstairs and went to find Kathy, who was seated by the television with both children at her side.

She looked up, an icy stare.

"Yes?"

"I would like to say goodbye to Ben, if I may," she said.

"Ben? Oh, he went into town with Roger early this morning. They're dealing with some glitch in the plumbing."

She waved a hand in dismissal.

Taking a deep breath, Emma steadied herself before the confrontation she knew would have to take place before she departed.

"Thank you for everything, Kathy. I'll miss the children. I'm asking one thing. Don't lie to Ben about why I left. That's all."

There was a slow blink, the eyelids at half-mast, accompanied by a smile that could only be described as an oily smirk.

"You must not hold my Christian values in very high esteem. Now why would I do something like that?"

There was no winning with this shrewd lawyer clothed in the innocence of blond hair and beautiful blue eyes, sitting on the couch with one tanned leg crossed over the other, her foot bobbing the dangling gold-strapped sandal. What else could Emma say?

"Well, it is time for my ride to show up, so I'll say goodbye."

"Goodbye, Emma."

Brent looked at her with a level gaze, then walked soberly over to her and threw his arms around her waist, pressing his head into her stomach.

"I love you, Emma."

"I love you, too, Brent honey. I'll miss you terribly."

She held it together even when Annalise came running. Emma lifted her to hug and kiss her, kissed Charlie Brown over and over, and felt secretly justified when she let herself out the door to the sound of Annalise's wailing and shouting for her to come back.

The Uber driver was uninterested, so she took the back seat gratefully and began to weep silently before they reached the end of the drive covered in oyster shells. Through her tears, she watched the vast restless ocean on one side, the glittering bay on the other, opened her window a few inches to breathe in the incredible scent that was the sea and the sand and the tall swaying grasses. She listened to the cry of the gulls, her own personal remembering carried on those wings, those mischievous eyes that darted left and right, scrounging all the treats they could find.

But the vehicle moved on, relentless in chewing up the miles that would separate her from the ocean, and Ben. They had never exchanged phone numbers or addresses, never thought beyond the summer. He would find her, if Kathy did not persuade him otherwise.

But Emma knew Kathy had the power to make him give up on her.

Or did she? How strong was a newfound love? She imagined a wobbly newborn calf, a fledgling unable to fly. But he was smart. Surely he'd put two and two together. Well, she knew it was all out of her control now, so she would have to shore up her faith and drive the piles deep below the sand so her house would withstand even the worst storm.

The journey was a time of reflection, one of soul searching and testing of her instability. As the miles rolled away, she finally concluded that everything, simply everything God placed in her path, was for her own benefit, good or bad.

If Kathy appeared downright unmovable, perhaps that, too, was for a reason.

She wavered between applying faith to the situation, and hating Kathy with an almost physical malevolence that made her grip her own hands till the knuckles turned white.

"I need to stop at the next available place," she told the driver.

"McDonald's okay?" he asked, glancing in the mirror, his eyes like two black buttons of kindness.

"Sure."

"You doing alright?" he asked gruffly.

"Yes, I am. I'm just crying because I was fired from my job," she answered, summoning an attempt at a smile.

He shook his head. "Too bad. S'way it goes. You do one job, you go to another. What's a person to do?"

"You are absolutely right," she said.

And he was. This short, fat man with the brown button eyes was like a simple angel of truth, sent to bolster her courage and make her realize how easy life could be if you did not get mired down in unnecessary thoughts and worries. This job was over, done with, so she'd get another. They chatted a little more, the driver introducing himself as Ryan, telling her about his kids who were now mostly grown up, she telling him about each of her siblings.

And suddenly she was shot through with a riptide of joy at the thought of Dena and the produce fields, her mother's cozy kitchen and her father's easy stride through the long rows of vegetables.

She would lie in her too-warm bed upstairs with hardly a breeze and be uncomfortable, but she would be at home where she was loved beyond reason. Her married sisters would come home and listen with sympathetic ears, and become outraged at the deceit and unfairness of it all.

At home, people were on your side. You could do no wrong. They would never for one minute think she had done anything wrong, certainly not what Kathy had implied. In the face of all this adversity, she would be alright.

If only Ben would . . . Someday, perhaps.

CHAPTER 11

Most of the way through Virginia she dozed fitfully, half-hearing the hum of the tires on asphalt, the drone of passing trucks, and the barely audible music from the car radio. As the afternoon wore on, she began to take an interest in her surroundings, the green rows of corn growing like a regiment, an army of tall green stalks that would bear the hard yellow ears in the coming months.

Corn, the mainstay of the farmers in Pennsylvania, she thought. It was such a normal everyday sight and occurrence, the rolling hills and wooded ridges with farms tucked here and there, the only close body of water a farm pond or a lazy creak meandering through a cow pasture.

A sense of loss settled over her as she compared her surroundings to the heaving ocean, the long sandy stretches she had walked with Ben. He had tried to become her best friend that night, and she had been about as romantic as a porcupine. She smiled, felt the beginning of hope.

She remembered the night spent with him. Was it really only night before last?

How could Kathy have made a decision so swiftly, sending her away like some criminal? She lamented her lack of a backbone, her willingness to comply, but knew it was for the best. Emma did not believe Kathy actually wanted Ben as a husband, but she was attracted to him, so she didn't want Emma to have him, either. She had seen it the first day, but didn't want to think ill of her new employer. Well, it was all unfortunate, horribly unfortunate, a good thing gone irretrievably wrong, and she powerless to set it right.

The sting of humiliation still smarted. Little Brent had heard them talking in the master suite, that was true, and there had been a bit of romance. And it was Kathy and Roger's house, and she shouldn't have let a guest spend the night—even use their bed—without permission. She had let herself get swept up in the pleasure of having him there in the same house, and in the process she had lost her good sense. But nothing more than a kiss had happened between them! Oh, but that kiss . . . it had meant something, she was sure of that. But what exactly?

She'd need her sisters to help decipher it all. The thought of her sisters, those deliciously irreverent, outspoken individuals she simply adored, was the one highlight of her ever-deepening gloom at the thought of her return. What would she tell her parents? How would she explain everything?

She breathed a small sigh and her eyelids drooped with weariness.

She watched with bated breath for the familiar rectangular glow of yellow light that meant her parents had not gone to bed. They came down the incline from Pebble Ridge, the lights in the valley welcoming her home. There were traces of twilight in the dark sky, where a graying pink color lingered in the west, the sun showing its reluctance to fade away until morning. The woods were dark and deep and a few stars already twinkled overhead.

"Here. Right, please. This is my home," she instructed, leaning forward to make sure the driver would not miss the entrance to the farm.

She felt a sob already forming in her throat.

They drove up to the sidewalk and Ryan pulled her luggage out of the trunk.

"Hey, girl, it's been decent. Hang in there."

They shook hands. She thanked him for a safe ride home, assured him she would hang in just fine. They laughed together and he held up a hand for a high five.

"Thank you again," Emma said. "You were great."

"Everything's paid. You're good to go," he said.

With that, Emma started toward the house, turning back briefly to watch the car move away.

She opened the door on the front porch, called, "Anybody home?"

Her parents had both been dozing on recliners, and now were snapped awake by Emma opening the screen door and struggling to draw the luggage in after herself.

"What? Who is it? Emma!"

Her mother was the first one to reach her, followed by her father in his white T-shirt, patched everyday trousers, and bare feet.

"You know, someone could rob this place, or set the house on fire and you would snore through it," Emma said.

"Why are you home? What happened?"

Her mother reached out for a warm hug, and Emma was drawn into the softness of her old cotton housecoat with the snaps down the front, the gentle, billowy arms like roll pillows, the scent of Bond's talcum powder and Dove soap. Her father stood, his hand shoved in his pockets, a genuine gladness etched in his face.

"I'm here," Emma said. "If you have something cold to drink, we can sit at the table and I'll tell you my sad tale."

"Emma, really. You didn't get fired, did you? How did you get here? Where is your driver?"

Mam poured Emma a tall glass of mint tea. "Here. Sit down."

Gratefully, Emma sat, lifted the glass to her lips, and took a long sip of the good *visa tay*. There was no drink in the world to compare with it.

She summarized the story, breaking down partway through, hiding her face in her hands and crying. Her mother's hand rested on Emma's forearm, her mouth turned down in a clucking motherly way.

"*Ach my, hesslich*. Well, it was not your fault. You couldn't help it that Ben helped you make that bed. Who . . . What kind of guy would do that, though?"

"Ben is so . . . well, he doesn't even know the word self-conscious. He has no shame. He's really funny and talkative, and doesn't waste time before he'll tell you exactly what he thinks."

"Is he . . . I mean . . ."

Her mother did not dare ask the question of whether he would qualify as a potential husband.

"He's very nice, Mam. We walked on the beach one . . ."

"I hope you didn't go swimming together," she broke in.

Emma laughed. "No, Mam, we did not."

But she did not tell her about the long and gentle kiss. Well, to start with it had been gentle, then . . . oh my, guilt flooded her.

"You look guilty."

"I am speaking the truth, Mam."

Her father caught her eye, winked and hid a mischievous grin.

"Where's Dena? Everyone asleep?"

"Dena is spending the night with her cousin Mary. She's been a grouch around here without you, and there was a spaghetti supper at the fire hall so we told her she could go."

"Mam, you know they're probably hanging out with boys this minute. You know how it goes with these fifteen-year-olds."

Her father nodded, smiled. "Perhaps we should have let you go to more spaghetti suppers."

Emma grinned, but her mouth trembled, went all lopsided and weird.

She shook her head, said wryly, "It's going to take more than a spaghetti supper, believe me."

"*Ach*, it will all turn out the way God intended. Every little twist and turn in the trial of life has a purpose. This too shall pass."

Emma climbed the familiar stairway and showered with cool water, then sank gratefully into the unbelievable comfort of her own bed. Long afterward, her parents sat together talking through Emma's situation, genuinely sad that she'd fallen hard this time. "The poor girl, and him being quite the chap the way it sounded."

She slept deeply, without dreams.

She awoke with the sound of the chugging diesel. For a moment she was back in the beach house, waking to the steady rising and falling of the waves. But as soon as she cracked her eyes open, she remembered everything.

Well, she was here now. This was her life, where she belonged. Almost, it seemed as if that time had never been. Only the remnants of a receding dream that left her with an unnamed regret, a remorse that stung worse than a hornet.

She rolled over, groaned. She had known him for such a short time, yet she could feel his sleeve against hers, his arm sliding gently around her waist. It had fit exactly, his long, slender fingers placed at her ribs. She touched the spot he had touched, grimaced with the pain of remembering.

Only now, with all these miles between them, could she fathom the depth of her feelings for Ben.

The sun was already illuminating her room, a fly buzzing, determined, at the window screen, the chug of the diesel, the clanking of milk buckets. A screen door slammed below her. Likely her mother, already in the garden, cutting spearmint for tea, checking the red beets for size, surveying the string beans and cucumbers.

She drew on her courage and strength to stumble across the hallway and into the bathroom where she gripped the edge of the sink and glowered at the reflection in the mirror. Bloodshot eyes, a pink peeling nose, chapped lips that had dried in the sun like cranberries, hideous freckles and hair that resembled a bottle brush.

Wow.

Back to the real world. That cliché was worn out like an old shoe rag, but it was certainly the truth. This was real. The familiar upstairs, way too hot for so early in the morning, produce fields that lay endlessly in long flat rows of vegetables to be pulled, picked, pulled into baskets or wooden crates, and left in the wagon tracks for her father. Backbreaking work that she didn't feel prepared for.

She yearned for the rumbling of the central air unit that would generate cold air through vents in the floor. CBS News on the television. K-Cups. The lazy days on the beach with Brent and Annalise.

She reached over to press the button on the battery lamp.

Oh great. The dumb thing was dead. Leave it to Dena to go flying off with her cousin Mary, and the only available bathroom light with a dead battery.

Well, she'd see by the dawn's early light, no doubt. She yanked a brush through her wild and unruly hair, then wet it with the palms of her hands and raked it into submission with her *schtrale*, the fine-toothed comb that every Amish girl used.

She heard the whisper of small bare feet. The bathroom door was pulled open slightly, and two large eyes peeped in.

"It's her!"

"What?"

"It's Emma!"

"Hey, you two. Hi! It's me. I'm back."

She caught Sallie and Amanda in a soft, sweet hug. They smelled of bath soap, their hair was *allus schtruvvlich*, sticking out every which way, and they were full of eager questions.

"It was great. I loved it. And look what I have for you."

They were impressed with the container of shells, impressed with Emma's knowledge of this faraway place that had been so fun for her.

These little girls need not know of the drama, the "mishap," as she labeled it. They wouldn't understand, and it wasn't worth upsetting them with a sad tale.

Breakfast was lively, the food good and hot and homemade. When Dena arrived, everything turned into bedlam, with Dena roaring her disbelief, followed by hugs and shrieks of pure happiness.

She sat down, heaped her plate with scrambled eggs and sausage gravy, drank copious amounts of orange juice, and then finally asked Emma why she was back so soon.

"We can talk while we work," Emma answered quietly.

"It's string beans and candy onions today," her father said.

"I *hate* picking beans," Dena groaned.

"Doesn't matter, you still have to do it."

Dena glowered and pouted, but that was the way of it. No matter if you disliked a job, it was there to be done and was not going away, so you may as well give up and do it. It was called work.

By ten o'clock, Emma felt as if her back would literally break in two. She sat on an upside-down crate, pushed back a lock of her hair, left a smudge of brown across her forehead, and sighed. She looked down the row of beans to find Dena sitting cross-legged between the rows, watching the antics of a group of swallows that followed an unseen whirlwind path in the sky.

The sun was already blazing hot and was not yet overhead, the afternoon promising even more heat. By the end of July, she would be used to the heat and the backbreaking work, but in the beginning, it was always like this.

Emma reached out, tried to pick the long, dangling beans from her perch on the crate, but then gave up and stood, bent her back, and kept going. She counted five bushel crates, filled to the top. By lunchtime, they should be finished, the candy onions a much easier job, for sure.

"Dena," she called, straightening her back.

"What?"

"If you'd get to work, we'd be done by lunchtime."

"Some things never change," she called back.

"Come on. My back is not used to this."

"Tut tut. Too bad. I can't help that you spent the month lying around on the beach."

Emma grinned, then squatted in the row, picking beans in earnest. It was true, some things never changed. Yet she felt different. She felt as if someone had taken the humdrum of her life and turned it upside down, shook out the contents, and replaced them with the splendor of the wide open ocean . . . and a tall, blond man with a sense of humor that filled up all her empty spaces.

If she was left with only the memory of him, it would be enough.

She had loved before, but not quite like this. Before, her love hadn't been returned. She hadn't realized how different it would be when the attraction was mutual, when two people felt destined for each other. She thought of his face, his touch, his wonderful laugh, the expressions that came and went in his eyes, everything. She grasped every moment greedily and stockpiled it against future loneliness.

Dena knew nothing about Ben, or she'd be right up here picking beans as fast as she could go.

When they finally entered the cooler interior of the house, there were bacon sandwiches and tall glasses of fresh-squeezed lemonade. Emma relished the food after a long morning of hard work, the satisfaction of having done a job well. Her father's praise rang in her ears. He'd said she was still one of his best pickers, but more than the words, it was his fond smile, his eyes twinkling with approval.

Then there was the announcement from her mother. The sisters were coming. They couldn't stay home and do their work with Emma here. Of course not. They wanted to be here, to hear her story firsthand.

Dishes were washed in record time. Emma went to wash up, rearrange her hair, and put on a clean covering and a clean dress, a new mint-green summer dress that would show off her tan. She smiled to herself, accepting this need to impress her sisters. They were a daunting force, a united front, with advice and opinions carried out freely, delightful in their constant attempt at shaping Emma's life.

They arrived together, the buggy stuffed with babies and small children hanging out the back window, waving and calling out. The second the horse stopped, two boys flung themselves out of the back window, stepped on the spring, and jumped off, narrowly escaping the sharp edges of the orange slow-moving vehicle emblem. They ran to Emma, who gathered them both in a tight hug.

Noah and Melvin, the twins, so dear and brown and skinny. She loved the little boys as if they were her own. At their birth, they'd struggled to survive, weighing in at three and four pounds. They'd had to stay in the hospital for about a month, and then Emma spent most of her summer helping out at their home, holding the two babies, washing and cooking and cleaning. Ruth had not been well, thin and struggling with postpartum depression, a horrible affliction for a young first-time mother. It had taken away her zest for life, her love for her husband or her babies, until she finally admitted she couldn't handle motherhood, weaving in and out of the dark place that bordered on being dangerous. The nutrition experts plied her with pills and powders and oils, took away gluten and dairy and white refined sugar, until their father stepped in and made her an appointment with a renowned gynecologist. She stopped trying to breastfeed the crying babies and was put on an antidepressant. The cost of the formula for the two of them was high, but every month there was cash in an envelope from an unknown source. Emma knew it was from her parents, but no one else needed to know.

And so Ruth struggled, but survived and finally blossomed. Her life righted itself and her husband accepted the fact that he needed to step up to the plate and do more to help out. And he did. He spent every night sharing bottle and diaper duties with his wife and nurtured and loved the twins alongside her.

And here they were, four years old, brown-eyed and towheaded, talkative and filled with energy.

Praise God, Emma thought. Truly she felt as if she could shout the Lord's name in thanksgiving.

"There you are, Emma!" Ruth called out, rushing to meet her, a baby in one arm, a diaper bag slung over the opposite shoulder.

"Hey, don't leave me alone with the horse," Esther shouted, her anxious face peering across the sweating animal as she loosened the traces. "Emily, get back in. I'll help you out as soon as I put the horse away."

Emma untangled herself from arms and diaper bags and babies, hurried out to help unhitch.

"Hi, Esther," she said.

"Hello! My, it is so good to see you. You're brown as an autumn leaf."

They took the horse into the barn, slipped off the bridle and put on the halter, gave him a long drink before leading him to an empty stall. Emma gave him a few blocks of hay and brushed off the front of her skirt before linking an arm in Esther's.

"It's good to be home, Esther."

"But why? What in the world, Emma? I thought you were staying till September. Mam told us you were back but wouldn't say one word more."

"It's a long story."

"Good. I can't wait to hear it."

Children and babies were deposited into the grandmother's waiting arms, duly fussed over, the candy jar brought out with packets of Skittles and Starbursts grabbed by the fistful, the mothers' intervention putting most of them back.

"It's too hot for coffee," Ruth moaned. "I just can't take this heat."

"Well, you're going to have to," her mother laughed. "July and August."

"I know. I'll get used to it. I told Emanuel we need to purchase one of those DeWalt fans for our bedroom."

"They're expensive," Esther broke in.

"If it's too hot for coffee, what will it be? Mint tea or lemonade?"

They all settled around the table, asking Emma to begin her story. It was harder than she'd imagined, the way she kept choking up, failing to conceal the depth of her emotion. She described the shores of North Carolina in detail, the house that was being remodeled, then finally got to the part about Ben.

"What?" Ruth asked, sitting up straight, the palms of her hands slapping the tabletop.

"You mean there's romance?" Esther squeaked, turning to pick up her fussy ten-month-old, Elijah.

"There is," her mother nodded solemnly.

"Why didn't you tell me?" Dena interjected, suddenly interested in the conversation.

So Emma went on to describe the walk on the beach, the determination to remain aloof. She went on to the night of the storm and its consequences.

For once in their lives, the sisters were speechless. Both of them opened their mouths for their opinion to be thrown out, but simply shook their heads.

"Wow," Esther said finally.

Ruth didn't manage a word.

"You know," her mother said quietly, "Perhaps it simply is not meant to be. God's ways are not our ways. His wisdom is beyond understanding."

"Exactly," Ruth said, her eye going to her mother's face with admiration.

"But still."

Esther's face held so much empathy, so much understanding.

"It has to be tough for you, Emma."

Almost, Emma succumbed to tears, only her pride keeping them in check.

"You know, I've always said, unlucky in love. That's me," she quipped, making a courageous attempt at lightheartedness.

"There is no such thing," Ruth said emphatically. "If this guy really, really wants you, he'll find you. There's no such thing as being unable to contact a person in this modern age."

"But I can see Emma's point. What is Kathy going to tell him?"

"Oh, it is just one big mess," Esther wailed, taking a piece of candy from her two-year-old, heading for the sink and a clean washcloth.

Dena sat at the table in her normal ill-mannered posture, one foot propped on the seat of her chair, her knee bent with her dress stretched across it, listening, eyeing them with the disdain of a fifteen-year-old who exists under her own self-made umbrella of teenage angst.

She snorted, lowered her eyelids to produce the full effect of the expulsion of disapproval.

"Whatever. I never saw a family as overboard as this one. Seriously. Everybody get a life."

Feathers were seriously ruffled after that, with Esther and Ruth gasping in disbelief, then giving the upstart little sister a piece of their mind. She had no idea what she was talking about, and she should learn to hold her tongue once in a while. Couldn't she think about someone else's feelings for once?

"What do you mean? The only reason Emma isn't married is because she is too picky. If one hapless individual asks her out and his pants are half an inch too short, he doesn't stand a chance."

Emma smiled at the "hapless individual." Dena was brilliant. Leave it to the younger set to speak the blistering truth, she thought wryly.

"Come now," Ruth defended Emma.

"Puh. You know Levi Esh? He's what? Twenty-six, seven? You couldn't find a nicer person. He shoes horses, and when he arrives at our farm, I make a point of being with him while he does Cheyenne. He's everything I would ever want, that's for sure. He's so talkative, so easy to get to know. Good-looking, strong. Think about it. He asked Emma, I know he did. What did she say? No. She didn't want to be called Emma Esh."

"Dena! I thought you said you wouldn't tell anyone."

"I just want everyone to know that I have no sympathy."

Esther winked at Ruth, and Ruth raised an eyebrow. Mam hid her smile behind her coffee cup. Leave it to Dena.

"Furthermore, there's Daniel Lapp. I would marry him in a heartbeat."

"Well then, you go right ahead. Marry away," Emma barked, a bit irritated now.

"I might just do that if I ever get a chance. I hope you have considered the fact that I might be found high and dry, just like you. What if none of the guys want to waste their time on another young woman who thinks she's too good for them? Think about it. I'll be sixteen in November and I won't stand a chance."

"Oh pooh," both older sisters said.

Mam sighed. "Well, at any rate, the summer's work is in full swing, and we're glad to have Emma at home. I wasn't too thrilled about that job to begin with. It was just too worldly, with all her time spent away from us."

"It was worth it. I don't regret my job at all. I loved the children, and I especially loved the place," Emma said.

"And you do seriously love him," said Dena in a mocking, theatrical whisper. "Oh, where are you, fair love?"

Everyone broke into genuine laughter, even Mam. Ruth and Esther wiped their eyes, said, "Hooo . . . Dena, you're a mess."

Dena was in her element now, having evoked the merriment she had hoped, so she continued.

"The elusive man remains on the long stretches of white sands . . ."

"It's not white," Emma told her.

"Whatever it is. He strolls alone in the moonlight, his heart aching, yet again at this desultory romance. Oh my love, where art thou?"

Everyone was in stitches now, even Emma.

Mam wiped her eyes, said, "Alright, enough now."

Emma wiped her cheeks with two fingers, blinked her eyes.

"I hope you find yourself in exactly this situation someday, and you will not laugh about it."

"Not me. I fully intend to have a drama-free rumschpringa."

Chapter 12

WHAT WAS THERE TO SAY? EMMA THOUGHT. WE CAN PLAN AND DREAM, but who is to know what God's plans are? Dena was so young and so brilliant, the world at her fingertips. Why burst her self-imposed bubble of overconfidence?

Only once was a person fifteen, perched on the high diving board before springing off and plunging into the frigid water called "rumschpringa." How to explain that word to Dena? Running around. It was, literally, that. You ran around in buggies to different homes, met single boys, you were introduced to dozens of girls you had never met before. Girls that were dressed in ways your mother would never allow, gorgeous girls who were so much prettier than yourself. You ran to the bathroom with a friend and tugged at your cape, replaced a few straight pins to make it all look a bit more like theirs. You turned your head this way and that, hating the way your hair was rolled all wrong, the way your covering looked limp and outdated. You longed for shoes with four-inch heels and a big white purse like that other girl's, the small black purse you owned suddenly seeming hopelessly old-fashioned. The purse had been chosen under your mother's conservative influence, and for the first time ever, you felt a sharp dislike of your mother. She was too bossy, too opinionated, and it was time she realized a few things about you.

You saw the ones who were popular, the ones who received the glances from the handsome boys. After that, you were crosshatched with discontent. It sprouted from your face in the form of red pustules that inflamed your low sense of worth, and you existed in this miserable bog until you chose to quit wallowing in the self-inflicted sorrow and get on with your life.

Rumschpringa wasn't that way for everyone, of course, but it had been for Emma. After doing it for ten years, all that angst seemed laughable, really, but those early years had been achingly traumatic.

Here she was, long past the time when most young men would consider her as a wife. She had seen the fruits of comparing one love to another, had been duly chastened by God during her stay in North Carolina.

Things had simply not worked out, she told herself, half-listening to the ongoing chatter surrounding her as she gazed unseeingly out of the kitchen window.

The heat was becoming unbearable, the kitchen like a steam bath, the humidity thick and uncomfortable, waves of heat sucking the small valance against the screen and blowing it inward. She thought of the central air unit whirring against the side of the house in North Carolina, the cold air blown through vents along the wall, the epitome of comfort on a day such as this.

"So, what are you going to do this fall?" Esther was asking as she brought empty lemonade glasses to the sink.

"You know, I have no idea. I am . . . was sick of my teaching job, but now that I failed at being a nanny, I might reconsider."

She imagined herself heading into midlife, her waist thickening, still holding court in the dusty classroom, cloaked in the memory of what might have been.

"You're a superb teacher. Why would you quit?" Esther asked, all kind eyes and growing concern.

"I don't know, to be honest."

"Did you pray about it?"

"Yes."

The word slipped out before she could retrieve the untruth of it. No, she did not pray about school teaching. She didn't say "Thy will be done," not wanting to spend the summer thinking of going back in the fall. This was the summer that was her last attempt, the last time she would be open to meeting someone.

She had met Ben, but to what end?

Surely God would not be so cruel to deny her the chance to reconnect with Ben. Her faith in a loving Father was sustainable, like a garden that produces well year after year. Grace and mercy rode on the wings of her prayers. Her prayers had always been unfettered by doubt. From the time she was a small child when her mother helped her say the "*Müde binn ich*" prayer at bedtime, she had never wavered in the childlike belief in God.

Or the fact that He loved mankind so much that He sent His Son, the only one He had, to be mocked and scorned and finally, die a gruesome death on the cross. And then He rose again to give light and life to everyone who believed. And there were many who did.

She thought of her life in His hands, cupped around her as she stayed nestled in His love. After her stay in North Carolina, she had felt as if God had taken those hands away, given her a small push, and allowed her to flounder around like a landed trout.

But please, please God. Give me Ben. Ben is all I want. Surely you have mercy. I don't want to lose him.

She knew she should give it all up to God's will, but somehow, she could not bring herself to think of giving Ben to God. To sacrifice a love as awesome and all-consuming as she had felt for Ben was unthinkable.

He had made her giddy with his presence. Her heart raced and her knees were fluid when he put a well-placed arm around her waist.

Oh, elusive love, so hard to have and to hold.

She pictured his pleasant face, the eyes filled with love, the blond good looks, the height and breadth of him. She longed to be in his arms, to hear him tell her she was beautiful.

He'd call. He'd write. He would obtain a phone number and address, scour the Pennsylvania directory until he found her. It was reasonable to be patient, reasonable to wait out her summer days at home.

Dena sat at the foot of Emma's bed, brushing her short, thick hair, wincing as she drew the brush through. Her tanned legs were like a pretzel beneath her, her strong young arms as shapely as a model's.

Emma glanced at the whacked-off hair.

"Why did you cut off all your long, gorgeous hair?"

"My covering fits better. Everyone does it."

"I can't see how you can get it rolled into a decent bob."

"I don't. I stuff it under my hairnet and draw it tight with the hair-pins. See, you're so old you don't even know what style is anymore."

Emma sniffed, indignant.

"I'm not exactly ancient, Dena. My covering fits as nice as yours. You don't have to whack off all your hair to have your covering fit nicely."

"I do."

She flipped her shoulder-length hair over one shoulder, and continued brushing. Emma watched with narrowed eyes, calmly appraising the way her long graceful neck was as exquisite as a young swan's. She was on the cusp of young womanhood, without a serious thought in her pretty head, as honest as a judge, as trustworthy as a thief.

"Dena, I worry about you."

Dena stopped brushing, opened her eyes wide to stare at her sister.

"Why would you do that?"

"I guess I've been through the mill, so now it's your turn and I know what it's like?" Emma said, drawing up the end of her sentence into a question.

"Oh really? English girl. Where did you learn to talk like that?"

Emma laughed, shook her head.

"You're hopeless."

"I can tell you right now that you can quit worrying. I like Nelson and he likes me, so no worries in that department. We won't date immediately, but my love life will be puzzle free. Uncomplicated. Slick as a whistle."

"Nelson who?"

"You don't know him."

"Well, who is he? I was probably his teacher."

"No, you weren't. He's in the other district. Raymond Look's Nelson."

Emma thought, but could not recall having met anyone from that family, hadn't known they had children old enough to be with the youth.

Emma put her book on the night table, got out of bed and went to the window, flapping her arms.

"It's so warm up here in my room. After living in AC, I can hardly take this heat at night."

"Welcome back to earth, sister."

"So what's Nelson like?"

"He's cute. He has black hair, cut short. Brown eyes, you know, handsome. He's not tall, though. Medium height. A little taller than me. He met me at a skating party, and says I'm funny. Likes to hang out with me."

"So the romance is effectively kindled," Emma said. "What was that whole row about me making it tough for you if you have this Nelson all sewn up?"

"What do you mean, all sewn up? That's a phrase out of the 1900s. Like I stuffed him in a pillowcase and sewed it shut."

"You might want to do that. Guys are elusive. They fade away."

"Nelson won't."

Emma looked serious. "I hope he won't."

"It's your name. You should be called Esther or Ruth. They were great loves in the Bible. Emma isn't even in that category. It's probably your name."

Emma reached over and threw a round decorative pillow at Dena.

"Get off my bed. Go to your room, okay? I need to get some sleep."

"Grouch."

"Sorry. Goodnight."

"Grouch."

"Maybe I am an old maid. A singleton. A leftover blessing. Whatever, I have every right to be grouchy."

"Because Benjamin, fair Benjamin, has not yet ridden his mighty steed in search of the beautiful Emma. The fairest in the land, the eyes like sapphires, the teeth as porcelain . . ."

She extended both arms, her hands fluttering dramatically. She flung her head to the side, her face raised to the ceiling, and said in a stage whisper, "Emma, my love. Whither hast thou vanished? I am but a lifeless vapor without thee . . ."

Another pillow was flung in her direction.

"Git. Go to bed. Go directly to bed. Do not pass go."

They were both laughing as Dena passed through the door of Emma's room. Emma reached out to turn off the battery lamp, pulled the thin cotton sheet to her waist, turned on her side, and was wide awake far into the night, reliving her walk on the beach, the thunderstorm, and the resulting dismissal.

A sultry night breeze riffled through the leaves on the old walnut tree outside her window, ruffled the sheer white curtains at her bedside. An owl hooted close by, likely in the white pine beside the front porch, the hated predator that frightened all the chickadees and cardinals away from the birdfeeders. A horse snorted in the barnyard, then moved away across a few protruding stones, his hooves hitting the heard surface. A car whined along the twisting road that led across the ridge. She heard the grinding of gears, the tone becoming an octave higher as it began its ascent.

It was far too warm to sleep. She kicked off the covers, flung herself on her back, and sighed.

She thought of a cold glass of ice water, a cold shower, the sensation of an icy wind off a cold lake, to no avail.

So what if Ben never contacted her? She'd buy a small house somewhere, continue teaching school, dig a bit deeper to come up with the willpower to exercise the proper amount of interest. She'd thought all that was over, but what else could she do?

She could work as a *maud*, but that was too close to being a nanny, which clearly hadn't been the right fit. She could work at the farmer's market, or in a restaurant. No and no. Possibly get her GED and be a caregiver in a facility for the elderly. No to that, too.

She spent the time between eleven thirty and twelve imagining her house. It would have to be a mobile home or a double-wide trailer given the small amount she had saved. Her income would not be enough to sustain a large monthly payment. But it would be cute and cozy and welcoming. She'd have her group of friends over quite often to make homemade doughnuts and fry pies. They'd sit around her breakfast nook to enjoy them with coffee.

Suddenly, she felt a heave of raw emotion, followed by the knowing that that was not what she truly hoped would happen. She wanted to be loved and admired, cherished by an attractive, worthy man, someone to share her life with, the intimacy of having a husband.

Was it too much to ask?

Her pillow was saturated with her tears before she fell into a troubled sleep.

She took to checking voicemails, found herself making excuses to get to the end of the drive first, her heart beating hard, waiting for the homely flat car that carried the rural mail. Neither one proved fruitful.

At the end of July, she told the school board she would not teach that fall, and regretted her choice the following week.

She felt adrift, loosened. She hoped to find a sense of belonging to someone or something, prayed for that voicemail or letter in the box, but there was none.

The days picking and sorting vegetables with Dena blurred into long weeks of heat, backbreaking labor, baskets of ripe tomatoes and cucumbers, bush beans, and corn. She literally saw rows of green peppers in her sleep, waxed and gleaming as they rolled on the conveyor belt. Her mind no longer hummed with anxiety, but her heart carried the dull pain of a half-healed wound. She could still visualize the slant of his nose, the quick humor of his widening grin, the easy way he had kissed her, as if he had done it many times before.

Why wouldn't he have kissed girls? He was older, matured, attractive, so of course he'd had practice. An unexpected jolt of irritation rippled through her veins. She saw herself as gullible, falling for his suave assertions, handing out compliments as easily as brushing a crumb from a sleeve.

But who was to know?

He had been sincere, at times. She could almost be certain of it, but never fully. As time went on, and there was no sign of Ben, or the fact that he had ever been in her life, her prayers turned doubtful, the uttered words containing more and more traces of disbelief, a soft, spongy faith that no longer held fervor.

Her best friend of at least ten years was Eva Kauffman, a tall, well-built girl of twenty-six, just like Emma. Dark-haired and dark-eyed, her face rounded after the birth of a robust baby boy named Elijah, she was Emma's sounding board, the recipient of aired grievances, self-pity, and total disbelief that it had happened again, "it" being cast aside after falling in love so hard it threatened a life sentence of incarceration of the heart.

Eva had married a young man two years her junior, not worthy of her, in Emma's opinion. Not that her opinion mattered after Eva laid eyes on Elvin. Emma and Eva turned into Eva and Elvin, who were married a year later and produced Elijah a year after that.

The wedding had been saturated with the intertwined E emblem, and of course, Emma was a bridesmaid, seated all day with Eva's much younger brother who had been less than thrilled to be *nāvahucka* (best man) with a girl as ancient and unexciting as Emma. She'd been his teacher, for Pete's sake, he whined to his mother.

That wedding, Emma cried discreetly into her lace-edged handkerchief when Elvin and Eva stood side-by-side and uttered their quiet vows. They were solemnly pronounced man and wife by the kindly bushy-haired bishop, who blessed them directly after that, and then the happy couple made their way back to their appointed chairs and kept their eyes downcast in the way that was good and proper.

Eva stole a glance at Emma, saw the reddened nose and the wet eyes, took a deep breath to steady herself, and vowed to stay loyal and true to Emma, to help find her a soulmate if it took every ounce of effort she could muster.

On this particular Sunday afternoon, Eva made sure there was a fresh jar of iced coffee in the refrigerator, the front porch was swept and scrubbed, the begonias and fiddle ferns watered and fertilized. Emma had a keen eye for these things, and Eva had been known to impress her with her flower growing skills before.

"Elvin, now, when Emma comes over, don't say anything about Abner Stoltzfus. You know how she is. There's no doubt in my mind that she'd consider marrying him to be 'settling.' She's sort of special, Elvin. I mean, she's a *lot* special. Smart, beautiful, classy. She's not a girl who will be content marrying someone like Abner. So just stay quiet about him, okay?"

Elvin, his round cheeks like polished apples surrounded by a healthy brown beard, slanted his own dark eyes at his wife and told her he would keep quiet if it meant so much to her.

"It does. And thank you."

Their shared smile held the old-fashioned value of giving in, one to another, the foundation for a strong and enduring union.

Emma bounded up the steps of her friend's house, eager as always. They met in a close embrace. Emma picked up the eight-month-old Elijah, who wriggled with delight at seeing someone he recognized, then leaned back into her arms to catch her eye before his little face burst into a huge smile for the second time. He snuggled against her shoulder, and Emma tightened her grip on the small body.

"He is the most lovable baby ever," she said, patting the rounded little bottom.

"He's ours, that's why," Eva answered, laughing.

"He's like me. He gets all that friendliness from me," Elvin told her.

Emma laughed. She'd often told Eva that her home was like a lighthouse that always guided her directly to their front porch.

"So tell me. Tell me everything again."

Eva led the way to the kitchen, a homey bright spot that held her in its coziness. She'd painted the old cabinets white, painted the walls and the woodwork in coordinating shades of gray, spread bright throw rugs across the worn linoleum, added her personal touches on the countertop. A bouquet of snap dragons and asparagus ferns were arranged in an antique vase, a woven runner spread neatly underneath.

"Iced coffee?" Eva asked.

"Oh, wonderful. Of course," Emma answered.

Elvin made his special popcorn, sprinkled liberally with sour cream and onion powder, an alarming river of melted butter and Parmesan cheese poured over top.

"You know your popcorn should be called 'Clogged Artery Special,'" Emma remarked, as she dipped a cereal dish into the bowl.

"Or 'High Blood Pressure Mix,'" Eva said, stuffing a large handful into her mouth.

"Ah, come on. A little butter never hurt anyone," Elvin said. "No worse than that coffee bomb you're drinking."

And so it went, all afternoon, three friends who had no problem speaking their minds, and no problem understanding each other's views and values.

The front porch was located to the west, with a large oak tree shading it all afternoon, a breeze coming from the north side, riffling the leaves and the ferns in their moss baskets hanging from hooks in the ceiling.

As it inevitably would, the conversation turned to Ben, whom Eva had labeled "that North Carolina fiasco."

"I refuse to think of that time in those terms, Eva. It was not a fiasco."

Her lips compressed in a tight line and her eyes flashed with rebellion as she pushed the white porch swing with one foot. An uncomfortable silence followed, an itchy blanket of outrage thrown across the porch by Emma's own hand.

"Well," Eva said brightly, recovering her composure after meeting Elvin's eyes in total agreement. The poor thing, she hadn't even started to give up.

Anyone who had fallen in love would have contacted her by now, if he was serious. Eva and Elvin had rehashed this with each other many times. When was Emma going to accept this fact?

"Well," she repeated, "why don't we just let sleeping dogs lie, then? Okay?"

"We should plan a vacation," Elvin said suddenly.

Eva's feet slid on the cement floor of the porch as she brought the swing to a stop, spread both arms to her side, palms up, in a gesture of helplessness.

"What? That came out of nowhere."

"I have two weeks paid vacation from my job."

"But we were going to work on the house."

"The house will be here when we get back."

"Okay?" Eva was clearly taken aback. "But, where would we go? The Outer Banks? Those houses are *hesslich* expensive."

"My boss owns a camper and he told me the other day we could borrow it—it's just sitting in his driveway and he doesn't know when he'll get a chance to use it. We could get a driver and pay for a spot along a river somewhere. A nice campground. With a pool, a golf course, hiking trails, you know. Maybe Virginia? Or Tennessee to the Great Smoky Mountains. Wherever we want. I could get Randy to drive. Emma could go."

"What? I don't care how big the camper is, it's too small to house me with all of you," Emma protested, thinking of the lack of privacy, the close proximity to bathroom and bedroom.

"No, Emma. It's not. That would be simply delightful. Let's do it, Elvin. Let's. When would we go?"

The remainder of the day was spent poring over dog-eared maps, atlas copies and calendars. They finally concluded the most accessible campground would be one in West Virginia, beside the Monongahela River. It was called Buena Vista retreat. The Appalachian Trail was less than a mile away, there was swimming and boating, a waterpark, and a good trout stream.

They grilled burgers in the backyard, brought out a bowl of potato salad and fresh-sliced tomatoes, a chocolate cake and raspberry jello. They discussed plans and Elvin promised to speak to his boss the next day.

After Emma left to go to the hymn singing, Eva fastened her brown eyes on her husband's face, and said she was going to invite her cousin, Elam Yoder's Matt.

"What?" Elvin's mouth dropped open.

"I am. I've got to get Emma's mind off Ben. You and I both know he would have found Emma by now if he was ever going to."

Elvin nodded soberly. "But Matt? He's at least thirty."

"He's thirty-four. He has a birthday in September and he'll be thirty-five. He's my sister Rose's age."

"But he's not Amish."

"So? He never joined a church, but he could. His whole family is Amish. He could be our driver! But Elvin, if you breathe a word of this to Emma, the consequences will be dire. She will not go if we even mention the possibility of a man."

CHAPTER 13

By mid-September, Emma had helped finish up much of the produce picking, cleaned the packing shed, and sewn a few new dresses and bib aprons.

Dena was upset, claiming the whole thing absolutely unfair. Whoever heard of not one, but two vacations in one summer? It didn't help when Emma reminded her that her first trip had not been a vacation. Dena replied that Emma should wake up and smell the truth now, because it was pretty rank, this old maid odor that wafted through the room.

"Spinsters go on cruises, they go out west, they spend entire winters in Florida, and you are exactly like them."

"You make the single life sound pretty appealing," Emma countered. But secretly she had started to question the vacation herself. What if she missed a voicemail or a letter from Ben? What if he showed up at her family's farm and she wasn't there?

But she did not want to back out on Eva, who was looking forward to this trip with an unusual intensity. So she placated Dena as best she could, tried to stop thinking about Ben, and packed her bag again.

The morning of departure she dressed in an olive-green dress that lent a golden hue to her dark tan and brought out the gold streaks in her auburn hair from her days in the sun. The day was one of those achingly golden days of late summer, when you could sense the dying of leaves and flowers, when the mandevilla and hibiscus in concrete urns were simply astonishing. Puffy white clouds scudded across the deep blue sky, and the black dual-wheeled double-cap pickup gleamed like alabaster as it slowly hummed up to the house.

She hugged her mother, said goodbye to her father, kissed the little girls, gave Dena a knuckle bump, and pulled her luggage off the porch and down the sidewalk.

The driver opened the door, got out, and helped Emma load her luggage into the back. She supposed he was Randy, the English driver she'd heard Eva mention in the past. He had driven Eva to the hospital when she had the baby, drove Eva to the mall to go shopping at Christmastime. She said he was always prompt and polite and she hated it when he wasn't available and she had to call someone else. Now Randy informed Emma that the camper was at Elvin's house and that they'd stop there next to hitch it up to the truck and pick up the family.

She climbed into the front seat, her large brown purse at her feet, adjusted the seat belt and settled in, happy to seize the day. The long hot summer was over, her bank account swelled with fair wages from her father, and she had enough cash in her purse to enjoy two good weeks with her best friend and family.

"Beautiful morning," he commented.

"Sure is. It would be cool to have this perfect weather for the next two weeks."

"Yeah."

She slid a sideways glance at him. He had deeply tanned skin, dark hair. He wasn't bad looking, though a little hairy. She liked his profile, with that cap pulled low like that. She wondered if he'd haul the camper to the campsite and return to his roofing job. *Surely he wouldn't stay. How awkward would that be?*

"Are you . . . will you be camping with us?"

Please say no, she thought.

"They invited me."

What? Why did they do that? Oh, for crying out loud. Seriously.

"I have my tent."

She didn't answer, trying to sort through the quick rush of annoyance, disappointment, and some other feeling she couldn't quite put her finger on.

"You don't care for the idea?"

"What? Oh no, it's okay. I wasn't thinking, I guess."

He laughed, a low rumbling sound. He turned the steering wheel to the left, his copper-colored hands and arms enormous, bulging with sinew and muscle, heaving black hair covering everything.

Their arrival at Elvin's place was announced by horn honking before Randy cut the engine and hopped out, greeting Elvin with shoulder slaps and hand-clasping. Eva was nothing if not exuberant. They hauled a mountain of luggage into the silver camper with black and gold detailing. It had the head of a snarling cougar painted on one side.

"Wow," Emma exclaimed. "It is beautiful."

"It's stacked with everything we'll need. Even popcorn and iced coffee."

"Great! Oh, this will be awesome," Emma said, climbing in and reveling in the pretty interior, the tiny refrigerator and stove, the blinds and table with upholstered three-sided seating.

She lowered her voice to a quiet, hissing whisper.

"Why did you ask the driver to stay? Where is he going to sleep?"

Eva hid her grin. Off to a good start.

"All set?" Elvin asked, sticking his head through the narrow doorway?

"Yes. I think we are. I can't think of anything we'll need, so if you'll get the car seat fastened, I think we can leave."

Elijah was seated and strapped in between Eva and Emma, with Elvin in the front with Randy the driver.

Emma noticed the black hair, the bulk of his shoulders, the expert way he dipped his head to pull out, checking the rearview mirror. There was a smooth transition from a standstill to a slow glide out to the road, more turning of the wheel before they were on the macadam.

It was exciting, this huge, thrumming diesel truck drawing the amazing camper, heading out to the mountains of West Virginia.

The morning flew by as they traveled on the interstate highways, exiting one to get on another, road signs and numbers blurring into a jumble of names and places. Elijah fell asleep, his little head lolling uncomfortably against the side of the car seat till Emma put a soft flannel-backed blanket next to his ear. Eva chattered on happily. Emma watched the late-summer landscape, aware of the black eyes in the mirror on the windshield that seemed to keep glancing at her. She vowed to change seats with Eva after they stopped for lunch.

She turned her face to the left, watched a small red car fly past, the two people in the front seat talking and laughing, followed by another. Everyone was a couple. Two and two. Everywhere.

"Denny's? McDonalds?" Randy called, checking the mirror as he prepared to exit.

"Doesn't matter," Elvin said. "You pick."

He drove with purpose, his wide shoulders and enormous arms turning the rig into the asphalt parking lot of a Chipotle.

"This okay?"

"I have no idea. Never ate here. But I'm anxious to try it," Eva said. Emma didn't say anything. Elvin was always happy, so he was game.

"What about you?"

Those black eyes were directed at her. *Oh, come on.*

"It's fine."

"You ever eat here?"

None of your business, she wanted to say. No, she never had, but she wasn't about to let him feel as if he was introducing her to some culinary experience, making her feel like a Crawford County hillbilly. So she didn't answer, and instead busied herself with the straps on Elijah's car seat.

She had to admit the food was delicious. Her taste buds sang with intense new flavors and textures, beans and rice and hot salsa and warm tortillas and nachos and fajitas. She loved it all, except for the fact that Randy sat at the same table. Drivers didn't usually do that, but she supposed he'd been their driver for so long, they'd become friendly.

While the women went to the ladies room to freshen up, the men strolled in the parking lot while the driver smoked a cigarette.

He exhaled, shook his head and said, "Whoo. Who is she?"

Elvin nodded, laughed outright.

"I told you, she's Eva's best friend. She had a rough summer."

"She doesn't want me camping with you. Should I just drop you all off and pick you up when you're ready?"

"She'll get over it."

That was all the time they had before they were joined by the women, Elijah perched on Emma's hip.

The driver dropped his cigarette, ground it under his heel, then bent to pick it up to deposit it in the trash.

Despicable man. Nasty habit. Emma was now feeling really peeved that she'd have to share this vacation with him.

He was looking straight into her eyes. A shock went through her body, a jolt of electricity as if she'd touched a hot fence.

"Did you enjoy Chipotle?"

She looked away. "I did. It was every good. Thank you."

And then he smiled with his even white teeth and his black eyes were squeezed into crescents.

"Good. Next time, you pick."

Another smile, and he hopped behind the wheel, leaving her standing on the hot asphalt before she remembered to open the door of the truck and climb in.

They were entering a scenic valley, completely surrounded by tall blue-green mountains, small white churches with steeples painted skyward, dirt roads, and small ramshackle buildings that caved in with rusty tin torn off and bent in two, beams and lathe revealed.

"Hey, Matt! Look at this," Elvin shouted, gesturing wildly to the right, where a herd of whitetails were grazing in the afternoon sun, antlers glinting white.

"Whoa!"

What? His name was Matt? Emma said nothing.

Eva stretched her neck to see the herd of whitetails, but at the speed they were moving, by then there was nothing to see.

"You need to slow down if you want to holler about a herd of deer," Eva said loudly.

Something was off. This man was not a usual Amish driver. *No one would ever talk like that to a hired driver*, Emma thought.

Eva smiled, slid back in her seat, and crossed her arms, clearly pleased with the adventure that had just begun.

The camping area was the most charming spot ever, surrounded by layers of mountains that rose in undulating waves around the little valley. The river flowed strong and wide, its colors changing from green to brown to blue, depending which way the sun and the clouds hit the water.

Willow trees hovered along the banks like a green fringe, the low-hanging branches dipping into the surface. There were acres of well-maintained lawn, forests to explore, a swimming pool, playground, all kinds of games and activities to enjoy.

Emma surveyed her surroundings, sniffed the tepid air, and could not help comparing this green world with the river and all its impurities to the wide open massive ocean, the sand, the smell she loved so much.

This was not what she had planned for the summer. This was like a mud puddle. She felt as if she was a rubber ducky being floated along by a child with a stick. She regretted coming to this place, did not want to be here living in these close quarters with this strange man.

She longed for the wide open space of the beach house and the ocean in front of it.

Her foul mood only escalated when Elvin asked her if she would be okay sleeping in the dining area, that the seats flipped over to form a hide-a-bed.

"Oh sure," she said sarcastically. "Just set your morning coffee on top of my sleeping body."

Eva raised her eyebrows. "Touchy, are we?"

She left them to their work, mumbled something about going for a walk, and left. She headed to the forest, not caring which trail she was on, or where it would lead. She never raised her eyes to greet any passersby, merely stumbled along with the huge chip on her shoulder, placed there by Elvin and Eva. Scheming, conniving couple.

The story of her life. Being prodded, pushed, paired with men she had no interest in meeting, let alone dating. She could not believe her own best friend had done it this time.

And he was old, and disobedient. She was no dummy. She could put two and two together. He was not a hired driver at all but some throwback from the Amish church, and Eva had thought surely Emma was desperate enough at this point that she might just fall for him. She could always tell the guys who grew up Amish but didn't join the church. They never dressed quite English enough, and never had quite the right English accent.

Certainly this guy was not husband material. Try and make a decent companion out of someone who hurt his parents, went his own way without a thought for anyone but himself. If they didn't make sacrifices in their youth, they certainly wouldn't for a wife, either.

She stewed as she walked, preparing the speech she would give Eva when she got back.

She found Eva at the picnic table, the others off exploring the grounds. Emma spoke sharply, fueled by the betrayal she felt by her best friend. "Look, Eva. If you think you can fix me up with this Matt, you don't really know me. I can't even believe you. How could you try to trick me like this, and after everything I just went through?"

Shocked, Eva recoiled, setting down the paper plates and sliding onto the bench of the picnic table.

It was a beautiful evening, with the glow of the sun that had slid behind the mountain leaving a golden residue, as if there was a kindness, a blessing left in its wake. The leaves fluttered gently, like a curtain of shimmering green. The scent of barbeque pits, gas grills, and charcoal fires mingled with the newly mown grass and dust from the horseshoe pits. Cries from the children at the playground carried across the camping area.

"Now just what do you mean by that remark?" Eva asked, working on the red twist tie that held the plastic from the stack of plates.

"You know exactly what I'm talking about."

The length of time it took her to reply confirmed her suspicions.

"Who is he?" Emma asked, biting her lower lip.

"*Ach* Emma, you're too shrewd. Alright, he's a cousin."

Emma's eyes flew open.

"What? A cousin? From where?"

"He's from Lancaster. Where else?"

"He's not Amish."

"I know. His whole family is. It's my mam's brother, Elam Yoder's boy. He's nice. He just never joined up."

"Really? And you think for one minute I would ever consider a guy who left the church like that?"

"Maybe." Eva defended herself, her eyes flashing as she met Emma's accusing stare.

She separated four plates, placed them on the table, and retied the twisty, carrying the stack back into the camper, before making an appearance.

"Okay, you can say what you want, Emma, but I'm going to give it to you straight up. This Ben should have contacted you weeks ago. If you're going to waste your time moping around for someone who I can hardly believe wants to get in touch with you, that's your choice."

A hot anger coursed through Emma, leaving her gasping open-mouthed, staring with hurt disbelief.

"You know nothing about us. About Ben," she shouted.

She turned on her heel, started off at a brisk walk, then began to run blindly, not caring where or when her destination would present itself. Eva was being unreasonable, cruel. Best friends did not throw matters of the heart around so easily.

She knew nothing. *Nothing.*

She slowed to a walk as she entered a woodland trail with a brown arrow marked "Clear Spring." She breathed deeply, then burst into a raucous sob that came from the fading hope in her chest, the place that kept diminishing every day, every week. When the truth of Eva's words settled in, it took her strength away and she sank to a bed of soft moss and leaves, drew up her knees, and wrapped her arms around them, her head laid sideways as the anguish welled up.

She knew, she *knew* Eva was right. But it would all take time, the acceptance of it, the letting go of a romance, a love so perfect it was too good to be true.

But still. Some girls waited years, and it all worked out in the end. Didn't it?

She would tell Eva it was not up to her to let her know when Ben was over.

And so her thoughts sliced through the situation like an old-fashioned crosscut saw. Back and forth, back and forth. Defending Ben one moment, letting go the next.

"Hey."

Annoyed, wanting to be left alone, she looked up, gazing with bleary eyes at none other than the annoying Matt.

"Go away," she said levelly.

He stood in front of her, his hands on his hips, his cap pulled low, and said, "Now why would I do that?"

"Because I'm asking you to?"

He continued to stand there, so she tried again, more politely this time.

"Go away, please."

"Is there anything I can do to help?"

"Of course not." Then, "You don't have a Kleenex, do you?"

He rummaged in his jeans pocket, came up with a rumpled paper towel, folded it in half and handed it to her, quietly.

She took it without looking at him, blew her nose, wiped her eyes, and sighed, a shaking sound that left him helpless.

"Thanks."

"You're welcome."

Then, instead of doing what she wanted him to do, which was to disappear, he lowered himself to sit beside her, saying nothing. She shrank away from him, her feet rustling the dead leaves.

"Want to talk about it?" he asked quietly.

"There's nothing to say."

Still he stayed.

"You know, this isn't working," Emma said, folding and unfolding the paper towel.

"What isn't working?" she asked.

"This. You being here."

"Why not?"

"They said a driver was bringing us. You know, hauling the camper."

"I am a driver."

"You're a cousin."

"I'm sorry I'm a cousin."

Her mouth twitched, but she turned her face away.

"So why is it so terrible that I'm a cousin?"

"It doesn't really matter, I guess. It's just . . . well, awkward."

"And why is that?"

Did he have to ask so many questions?

She spat out a small sound of exasperation.

"You just don't get it. Eva is . . . well, you know. Matchmaking."

"Oh, come on. You're kidding me. She knows I'm not Amish. I have an English girlfriend. Sort of. Why on earth would she try to get us hooked up?"

She turned to glare at him. "I hate that phrase."

"You hate a lot of things. Me included. Look, I'm innocent. I have no intentions of becoming romantically involved. Trust me, okay? I've been bitten a couple of times, so don't worry. I don't plan on returning to the Amish and have no plans to ask an Amish girl, either. So relax."

A silence settled over the two of them, a subtle veil of acceptance, one of the other. At long last, he sighed, grabbed a twig and began stirring the old growth of leaves.

"So is that why were you crying?"

She told him the honest truth. Told him the misadventure that happened in North Carolina, ending with the worn-out excuse that Ben must have been too busy to hunt her down.

He did not say anything for a while. Finally, he got to his feet, reached for her hand to help her up. She placed her hand in his and sprang lightly to her feet. He released her, and asked if she wanted to walk a little farther down the path.

"It will soon be dark," she said, looking around.

"Not yet. There's a long twilight on account of the mountain."

"You sure?"

"I'm sure."

CHAPTER 14

W HEN THEY STOOD SIDE-BY-SIDE, MATT WAS NOT MUCH TALLER THAN she was, which was disconcerting, having his face almost to her level. When he tilted that cap, a tumble of black curls fell across his forehead and over his ears. She watched as he ran a hand through his hair before replacing the cap, tugging it low over his forehead again.

His hands were immense, dwarfing the bill of his cap. They were covered in fine black hair, his forearms covered in a thicker layer of them. He walked with an easy gait, yet seemed to cover a great distance with a small amount of effort. Emma found herself quickening her pace, her breath accelerating as the terrain slanted uphill.

"I want to show you something," he said.

They continued on in silence, but said hello to passersby, smiling hikers, or vacationers who seemed to be happy and relaxed.

They rounded a bend, moved down a short incline, and came upon a hidden forest pool of crystal clear water that ran down from the mountain, across a pile of boulders and smaller stones, a fringe of fern and lilies of the valley, pale green moss and skunk cabbage surrounding it like a woodland scarf. She listened to the twittering of tiny wrens, the sharp shriek of a perched hawk.

Emma stopped, her eyes opening in astonishment.

"It's so perfect," she breathed.

"See the cup on a chain? We can drink this water."

"How many other people have been drinking from this same cup?" she asked.

He shrugged, said "suit yourself," and bent to fill it, taking a long drink, the cup disappearing beneath the bill of his cap. Instead of offering her a drink, he replaced the cup, turned to find her facing him.

"My turn."

"You're going to drink from it after I did?"

She lowered her eyes, motioned with her fingers.

He filled the cup and watched as she drank the pure, sweet water. Her eyes were downcast, a pull of wind moved a stray lock of hair across her forehead.

He noticed her freckles, the way her eyes were the same color as the pool of water, the way her long slender fingers curled around the tin cup.

"Thanks."

She handed the cup back without looking at him, then turned on her heel, saying the trail was barely visible, and that darkness would overtake them if they didn't get back. He told her it was darker by the mountain, especially beneath the trees, that if she'd be out in the center of the valley, the sun would still be shining.

"It's pretty dark here, though," she insisted.

"Would you like to sit here awhile?" he asked, motioning to the hewn log bench by the spring.

"Not really. It's getting dark."

"We might be able to hear a whippoorwill," he said.

"Really? I never heard one."

"Come here. Sit."

He sat down, patted the space beside him, so there wasn't much to do except sit on the bench, which was much too close, as far as she was concerned. She sat as far away as possible, crossed her arms tightly around her waist, her eyes darting first one direction then another.

He laughed, a low sound.

"Mind if I smoke?"

"Of course. Why would you ruin this perfect area with all those toxins?" she asked primly. She seriously detested that low-classed habit, figured he had no business even thinking about it. Not with her, anytime, anywhere.

He raised both eyebrows, drew his upper lip across his lower lone, but did as she asked.

"So now, this Ben. Tell me how long you're planning to wait. Like, forever? A year?"

"Why do you want to know?"

"I'm curious."

"Well, for a long time," she said very seriously. "It's not as if I had any other prospects. I mean, he was nice. He was sincere. If it . . . well, if Kathy wouldn't have ruined everything, we'd have been together all summer. Probably married eventually."

He hoped this Ben would be discerning, watchful, because he could easily be prey to this Kathy's prowess. Matt had seen some things since being out in the world.

It was the way of it, after being released from the old-fashioned values of the Amish in which he'd been raised. He had resisted authority, the demands of a father who was not accustomed to his wife or children disobeying his orders. When his son showed signs of rebellion, he brought the hammer of authority down without mercy or understanding.

But that was only a part of it.

"I think you should wait. No decent guy would fall for this Kathy. She's married, right?"

She nodded. "They have two beautiful children, Brent and Annalise. That's the hardest part. I miss them."

"More than Ben?"

"In a different way, of course."

He liked her musical voice, the way it rose and fell, the way her hands demonstrated her feelings like fluttering birds. Clearly, she was suffering, desperate to be courageous, but hurting in spite of it.

He sighed.

"Yeah, life can be tough. But looks like you're doing a great job, keeping your head above water."

She gave a low laugh.

"It helps, now that I don't have to worry about you wanting to . . . you know."

She broke off, clearly embarrassed.

"No, no worries in that department. Absolutely. Sheila's a great girl. We've been seeing each other for close to a year."

"What is she like?"

"She's short, dark-haired like me. She's cute. Works in the lab at Lancaster General."

"Will you ask her to marry you do you think?"

He held up one finger. "Listen."

She held very still. As clear as a bell, the whistle came.

Whip-poor-will. An answering call came from father away.

Whip-poor-will.

Emma gasped audibly. In the waning light, she turned to him, her eyes shining with the amazing sound of these small, secretive birds.

"It's so clear. Almost as if they're talking," she whispered.

"It is beautiful, their call, but they are quite common looking. A brown bird with a rather large beak and flat eyes. Have you ever seen one?"

"Yes. In a nature book at school."

"You taught school?"

"Ten years."

He whistled, a low sound of surprise. "Wow."

"We should get back. It is dark for real now."

Reluctantly he got to his feet, stretched, and agreed.

"Give me your hand."

"Why?"

"I'm afraid you'll wander off the trail."

Emma laughed and told him to go first, she'd follow, and then she hurried to keep up. She'd never seen anyone cover more ground in such a short time without all out running. She kept her eyes on the trail, trying to see the tree roots and small stones on the path so she wouldn't trip.

He called back, "Careful," just as her sneaker caught on an extra-large tree root, tripping her as efficiently as the hook on a cane. She flopped flat on her stomach with a clumsy expulsion of breath, feeling very much like a freshly landed fish.

He knelt at her side, relieved to see her laughing. He touched her shoulder tentatively, asking if she was alright.

She rolled over and sat up, laughing even harder, her merriment catching him off guard till it finally sank in.

"Whoo-ee! What a flop," she gasped. "Wham. Down I went."

"I should have been more careful," he said, ashamed now.

"Nah. Let's keep going, I'm fine."

"You sure?"

"Yes."

"Give me your hand."

So she did this time, and he held the lovely slender fingers in his own massive ones.

The campfire was a beacon of welcome on their return. The little boy had already been put to bed, leaving his parents basking in the fire's warm crackling glow, relaxed and happy to be spending time together.

At their approach, they looked up, eager to know where they had been.

"Hiking. We met up on the trail," Emma informed them, in what she hoped was a no-nonsense manner.

Eva gave her a piercing look, as in, *you'll tell me later, right?*

They were starved, and fell on the mountain pie makers, filling them with the slices of bread, ham, cheese, mustard, pickle relish, and whatever they could find to produce the wonderful campfire concoction. They feasted on potato chips, pickles, chocolate chip cookies, and kept up a lively banter as darkness fell heavily.

"So Randy the driver is actually Matt the cousin," Emma said sourly, though by now she didn't feel nearly so upset by the whole thing. Still, Eva and Elvin deserved to squirm a little.

Elvin looked at his wife and she looked back at him, guilt making both of them a little twitchy. They said nothing.

"Sorry, I don't mean to be a problem," Matt said, leaning back in his chair, crossing his arms behind his head. But his voice made it clear he didn't actually care whether he was one or if he wasn't.

Emma kept her eyes on the fire.

Eva broke the silence, throwing up her hands. "Oh, everybody just get over it. We weren't trying anything. We just thought you would enjoy the vacation, Matt."

He grunted in response.

Emma blurted out, "He has a girlfriend, for your information."

No response. Elvin, apparently, decided to change the subject.

"So why didn't you ever join the church?" He was stripping four golden marshmallows from a forked stick.

"Personal question. Make me one of those, Elvin."

"But why didn't you?" Eva persisted.

There was a long silence.

"I guess because I never felt as if I fit in," he said finally.

"You wanted to drive a car, right?"

"Not just that. I have nothing against driving a horse and buggy at all. I like horses. Especially these high-stepping ones they're driving nowadays. But after I found out I was adopted, I felt as if I was living a lie."

Elvin shook his head.

"Yeah, that wasn't handled right. You should have been told before you started school, especially since so many other people knew. I remember the way it used to bother me a lot."

"How did you find out?" Eva asked.

Elvin handed a graham cracker spread with peanut butter and a chocolate square to Matt, who left his chair to scrape off the burnt marshmallow, lifted his face to insert half of it into his gaping mouth.

Matt chewed, swallowed, looked around for a wet cloth to wipe his fingers.

"I got in a fight in vocational class. I won, but the other boy yelled the truth as he was walking away. I went home and asked my mother, who turned white and plunked down in a kitchen chair. She never could explain to me why they hadn't told me sooner."

"I remember. You stayed living there until you were nineteen or twenty, right?"

"Something like that."

"Where did you go?"

"Just down the road. I had a good job. The same one I have now."

Emma wanted to ask what he did, but figured he didn't need to know she was even mildly interested. She could not imagine what he would have gone through, at that age. Adolescents were already an insecure bunch, or at least she had been in vocational class. After eight grades in a one-room school, being well-acquainted with all your classmates, you were thrown into a school basement with fourteen-year-olds from the far reaches of the community, and it was a real jolt. After the age of fifteen was reached, you were finished with school, sent to work on the farm or wherever employment was legal. Equipped with basic arithmetic, spelling, reading, rules of driving a horse and buggy, German reading and comprehension, every young person was expected to thrive within the community, and most of them did. Everyone had the security of knowing what was expected of them, where they would belong in the future, living in a close-knit circle of family and friends.

But to find out you were not born into the Amish family, to know somewhere there was another family who did not adhere to the *ordnung* and chose not to keep you for whatever reason, must have been traumatic.

Emma looked at him, found him staring into the fire with a dark brooding look. She wanted to know who his original family was, where they lived, and whether he had ever found them. She weighed her curiosity with her pride. Curiosity won.

"Do you . . . did you ever find your biological parents?" she asked, her voice gravelly, so that she had to clear her throat.

He never raised his eyes, just leaned forward to grasp a metal stick and thrust it into the fire, sending up a shower of sparks.

"My mom. I found my mother."

His voice was low, and he did not raise his eyes but continued stirring the fire. He offered no more information, and no one made an attempt to question further. An uncomfortable silence settled over the group. A nighthawk called its plaintive cry, followed by an echoing one. Matt dislodged a log that fell into the red hot embers, scattering the flames.

Eva rose from her chair, turned to collect plates, marshmallows, and crackers.

"I'm going to call it a night," she said.

Her husband rose to help.

Emma looked up. "You can get to bed first. As soon as the coast is clear, I'll use the shower. If there's any hot water left over."

"Feel free to use the facilities the campground provides," Eva answered, a bit prickly after the tone of Emma's voice.

Emma wished she'd have brought her own tent. Why had she thought there'd be more space in the camper? She remembered the luxurious beach house with her own bedroom and bath.

After the couple disappeared through the side door of the camper, the silence became even more intense. Emma willed Matt to get up and go to his tent, wherever it was situated. Even better, he could simply get into his truck and drive home. She did not like this arrangement at all, could not imagine getting a good night's rest on that stupid fold-out by the table.

She wanted to go home to Dena, her mother, and the rest of the family in the comfortable farmhouse where nothing was awkward or uncomfortable, where the sound of children and laughter filled up all the empty spots. Where life was predictable, scheduled with hard work, meal times, and companionship.

"I should not have agreed to this," she said, without thinking.

He gave a low laugh.

"Not because of you. It's this nighttime situation. It's awkward."

"You can have my tent. I'll sleep in the truck."

"Of course you won't."

"You want me to stay?"

"No."

"You're not afraid of the dark?"

"No."

When he got up and left without further words, she was surprised. He could have offered a goodnight, couldn't he? She thought of the easy banter with Ben, the way he kept talking, entertaining her with his easy opinions, so that conversation was as easy as the ebb and flow of the ocean.

A searing sense of failure was followed by the heaviness of missing him, longing for his good looks and yes, his touch.

Where was he? Did he ever think of her? Her mind sought every rational avenue of excuses why he had not contacted her the remainder of the summer.

Perhaps he wanted to finish the work in North Carolina before dedicating his life to her. Even now, there would be a letter in the mailbox at home. He would be coming to Crawford County. He would. By Christmastime they would be dating, perhaps a wedding in the spring. She would wait till fall, if he wanted to get married in the traditional month of November. For the hundredth time, she dreamed of how she would feel, standing beside his tall, handsome form as the bishop solemnly pronounced them man and wife.

She lowered her hand on her drawn-up knees and whispered, "Ben. Ben."

"Sorry to bother you."

She sat up quickly, to find Matt standing on the other side of the campfire, holding a backpack.

"You don't have an extra toothbrush, do you?"

Oh, for Pete's sake, she thought. Use your hairbrush.

"I don't."

"It's okay. I'll drive to town. I think I remember a Wal-Mart."

"Now? It's late," she said.

"They're open. Want to ride along?"

Emma surveyed the camper, could still hear Elvin and Eva's low voices. She thought about how she had only brought light pajamas and no robe. Not very modest.

"I could buy a robe. Looks like I'll need one."

"Get your purse."

That was how she found herself in the front seat of the pickup truck, headed out the gravel drive and onto the macadam road. He did not speak, so she offered nothing, either. If he was comfortable this way, she would be, too.

The road stretched in front of them like a moonlit ribbon banked by trees on either side, the tall mountains appearing black, formidable sentries of the night. There were no oncoming vehicles, only an occasional speed limit sign or an advertisement on some bedraggled billboard. The wheels hummed steadily, the slightly open windows providing a soft hissing sound.

A large yellow deer-crossing sign appeared on the right. Emma had just opened her mouth to speak when her eye caught a movement on the left. She screamed as a huge animal lunged from the trees, was suspended in mid-air before Matt hit the brakes, turned the steering wheel to the right, trying to avoid the impact, and failing.

The right wheel skidded across the shoulder of the road as the large, antlered deer hit the fender, was thrown across the hood and up against the windshield.

Matt fought for control, but they ended up in a steep forty-five degree angle down a small ravine by the side of the road, the restraint from their seat belts their saving grace.

Emma experienced a stabbing pain across her shoulder, the belt across her stomach leaving an uncomfortable ache.

"You okay?" Matt asked, reaching over to touch her shoulder.

"I think so," she answered shakily.

He reached to unfasten his seat belt, then tried the door, which opened easily although at a strange position. He slipped out, then looked back.

"Just stay where you are till I find out how bad it is, okay?"

She nodded, but hadn't really registered what he was saying.

She shoved both feet against the floor to loosen the seatbelt, then tried the door, which seemed to unlatch and swing out alright. Gingerly, she turned, winced as she moved her left arm to hold on to the door handle as she slid to the ground.

The grass in the roadside ditch was wet with dew, but the night was warm, so there was no need to grab a sweater, although she found herself shivering.

As headlights appeared behind them, she saw the bulk of the dead deer on the road, watched as Matt stepped out to flag the oncoming vehicle. She was relieved when the car slowed, drifted off to the side, and came to a stop. A door swung open, followed by the form of an extremely overweight man who shouted in a stentorian voice, words Emma could not understand. He lumbered over in a rolling gait, stood over Matt and continued his unclean diatribe.

Emma wanted to crawl under the pickup truck, or creep away into the bushes, but she stayed where she was, watching Matt as he stood, absorbing the bitter tirade, his hands by his sides.

She thought of his strength, the ease with which he could push this man out of the way, or worse.

"Look, if you'll give me a minute, I'll have him off the road, okay?" Matt spoke in an even voice, but Emma could hear that he was restraining himself.

The man yelled something about flashers and cones, then stood watching as Matt walked away, careful in his approach of the dead deer, before grabbing the antlers and dragging him. It took a few tries, Matt heaving against the enormity of the deer, but eventually he got it all the way off the road, then turned to join Emma at the truck.

"You're sure you're okay?" he asked.

"Yes. There's nothing wrong with me except I'd like to punch that . . ."

Matt gave a low laugh.

"Not everyone is a Good Samaritan, Emma."

They watched as the angry motorist returned to his car and sped off, spinning gravel. They walked over to see the deer, with the aid of a small flashlight, a nice eight point buck that had met an unfortunate death.

"Poor thing," Emma murmured. "He just wanted to cross the road."

"He should have waited," Matt said dryly.

"But still."

"Look, I'm going to back this truck out of here, if I can. If not, I'll have to call someone."

Emma walked up to the side of the road, waited in the eerie silence till he entered the truck and started the motor. She didn't like the black mountains looming over the dark forest, or the strange ribbon of road that contained massive men who shouted obscenities for no reason other than a hapless deer being killed. She had not been raised in a culture where things like this were everyday occurrences, and she felt dirty. Cursed.

Matt shrugged it off as if it was nothing, and perhaps to him, it wasn't. She couldn't help but admire him for the quiet, even way he'd simply gone about his business and ignored the words that assaulted him.

She moved away as the night was illuminated by a pair of headlights approaching, followed by the whine of a motor. She shrank back as far as she could, wishing Matt was not in his truck. She did not breathe easy until the car flashed past, leaving the night silent except for the tired chirping of crickets, the other insect sounds that seemed strangely comforting now. She watched as Matt kept trying to move the truck, easing on the gas, backing it up out of the ravine.

She found herself holding her breath as the truck inched backward, rocked, settled, and stopped. Then again, just as Emma thought he was attempting an impossibility, the left rear wheel caught on a rock, giving him the traction he needed, and in one attempt the truck came up and out of the ravine.

The door was flung open, followed by Matt, who went around to the front, bent to inspect the damage, which was surprisingly minimal.

He gave a low whistle. "Not bad."

"I thought the windshield would break," Emma offered.

"We're lucky. You brought me good luck."

Emma did not know what to say to that, so she said nothing.

"You don't believe in luck?" he asked, as they fastened their seatbelts.

"Well, yes. But I think God controls everything."

"Not for me, He doesn't."

His words were bitter, laced with irony.

"Of course He does. He cares the same for all of us."

Matt pulled out onto the road, swung right, and sped up.

"See, that's what I don't get. It's all God this and God that, how He cares so much, does this and does that, and all of it is like a puff of smoke. There's nothing to it."

For the second time, Emma was shocked. How could he spout off like this? He had been raised in an Amish, God-fearing home.

"You're wrong, Matt. There is something to it."

"Well, I disagree."

They moved through the night, surpassing the speed limit, his profile like stone. He offered no conversation and neither did she.

Chapter 15

They passed a Sheetz, a Kentucky Fried Chicken, a few garages. There was litter lying about like strange birds, flapping each time a car or truck passed. Cars filled with young people moved beneath the yellow streetlights, music turned up so high Emma could feel its repercussions. At the stoplight, an eighteen wheeler moved in beside them, the diesel engine throbbing.

"I'm no atheist," he offered. "I just don't believe God cares for someone like me."

He looked over at Emma, and she looked at him. She smiled, a smile of genuine feeling that illuminated her face. He could not look away.

"There's good news for people like you."

"Are you an Amish evangelist?" He laughed, then immediately felt badly for mocking her.

"The light's green," she said, just as a horn honked behind them.

It was awkward walking around Wal-Mart with someone she barely knew, looking for an item located in women's sleepwear. She was grateful when he said he'd meet her at the bench out front.

She chose a simple white robe of polyester and cotton, an inexpensive thing that would serve the purpose of retaining her modesty, and found him waiting for her at the promised spot, a small bag protruding from his shirt pocket.

"Find what you needed?"

"I did."

"God was with you, wasn't He?" Matt asked sarcastically.

Deeply hurt, Emma said, "Stop that," and kept her eyes averted as they crossed the sidewalk and climbed into the truck. He offered no apology, and she did not try to ease into a forgiving conversation.

In the morning, she was peevish, having slept very little. The air was damp and gray, her coffee was too weak, the campfire was blackened and soggy, and no one else had stirred so far. She tried lighting a fire, with no luck, then settled into a camping chair with both hands wrapped around the lukewarm mug of coffee, staring into the charred, cold ashes.

With all her heart, she did not want to be there.

Her friends had a lot of nerve, asking her to accompany them to some remote camping area with a guy who turned out to be a genuine nutcase. All of it, the summer in North Carolina especially, seemed to choke the last shred of hope and goodwill toward anyone or anything.

She stared into the cold ashes, shivered in the moist air of morning, then whispered a prayer to get through the day. *Just help me get through one day at a time, dear God. You know I don't want to be here, you know what I do want, so please, please let Ben contact me. Keep him safe and happy, and if it is Thy will, help us to get together. You know I love him.*

Chilled now, she got up and crept softly into the camper for a blanket, a light throw she'd seen Eva unpack, then returned to the camping chair. She looked up to find Matt returning from the camp store, carrying a cardboard tray containing two large Styrofoam cups. He was wearing a T-shirt with a plaid flannel shirt, unbuttoned, a clean pair of jeans, and his hiking boots. His hair was still wet and it sprung into tight, glossy black curls. She watched his approach, that lumbering gait, as if his upper body was too heavy for his knees.

"Good morning," he offered. "Sleep well?"

"I did not."

He laughed, the low, rumbling, mirthless laugh.

"We'll go get you a tent and an air mattress."

Wonderful proposition, but she shook her head. Elijah had woken three times, the camper shook with even light footsteps, Elvin snored like an old dog, and Eva coughed all night. But still. She didn't need a tent.

Her eyes were heavy with lack of sleep, itched and burned. She drew up a fist to rub at the left one, grimacing.

"I brought you a coffee."

She looked up, blinked.

"Thank you. That was very thoughtful."

She picked up her mug and dashed the contents to the ground.

"Cold and weak," she said. Then laughed. "Like me this morning."

He came close, handed her a cup. She smelled aftershave, or cologne, an earthy woodsy scent.

"This should be hot."

Then, "I put cream in it, I saw you do it at Sheetz."

"Perfect."

She took a sip. It was hot, and very good. She smiled at him as he sat in the opposite chair. He smiled back, a small, hesitant kind of smile that did not reach his eyes.

"What's on your busy schedule today?" he asked.

"Not a whole lot of anything. I suppose it depends a lot on them." She rolled her eyes to the vicinity of the camper.

"You don't enjoy camping?"

"I don't want to be ungrateful."

He shrugged his massive shoulders. "Makes no difference to me." Then, "Go hiking with me."

"To where?"

"I'm planning an all-day hike. Maybe find the Appalachian Trail."

Emma considered this. It would beat sitting around the campfire all day, although she wasn't sure she wanted to be in this man's company for an entire day. She wanted to go home, check her mail, find out if there had been messages left on her parents' voicemail. Perhaps he had tried to tell her his summer job was over and he was ready to come to her valley, in Crawford County.

She drank her coffee as she mulled over her options.

"What about Elvin and Eva?" she asked. "They couldn't go very far with the baby."

As if on cue, Elvin appeared at the door of the camper, his hair disheveled, snapping his suspenders over his shoulders. He was wearing a red shirt and black Amish trousers, which Emma thought was a bit inappropriate for a camping trip.

She thought of Ben and his blue denims from Gohn Brothers in Indiana. She remembered the way he walked, remembered the fit of his clothes, the graceful gait, the polo shirts he wore with his old pair of brown suspenders, the easy way he flipped his hair off his high forehead.

He had wanted her, had truly made her feel as if she was the special woman in his life.

She did not hear the easy banter between the two men, but gazed at the dead embers of the campfire as she sipped the good hot coffee.

"What's with the maiden made of stone over there?" Elvin called out. Emma blinked her eyes, came back to reality, waved a hand in dismissal.

"Give me your coffee," he said, walking barefoot over the gravelly area. He bent over, grimaced, picked his way across the areas that contained the least amount of stones.

"Ow! Ouch."

Matt caught Emma's eye and smiled, then burst out laughing. Emma found herself laughing without wanting to, which made Elvin look from one to the other.

"What?" he asked.

"Shoes?" Matt asked.

"Didn't get that far. Emma, share your coffee."

"There's a good coffeepot in the camper. Make your own."

"No wonder you're not married. A good wife would get up and make her man coffee," Elvin joked.

"You're not my man," Emma answered easily.

Elvin opened his mouth. Matt held up a hand.

"Don't say it."

The door of the camper swung open, with Eva carrying the little boy, her hair uncombed, a blue bathrobe belted around her waist.

"Coffee's on!" she called. "Here, Elvin, come take Elijah so I can get dressed."

"Good morning!" Emma called out.

"Good morning to you, dear friend. And how was your night?"

"Okay."

"Just okay?"

"Not much sleep."

The morning was spent preparing breakfast over the campfire. Eggs, ham, and cheese between two slices of bread, toasted to perfection in the cast iron mountain pie makers held over the good hot embers. There was plenty of coffee, grape juice, and the shoofly whoopie pies Eva had brought.

Plans were made to hike the surrounding trails, with Elvin boasting about being able to carry his son on his backpack all day if he had to. They packed light food, water bottles, tea, and Coke, then set off at a respectable pace, Elvin easily carrying Elijah perched high on his back.

Eva and Emma fell behind the men, engaged in a serious conversation as they walked along. Bits of gossip, news of the community, Emma's refusal to teach school, and finally, to Ben.

Birds trilled and warbled, fluttered in bushes and treetops. Bold chipmunks sat in the center of the trail till they were almost upon them, then dashed off into the undergrowth with the speed of lightning.

Squirrels peeked around tree trunks, chirring indignantly, before racing along branches to leap like acrobats onto another tree, then another. Emma wished for a good pair of binoculars after an orange bird called a beautiful note from high up in the treetops.

"It's a Baltimore oriole," Eva said, stopping to crane her neck.

"But there's no black," Emma protested.

Around them, the forest became increasingly heavier, the level land turning into hilly terrain, dotted with jagged gray rocks that rose randomly, as if someone had dropped them from the sky years and years ago, the undergrowth now holding them hostage. The scent of pine needles was prevalent, and they soon came upon a thick stand of white pine, the needles carpeting the ground beneath them.

Emma sniffed with appreciation.

"Break time," she called out.

The men stopped, turned, and came back. Elvin looked flushed, a bit pained, and immediately divested himself of the cumbersome backpack. He lowered his son to the ground, flexed his shoulders, and grimaced.

"That thing gets heavy," he said.

Emma produced the granola bars and bottles of water, before turning to find a comfortable place to rest. Matt shrugged off his flannel shirt, placed it on the bed of pine needles and suggested she sit there, noting that the pine needles had sharp points. He was completely unselfconscious—it was merely a gesture he would have done for a child, or Eva.

She sat gratefully, with a murmured thanks, turned to meet his eyes, but he was occupied with the wrapper on his granola bar and didn't notice.

Eva asked her to move over and share her blessings. Elijah set up a howl after being freed from the confines of his backpack only to find the pine needles sharp and too slippery to support his crawling.

Before Eva could get to her feet, Matt reached him and scooped him into his arms.

"Poor guy. This is not a good place for little boys, is it?"

He held him, smiled down into his astonished eyes. Elijah reached up to pull down the black curls behind his ears.

"Ow!" Matt cried softly, teasing him.

Emma watched the muscles of his arms turn into cords of strength, the T-shirt doing nothing to hide them.

She looked away, stunned by the sheer masculinity. And she couldn't help watching as the little boy giggled and squirmed, grabbed at more black curls, clearly enthralled with Matt. When they sat down on the ground, Matt shared the granola bar with him, breaking off small pieces and placing them carefully in his mouth.

Elvin rubbed his shoulders with the palm of his hands.

Matt watched, offered a turn with the backpack, which Elvin accepted.

Back on the trail, they found a marker saying the Appalachian Trail was straight ahead, which would take them to the top of Gobbler's Knob, but the trail to the left would take them to Iver's Hollow, the place on the map that showed a small lake and a rest area of sorts.

They decided to tackle the mountain, then visit the lake on their return. The climbing was more than Emma had bargained for. Eva gasped and hung on to small saplings, opened her mouth and panted without a trace of embarrassment. When they stopped to breathe, Emma massaged the calves of her legs, which felt as if they would burst into flames.

Elvin did his best to act as if he was in good shape, but his chest was heaving, his shirt buttons open. Matt stood solidly, his foot propped on an outcropping of stone, the baby sound asleep in his papoose-like gear, looking as if he had not taken more than ten steps. Emma thought of his smoking, pictured his blackened lungs and his impaired breathing, but saw no sign of either one.

"I cannot keep going at this pace," Eva wheezed, clutching the sapling, bent over as she gasped for air.

"Of course, we'll slow down," her husband said.

She smiled at him gratefully, and he gave her a look that was full of unspoken endearments. Emma watched this exchange, thought how Ben had said so much with his eyes, making her feel as if she was the only person he would ever want to be with.

She had been loved, admired, cherished. If things did not work out this time, she would never marry. She'd remain single. She had been in love twice, had the love reciprocated once. That was more than many people could say.

"Onward ho!" Elvin shouted, drawing his wife to his side with an extended arm, smiling into her flushed face. Eva laughed, then set off with her husband at her side, happy to match her step with his, which left Matt standing on the trail, waiting for Emma.

"How are you doing?" he asked.

"The back of my legs are sore," she said, sheepish now. "I thought I was stronger than this, the way I work at the produce farm at home."

"Bending over and carrying things uses different muscles than climbing a mountain," he said, defending her.

"I guess you're right."

"It would likely help if your ankles were supported with hiking boots."

She nodded. She had paid almost a hundred dollars for her sneakers and they had served her well, but he was right that they didn't offer any ankle support.

And still the trail became even steeper, rising straight ahead, beckoning them to test their endurance, silently mocking their so-called fitness. Determined to show her strength, Emma matched his stride. They both laughed when Elvin and Eva slid to the side and sagged to the ground.

They teased them without mercy, then kept walking to show them up and thus were subject to breathless wails of outrage.

They were both laughing helplessly as they kept their pace up, ascending the murderous trail in good time. Weak calls from Elvin and Eva finally slowed their pace.

"You two are show-offs," Eva panted, mopping her flushed face with the hem of her apron.

"This is brutal," Elvin said.

When they finally reached the summit and found the low stone wall surrounding the lookout, with the Blue Ridge Mountains stretching away into the hazy distance like an undulating carpet of green, the physical exertion had been worth the climb. They stood as a group, spellbound.

The sky was cobalt blue, with wisps of white like torn quilt batting. A vulture circled, floating on warm air currents, on the lookout for some unfortunate animal, or one that already had been turned to carrion. Hawks flew in straight lines, intent on finding dinner that scurried beneath fallen logs or rock crevices all too son.

Emma thought of the thousands of years these hills had endured. It was a vast tract of unspoiled wilderness that counteracted all the symptoms of manmade tarmac and diesel fumes, of overheated and overcooled mega cities built by the ingenuity of man to provide easy access to material things that would make life even easier. The pursuit of ease, a luxurious lifestyle meant to make everyone happy and content—lofty goals that were loading the atmosphere with dangerous carbons that were already destroying natural beauty such as this. Some thought global warming was only nibbling at the edges of security, but scientists knew what was going on, and the outlook was grim.

Emma kept her thoughts to herself now, as she usually did. A woman's views were never taken too seriously, especially in matters of science or politics. Being a schoolteacher, Emma was widely read and formed her own opinions on many subjects, but mostly she kept them to herself.

"That's a lot of unspoiled land," Elvin said finally.

"Bunch of trees, that's for sure," Eva echoed.

"You have to wonder how many Native Americans wandered around down there," Emma offered quietly.

"What a teacher. You're always thinking of history," Eva teased.

"Seriously though. They were here first."

"They should still be here. It's completely unfair that we're here and they're not," Matt said.

Emma looked at him, taken by surprise.

"Not many people agree with me," she said.

He said nothing, just kept looking out over the vast beauty with squinted eyes. He still wore the heavy backpack with Elijah asleep in it. He stood with ease, his thumbs hooked in the belt loops of his jeans.

"It's too beautiful," said Eva. "I'm going to burst into tears at the awesome wonder of God. He is beyond comprehension. Imagine, guys. This is a very tiny portion of the earth. And think of all the people that have lived and died since creation, yet He knows how many hairs were, are, and will be on everyone's head," Eva said, becoming emotional now.

Elvin grinned. "He might not know how many are on Matt's arms and chest."

Matt laughed good-naturedly, taking the joke for what it was, a simple jibe.

Didn't the man have an ounce of guile in his body? She couldn't imagine her own brothers taking that lying down.

The return trip was easier, going down, for a while, till the pressure on her knees became uncomfortable, the toes on her right foot burning as they were pushed against the fronts of her sneakers. Elijah woke up and kept hitting his mouth on the aluminum bar of the child carrier, crying out in frustration every time it happened. Matt stopped, took Emma's empty backpack, and wrapped it around the offending bar, before continuing down the trail behind Elvin and Eva.

For whatever reason, they walked in pairs now, Matt staying with Emma. Husband and wife wanted to be together, Emma reasoned. Matt was actually good company, remaining quiet much of the way. She kept her eyes on the trail to watch for stones or roots, placing one foot in front of the other. She was thinking of the panoramic view from the mountaintop when she asked suddenly, "So what do you think of global warming?"

He looked over at her. "Where did that come from?" he asked.

"You're answering a question with a question. That is so irritating. I was simply wondering. I was thinking of the oxygen those trees, these trees, put into the atmosphere. You know, balancing the effects of carbon emissions."

"Sorry to irritate you," he said. "But yeah, there is definitely something to it. We're doing a good job of ruining the good earth."

"Really? You think that?"

"I do."

"It's funny, being Amish. You know we're a simple folk, set in our old traditions, and sometimes it feels like people are afraid to think outside our little bubble. Do you know how many times I grit my teeth when someone comes to school with a buggy full of children, yelling about the cold weather, and 'where's the global warming now?'? No one takes it seriously."

"I take it you do?"

Impassioned now, she launched into how politicians could change emissions policies, which led to a lively debate about the president, the problems with a two-party system, the role of the electoral college.

Matt shook his head. "Pretty weighty matters here. I've never heard an Amish girl talk like this."

He knew he was falling for her, and told himself to back off. He couldn't see himself returning to the Amish fold, ever. After ten years doing what he wanted to do, how could he return to all those silly rules?

"Amish women aren't all stupid, if that's what you mean. We're just taught to submit to our men. And believe me, that doesn't mean what most people think it does."

"You don't believe in submission?"

"Only if the husband gives his life to his wife, the way Christ gave His for the church."

"Wow. Tough call."

Emma laughed. "You wouldn't do it, give your whole life, for me?"

When he said nothing, she glanced at him, sideways, and found his face darkened by an unnamable emotion, almost like pain. She couldn't have known the internal struggle he felt in that moment, imagining giving up his car, his job, everything.

"Sorry," Emma murmured. "I didn't mean anything by it."

He shook his head. Suddenly, he reached for her hand, held it so tightly she bit down on her lower lip.

"I'm sorry," was all he said.

CHAPTER 16

WHEN THEY ROUNDED A BEND AND SAW ELVIN AND EVA STANDING IN THE trail waiting for them, he dropped her hand abruptly. Eva hoped they'd been far enough off that no one had noticed. It had felt right while they were out of sight, but now she scolded herself. What exactly was she thinking?

"We're heading to the lake," Elvin informed them when they got closer. "You still okay carrying Elijah?"

"We're great," Matt said. "Lead the way."

As they started off again, Emma realized Matt was slowing his steps, so she matched his pace, and soon Elvin and Eva were out of earshot again. But almost immediately, Elijah began fussing. He started by kicking his feet into Matt's side, followed by unhappy grunts, which soon escalated into howls. So they hurried and caught up to Elvin and Eva quickly. They all stopped and transferred Elijah and the backpack to the Elvin's shoulders. After a graham cracker and a drink of apple juice, they were off down the trail.

Matt sighed, flexed his neck, then smiled at her. "Race you," he said unexpectedly, taking off at a sprint now that he was no longer burdened by the backpack.

"What?" Emma laughed, chasing after him as fast as she could. "Cheater!"

There was no way she could catch up, but it felt good to run, plummeting down the trail, dodging jagged stones and roots, her covering loosening with every stride. Matt was out of sight in no time, but eventually she rounded a bend and saw him sitting on a rock on the edge of the trail. She slowed to a stop, breathing hard, sweat dripping from her forehead.

"What took you so long?" he teased.

She was breathing too hard to answer, so she just made a face and reached up to pin her covering back in place.

"Let's walk," she panted, once she could, and he stood and joined her.

They walked in silence for a while, each lost in their own thoughts. Then suddenly she spoke, feeling bold, adrenaline from the run still fresh in her blood.

"So why were you so sullen before, when I mentioned giving yourself up for a wife. You know I was just joking, right?"

"Yeah," he answered. "Nothing really."

She figured he'd probably been hurt by a girl at some point. "Well, I let myself get burned twice," she said, trying to make him feel better. "I really thought Ben was special. But I'm not dumb. I mean, I still sometimes think he's going to write or call, but Eva's right. He would have by now if he was going to."

He stopped walking. She turned to find him looking at her with soft, earnest eyes, eyes that were the color of dark honey.

"Ben's an idiot."

She smiled a very small, very wobbly smile, then bowed her head as the honey gold of his eyes stripped away the pride in hers.

The evening at the lake was a blur. Emma was starved, her feet aching horribly. Elijah got on her nerves, and Eva was acting like a sixteen-year-old girl, throwing mud at Matt, shrieking and running when he came after her. Elvin drank all the Coke, and the mosquitoes were so abundant she accomplished nothing by swatting continuously. When no one made an effort to continue on home, she set off by herself.

She had no idea who or what had brought on this dark, suffocating mood. She was tired, in a good way, physically, but her heart and mind felt like they were trapped in an airtight container, slowly suffo-cating. She reasoned she needed a good night's rest and was showered and had her bed made up before the others got back to the camper.

She did feel better in the morning, and that day and the next followed in slow rhythms of hiking, fishing, relaxing around the campfire. Elvin decided to rent a pontoon for fishing. The price was outrageous, but he shrugged his shoulders, said it would be worth it, that Elijah would love it.

Eva packed the diaper bag while Emma gathered food for the day into the cooler. Today they'd be fishing, and tomorrow they'd pack up and clean the camper to leave the following day. The men were in high spirits, thrilled to be going pontooning on a lake. The only downside was the weather. Matt checked his phone, announcing it forecasted rain and high winds, and suggested they should put it off till the following morning, but Elvin would have none of it. It was barely cloudy, he said, and a stiff September breeze never hurt any-one. Eva told him if they tipped and she drowned it would spite him terribly, whereupon he threw his arms around her and told her he would never put her in that kind of danger.

The sky was the color of sheep's wool, a dirty white with jagged rips of blue. The wind was soft, so Emma put on a windbreaker and wrapped a light blue scarf around her neck. The water was a deep greenish gray color, reflecting the overcast sky. The trees surround-ing the lake appeared to have been brushed with occasional strokes of yellow and orange, an occasional scarlet, but mostly the trees retained the chlorophyll of the summer green.

The pontoon boat was like a large room on two upended canoes, with a sturdy roof on poles, soft vinyl benches, and blue outdoor car-peting. It was white on the outside, quite streamlined for a pontoon. Matt called it a yacht, pretending to offer champagne as the others climbed on, making the three of them laugh. Elijah laughed too, mimicking the adults.

As the boat sliced through the water, the spray shot up on either side, leaving a long wake behind them. The breeze was strong, and

Elijah gulped, turning his head toward Eva's chest when the air became too much for his little lungs.

They found a quiet spot beside a few willows, the branches trailing in the deep green water. Matt killed the motor, then hauled the anchor overboard before diving to beat Elvin to the fishing rods. Arguments ensued over real bait versus artificial, night crawlers versus spinners. Eva quietly went ahead and baited her hook with canned corn she'd sneaked into her tackle box, winked at Emma, and cast expertly on the opposite side of the boat.

Emma played with Elijah, insisting that she didn't fish and was happy keeping him entertained.

"Come on. Just pull up one of those darling night crawlers and spear him with the hook," Elvin barked happily.

Emma shook her head.

Matt settled the fishing rod in the bracket, pulled up a chair, and leaned back, his hands propped behind his head. Elvin followed suit. The only sound was the gentle lapping of waves against the side of the boat, the rustle of the willow trees, and Elijah's happy chatter as he played with his toys.

A yelp from Eva surprised them all. Down came Matt's legs, the chair crashing to the floor.

"Fish on!" Eva yelled.

Emma watched as the tip of the rod bent like a macaroni noodle, then jiggled and shook as she grabbed the handle, grasping it firmly before slowly working the reel. Both men stood at attention, their eyes riveted to the almost invisible line that stretched out into the dark green water.

Eva bit down on her lower lip, concentrating as she worked the reel. Finally she settled the handle on her upper leg, for stability, and shouted, "It's no small fish!"

"I can tell," Elvin said, fairly dancing around on tiptoe in his excitement. The rod bent almost in two, Eva gave the fish more line, then worked the reel faster.

"He's coming in. Get the net," she said, now out of breath.

"Want me to take a turn?" Elvin asked, hovering.

She elbowed him away. "This is my fish."

And it was. She landed a beautiful largemouth bass, all green and silvery scales that rippled beneath the cloudy sky, the frightened yellow eyes and huge gaping mouth gasping for air. Emma hoped it would be a catch and release, but no, they were looking forward to an old fashioned fish fry with thick white filets rolled in cornmeal and cracker crumbs, fried in oil and eaten with fresh coleslaw.

They held him aloft, admiring the poor gasping fish before putting him on ice in the massive cooler. Emma did her best to be a good sport, but it seemed cruel.

Elvin told her God put those fish in the water to sustain man, that was the order of His law. Emma argued that we have cows and pigs and chickens to eat, which are killed in a humane manner, instantly, while the poor fish lay gasping on ice, which was unfair.

Eva giggled. Elvin rolled his eyes. Matt smiled and reminded her that Jesus ate fish with his disciples, which Emma couldn't argue with.

She thought how they had come to know each other pretty well these two weeks. He'd make a good husband for some English woman. She hoped his girlfriend would treat him well.

The trip home proved uneventful, everyone tired out and sunburned, the prospect of returning to the real world a bit daunting, with all the rest and relaxation behind them. Elijah was cranky in his car seat and kicked and twisted his small body against the restraints until he fell asleep. Matt drove, keeping his eyes on the road.

The camper was taken to Elvin and Eva's home to be cleaned and unloaded. They invited Matt to stay for the evening, but he said he needed to get back, he had a list of jobs in the morning.

Emma found herself watching his face, wondering if he'd offer his phone number or some way to stay in touch. But he simply said goodbye, thanked them all for a great time, and drove away, heading back to Lancaster.

"Well," Eva said brightly. "There he goes."

Elvin grinned, shook his head. "He's a great guy. Can you imagine carrying Elijah all day?"

"Not all day."

"Almost."

They set to work, Emma pitching in with the cleaning of the camper, the sorting of food and clothes. She was eager to return home, but felt it was her duty to help her friends before she left. After all, they'd paid most of her expenses, so it was the least she could do. The past two weeks had proven to be much more rewarding than she had ever imagined. Her friendship with Eva had deepened, her respect for them as a couple had been set in cement. Her highest aspiration was to build a union with a good man such as Elvin.

Oh God, lead me to Your will. Take me beyond the physical attraction, lead me to real love, the kind that is deep and enduring and forever. Thank you.

She whispered this as she worked, adding silently, *Or if I am to be single, please help me to accept that.*

She could not place her finger on what it was exactly, but the trip had been a time of reflection. It was as if she had let go of something, opened her hands to allow something to escape her palms, then turned away from that to find her world opening up with colors suffusing the gray parts.

Where would Matt go once he arrived in Lancaster? He had never mentioned his location, if he lived alone, or with whom. Perhaps he lived with this Sheila.

She asked Eva, who turned to her with a look that could only be described as triumphant.

"He has an apartment somewhere. His address is Ronks something."

"Ronks is a huge area."

"So why do you want to know?"

"There is a thing called curiosity. I'm merely being curious, okay?"

"I have his phone number. Do you need it?"

"Of course not."

Her family was overjoyed at her arrival, plying her with dozens of questions, the little girls hopping around her like two bunnies, grabbing the package of oversized balloons she had brought them, unwrapping the lollipops, and running outside to continue their swinging.

Produce season had come to an end, except for late pumpkins that lay on the frostbitten vines in great colorful piles. Huge heads of cauliflower were cut and brought in to be pickled, cooked, eaten raw with ranch dressing, even boiled and mashed like potatoes.

The fields were tilled, a late rye planted, and everyone could breathe easier, count the profits their hard work had brought, and call it another successful season.

Her mother brought the stack of mail she had kept for her, then busied herself at the kitchen sink with eyes in the back of her head, her ears straining to hear. The rustling of paper stopped, as did the paging of magazines.

A plain white envelope with no return address.

Emma's breathing became shallow puffs that left her face erased of color. Slowly she slid a straight pin out of her covering and poked it along the top of the envelope before slinging it from end to end. One piece of folded paper. Her eyes went to the signature.

Ben Glick.

He had written to her, after all these months. Blood pounded in her ears as her eyes darted from sentence to sentence.

His work in North Carolina was not finished, so he could not return just yet. He inquired about her health and well-being and told her he thought of her often, but the way things looked now, he'd be there till Christmas. As an after-thought, he mentioned the fact that the rest of his crew was going home the end of the week.

Could she come down sometime? The beach would be deserted through October, pretty much.

He didn't say he missed her, but surely that was what he meant when he asked her to come to North Carolina.

Her head spun as she made immediate plans.

She stared into space, the letter in nerveless fingers, her thoughts arranging, rearranging.

"Mam," she said finally.

Her mother turned from the sink, wiping her hands on a dish towel.

"Mam, Ben wrote to me."

Wordlessly, then, she handed the letter to her mother, who restrained herself from devouring it too eagerly. Her brows knitted, the hope of finally seeing Emma married dissipated as she read. Slowly she lowered herself into a kitchen chair, took her time to read it again.

It broke her heart, the desperation in her daughter's eyes.

"Should I go?"

There was an uncomfortable moment when her mother hesitated, and Emma knew the space of silence meant no, but could not bring herself to accept it just then.

"I guess that's up to you. I'm not sure that I would. If he is truly interested, shouldn't he be coming here? He's hardly making his intentions clear."

Emma could not absorb her mother's words. She had prayed to God, and He had answered. Ben wanted her, and that was all that mattered. There was one small glitch, though. Ben had left no return address and no phone number, which was puzzling, but understandable, knowing him. A soft smile turned up her lips, as she prided herself on how well she knew him. His passion for life, his infectious grin, the slaphappy camaraderie of his persona.

She would surprise him. She had a plentiful nest egg in the bank. What was the cost of a driver if it meant her heart's desire would finally find a resting place?

She went to church and talked to Eva, who wiped Elijah's face with a baby wipe before spooning more sweet potatoes into his mouth.

"I don't know," she said quietly.

"Don't give me that same spiel my mother did, Eva. You don't know Ben the way I do. Look, he wants me to come down, and that says it all. Right?"

Eva ate some of the Gerber sweet potatoes, made a face, and said she had no idea how her son could eat that stuff.

"You didn't answer my question."

Eva cast her a look that could only be labeled as irritated.

"Just chill, Emma. Take it easy. This is not something to be decided on immediately. Give it a month, at least. And keep praying. God does not always answer our needs quite so soon, or so . . ."

Emma broke in.

"Or so what? You just can't accept this because it's not what you want, right?"

"Come, time to eat."

The lady of the house came to steer them in the direction of the women's table, where they took their place in the line of women and girls, sliding onto the benches set on either side of a long table, cutting off the conversation effectively.

Emma found herself without appetite, a sick feeling of dread building up in her stomach. First her mother, then her best friend. Why couldn't they see it her way?

She spread a slice of homemade wheat bread with cheese spread, cut it in half and chewed slowly. She speared a pickled red beet with the tines of her fork, brought it to her saucer and cut it in small pieces with her knife.

"Coffee?"

Behind her, a young girl held the coffeepot aloft. Wordlessly, she handed her the green melmac coffee cup, received it back before scooping up dry creamer and swirling it into the black liquid.

"I heard you went camping," Rachel Zook commented, on her right.

"We did. Elvin, Eva, and I."

She affirmed the vacation was good, and yes, she was glad to be back. But she didn't offer any details, didn't ask Rachel about her own fall plans. Her thoughts were on the beach in North Carolina.

Her words to Eva were clipped and short as she said goodbye later, glad to go home to her room and figure out the details of her upcoming trip, returning to the place and the man of her dreams.

She applied for and got a job caring for a neighbor lady who lived alone and was approaching ninety years of age. Her name was Anastasia Gilbert, known by most as Anna Gibbs. She was under five feet, had a small frame, and had her hair done every two weeks by that hairdresser in town that charged an arm and a leg and didn't use the right hair color.

Her hair shone bright blond, and everyone on God's green earth knew her hair wasn't that color. She didn't need a caregiver, she got along fine on her own, but she just needed someone to help out with a few things here and there. She had no children, no relatives close by.

Her house was like a gingerbread house, complete with trim work, porch posts, and railing painted white against an apple green porch.

White shutters accentuated the green painted stucco, giving the house an aura of being in a fairytale, the porch being deep and wide, filled with ceramic pots in colors of the rainbow, huge ferns drooping over their sides. Wicker furniture of every size and description was placed hapharzadly and filled with the neighbors' cats or the three of her own.

Emma loved Anastasia Gilbert from the first day she met her. She had come over from Russia in 1945, after the war, with her parents and one brother, who were all dead and gone, may they rest in peace. She'd married Thomas Washinger, and when he died, she'd waited a year before marrying William Gilbert.

Anna and her family were poor as church mice when they arrived in America, but her father had worked hard and done well with the dry cleaning business and sent her to college, where she'd got her degree in English and went on to teach high school literature.

When Emma took the job, she explained she would need the last five days of October off, having planned a trip to North Carolina during that time. Anna had agreed, eager to have her start. So Emma spent her days with Anna from six in the morning till six at night, cleaning, baking, doing laundry, ironing, or just sitting and talking.

She loved the cluttered interior of the small green house, the deep carpeting that silenced footfalls and invited the cats to lounge in puddles of sunlight. She hoisted the clumsy Rainbow vacuum cleaner out of the hall closet and into each room every single day, vacuuming the accumulation of cat hairs with its quiet power.

Anna called Emma "Emmaline," which felt to Emma like a term of endearment. Emma would come home in the evening and tell her mother what a sweet and smart woman Anna was, and Emma's mother was glad to see her find contentment in her new job. Emma's mother dismissed the ever-thickening cloud of worry about this Ben and tried to place her trust in Emma's own sense of direction. Surely she wouldn't actually go to North Carolina to chase the man. A mother's anxiety is best swept away by frantic housecleaning, and the house had never looked quite so clean.

CHAPTER 17

Eva was happy to hear about her friend's new job, the lively description with which she entertained her, tales of the old lady's whimsical traits, the coziness of their breakfasts and shared lunches.

And then the bombshell was dropped.

"Only a few weeks until I leave for North Carolina!"

Shocked, Eva stared, her eyes bouncing in her head.

"You haven't given it up?"

"No."

A moment of silence settled between them, during which Eva held back a tirade of frustration over her friend's stubborn and idiotic pursuit of this man, and instead simply said, "You're not going alone."

It was a statement. An order.

"Why not?"

"Emma, you can't go all that way with a driver. It would cost you a thousand dollars."

"That's my business if I want to pay that much."

"True. Elijah, no no. Here, give me that."

Eva got up, reached to take an empty cupcake wrapper out of his hand, which sent him into howls of indignation.

"Give it up, little guy. Here."

She plopped him in his high chair, upended the Cheerios box onto his tray, and scattered them appealingly.

"You want my honest opinion?"

"I don't know if I do."

Outside, the autumn rain slanted in from the northeast, sending brilliant yellow maple leaves into a golden carpet at the foot of the tree. Birds pecked halfheartedly at glistening wet sunflower seeds, and a soggy downy woodpecker hammered away at crumbling suet at the birdfeeder.

It was on a Saturday afternoon, when Lutheran Care sent the night caregiver early, giving Emma a break from her usual routine.

Eva had invited her for pizza, with Elvin being on his annual archery hunting spree.

"Well, it doesn't matter if you do or if you don't. Here it is. Don't go."

"Why do you say that?"

Emma lifted bewildered eyes, hoping Eva would take pity, come to see it her way.

"Look, there are plenty of red flags planted all over. For one, did it ever occur to you that not many respectful Amish guys, after only knowing you a few days . . ."

"Weeks."

"Weeks. Whatever. Would come into a bedroom to help make that bed?" Here she lifted both hands and waggled two fingers. "I'm sorry, but I had a problem with that scene all along. Then he got all romantic? Really? To me, that was simply pushing the envelope. And he should have been the one to talk to Roger and Kathy, to come to your defense. To make this right. I mean, of course they weren't pleased you had a man there overnight! But he could have apologized, said it was all his fault, which it was."

"But Eva, you don't understand. Kathy didn't like me. She was jealous of Ben. She didn't want us together."

"A married woman? Now right there is the biggest red flag. Don't you think Ben could have set her straight, told her he had absolutely no interest? You can't tell me Ben did not flirt back. Maybe you didn't see it, maybe it was only when they were out of your sight, but believe me, Ben could have put a stop to her inappropriate affections if he had wanted to."

Emma toyed with the handle of her coffee cup, her thoughts seeking an avenue of release. No one understood the power of Ben's attraction, what she had felt with him.

A stiff silence followed. One that was broken only by the cheerios being picked up and dropped by Elijah's chubby little fingers.

"You want me to like Matt."

"I'm sorry about that. I thought maybe he would take your mind off Ben, but I didn't really think it through. I know you would never leave the Amish and he has no plans of returning. Besides, I didn't know about this Sheila."

"Do you think he would take me to North Carolina?"

"He might. I mean, not alone. But maybe if Elvin and I could go. We could only go from, say, Friday morning to late Sunday night. You'd have to pay our motel room. We're broke after that vacation. Boy, people would really talk, traipsing off to the Outer Banks a month after our camping trip."

Emma smiled. "Call Matt, see what he says. Right now. I'll watch Elijah."

So Eva threw a light jacket over her head and ran across the yard to Elvin's office that housed the lone telephone. A few minutes later she dashed back through the rain, her eyes fairly ablaze with excitement. Yes, he would go, in fact he agreed immediately. Wasn't that absolutely great?

Emma was more than pleased and began to plan ahead, thrilled to think of the upcoming trip turning into a reality. The thought of seeing Ben was the spontaneous energy that fueled her days until the week arrived.

She told Anna at breakfast the following Monday, who drew down her white brows and pouted into her bowl of rolled oats.

"How long did you say?"

"Just a couple of days," Emma said, watching the way the light and shadows played on the kitchen wall as the wind tossed leaves in the air outside.

"Two days?"

"Friday afternoon and Saturday. Part of Saturday."

"I don't believe you should go."

"Why not?"

"Because you might drown."

"I won't go swimming."

"I still don't like it. In the old days, we never went on a car trip. We worked. All day long, six days a week. How do you think my father was so successful with the dry cleaning? We all worked, that's how.

"I'm sure you did."

"I did."

Emma washed dishes and cleaned the stove and refrigerator while Anna took her morning nap, then got on her hands and knees to scrub the tiny kitchen floor. In her head, she planned her wardrobe, what she would pack, what she would wear on the Saturday they would arrive. She knew he would be working, she could hear the shrill saw, the pounding of hammers, Kathy and Roger bent over a sawhorse and plywood table, following the print of the house. It would be awkward to see Kathy again, but that faded in her mind in the light of reuniting with Ben. Like a dream, an undeserved fantasy, she would be allowed to return, look into those eyes and feel anchored by the love she found there. A love meant for two of them, both ready to be married, to serve God the remainder of their days, bringing children into the world, teaching them to love the Lord, to stay in the Amish church and help to build it into the future.

Oh, she would be blessed among women, as the Bible said.

The day came, finally. The air was crisp and cold, leaves swirling haphazardly around the lawn, when the black pickup truck chugged to the door. Matt got out, went around to open the door, just the way he'd done before. This time, he seemed strangely familiar, as if she'd known him for a long time.

The truck was filled with happy banter, four friends who continued a relationship where they'd left off. The miles drained away, and when they stopped for lunch, they were all laughing and talking.

Lunch was relaxed, and Emma felt she could be herself without fear of being judged or ridiculed. Matt watched her from beneath the brim of his baseball hat, his eyes soft. He had made it clear that he thought Ben was crazy, but here Ben was now, coming through for her, inviting her back. The satisfaction of being right and the anticipation of seeing her love, of the glad embrace they would share when she showed up, lit up her eyes and gave her whole being a happy glow.

Matt had tried to get Emma out of his mind. He'd even opened old avenues of prayer that hadn't been used in a decade. He didn't really believe God would listen to his prayers, but he figured it didn't hurt to try.

He knew she loved someone else, and yet he could not forget her. In fact, he had fallen for her pretty hard. He even imagined returning to his roots, the church services and the Pennsylvania Dutch, the rules and regulations. Emma was unlike anyone he had ever met before. He had realized that while they were together, but when he returned home after their camping trip, he felt it even more keenly. He missed her quick wit, her strong views, her bright eyes. He missed drinking coffee together by the campfire, discussing politics, making her laugh.

He had gone to visit his adoptive parents. He'd walked into his old room, wandered around the farm, and searched his soul for a reason not to come back and make his parents proud. He'd looked at the eighth grade diploma from Hickory Lane School, hanging there on the wall above his bookcase like a sign of his past.

He'd been born into the world to a mother who was not yet sixteen, and given up for adoption. His adoptive parents had raised him lovingly, showering him with privileges and affection, leveling it all out with good old-fashioned discipline. When he discovered he wasn't their biological child, they had helped him trace his roots, allowed him to seek the truth, supported his genealogy search.

He was Italian, for the most part. That was where he got the dark hair and skin. His father was a boxer, of sorts, in some area of the Bronx. He hadn't been able to get in touch with him, but he did meet his mother. She was a shy woman, short of stature, black-haired, courteous, but she hadn't shown him any affection. She told him she was glad to see him, but that he did not want to live in Harlem, that New York City was no place for an Amish boy. He told her he wasn't Amish anymore, that he'd live with her, take care of her. She told him to go back where he came from and to have a good life, and that she meant it. She said he didn't want the kind of life she lived.

So he'd driven out of New York City in his black Volkswagen with the music turned high and the Statue of Liberty to his left with the glistening waters of the Hudson Bay and the sun on his shoulders, determined to get on with his life. What else was there to do?

He settled into an apartment close to Smoketown and continued the job he'd always had. He liked delivering and setting up all sorts of storage sheds and garages, playhouses and gazebos. It was good work and he got along well with the crew, so why leave? Plus, the pay was good and his savings account had swelled to a sizable amount.

Working hard and enjoying weekends however he felt like it had kept him pretty content for the last decade. But since the camping trip, he had felt lonely and disoriented, a little lost. And so when Eva had called, asking if he wanted to drive them to North Carolina, he had said yes without even considering that he'd be putting himself through more heartache, watching Emma chase after the love of her life. But at least he'd get to be with her for the trip. And although he wasn't eager to meet this Ben character, he did feel some protective instinct to make sure he wasn't a total jerk. Maybe if he saw Emma happily reunited with a really great guy, if he could be sure he'd love her the way she deserved to be loved, then he'd be able to let her go and return to life as a free man, a hardworking, worldly bachelor. At least he would try.

They arrived at the bridge that led to the Outer Banks in late afternoon. Emma became quiet, pensive, her face pale and upset.

"You know where you're going?" Elvin asked over his shoulder.

"I do. Keep going. You can see the ocean before too long. Bay on the other side. Um . . . Matt, do you mind stopping somewhere so I could, you know, freshen up?"

He pulled into the parking lot of a gas station, peering through the glass of the convenience store and noting the half-asleep figure behind a plywood counter. The bathroom was accessible and fairly clean, for which Emma was thankful. With shaking hands, she brought out her fine-toothed comb, a small travel-size hair spray, and proceeded to alter her travel-worn appearance.

When she returned, Matt did not glance at her, merely asked if everyone was set before starting up and driving off. Emma noticed the lack of conversation, and thought perhaps everyone was exhausted, like Elijah, who was whining and throwing his toys on the floor.

There were a few exclamations when they got their first glimpse of the ocean, but in general everyone was acting as if they were going to a funeral. Well, it was understandable, the way they all disapproved of her actions, coming all this way to meet Ben.

As the road wound between the two bodies of water, the familiar scent wafted through half-open windows. Grasses and scrubby pines gave way to sand dunes, wooden slat fences, an upended dinghy, with water everywhere.

"Another mile," Emma said, breathless now.

No one replied, so she said it again, only a bit louder.

"Sure, yeah," Matt answered. "Right or left?"

"Left."

And then they reached the end of the drive, crunched their way to the house with the massive front steps, the structure supported on the thick piles. The dull thumping of the waves greeted them, the grasses bending and swaying like hula dancers, the screaming seagulls dipping and cavorting in the skies.

A child shouted somewhere by the ocean, another answered.

There was no welcoming golden light from the rectangular windows, no white SUV parked in the driveway.

"They're likely over at the new house," Emma said, her voice barely above a hoarse whisper.

"You want me to drive over?"

"No. No, I'll go."

She was out of the truck like a vapor, disappearing around the corner of the house.

Emma's heart was banging in her chest, so that she held a hand to it, palm down, to steady herself before knocking on the huge door. She saw the white SUV then, parked at an angle in the carport below the house.

She knocked again. When no one answered, she held her hands to the side of her face to peer through the glass door. The interior of the house appeared to be nearing completion. Maybe they had moved in already. Soon, Ben would be coming home, or going home to Lancaster County.

The idea of a future with him lent wings to her feet as she ran down the steps, eager to check the adjoining house one more time. The car was here, so someone had to be around somewhere.

She turned to the sight of the wooden walkway, the familiar grasses that rustled in the sea breeze, the romance that was sure to follow. When had she ever felt such confidence, such solid hope? She inhaled deeply, the scent of salt water, the endless sand, watched as the gulls cried and lifted their wings at someone's approach.

Someone . . . wait.

It was Ben, a shirt flapping loosely around his swimming trunks, a towel draped across his shoulders. Her glad cry caught in her throat at the sight of small, blond Kathy, a white cover-up belted around her swimsuit, their hands entwined.

She was halfway up the stairs to the house, and for a moment, shock sent her sense reeling, so that she clung to the railing. She felt the prick of a sharp splinter from the weathered wood, which brought everything into focus.

Her first instinct was to flee, to become invisible. She turned to make her way down the stairs and back to the truck, before a grim determination made her stop. She would not slink away like some guilty varmint.

Slowly, her feet like a dead weight, she made her way to the top of the stairs to turn in their direction, her bright skirt billowing in the strong breeze.

How long till he spied her?

She didn't know, but at the time, it seemed like an eternity, a time when she experienced the deep and awful sinking of her hopes and dreams. Her heart had been wrong, and her friends and family right. Her love had been a folly, an attraction meant to be dashed to the ground.

He caught sight of her. She waved, a pathetic, faltering lift of her right hand. He turned to speak to Kathy, released her hand.

On they came. A large gull that dipped close, his yellow eyes accusing her of invading the world that had never been hers.

"Hey," Ben called out, his eyes never leaving her face.

Slowly, she made her way down the stairs, her head spinning as her breathing came in short gasps. She stood, leaning on the post at the bottom of the stairs for support, said hello.

"Hi, Emma. Imagine seeing you here," Kathy trilled.

She ignored her, turned her eyes to Ben.

"You asked me to come here," she grated, low and ominous.

"I did?"

"You wrote to me."

"Oh, right. I felt badly about how things ended and wanted to make things right."

"Make what right?"

"You know, our fling. Whatever it was."

He was uneasy, stepping from one bare foot to another.

Kathy seemed at ease, smiling at Emma with unbelievable audacity as Ben fumbled his excuses, guilty and miserable as Emma stood firm, her eyes burning with the hurt that only a flagrant display of betrayal can achieve.

"You can stay with use for a while," said Kathy, eagerly, like she really meant it. "You know there are no hard feelings. Roger will be back with the kids tomorrow afternoon. They'd love to see you again. Do stay for a few days. How did you get here?" She bent backward to peer around the stairs.

"Oh, you brought friends. Do tell them to come in. We'll throw something on the grill, have a party!"

Emma was dumbfounded. It took her a moment, but when she spoke her voice was strong. "I don't think so. I'll be leaving directly. Ben, you know what you are doing is wrong. I hope you can live with yourself the rest of your days."

His face was a bland mask of denial, a mockery of feigned inno-cence. Kathy smiled sweetly, but Emma could feel the undercurrent of victory.

Emma pushed past them, her walk to the truck hindered by the loose sand that constantly blew in around the piles. She reached for the door handle, yanked it open, sat down hard and said, "Go."

No one spoke. Matt turned the truck back to the road, turned right onto the macadam, and moved off slowly. Eva cast a sideways glance at her friend, who was as pale as she had ever seen her, the freckles on her nose like bits of copper paint. Her eyes were large and dark, giving nothing away.

Matt drove steadily as the sun slid lower toward the sea. The bay rippled and glistened, the white sails on the small sailboats like handkerchiefs floating above the water. A large fish crane lifted off, flapped its immense wings with a slow, graceful movement, as if it were waving a sad goodbye.

They stayed in the town of Point Harbor for one night.

Emma booked a separate room for herself, knowing she needed space. She did not speak to anyone but was like a shadow, a wisp of fog. When everyone discussed a place to eat, she felt the bile rise in her throat.

"You okay?" Eva whispered, grabbing her hand and squeezing. Emma nodded.

The table in the quaint restaurant was round, and Emma found Matt across from her, the moving lights of boats coming in to the docks illuminating the background, so that his face was often in shadow, with the dim yellow lights that hung above the table. For this, she was grateful.

Elvin kept the conversation going with comments about the prices on the menu, the unusual items, and how he'd love to live here.

"We could move down here. Start an Amish settlement, couldn't we?" he chortled, lifting his drink and wiping the tabletop with his napkin.

"Elvin, seriously. Do you have any idea what a house would cost here? And how would you make a living?" Eva asked, always the realist.

"Hurricanes go through here, don't they? Plenty of carpentry going on."

Emma toyed with her drinking straw, watched the swirl of ice in the dark tea, and half wished that a hurricane would come through tomorrow and blow her off into oblivion.

She ordered a small salad, choked on a slice of cucumber, then laid down her fork and asked to be excused.

"Emma," Eva said quickly.

"I'll be alright. I'm not hungry. I'll just find a bench somewhere."

"Where will we find you? Do you know your room number?"

"I have this," she held up the card that would open the door to her room.

She made her way blindly across the room, her lifted shoulders and hurried gait giving away the tension of her afternoon. Matt leaned back in his chair, watched her go with eyes that gave nothing away, but Eva saw the twitch of his lips, the downward turn at the corners, and was not surprised when he lifted a blue men's handkerchief out of his pocket to blow his nose very quietly.

Emma moved along the sidewalk without seeing, bumped into a lamp post and stopped, a hand going to her forehead. She grimaced at the exploding pain, looked around in embarrassment, hoping no one had witnessed it.

And then she sat on a bench, overlooking the channel as night enveloped the town by the ocean, the street lights shining their reflection on the dark water. She allowed her mind to become still and quiet before she bent her head to her knees and began to accept the loss of her castle in the air.

CHAPTER 18

Eventually, she wandered back to the hotel, a square beige-colored structure that rose above the smaller houses of business, the blue neon sign with orange letters erasing the authenticity of the small harbor town.

She tried to sleep, but her room was stifling, choking out the bit of living breath she had left, so she showered, dressed in a clean blue dress, as light as the sky, twisted her hair into a ponytail holder, and let herself out the door, careful to keep the plastic card in her pocket. She moved across the walkway and down the steps, then out onto the street, now mostly empty. Strangely, she was not afraid, not in this cozy seaside town filled with friendly tourists.

She walked along the sidewalk, sniffed the salty air appreciatively, then remembered her walk on the beach with Ben, the afternoon and its humiliating aftermath, the dead silence in the truck. For once, Eva had been speechless, and luckily, Elvin kept all his smart remarks to himself. But once she found a park bench beside the water of the bay, she folded herself into it and gave way to tears.

She cried quietly, reservedly, as if she was afraid to let go, afraid she would howl and wail at the loss of her dreams. What if, though? What if a year went by and Ben saw the error of his ways, repented and came clean, lived with a deep chasm of remorse? Then what?

She shook off this thought, recognized the tempter's smooth wheedling tone. Her feet on solid ground now, she realized she'd never be able to trust Ben, even if he were to repent and beg her forgiveness. She could never go back.

A large white boat came slowly along the channel, lights everywhere, the occupants sprawled on chairs or hanging from the railing, talking and laughing as they moved slowly past, leaving a V of ripples in their wake.

She wiped her eyes to see more clearly, honked into the soggy Kleenex, then sniffed as someone sat beside her.

Just stay over there, she thought, as she gave her nose a final swipe. She shivered. It was decidedly wet and chilly, here by the water. She should have brought a sweater. She glanced at the person beside her, surprised to realize it was Matt.

"Matt."

"Thought you might need company."

She gave a low laugh.

"I'm not real good company myself."

"I figured."

He leaned forward, his elbows on his knees, his head bent. She saw the glistening light on the wet dark curls. No hat.

"I couldn't sleep," she offered.

"Yeah."

She sat back, shoved her feet below the bench and wrapped her arms around her waist, seriously chilled now.

"Cold?" he asked.

"Getting there."

"You want my hoodie?"

"Then you'll be cold."

He was already on his feet, pulling it off, then turned to hand it to her. She snuggled into it gratefully, wrapped it around herself, lost in the scent of his woodsy, earthy cologne.

"Better?" he asked, before sitting on the farthest edge of the bench.

"Definitely."

Emma appreciated his silence, his lack of any attempt to entertain or distract her. He merely sat with her, watched the lights on the water, the occasional boat slip past with only a muffled sound of the motor, a small splashing as the water hit the sides of the walkway. The stars were only visible directly overhead, the yellow light from the street lamps effectively dimming them. Behind them, late stragglers made their way to their consecutive rooms or homes, quiet conversation or only the sound of shoe soles on cement accompanying them.

Emma had no desire to return to the cloying emptiness of her room, or to sit here on either side of a park bench in the damp chill of this unforgettable evening. She told herself sternly that it was time she went home with her family and stayed here, stayed in close proximity to everything her parents had taught her about hard work, dependability, and most of all, to live constantly seeking God's will.

Matt cleared his throat.

"Do you want to talk about it, Emma?".

She gave a short, harsh laugh.

"Why would I?"

"So it was pretty bad?"

"You saw him with her."

There was a dead silence at the opposite end of the bench.

"You know," he said finally. "What hurts the most is the sense of betrayal. It's painful to know how much you love, did love, while the object of your affection tosses that away with the flick of a wrist. Just like that, it's over, and you realize your love was one-sided, an impotent thing that was never meant to be. You hate yourself for your self-delusion, building air castles in your head. Believe me, I know."

Emma crossed her legs, said nothing.

He continued. "So that said, let me ask you something."

She kept her silence intact. One foot bobbed under her skirt, the only sign of life from that side of the bench.

"Do you believe in an English person being Amish?"

"You're not English."

"I am not Amish, either."

"You were born and raised in an Amish home."

"Raised. Not born."

"Big difference. You aren't English, Matt. What our parents instill in our minds and hearts will be there till the day we die, I don't care how we dress or what we drive or which label we apply to ourselves. It's a culture, a way of life, a whole heritage that gets into our veins, runs in our blood. We really can't help who we are."

"But what about my lineage? My DNA and all the genes that make a person?"

"What are you getting at?"

"I'm trying to see if the bridge will hold if I take the first step."

"What is that supposed to mean?"

He gave a short laugh.

"I know I have no right, with my birth and the way I have been living. I also know it's too soon. But after this night, I don't when I'll see you again."

He stopped. She could feel the tension, the line that hummed between them like a live wire. Dangerous and untouchable.

"But if you will give me a chance to return to my home, to do some serious soul searching, would you ever consider me? I haven't stopped thinking about you since the camping trip. I told myself to disappear, stay out of your life. But then Eva called, and I'm thrown right back in the ring. I know you have no interest, and would be happy to see me fall off the edge of the world, but I can't go home without telling you how I feel. You don't have to say anything now . . ."

When her silence stretched awkwardly, he got up and began to walk way. He reached the sidewalk, turned right before she called out.

"Matt?"

He stopped, his back turned.

"I can't think straight. Come back? Let's talk."

He came back, sat heavily on the bench, as if his legs would no longer hold him.

"It's going to take time."

"I'm aware of that."

"I know you are. And it's kind of you to consider my point of view."

She gave a low laugh, shook her head ruefully.

"I know that Ben's character is too questionable to consider a happy ending, ever."

Her voice thickened, caught on a sob. She tried to continue, to tell him the rest of what she was going to say, but found herself in so much misery, the tears unstoppable now. So she got up and started walking, not caring which direction she was headed, or what the outcome would be.

He caught up with her, walked beside her without speaking, quietly handed her a large blue men's handkerchief that was infused with the same woodsy scent that seemed to be his trademark.

She took it gratefully, then stopped.

"Let's go back, okay?"

"Back to the hotel, or the bench?"

She laughed, then her voice caught on another sob.

"I don't know. The bench. I guess. Like two homeless people."

"We aren't exactly homeless."

"I know."

This time, they did not sit far apart, but side-by-side, for warmth or for comfort, or for the unknown fact they simply needed each other to get through the night. They talked, then, not of the matters of the heart, but mundane subjects that brought a kind of comfort both craved. They talked about the beauty of the ocean, laughed about how odd they must look together to the occasional passerby, told stories from work, their families, their childhoods.

After a while, there was a lull in the conversation, and Matt cleared his throat awkwardly. "Emma, I have to tell you something."

"What now?"

"There is no Sheila."

"What?"

"I mean there is, but we're not dating, we never were. It's like a 'sort of' lie. I guess because you were so upset about Elvin and Eva throwing us together. I stretched the truth so you'd be more comfortable. Sheila is an acquaintance, that's all."

He grinned a lopsided grin, and she responded with a small one of her own.

"It's not funny," she said sternly.

"Then why are you laughing?"

"I am barely smiling."

"Look, sometimes a guy has to do whatever it takes, you know?"

Emma sighed, looked into his eyes to search for hidden guilt or deception, but the only thing in his eyes was the golden light fringed by dark lashes. She wanted to be a little mad at him for lying, but all she could feel was relief that he didn't have a girlfriend.

The waters of the channel were as still as glass, the street lamps casting yellow cones of light across the surface. When Matt yawned, then stretched, Emma asked if he thought there might be an all-night coffee place somewhere. He grinned, checked his watch, and told her it was early morning. Another hour and they should have no trouble finding coffee.

They found a tiny place, with only one square of yellow light from the window, a sign that simply had "Harbor" written in black letters on a blue background. The interior was dimly lit, with one small room that held a scattering of small tables, a high counter which housed a display of what appeared to be pastries. The aroma of fresh coffee was a heady smell that made Emma grab for Matt's arm.

"Mmm. Oh my word. This is serious coffee."

He grinned at her, then took her hand, squeezed it before immediately letting go.

"Good morning! How's it going?"

"We're good," Matt said. "And you?"

"Lovely. Wonderful. Great day to be here. Coffee?"

"Two regulars."

They bent to survey the pastries, settled on a chocolate croissant and a cheese Danish. Emma was reeling with fatigue, chilled to the core, and wrapped both hands around the large cup of strong coffee and smiled back at Matt.

"So we're friends," she said.

"We are friends. At least for now?"

"Remember," she reminded him. "There's this little thing called the will of God and we're supposed to wait till we feel His calling. Or weren't you serious about remembering your mother's Bible stories?"

He toyed with his stirrer before he nodded slowly.

"Yeah. I am. But I've been pretty bitter for a long time. I told you, I'm not sure God will take me back."

"Not on your own merit. Jesus is the doorway."

"Yeah."

His features darkened, as if a shadow had passed over him, a certain weariness to the wide set of his muscular shoulders.

"I don't know. Even the name of Jesus is tossed around in the world like any other swear word, so to be . . . I don't know. My Amish life seems so far removed from . . ."

He stopped.

Suddenly, he reached across the table, put his hand on both of hers, his voice catching when he said, "I don't really know how to do this."

"Well, you can't place me in the spot where Jesus belongs. You have to put Jesus first. You realize that's why our other relationships failed—neither of us were really seeking God's will."

He gave her a skeptical look.

"Now you sound like an evangelist."

"Maybe. I'm just tired of things not working out, that's all."

"Which means you're hoping it will the next time?"

"Honestly, I don't know if there will be a next time. I need to get some rest. I'm going back to my family and my job and I'm just going to stay put for a while. No more adventures."

"Well, then I will do the same."

But the coffee shop held an aura of warmth and companionship, if not of romance. When they returned to the hotel to find a frantic Eva knocking on the doors of their rooms, they looked at each other and burst out laughing. "It's not funny," she shouted. "Where were you? Elvin is fit to be tied, Elijah is throwing up with the stomach flu, and we need to get on the road as soon as possible. Elvin's boss says he needs him on a job as soon as he can get back—someone else called in with the stomach bug, too."

Anna was glad to have Emma back. She immediately told her about a mouse behind the sink and how the scratching sound was driving her mad. Emma found an old wooden trap in a drawer full of random junk, set it with a dab of peanut butter, and placed it behind the bottles of cleaning products. Anna was relieved, almost excited about the mouse's upcoming demise.

"God did not intend for mice to live in the same house as humans, the dirty little rotters."

"Oh, but they're cute. Especially the deer mice, the brown ones with white feet," Emma laughed, wielding her dustcloth across the top of the hutch in the kitchen. Two small vases held plastic artificial daisies coated with a furry layer of dust, which Emma removed, took to the sink, and swirled in the dishwater.

"Here, now," came the strident voice from the kitchen chair. "Don't you break my flowers. My niece gave them to me in September of seventy-nine, for my birthday."

Emma assured her they would not break and that they would look like new once they dried. Anna made sure that Emma replaced the stack of *Good Housekeeping* magazines from the nineties once the area was clean, as there was a recipe in the third one down that she hadn't copied yet.

Emma was happy, she realized. She couldn't understand it, but she was willing to recognize this new sense of joy as a blessing, albeit a mysterious one.

She still felt the sting of Ben's betrayal, of her own miscalculation of his character, but in some ways she was glad she had arrived at the beach house right when she did. There could be no doubt in her mind now, no second guessing his intentions. No man, of any religion or without it, could justify those actions, so Emma found it easier to dismiss the summer and their brief relationship as one of learning.

She'd been placed in God's schoolhouse, given difficult assignments, and through it she was learning more about His plan for her life. More than ever, she felt like she'd been taken under the mighty wings of His love and rest.

Anna Gibbs was a treasure, with her sweet puckered face and her increasingly humorous view of the world and its inhabitants. Anna knew she could make Emma laugh easily, which really brought her charming sense of humor to life, her little eyes sparkling as she spouted off and waited for Emma's bubbling laugh.

The morning was pleasant, the kitchen warm and sunny as the wind battered the brown oak leaves against the side of the white bungalow. The teapot was filled with the black Russian tea, sending out the herbal aroma she had come to enjoy. Emma used sugar, to Anna's constant chagrin; the old woman would shake her head and saying no real tea drinker took sugar, only milk.

"Stop, stop," Anna shouted in her little bird chirp, watching Emma spoon the sugar into a steaming cup.

"The sugar. You'll get the diabetes. All you Americans have the diabetes. Too much sugar."

Emma was enjoying her morning tea at ten o'clock, the way they always did, and she was not about to drink it black for her sake, and told her so, reaching across the table to touch the arthritic old hands.

Anna inclined her head, glared at Emma, and said she may as well go stick her head in the sugar canister and start chewing, which brought the results she'd been hoping it would. Emma shook a finger at her, while choking on a mouthful of tea, and Anna's beady little eyes shone with pleasure.

Emma worked her way through the small square rooms, washing anything washable in the sink, air drying the items on towels spread on the counter. She wiped and polished, ran the ancient vacuum cleaner that kept making odd pinging noises and spewing dust from places that were supposed to be tight. She shut it off, then peered around the corner to see if Anna was awake. This thing needed serious attention, and it was time Anna realized it.

But the elderly lady was sound asleep on her recliner, her head resting on a plump pillow on the right side, the television turned so high it was uncomfortable being in the room. Emma walked over and sneaked the remote from her lap, had just found the volume button when she heard a crackly, "Give me that."

"You were sleeping," Emma defended herself.

"No. I was not. I just had my eyes closed to rest them for a while. Why would you try to snatch the remote?"

She glared at Emma like an outraged little bird.

"It was really loud in here."

"You didn't need to be in here while I was sleeping."

"Okay. Sorry."

"You should be. Now get on with whatever you were doing while I finish my nap."

"The vacuum isn't working right. Could we take it somewhere to be fixed, or have someone come look at it?"

"Oh, just let me look at it. You're likely not doing something right."

She heaved herself from the chair, before she slid back into it. She lowered her head and ran her hand across her eyebrows, but said nothing, merely grabbed the arms of the chair and tried again. Emma put a hand beneath her elbow to stabilize her.

Anna tottered across the room, her feet dragging on the thick carpet, stopped to survey the top of a dresser, ran a hand lightly along its surface.

"You make my furniture look like new," she said, as if to herself. "This dresser came from a used furniture place when we lived in Queens. We paid two dollars and fifty cents for it."

She moved on, then bent over the vacuum cleaner, pressed the start button, and stood back as the dust particles blew out.

"You have an obstruction here somewhere. Here, you have to take this apart."

She bent over, tugged at a seal where the hose went into the vacuum. Emma felt uncomfortable, seeing her bending over without support, but stood back to allow her space. When Anna straightened, she reached for support, and when there was none, she grabbed at the emptiness around her before she went down. A frightened cry emerged from her lips as she fell hard across the edge of the vacuum.

There was a sickening crack that could only be the breaking of a prominent bone, followed by a cry Emma would never forget.

She tried to gently move Anna off the vacuum, but was only met with wails of anguish, her poor old heart barely able to support her voice. Emma knew to dial 911, which she did with shaking hands.

The desperate cries from the poor suffering Anna were almost more than Emma could bear. It seemed as if hours had gone by before she finally heard the distant wail of the sirens. If only she hadn't mentioned the disabled sweeper, if only she had not allowed Anna to walk without her cane.

The medics arrived, rushed into the house with professional speed and caring, lifted Anna off the sweeper amid her piercing cries.

Emma felt weak with the horror of listening to Anna's terrible distress, but there was nothing to do but stay out of their way and answer questions.

Eventually she was placed on the gurney that would take her away. Her eyes were closed, her lips moving silently. Emma could never be sure if she was praying or mumbling words to herself, but she opted to believe she was praying.

She rode in the front of the ambulance, silently clutching one hand with the other, answering the driver's questions as best she could, her mind in the back with the frightened Anna. Once at the hospital, she stayed right by Anna's side. The X-rays showed a broken hip, badly fractured in two places on account of her aging joints weakened by arthritis. She was taken into surgery immediately. Emma called her parents, asking them to send a driver with clothes and toiletries so she would be able to spend the night at the hospital with Anna.

When both parents showed up later in the day carrying a small overnight case, Emma was so grateful. The sight of the two Amish people, dressed in the traditional black, so clean and well dressed, so dear, with eyes alight at the sight of her, brought quick tears to her eyes. If the whole world crumbled around her, she still had her parents to bolster her courage.

She extended both hands to them, saying, "Glad to see you. It was so awful the way she suffered."

Her mother put a hand to Emma's back and rubbed softly.

"I can't imagine, Emma."

Her father smiled kindly, looked at her with so much empathy Emma thought surely God must look something like that.

"Thanks so much for coming. You can't know how much I appreciate it."

"You know we'd do anything for you, Emma."

And Emma knew they surely would.

CHAPTER 19

ANNA GILBERT STAYED IN THE HOSPITAL FOR ALMOST A WEEK, WITH EMMA spending her days by her bedside. After the first night sleeping in the chair next to Anna's hospital bed, she decided Anna was in good hands with the nurses and doctors there and spent her nights sleeping at home.

She wavered between wishing she had never taken the job of being a caregiver, to hoping she'd be able to continue caring for Anna's needs so that she would not have to be taken to a home for the elderly.

The November rain poured from leaden skies as Emma stood at the floor-to-ceiling windows at the end of the hospital hallway. The brown river snaked through the city like a glistening serpent, sluggish and filled with waste from a variety of industries that lined its banks. Tall buildings thrust their way into the churning gray clouds, the bare branches of trees lining the riverbank like dark crocheted lace. Overhead, black crows spread their wings and circled, dipping their wet wings to turn this way and that, coming so close to the window Emma could see their malevolent yellow eyes glaring through the rain.

Below her, pedestrians with bright umbrellas appeared to be moving flowers in brilliant shades of pink, yellow, and orange. Traffic splashed silently through the waterlogged streets, stopping and starting at various signals. Emma shivered, grateful for the warmth of the hospital, the lights and sturdy walls and roofs that kept her dry.

She turned to make her way back to Anna's room, feeling mildly discontented, as if the day was turning into a long gray parade of uneventful minutes. She smiled weakly at a passing doctor, said hello to a familiar nurse. She heard the sound of an IV pole being monitored, cringed at the annoying beeps. A man with wide shoulders and a familiar gait stepped off the elevators and looked in her direction, without seeing her. He bent to check his phone, then walked resolutely in her direction.

Matt! He stopped, recognized her. His eyes opened wide.

Emma was astonished at the strong wave of pleasure she felt at the sight of him. So soon. They had parted with the sense of it being a long length of time before they would meet again, if ever.

But here he was.

"What are you doing here?" she asked, extending her hand.

He had no words, didn't bother answering, simply took a few steps and folded her in his strong arms. Her chin rested against his shoulder. She felt the whisper of the dark curls, caught the scent of the woods and damp earth, felt his leather jacket, his massive hands on her slim waist.

She didn't pull away. In fact, it never crossed her mind to try and break free, couldn't care less what anyone thought. When his arms tightened, she slid hers around his heavy, powerful arms.

After too long, they both stepped back reluctantly. They held the embrace in their eyes, one knowing the other felt the same.

"My mother had gallbladder surgery," he said, quietly. "Why are you here?"

"The woman I'm caring for fell and broke her hip. She's recovering from surgery. Today we find out if she has to be put into . . . you know, a home. She'll go kicking and screaming, believe me." She paused, absorbing the fact that they'd run into each other in this strange way. Her thoughts seemed to be piling on top of each other. "Is your mom okay? Are you staying at home, then?"

"Yes, she's going to be fine. No, I'm still living in Lancaster."

Disappointment plunged its sharp saber into her spirits. So he hadn't taken anything seriously, none of the conversation about God or returning to his roots.

Emma became aware of the passersby looking in Matt's direction. Obviously, some of these nurses found him attractive, the way they threw backward glances after the first look. He seemed unaware of anything unusual.

She looked at him, really looked. Attractive, yes. But also absolutely unattainable. He had chosen to be English. He was off limits. They could be friends, but no more.

"Look," he said. "I'm going to visit my mother. Are you free to grab a bite later? Can we meet at, say, five or something?"

"I have a driver picking me up at seven."

"You can cancel, can't you? I'll take you home."

The thought of spending the evening with Matt was so refreshing that she smiled genuinely into his eyes without reserve. "Meet you here at the elevator at five."

He looked deep into her eyes and said, "I'll be here."

The afternoon crawled past at a snail's pace. Emma watched the almost imperceptible jerk of the long black hand of the clock moving from one to one fifteen. She had helped Anna with her lunch tray, rang for the nurses when Anna needed to use the bedpan, then ate her own bland chicken noodle soup and grilled cheese sandwich. She helped Anna put cream in her coffee, turned the television on, turned up the volume until a large nurse came in and told her that was not allowed. The nurse was then berated harshly by the small rotund woman in the bed who told her this was exactly what was wrong in America, everybody bossed each other around over the stupidest things, and she was having none of it, broken hip, toe, knee, or arm.

Emma looked out the window at the rain that was carried on the current of a strong wind, thought of long winter evenings at home, wondered what the future would hold for her. Well, you simply never could tell about anything, could you? She had been determined to rest, to pray, seek God's face and get it right, and fully intended to do just that. And here she and Matt were, thrown together again, here at the hospital of all places. *Huh*. She shook her head.

She just needed to trust God, let Him carry her whole load on His capable, almighty shoulders. She smiled to herself. How precious was this thing called faith? To believe in a higher existence, to believe your life was directed by none other than a living God who knew exactly what He was about.

She took a long time beneath the fluorescent lights in the bare, sterile bathroom, washing her face, combing her hair just right, wishing she had not worn the limp forest-green dress that had seen dozens of washings. Nothing to do about that now, so she turned to Anna's bedside and was met with a piercing look and a sour disposition.

"Either you fell in love with the doctor or you have a young man somewhere," she remarked drily.

"Neither one."

"Is too. No one spends that long in the bathroom without something up her sleeve. You look all spiffy."

Emma said nothing, which was a big mistake. Anna became absolutely determined to know why she had been in the bathroom so long.

"It's nothing. My hair was coming loose from the hairpins, and it was driving me crazy, that's all."

"I don't believe it."

"So what am I supposed to say?" Emma asked.

"The truth."

A gnarled finger was held up, waggled in her direction.

"You can't fool me, Emmaline Beiler. There's some young man coming to take you home. Am I right?"

Emma laughed, agreed, and said yes, there was.

Anna hooted like a screech owl, so pleased to have extracted this bit of information all by herself. When Emma gave her a goodnight hug, she cackled delightedly at her own cleverness.

"You'll tell me all about it, right?"

Emma said she would, then remembered the fact that no doctors had been there, nothing had been discussed about her impending release from the confines of the hospital. As she had feared, a trio of doctors appeared a few minutes before five, intent on allowing Emma to help with decisions.

She restrained herself from watching the clock and listened respectfully as the doctors informed them of the need for a stay at a facility for rehabilitation, that Anna's insurance would cover it, and if she had a trained caregiver she would be allowed to enter her own home after three weeks of rehab.

All this had taken almost thirty minutes, so when Anna managed to escape she found the hallway around the elevator empty. Her heart pounded with anxiety and disappointment as she realized that he'd waited, given up, and left.

His phone number was at home in her address book. For a wild moment she used all her brainpower, desperately trying to remember.

Three five two. Yes, that was right. But eight zero five nine? She hurried back to Anna's room, grateful to find her asleep, lifted the receiver of the telephone, and dialed with hands that shook so badly she could barely accomplish the task.

"Sorry, we cannot complete this call . . ."

"Sorry this call cannot be completed. Please try again."

On the fourth try, she got it right.

"Hullo?"

She sagged with relief when she heard the low voice, steadied herself to say, "Matt?"

"Yeah?"

"It's me, Emma. I'm sorry. The doctors came in to talk about Anna going to rehab, and I couldn't get away. Are you still in the hospital?"

Did she detect a choking sound, or was he merely clearing his throat? He did not answer immediately, and when he did his voice was strangely different.

"I'm actually in the parking lot, on my way to the car."

"I'll meet you at the front entrance."

She was breathless by the time she'd flown down the long corridors and burst out into the cold rain to find him, finally, his shoulders hunched inside his leather jacket, his hands stuffed in the pockets of his jeans.

He reached for her hand. She gave hers to him with so much will-ingness, and was led through the cold and the dark to a small white car.

"Whew," she breathed. "Wet, wet."

"Sure is. Here, let me get some heat in here."

His hand was much too close to her knee, so she drew it back. He laughed good-naturedly, then put the car in reverse, turned, and drove through the rain that still poured from the sky.

"Don't worry about your knee. I'm perfectly respectable."

"Of course you are. It was involuntary, to give you room to find the heater thingy."

"You sure?"

"I am."

But the car was much too small, and Emma was caught unpre-pared for the strange way her heart pounded, or the intimacy that made her catch her breath.

The only sounds were the hissing tires on wet asphalt, the swish of the windshield wipers, and the barely perceptible car radio.

"Where to, Emma?" he asked.

"Oh, I have no idea. I'm not well acquainted with Rock City."

"How about here? It's nothing impressive, but it'll be open late. A cup of coffee would be just great."

"Sounds good to me."

The coffee was liquid gold, the bowls of potato soup like ambro-sia, the table between them an annoying obstruction.

"I thought you'd changed your mind," Matt said, with a counte-nance so humble she had to restrain herself from touching his face to convey her feelings. She confessed the fourth sequence of numbers, the hopelessness of not having the number he had given her.

"You need your own phone."

She told him that she really didn't. The phones and computers were tearing at the Amish church like the fangs of an invisible wolf. She just needed her phone book, that's all.

"You wouldn't get a phone?"

"No."

"I do respect and admire that, you know."

"Well, I simply don't need to help the damage along, to help destroy the foundation of what our forefathers have suffered to bring the religious freedom we enjoy today."

"For me, though, the phone will be the hardest thing to give up."

"Have you counted the cost, then?" she asked.

"I am working on it."

They talked as the rain lashed against the windows of the diner. They shared memories of childhood, discovered mutual friends, found the time disappearing at a surprising rate.

"You think your parents will worry?"

"I left them a message. But yeah, I should go, probably. I know my mother does not sleep well until I arrive."

He helped her with her coat, paid the bill, and put her in the car. They were quiet now, but with a new companionable silence, a relaxed knowing.

When they peeled up to the sidewalk, the house was dark, every window glistening with rain. The trees in the backyard appeared to be waving skeletal fingers, black and cold.

Emma shivered.

"So this is goodbye?" he asked quietly.

"Matt, it's up to you. I'll be honest. I'm right here. I'm not going anywhere. But I can't think about dating until . . . until you decide if you're returning to your roots."

He nodded. "So you won't change? That's not an option?"

"I'm sorry, but no. I'm committed to Christ and to the church, so I plan on staying steadfast till the day I die. It really is up to you. If it's too depressing for you to change your way of life, then I'll move on."

She was enormously grateful for the dark interior of the car to conceal the way her face heated up.

He gave a low laugh, then turned sideways in the driver's seat, resting his elbow on the steering wheel.

"Look at me, Emma."

She would not obey, afraid of the consequences. So slowly, he lifted a hand to her face and gently turned it. He cupped her chin, then tilted his own face just right and leaned softly forward until his mouth found hers, as lightly as a whisper.

He drew back, and when she leaned forward ever so slightly, he whispered her name, still gentle and calm. She found his eyes, glistening with emotion, before he found her mouth for the second time, claimed it with his own, and Emma was whirled away into a place where she had never been. Not with Sam King and certainly not with Ben.

This was entirely different. It was as natural and as right as the moon's ascension into a cloudless night, as real as the flight of two turtledoves. There was a dimension of concern and caring, the promise of better things than a life lived alone.

"Matt, Matt . . . I . . ."

She put a hand to his chest, that wide solid space.

He said nothing, merely sat and waited until she spoke.

"If you still feel I'm worth it, I'll wait."

She was unprepared for the response, which was a long trembling intake of breath, before tears trembled on the edge of his thick lashes.

She reached out to wipe them away, and with a low sound he held her tightly against him, whispering words she could not comprehend.

"Emma."

Only her name, but a crown was placed on her head.

"You know I'm not worthy of you. You don't know me at all."

"I might not, but I know enough to have the confidence to give it a whirl."

"Thank you."

"So, it's settled, then, right? We'll keep in touch, see how it goes. And I'll be right here in little old Crawford County while you go back to Lancaster County and . . ."

He shook his head.

"I don't know, Emma. It will be too weird. Giving up all of this," He waved his hand across the car's interior.

"It will be weird. But we'll give it time."

"Years? Months?"

"It's up to you."

And so began the winter. The days were long and dreary, the only thing to look forward to the phone calls from Matt. She missed her time with Anna, but instead spent her days at home with normal household chores, sewing, quilting, learning the art of appliqué. But she was restless, her sharp mind bored.

Anna came home after Christmas, the rehab having gone poorly, which lengthened her stay considerably. She sat in her old green recliner with the lace doilies draped across the arms and proceeded to outline every detail of each therapist's failures, the doctor's inadequate education, and the rest of the residents' stupidity.

"It's torture, that's all it is. It doesn't matter how much you yell or carry on, they ignore you and you have to do what they say. And the tea?" She spat. "Puh. Like dishwater, it was."

Emma smiled, told her she'd heard plenty about rehab, but it was indeed very necessary for someone who needed to strengthen limbs.

"I don't need strong hips. My legs carry me to the table and the bathroom and back again. All that stretching and pedaling was absolutely unnecessary. It's a money racket."

She shook her little fist into the air.

Her indignant displays decreased as the winter progressed, and her sense of humor nearly disappeared. Emma sensed a weakening, an overall lethargy that had not been evident before, so she called her doctor, who advised weekly visits from the hospice center. As the cold strengthened in mid-January, Anna mostly slept the day away, waving a tired hand at her dinner tray, refusing the many strong cups of black tea.

At home, Emma rested over the weekend, while the visiting nurse took over, allowing her time to restore her spirits before entering

Anna's house the following Monday. She seldom saw Elvin or Eva, but found out through her mother that Eva would be having another little one in April.

"Why don't you visit them more often?" her mother asked, sitting at the kitchen table with a bowl of hardboiled eggs, breaking the shells with her thumb.

"Oh, I don't know. I guess since I'm still single and she's a mother with a life of her own, we just don't have that much in common."

"That doesn't sound right. I think it's something else," her mother said, throwing another slippery white egg in a bowl.

"What are they for?" Emma asked.

"Church."

Most members brought a dish to church to share, along with bread, peanut butter spread, or spreadable cheese.

Occasionally, as a treat, someone would bring seasoned pretzels or red beet eggs that would be eaten with the usual lunch of coffee and snitz pies, which were pies made of dried apples, apple butter and applesauce, brown sugar, and cinnamon.

"You're always taking church food," Emma commented.

"Oh, it's what I do. I'd feel empty-handed going to church without something."

Sally and Amanda giggled together in the playroom, piecing a puzzle on the child's table. They sat in the glow of the winter sun, their blond heads like golden halos, their red dresses matching the stiff blooming poinsettias on the sewing machine top.

"Hey, girlies. You want an egg?" their mother called.

Sally gasped and came running, but Amanda wrinkled her nose.

"Eggs are not good," she said in a very sure voice.

"Sally likes them."

"Good for her."

Emma caught her mother's eye and they shared a smile. Sometimes, at moments like this, Emma felt as if she could burst with her secret, and yet was too unprepared, too vulnerable to be on the receiving end of their disapproval, their worries and senseless anxieties. Parents were supportive until something a tiny bit out of the ordinary was placed in their lives, and it was blown all out of proportion, as Matt would surely be. He just would not be safe enough or Amish enough to suit their specifications, and certainly not her sisters'. Matt was the reason she didn't spend more time with Eva, too. Although Eva would be thrilled to learn she and Matt were still speaking, she would blow it all out of proportion the other way, planning their wedding and naming their children, and Emma wasn't ready for that, either. For now, she needed to keep quiet about Matt.

She attended church services on a neighboring farm, the people hurrying into the house in the freezing wind, divesting themselves of black shawls and bonnets before rubbing their hands gratefully in the heat of a coal stove in the laundry room. The sermon was inspired, but she kept drifting into a half-awake state that contained the voice of the minister, but not much comprehension. She would awaken with guilt and keep her eyes focused and alert, before drifting off again.

It was the small amount of deep restful sleep she received during the week, with Anna becoming increasingly demanding and restless. Some nights Emma declared she would no longer allow this, but Anna would not accept anyone other than Emma since her fall. Emma had committed to Anna's full-time care, except on the weekends, but it was taking a toll on her strength.

Her friend Esther asked her to go along to the youth's gathering, followed by the hymn singing. The cold, the long ride in a less-than-accommodating carriage, plus the boring wintertime supper get-together was certainly not something she looked forward to, but she relented, being frightened of her own "old maid" style. She was getting old, dried up, almost thirty, she reminded herself.

And so she went, dressed in a pretty shade of lavender, and played so many games of Rook she felt like a cawing black bird herself. She ate two plates piled with food for supper, then became so sleepy she seriously considered going upstairs and finding an empty guest room. Instead, she endured the silly flirtations of young men much her junior, felt like their mother, and wished them out of the room. She sang the German hymns, yawned in between, and was grateful when Esther came to tell her it was time to go.

She realized then, that rumschpringa was indeed a thing of the past. She would never again feel that thrill of being around different young men, enjoying the attention of being the pretty girl in the room, the banal words and empty giggles and batting of eyelashes. This revelation filled her with a new longing for Matt. Matt was all the things these young men were not—he was mature, having lived some really hard things and come through them kinder and wiser. He was hardworking, thoughtful, and interested in her ideas and opinions.

She stopped herself there. He lacked one thing that these other young men did have, and that was his faith. Unless he was willing to commit to the church, she would not—could not—let herself pine for him. She'd be a fool to let her heart go there, only to be broken yet again. This time she was determined to take one day at a time, trusting that God's timing was better than her own.

She kept his letters, of which there had only been two. Her mother had not noticed either, which was unbelievable, really. And only once had she been caught on the phone with him, when the little girls came crashing into the office looking for a sled, but they didn't seem to care who she was talking to. Mostly Emma and Matt spoke while she was at Anna's house, late in the evening after Anna was fast asleep. She told him not to leave messages at her home, a request he seemed to understand. They talked about their work, their families, ideas and opinions. But rarely did they speak of his faith. Emma knew better than to push him. He had to come to his own conclusions in his own time, and for now at least, she would wait as contently as possible.

CHAPTER 20

MONDAY MORNING BROUGHT A FRESH OUTLOOK, AN INCREASE IN HER energy. Emma was determined to throw herself into the care of the elderly woman who was experiencing many hours of discomfort now. Anna's legs were restless, her incision was increasingly itchy, and her breathing became steadily more labored as time went on.

Emma swept the snow off her boots with the corn broom that hung on its peg beside the front door, then let herself into the living room as quietly as possible. The overnight nurse was awakened and on her feet, smiling as she put a forefinger to her lips.

"She's asleep," she whispered.

"No, I am not," came from the recliner. "Everybody says I'm sleeping when I'm resting my eyes."

"Good morning," Emma said softly, bending to kiss the soft leathery cheek. Up came the two arms, weak and frail, to pat Emma's back, with a resounding "Glad to have you back, sweetie."

"It's good to be here."

Emma patted the heaving shoulder, straightened the collar on her housecoat.

"You go ahead and rest your eyes, okay?"

Anna nodded, and was instantly asleep.

"So how is she?" Emma mouthed, spreading her hands and lifting her shoulders.

"I'm just fine," came the strident voice from the recliner.

"Here. Someone get over here and take the doilies off these arms. They're nothing but a nuisance. Don't throw them in the trash. Put them in the washer with the whites, but not in the dryer. They have to be air dried. There's a bottle of blueing under the sink, you need to put that in the rinse water. Liquid starch to soak them in before ironing."

Her voice was being punctuated by small gasps as her lungs struggled to supply the necessary oxygen.

The caregiver from hospice looked at Emma and they shared a grin before she let herself out. Emma carried out the directions Anna had given her and returned to the living room to find Anna sound asleep this time.

So she went about her Monday duties, which weren't much—a few dishes to wash, a bit of ironing, checking the refrigerator for milk or eggs.

She found herself distracted, easily bored, pacing restlessly from room to room.

What if Anna passed away? What would she do next? She thought of Matt, imagined him returning to the community, moving in with his parents again. After all this time, would it be possible?

She was determined to stay patient, to keep herself from asking too many questions, give him all the time he would need to reconcile himself to the Amish church.

Did it have to be the Amish church? She could leave to join him, attend any of the churches that dotted the land from one end of Pennsylvania to the other. There were Christians of all kinds, none necessarily better than another. What was keeping her from leaving?

Before the thought was completed, she knew the price would be far too high, leaving everything she had ever known. She could never place that kind of deep and lasting sorrow on her parents' shoulders, then live with the guilt of having done just that.

Baptism into the Amish church was no trifling thing, with the solemn promises made to God and to man. It was marriage, of sorts, and leaving was as unthinkable as divorce, a true horror in the minds of the plain sect, their conservative shoulders shuddering at the mere thought of it.

It was totally forbidden. To leave the Amish way of life, to enter the mainstream, was viewed as a spiritual adultery by the steadfast members of the plain people. It was better to stay, to honor her conservative parents, to bring them joy, so that the days would be long in the land in which she lived.

But what if, in the end, Matt simply could not trade his truck, his job, his life for one he had completely denounced, to return to what he had condemned? Would it be easier for her to leave the church than it would be for him to return to it?

But how could she disobey parents who loved her so deeply, who cared for her from the time she was born? To disobey them would be a disobedience to God, which was a blatant, in your face, transgression.

Yet people did it. Young families were leaving almost weekly. Young men chose to keep their vehicles and joined a liberal church where such things were allowed. The parents cried, pleaded, and sometimes turned against their own offspring with a bitterness that tore their hearts into unhealthy shreds, left them dry and aching with sorrow.

Emma sat toying with a buttered muffin, her coffee gone cold, a sickening grip taking her appetite. If her mother knew how very close she had come to telling Matt she would make it easier for him and break away from tradition herself . . .

And then Matt stopped calling and stopped returning her calls. A week passed, then two, then three. She checked messages obsessively, sat by the phone imagining it would ring. She was tempted to purchase a cell phone, send him her number. Where was he, and why did he try to stay away? Just like Ben. The thought made her feel ill, her stomach clenched.

Anna Gilbert had roused her stubborn will and was walking around the house again, railing against the food Emma cooked, the smell of the bathroom cleaner, the unnecessary noise Emma made when she washed dishes, and of late, she was using too much detergent when she did a load of whites. Emma took it all with an absentminded good humor, her thoughts far away as she peeled carrots for the vegetable soup she was making, listening to the dripping of the water from the eaves as the snow melted on the south side of the house.

"I'm itchy. My underpants make me itchy," Anna said with all the force she could muster from her worn-out lungs.

"Alright," Emma said cheerfully. "I'll use only half a cap instead of a full one."

"Don't put too many carrots in the soup. They look like pennies when they float around in tomato sauce."

"I can grate them if you want me to."

"What? Of course not. I don't want sawdust in my soup. I hate carrots, doesn't matter how they're cut."

"Well then, we won't put any in the soup."

She wrapped the carrot in plastic wrap, placed it in the drawer of the refrigerator and began to peel potatoes. She hummed as she worked, the sun spreading a new warmth as the water dripped on the back patio.

She imagined this cute house being her own. The arborvitae in the backyard would be a perfect backdrop for a garden shed, with stone walkways and all sorts of raised beds filled with vegetables and herbs. Flowers and bushes everywhere.

Only a few miles from home, she could visit her mother easily, either with a horse and buggy or a scooter. She tried to picture Matt living there with her, but the thought sent an ache to her heart that was too much to handle.

"That is enough potatoes. Too many potatoes in vegetable soup makes it starchy. I can't have all that starch."

Anna had settled herself in the living room, gasping for breath as she did so, and Emma had no idea she knew how many potatoes were going into the soup.

"You have eyes in the back of your head," she called out.

"I do, don't I?" Anna cackled, pleased to prove herself one step ahead of Emma, no matter her age or her state of health.

The vegetable soup filled the house with a pleasant aroma, and when it was ladled into ceramic soup bowls, with a small dish of saltines, one of applesauce, and another of the sour pickles Anna loved so much, she ate with a good appetite, but was stingy with her praise.

"Too much beef broth," she growled. "It's greasy across the top." But she ate three helpings.

Valentine's Day came and went, leaving Emma harboring a certain sad wistfulness. She had never felt more alone.

Anna continued her streak of good health, feisty now, with the ability to push the wheeled walker around the house. By the week's end, she told the hospice caregiver not to come anymore. She could stay by herself for the weekends, and no one was going to change her mind, either.

"You can't do that," Emma gasped.

"I can and I will."

Hospice could get in trouble for leaving her alone, they told her, but nothing made any difference. From Saturday night to Monday morning she was on her own, absolutely capable and without a problem.

Emma told her she would camp out in her backyard, but was met with hoots of mirth.

"I'll be fine. You just go on home, dearie."

There were tears in Anna's eyes as Emma bent to hug her goodbye, so Emma patted her shoulder, told her she loved her, and let herself out the door, pulling it softly behind her.

The gray days of February were accented by lowering clouds that roiled in the sky without expelling any rain. Damp and cold, with half-melted snowbanks pocked with salt and gravel like bad acne, mud and flat brown grass that lay by the side of the road like dejection in vegetable form.

She had hoped for a message, a letter, a card for Valentine's Day, even a small note of remembrance, but there was nothing. Her little sisters had a head cold and a high fever. Her mother had cut her thumb on a piece of broken glass so badly that she had four stitches put in at the local trauma center. And her father was in an ill temper, having lost his best driving horse to colic, the result of a gate left open in the barn.

Emma noticed the stickiness of the kitchen floor, the unwashed dishes, the laundry that had not been folded, asked where Dena was in clipped tones that gave away her disapproval.

"Now don't you come home in a mood," her mother warned. "Dena works at market on Saturday, remember?"

"Market closes at three."

"Four. She doesn't get home until six. And now she's upstairs getting ready to go out."

Emma marched up the stairs, doing nothing to soften her footsteps, went to Dena's room and banged on the door.

"What?" Dena yelled.

"Let me in."

"It's not locked."

Emma let herself in to find Dena in front of a full-length mirror, adjusting the hem of her dress, which hung very close to the soles of her shoes. The color was a shrieking shade of orange, a *verboten* color.

There was a pair of Converse sneakers, still in the box, thrown across her bed, along with the contents of a purse that could have carried a full-grown dog if the need arose.

"Hi!" she said brightly. "I didn't know you were home."

"Yeah well, I usually come home on Saturday. What is up with the messy house? Why couldn't you wash dishes, at least? Mom cut her thumb, you know."

"So? She collected my money easily enough with that busted thumb, so she can do her own dishes."

Dena turned from left to right before pulling a black sweatshirt over her head, facing the mirror and smoothing the sides over her hips.

"Where's your apron?" Emma barked.

"I'm not wearing one. We're going bowling."

"What? Seriously, Dena, who do you think you are? Do you think Mam is going to let you out with that awful dress and no apron?"

Dena whirled to face her, her hands on her hips.

"You're not my mother, or my fashion police. I'm sixteen now and I can do anything I want."

Emma picked up the shoes, raised an eyebrow.

"Cool, aren't they? The guys love girls in Converse sneakers."

"Dena . . . who made your dress?"

"My friend Kaitlyn."

"Who is she?"

"You don't know her."

"Is she from around here?"

"Course. Elmer King's Kaitlyn. Look, I hafta hurry, okay? I'm not in the mood to be questioned, so bug off."

With an arrogant shake of her hips, she turned to spritz cologne, then leaned in to the mirror, holding the battery lamp above her head as she turned from left to right, checking the condition of her hair.

Slowly Emma sat down on the bed, a weary sigh escaping her. She was dumbfounded. When had her little sister turned into this weird orange disaster she didn't even recognize?

"Dena," she said quietly.

"Hmm?"

"Don't you think it's time to slow down? Surely Mam and Dat don't want to see you leave the house in that dress, without an apron? And those shoes . . ."

Dena tossed her head, then stuck her face close to Emma's.

"I told you to bug off. Leave me alone."

Emma left the room. With a heart already filled with disappointment, she felt a crushing sensation in her chest as she filled a bucket with soapy water to wipe the kitchen floor. She did dishes afterward, until every countertop was empty and gleaming, then tackled the huge basket of unfolded laundry, a grim slash where her normally cheerful mouth would have been.

True to her word, Dena had left with no resistance from her parents, one with his nose in a book, the other drowsy from the Tylenol with codeine for her pain.

It was almost eleven when she fell into bed, waking to find the steely gray light of another morning, another Sunday at home, with no prospects of anything ever changing.

She read passages from her Bible, the story of the traveler who had been helped by the good Samaritan, and another chapter in John about the truth of the gospel. She found a sense of wellness, the always new spiritual truth written in the sacred text, so she was better prepared to meet the day and the undoubted challenges she would face.

Her own disappointments rode her shoulders like a thick wet shawl, chafing and miserable, but she would place her trust in God and be content to live among those she loved, and be thankful, above everything.

Her mother was bravely spreading slices of bacon on a jelly roll pan, wincing with each movement of her swollen thumb.

"Here, Mam. You sit down. I'll get you a cup of coffee."

Emma was all brisk efficiency, finishing breakfast, bringing a tray to Sally and Amanda, combing their hair before peeling it back into tight ponytails. They wrinkled their noses at everything except the pieces of fruit, small orange sections and grapes.

Her father thanked her for the breakfast, said it was like Mam's. Emma looked at him appreciatively, her eyes smiling over her coffee cup.

"I get plenty of practice, cooking for Anna."

"You must. I don't remember you being able to make pancakes like that," her father told her.

"Oh, she taught me. She'd never use boxed pancake mix."

And then she told them about Anna being on her own for the weekend, and how unsettled she felt, but those were her wishes, so she honored them.

"Will you stay on there until she passes," her father asked.

"What else would I do?" she asked.

"I suppose."

Her mother cleared her throat. The silence hung awkwardly.

"I know. You'd love to know if there are any marriage prospects."

"Oh no, no," her mother said, quickly righting the cart that had already spilled its contents.

"Come on, Mam. You know it's true."

"So what about this Ben? Never heard from him again, have you?"

"Ben? What Ben?"

She laughed a little, and then found herself telling them everything. She launched into a vivid account of her camping trip with Elvin and Eva, the return to the Outer Banks and the subsequent revelation of Ben's liberties with Kathy, the night with Matt.

Her mother literally shivered.

"Emma!"

"But Mam . . ."

"Emma!" she repeated.

"See, this is why I don't tell you anything. You're going to think Matt is horrible and untrustworthy because he left the Amish. He left when he found out his parents had basically lied to him, not telling him he was adopted."

"Right there is my first warning flag," her mother said forcefully, her eyes bright with passion. "No parent is perfect. That doesn't mean you go English. It's a bad sign. A bad start."

She spread her lips in a thin line of disapproval, that rock hard stance that left nothing to chance. Her father leaned back in his chair, saying "Why can't you date a normal fellow?"

"Then find me one, Dat. In all of Crawford County, this little settlement in the middle of nowhere with not one young man who would be mildly interested in an almost thirty-year-old."

He pursed his lips, then raked a hand through his hair.

"I believe there would be plenty. However, they know their attentions would hardly be appreciated."

"Who? Just tell me who." Emma growled.

Her mother changed the subject, before her father came up with an answer.

Like a small nervous bird, her mother hopped from one question to another, firing them off with quick precision.

Who were the adoptive parents?

On receiving this bit of information, both eyebrows were raised on her mother's face, her father's countenance changed from displeasure to surprise, and he gave a low whistle.

"I know them," he said. "I remember when they adopted him. They lived in our '*nāva dale.*' Oh, it was quite the talk of the town for a while, this black-haired boy with so many curls."

"It is, indeed, a small world if you're Amish," her mother said, giving a low laugh.

"We all live in one fish bowl," Emma said sourly.

"Not quite."

"So, are you dating?" This from her mother, who was loading her machine gun for another round, ready to fire questions.

"No. We are not. He is . . . I guess you would say, checking to see if he can make it. I mean, returning to the Amish. He's thirty-five years old, mind you, so he has a few years under his belt."

"It won't happen. How could it? It never works out."

Her mother's pessimism left Emma with all the oxygen taken out of her lungs. For a moment, the dreary kitchen faded away and she actually thought she might faint.

"He was raised Amish," her father reminded her.

"Doesn't make a difference," her mother answered, shaking her head with an air of dismissal.

"Well, I'd say give it another year or two," her father said, then left the table to go out and check on Benjamin and Lloyd, who were in charge of doing the feeding on the Sunday there were no church services, leaving Emma with her stern-lipped mother and absolutely no hope of ever finding approval, the word "English" branded into her conscience with a red-hot iron.

CHAPTER 21

EMMA FOUND THE DOOR TO ANNA'S HOUSE UNLOCKED, BUT THERE WAS NO welcoming call. She slowly opened the door, called a bit louder, but the only sound was the hum of the refrigerator, the metallic ticking of the old grandfather's clock in the dining room.

"Anna?"

The recliner was empty, the usual array of Vaseline, cough drops, pills, hand lotion, and reading material carefully set in order. The house did not smell of cooking odors, only a faint lilac scent.

Her heart was pounding as she opened the door to the bedroom, and she was already crying when she found her beloved old friend curled in a fetal position. Slowly, she bent and placed a hand on her cold shoulder, smoothed back the silver white hair as tear drops fell on the waxen cheeks.

"Goodbye, Anna."

As she wept quietly, she realized Anna had known the end was near, and wanted to be alone. She had her ways, and her faith. She would have faced death with the same bravado she faced everything else, bless her heart. Emma had no reason to believe anything but the fact that Anna had met her Savior, the One on the cross, the One whom she trusted with the same feisty life she had lived fully.

There was a scattering of friends and acquaintances at her visitation, and her funeral. The obituary appeared in the daily paper, but very little could be written about her, with her extended family mostly in Russia or surrounding countries.

Emma cleaned her house, set out cupcakes and small sandwiches, bowls of potato chips and pretzels with cheese. Her mother brought a casserole and a kettle of chicken corn soup, with a reluctant Dena in tow, pouting at the prospect of being at this crazy old lady's house.

The small house filled up with Anna's friends, the cashier at the Rexall drugstore, the nurses from her family doctor, old friends who had gone out to eat with her, who had whooped and hollered and laughed at her offbeat sense of humor, gladly accepted her offer to pay for their dinner, and who were blessed to have known her.

Dena offered them tea or coffee, with Emma bearing a tray of delicate tea cups. They were both dressed in the traditional funeral black, with the white head coverings, the strings tied neatly in front.

They were examined through various bifocals, eager eyes that appeared birdlike behind rolls of flesh, their lips pursed in consideration of these Amish girls.

"Now, which one was Anna's care person?" the first one asked.

"It was me," Emma said softly.

"You? Is this your sister?"

"Yes."

"I'm Dena," she informed them.

"Let it be known, you did a wonderful job."

Up came a moist hand that clasped Emma's forearm, followed by the sharp intake of breath that preceded a sob. Emma clutched the tray tightly, thinking of the porcelain teacups.

"She was a character, you know."

Emma smiled and nodded. "She certainly was."

"Who is going to get her possessions?" the lady asked, dabbing at her eyes with the corner of her handkerchief.

Every eye was turned in her direction, as bright as small flashlights, anxious to know if they would be the recipient of one valuable thing, of which there were hardly any.

"I have no idea. She never spoke about such things, really."

"Does she have a will written up? You know, a legal document that will legally dispose of her worldly goods?"

"Oh now, Malverda, stop digging for gold. She never mentioned a word about her monetary worth, so let it go. We're here to celebrate her life, and it was a long good one."

Emma was stopped at the door by a frightening lawyer who loomed above her like some somber apparition of doomsday.

"Miss Beiler, I gather?"

"Yes."

"Tomorrow at two o'clock in the afternoon, I have a half hour set aside for the reading of Anastasia Gilbert's will."

"Oh. Do I need to be there?"

"I assumed you knew."

"No."

"I believe you and the gardener."

Confused, Anna looked up, way up, to meet eyes that were surprisingly kind.

"Gardener? I don't believe there was a gardener."

"Someone who cared for her grounds?"

"Grounds? There is only the small area surrounding the house."

"You will find out tomorrow, then."

She and Dena worked side by side, washing dishes, mopping floors, setting the small house in order before they locked the doors and left the house.

The hills and wooded ridges of Crawford County were covered in a thick mace of gray and black branches, the floor beneath them coated with the dead undergrowth and a thick carpet of leaves that would decompose into the soil till another growth, another fall would replace them. Starlings sat on telephone wires, squawking their voracious discontent before flapping busily into the distance.

The clouds hung thick and gray, without a breeze, the air heavy with the residue of the late morning frost. On days such as this, when the still air claimed its hold on winter, pushed back the hope of spring, Emma struggled to keep a deep sense of despair at bay. How was she to make sense of her world, with doors opening and closing so swiftly? When one occupation was rudely snatched out of her grasp, only to be led to another, which was taken away again so soon?

She had closed the door and turned the key on being a teacher and was confronted with the prospect of being a nanny, a worthwhile and very lucrative position, one she was proud to hold. But that was slammed in her face by none other than the amorous Ben in all his untruthful sweet-talking. A paid caregiver was as worthy a title, and here again, the door was closed none too gently by her friend Anna's death.

Dena was driving, as usual, hanging on to the spirited horse with her strong young arms, applying the brakes now as they made their way down Fogel's Hill.

"Ease up on his speed," Emma directed. "You know he stumbles easily."

"You wanna drive?" Dena asked, handing the reins to her.

"No, of course not. Just slow him down. Didn't Dad ever tell you it's hard on a horse's feet to run downhill with any amount of speed?"

Dena shook her head.

"Dad doesn't talk to me the way he talks to you. He barely talks to me, ever."

From the backseat came the strident voice of their mother, squeezed in amid various boxes of leftover sandwiches and pastries.

"Dena, going around with that air of indignation is why he won't say much. You're so sixteen going on eighty."

Emma burst out laughing, loving every minute of her mother's unusual outburst.

"About time, Mam," she applauded, clapping her hands.

Dena ignored both of them, concentrating on her driving skills as they reached the bottom of the ridge, steadily following the country road as it wound in and out of woodlots and barren fields that lay brown and dormant.

"I hate February," announced Dena.

"Hate is a strong word."

"I do hate it. There's not enough snow to make the world look fresh and clean, not cold enough to go ice skating, and not warm enough to play volleyball, or baseball, or anything."

"March is just around the corner," Mam said evenly, her voice barely tolerating the young daughter's sense of discontent.

The horse's gait picked up as they turned right onto the road that wound its way past their farm. He knew he was arriving home where a good feeding of oats and corn with a nice block of timothy hay awaited him, so he tugged at the reins as his speed increased.

"Dena," came the expected warning from the back seat.

"I have him under control," she called back, but she loosened the reins to wrap them around the palms of her hands for better discipline of the energized driving horse.

"Need help?" Emma offered.

"I got it," Dena replied, but her arms were stretched out, the pressure from the bit in the horse's mouth inducing all her strength.

They took the turn at the driveway with a sliding of steel wheels on gravel, causing a slight squeak of fear from the back seat.

The house and barn appeared like a harbor, a haven for travelers, a place called home, nestled between wooded ridges like a colorful bosom of rest.

What was there to worry about on a gray, frosty day in February when she rode in a buggy with her mother and sister? Doors would open and close in her life, yet there remained one true thing. God on His throne, home would always be tucked in these hills, and trust was the foundation of her wellbeing.

She hired a driver to take her to the lawyer's office, not wanting to drive through the bustling streets punctuated by red lights and cross traffic with a horse who sometimes bolted at an approaching truck.

She was ushered into a luxurious office that smelled of fine leather and Scott's Liquid Gold, that moisturizing furniture preservative that had its own distinctive odor. An aging gentleman rose to greet her, dressed in clean overalls and a Carhartt jacket, his bill cap held self-consciously in the opposite hand from the one he extended.

"Good afternoon, young lady." His voice was like a rusty pipe.

"Hello. You must be the gardener?"

"I am Clyde. Clyde Armstrong. I worked for the Washingers when Anna was married to Thomas, and then I worked for them when she married William Gilbert. Wonderful people."

"Yes, of course. I never met the husbands. Either one, of course. I knew Anna for only a short time."

"Yes, yes," Clyde shook her head, affirming her words.

The lawyer hurried in, made the proper introductions before immediately applying himself to the job at hand, opening a file, shuffling papers before sliding his glasses down his nose and clearing his throat.

Emma sat, stunned and shaken after the reading of Anastasia's last will and testament.

Anna had owned a sprawling estate in Alexandria, Virginia. A breathtaking amount would be gathered from the sale of it, which would be divided equally between the gardener, Clyde Armstrong, and the caregiver, Emma Beiler. The small house on an acre of ground would be deeded to Emma Beiler on the day of this reading, with both vehicles, the Cadillac and BMW, going to Clyde.

The remainder of the estate, which was vast, would be presented to John Hopkins University Hospital and Penn State University.

Emma kept her eyes downcast, her heart pounding, her hands knotted into fists.

"There is no mistake?" she asked, in a voice bereft of strength. The lawyer shook his head, said no, there wasn't.

Clyde Armstrong reached over and took her hand, squeezed it gently with his own dry gnarled, work calloused one, and said, simply, "Be thankful."

The lawyer wasted no time before exiting, leaving the promise of signing documents and a deposit made in their accounts, and was gone.

Emma found her knees without strength, had to sit back down after leaving her chair. Clyde reminded her to give ten percent to the Lord, as he surely would, then his old mouth trembled and wobbled as tears coursed down his withered cheeks.

"Forty-two years of love. It wasn't work. It wasn't a job. I loved every minute of it. Mowing and digging and trimming. I planted, washed windows, replaced things, built things. My heart was content with the wages I earned. My children grew up, went to college on scholarships, my Barbara never needed a job. They were good to me. Everyone was always good to me, and now I'm blessed with all this money I'll never know how to spend."

Emma returned his clasped hand with pressure of his own.

"I don't know what to say."

"It's a bit of a shock, I know. But praise God. I'll retire, buy my own place, with my own garden. I'll putter around in it till God calls me home."

"I guess I own a house, too." It felt unbelievable, saying that.

"Not just a house," Clyde chuckled.

They exchanged addresses and phone numbers, then said heartfelt goodbyes. Emma walked down the steps and to the waiting vehicle as if she was in a dream and some unexpected noise would break the quality of it.

At home, it was bedlam, her father trying to insert words of wisdom, her mother absolutely sure she would go "English" with all that money, and what earthly good could ever come of it? This was said with her eyebrows raised and her mouth in a tight line of anxiety that bade no well-wishing for anyone within eyesight, not even the family dog or the slinking barn cats.

Dena said she was going to buy a car, a green Jeep with the top down and drive it to California to become a surfer. Her father eyed her with distaste, opened his mouth and closed it, before sinking wearily into a chair. Her mother gave up collecting her wits to cook a decent meal, made a stack of pancakes and scrapple for supper, served sliced bananas and peanut butter to make up for the unhealthy fare, then came down with a whopping migraine and went to bed.

Steven and Abram came home from work, were incorporated into the chaos, and responded with raised eyebrows that hovered over rounded, disbelieving eyes and mouths opened with astonishment. They too planned the lucrative maneuver of purchasing the best Friesian stallion in the world, said they would raise colts of world renown, or perhaps open a welding shop to make the most competitive railing anywhere.

Dena told them the stallion would die and they couldn't weld a stitch, which led to a whole new level of contention, till their father put a stop to it, saying no one was going anywhere or doing anything without Emma's consent, and if she knew what was good for her, she'd put the money away to draw interest, to which Emma agreed and everyone eventually ran out of steam and fizzled off to their showers and beds.

In the morning, a whole new chapter began, with her mother coming to the realization that this was *unfadient gelt*, unearned money. She frittered away as they washed the breakfast dishes, spouting off Bible verses and dire premonitions sprinkled with myths and old wives tales.

"It's like gambling," she said. "It's forbidden! Suddenly there is this pile of money you did nothing to earn, this little house dumped in your lap, and Lord knows what will happen. You might get cancer or something if God truly does not want you to have this *unfadient gelt*."

"Mam!" Emma shrieked, her hands over her ears. "You are so Amish!"

"What's that supposed to mean?" Mam looked shocked, hurt, confused.

"So wary of everything. So sure everything comes with a warning label. Perhaps, Mother, this is a gift from God. And did it ever occur to you that this might not mean very much to me? That I would rather be happily married with children than anything else? Do you think Esther and Ruth 'earned' their good husbands, and I just haven't earned one yet?"

"I'm sorry."

"Don't be sorry. Just stop. Okay? We don't get to choose which blessings God gives us."

Spring was a soft, colorful benediction, a blessing that rode in on a warm breeze and gentle rain. Smiling daffodils and laughing tulips swayed and danced in the breezes. Lawnmowers buzzed across arrogant growth of bold green grass, leaf blowers and rakes made short work of winter's leftover debris, brown leaves that had been abused by strong winds, harsh snow banks, and a violent spray of salt and calcium to melt ice on the treacherous country roads.

Emma had never been happier. The small green house was a little haven, a place to make her very own. The necessary papers had been signed, the amount put in a trust fund, and the small green house was hers to enjoy.

She hired contractors, after her father's advice. He said he was a farmer, not a carpenter, but that she should give Steve and Abram a chance, which she did.

The green siding was removed and replaced with dark gray, with wide white trim around the newly installed, larger windows. The front porch posts and steps were replaced, stone laid on the front walls and down the steps. Partitions were removed, new plumbing and wiring put in, old carpet taken away to reveal narrow boards of hardwood.

All this took up Emma's time, her energy and thoughts. Matt was fading from her mind all through the summer, like a painting exposed to the elements too long. He was still in her heart, and often in her mind, but a relationship unattended will fade away of its own accord, especially when the nurturing is directed to another project. She stopped checking voicemail, the letter box at the end of the driveway held no excitement.

But she knew that what they had shared had been real. The love had been built of honor and respect, not merely attraction, and sometimes when she allowed it, a rush of anguish and lost hope overwhelmed her.

The brothers persuaded her to build a screened-in porch with a stamped concrete floor, build a brick walkway to a garden shed a few steps down, surrounding it with trees, shrubs, and flowers.

"That could wait, couldn't it?" she asked.

"Why wait? It'll be done before the snow flies," they answered, eager to keep collecting the bonus wages they made by working every evening and on Saturday.

So Emma agreed, but only after the new cabinets were installed and the painting finished.

The interior of the little house now held an open floor plan, with freshly painted white woodwork and doors, soft beige walls and the original hardwood flooring. She had white kitchen cabinets with a small island, a large, low window above the sink, and she was absolutely thrilled with the results.

Her family helped her move in, lingered in the glow of a golden autumn afternoon before making their way home across the ridges and fields between them. Dena threatened to run away from home, go against her parents' wishes and live with Emma, but finally compromised on just spending most of her weekends at the little house.

The first night Emma stayed there by herself, every popping sound, every creak or rattle startled her into a rigid state of wakefulness. She checked the lock on the front door twice, stopped to watch the shadows created by the pine trees in the side yard, the moon sailing uninhibited across a starry sky, shivered, and scuttled back to the safety of her bed.

The next morning, her mother dropped off a letter that had arrived for her.

The single piece of notebook paper said he still loved her and would never forget the times they spent together, but that he could not give up his vehicle or his job. He did not believe he had to return to the Amish to fall into God's good graces, but that His love would expand his world beyond the confines of tradition.

That was all.

Emma wept. She sobbed out loud in the shower, her tears mingling with the shampoo that ran unheeded down her face. For at least a week, she woke every morning with red swollen eyes and a large purple nose, drank her coffee as her nose burned in the way it does before another onslaught of fresh sorrow.

She missed Matt a hundred times more than she had ever missed Ben. Or Sam King, for that matter. She missed the dark curly hair that smelled of wood and pine trees and wet soil. She wanted those massive arms around her, a promise he would return to the Amish and drive his horse and buggy without looking back.

Would she ever be enough for anyone?

Dear God, what am I supposed to think anymore?

She was horribly tempted to leave the Amish tradition. She even thumbed through the catalogues that came in the mail, still addressed to Anna, all touting their English clothing—the stretch polyester pants in lavender and mint green, the sandals and T-shirts in colorful hues.

What would Matt say if she showed up at his door, dressed in English clothes, her long hair flowing around her shoulders?

Oh, what was this world, anyway? Why did everything have to be so complicated, so out of kilter? She cried into her coffee as she stared blearily out across the unfinished back porch.

This screened-in porch and brick sidewalk deal was dragging on far too long. What were these guys thinking? Already, the red and yellow leaves were being dashed to the ground by a good strong wind, which meant winter was not far behind. She did not want a poorly done concrete job, or bricks that were slapped down in a hurry, to be heaved out by winter's freeze.

She turned to the kitchen table, sat and surveyed her small home with appreciation. Everything about it was so perfect. She was surrounded by objects that she loved—a potted fig tree, a healthy fern in a gray, stonewashed pot, a painting of the sea grass she loved, a blue pottery vase holding a single late-summer black-eyed Susan from the yard.

She had no idea she missed Matt so horribly until all hope had been crushed. Yet she reminded herself that she had never been more joyful than working on this house, never felt more complete than when she was in the middle of dust and dirt and the whine of saws and the dull thump of hammers.

Suddenly, it occurred to her that perhaps she could put to use all these skills she had acquired and make a living by it. She didn't need to make money anytime soon, but she needed a purpose, and perhaps this was it.

CHAPTER 22

A YEAR PASSED AND SHE PURCHASED A SMALL CAPE COD–STYLE FIXER-upper with swaths of shingles torn loose by years of blustering winds, shutters in disrepair, a rusted mini-van in the backyard, and trails of rodents and feral cats along the perimeter. There were broken windows, screens that hung in shreds, busted walls and a kitchen blackened with grease.

She employed her two brothers, Steven and Abram, and together they started their journey as house flippers. They shouldered their way into the front door and took stock of the situation, disappearing down to the cellar, knocking around on the floor joists and talking loud and fast. Energy flowed as they took the stairs two at a time, walked around the tiny rooms discussing insulation, flooring, outlets.

Once they had a plan, Emma worked side by side with them, caulking, painting, cutting siding, learning how to wield a hammer with the proper swing. Since the house was situated only a half-mile away, she rode her scooter over every day, a Thermos of ice water in the basket.

She became quite attached to her brothers and Dena, who was quick to offer her assistance, which meant a day away from the vegetable fields. The time spent with her younger siblings helped her to accept the loss of Matt, who had now largely faded back in time with Ben and Sam. At least until Dena had her first date, which was cause for joyous celebration from most of the family all week long. But Emma found herself saying cutting remarks she regretted later.

At one point Dena growled, "Stupid old grouch."

"Well, you can't let that white smear of paint dry on the off-white wall. Get that wet rag."

"If you don't like the way I paint, do it yourself," Dena yelled, throwing down the brush, and stalking off.

Emma fumed, wiped the offending paint off the wall, and burst into tears of frustration. Nothing was going as planned, the drywaller having been delayed two weeks, the ancient varnish on the plank floors gumming up the sander belt until everyone had to admit the floors had to be painted or covered with vinyl. Emma said she absolutely would not allow carpet.

She was happy for Dena, wasn't she?

But she fought jealousy all week. Here she was, thirty years old in a few months, with lines appearing around her eyes and mouth, her hair less luxuriant, aging in recognizable spurts that seemed to seal her fate.

Dena was outwardly disobedient, hopelessly fancy as far as her Amish sense of conservation went. She owned dresses in colors and fabrics that Emma would never have been allowed in her closet, and here Dena was parading around the kitchen for her younger sisters to see, with Mam turning a blind eye and Dat with his nose in the *Botschaft*. Her shoes were simply unbelievable. An array of white, orange, pink, and blue. How many pairs of shoes could she even wear?

If Emma complained, her mother set her straight by saying they had to take care of Dena, she was a rebel and could not be confronted with the same stringent rules that worked for the boys. If they lost the love and respect between them, all was lost.

Emma justified her grumpiness as she worked side by side with Dena, made attempts at small talk which fell flat, and finally accepted the stony silence as a boomerang of her own making.

But there were good days with Dena. Days when Emma listened for hours on end to Dena's descriptions of her boyfriend, dizzying accounts of the whirlwind weekends racing around in their horses and buggies, the carefree inhibitions of being sixteen years old.

One day Dena spoke up out of the blue. "Why don't you date Elmer Zook? He's not half bad."

They were seated at the white folding table, eating bologna and lettuce sandwiches, a bag of chips on the bench between them. They had been finishing the doors of the kitchen cabinets, one of the last tasks to be completed before Steven would assemble them and cleanup could begin.

"You want to ask him if he'll agree to go out with me?" Emma said, her voice sarcastic and full of weariness.

Dena looked at her. She saw that Emma's eyes contained a deep inner sadness that was staggering. She looked away. "I see what you mean. Amish girls don't go around asking guys out, do they?"

Emma shook her head, gave a short laugh.

"I'd be labeled as desperate, and there goes any chance that might have been lingering somewhere."

"Absolutely," Dena said, nodding her head. "But who knows? I could pull a few strings, put a bug in a few ears."

And that's exactly what Dena set out to do.

Young, popular, already dating, everyone loved Dena, and Dena loved everyone else. She made a perfect matchmaker.

Meanwhile, Emma went on her way, working long days toward the completion of the now-charming house. It was truly a stunner, with white siding and the original wooden shutters painted a perfect shade of gray, the brick walkway pressure washed and adorned with hydrangea and roses, clusters of boxwood and daylilies. They painted the front door a rich shade of green, put urns on each side and filled them with caladium.

The real estate sign was put in the front yard and cars began to creep past, curious onlookers pressing their faces to windows.

When the cold winds blew down off the ridge, the realtor had so many showings, he called Emma about possibly raising the price.

She had kept a careful account of all the expenses, the hours of labor she had paid out, so she knew she was well ahead of all the money she had invested. She didn't feel right raising the price. "Let's let some young couple have it," she said. "No sense sinking them into deep debt."

So the deal was done, leaving Emma with a tidy profit, even after giving her brothers and Dena extra money beyond the wages for the hours they had put in.

And then they went on to the next house, a derelict old brick rancher that sat in the woods about five miles to the east of Emma's house, over along Pottstown Road. Emma's first thought at the sight of it was the fact that it looked ashamed of itself, the junk and the weeds and the rusted cars like a giant "keep away" sign. She pitied the house, which was an emotion so silly she'd never tell anyone. The house was in foreclosure, so she was able to purchase it for a song, she told the boys.

She never gave away the price, or the amount of profit, knowing the family's tendency to give their opinions, wanted or not. It was simply so much easier to keep things to herself.

It was a cold dark evening in December when Elmer Zook walked up to her front door and placed a well-directed knock on the side of it, stepped back, rocked on his heels and waited. When there was no sound, he repeated the maneuver before stepping back.

Now he heard the sound of footsteps, saw a face appear in a small window, and then the latch was turned.

"Good evening, Emma."

"Elmer? What are you doing here?"

"Actually, I'm not sure."

They both laughed, a pleasant, if nervous sound.

"Well, come in, it's cold outside."

She stepped back, opening the door wider, allowing him room to enter. He was tall, with brown hair cut in the style of the Amish, his cheeks flushed with the cold, his brown eyes curious, alert, like a well-trained dog, Emma thought.

"You have a very nice place here."

"Why thank you. I appreciate that. We put a lot of work into it."

"I heard. You did another house, right?"

Suddenly she remembered. Dena! She hadn't thought she was serious. She felt her face flushing, felt the heat suffuse her cheeks before she could turn away.

"Yes, yes. We did. My two brothers and I, and Dena."

"Looks like they know what they're doing."

"You mean . . . ?" She spread an arm to show the interior.

"All of it."

"Oh, well, it was me," she laughed. "I designed the inside. Actually, I picked the colors for the outside, too. And for the house we just flipped, I did a lot of the work."

She didn't want to boast, but she wasn't about to let her brothers get all the credit for her hard work.

He smiled. He shifted his weight from one foot to the other, then cleared his throat.

"So, the reason I came over . . . I would like to ask you to the contractor's Christmas banquet. I work for Keystone Structures and thought perhaps you'd enjoy it."

Emma smiled. "You're supposed to bring a girl, right? If you can find one, that is."

He smiled back. "Yeah. Sort of like that."

"Okay. I'll go with you. Am I there for decoration, or for business purposes? I don't really need a new contractor—my brothers and I make a good team."

She sounded ruder than she intended.

"I thought we might enjoy each other's company," he said, without a trace of defensiveness.

"Thank you," she said, more humbly.

"Six o'clock? Friday night the eighteenth."

"I'll be ready."

"Sounds good. Have a good night."

"You, too."

She closed the door gently, sagged against it, blew out a long, slow breath. She knew it was all Dena's work, but whatever. It might be fun to go. But she had no heart to make another attempt at romance. Elmer was nice enough, and at this point the fact that he was five years her junior didn't seem like such a big deal. Somehow, the older you got, the less age seemed to matter. Within reason.

Her sisters planned a day of cookie baking at Ruth's house, so it was off to the home place to pick up her mother and Dena. The hired driver showed a lack of interest in anything Emma tried to say to him.

"Where to?" were the only words out of his mouth, the unloading of the van left entirely to themselves, the hearty thank you's received with a grunt.

"I don't know why you called him," Dena complained.

"I couldn't get anybody else. Everyone's busy at Christmas," Emma said.

The sisters were already bustling around Ruth's kitchen, setting out the coffee urn, mugs, an array of breakfast foods.

Esther greeted them warmly, hugged them closely, and fired questions without reserve. Ruth was already flushed, gamely trying to produce a new breakfast quiche, which Dena said was simply a fancy name for eggs slopped into a pie crust, causing Ruth to draw her lips into a firm line before barking some retort in her own defense.

Emma hugged the nieces and nephews, each one so precious, then sat at the table, cradling the six-month-old baby in her arms.

Would she ever have a child of her own? She knew she wanted one, or two or even more, but the possibility of that seemed so remote.

She felt a sickening despair at the thought of next Friday evening. Elmer was a good man—devout, hardworking, safe. He would make someone an excellent husband. But could she make a good wife? Would she be able to love him? These days, she was always telling herself she could accept life as a single girl, especially now that she had her mind and heart occupied with the business of renovating old houses. This was not just a job—it was her new life's purpose.

But when she held a small child—a warm, squirming baby that cooed and smiled and smelled of Johnson's baby lotion and that warm, damp smell all babies were born with—she felt the longing to be a mother as strongly as she ever had.

Her thoughts took on the usual prayer. *Thy will, Lord, not mine. I don't know why my life is so filled with bad luck when it comes to romance, but I will place my trust in Thee.*

"Earth to Emma. Beep-beep-beep," Dena said loudly.

"I'm here. Stop saying that. It makes my toes curl."

"Then stop staring off into space."

Dena looked around to make sure she had everyone's full attention, before announcing the upcoming event with Elmer Zook, then basked in the audible gasps of astonishment, the high fives from both sisters.

"It's perfect. Absolutely perfect," Ruth said, setting down a casserole dish containing the flattest French toast Emma had ever seen.

"Why didn't we ever think of Elmer Zook? They say he owns his own farm already. Milks cows."

Emma thought of herself tying a bandana around her head, slipping her feet into Muck boots that never were completely free of the rancid odor of cow manure. She thought of bawling calves and their wet tongues that were as strong as an arm, slurping at anything they could find, the flies and the runny bowels called scours and the mud and the rain and the sound of dozens of cloven hooves squishing into the slimy smelly mixture of mud and manure.

She squeaked softly, "Does he milk cows?"

"They say he owns his father's farm, so it must be his dad does the milking."

"He must work for this Keystone place, right? Or else he wouldn't be going to a Christmas banquet," Emma said, realizing how desperately she did not want to be a farmer's wife.

"You're right," Ruth said. "Alright, everyone, dig in. There's more coffee brewing, so help yourself."

They dug in, finding solace in the familiarity of sharing breakfast.

"So, do you know how I got Elmer to ask Emma?" Dena asked, looking around to make sure she had everyone's undivided attention.

Her mother's eyes opened wide.

"You mean you had the nerve to set this up?"

"Of course. It was really easy."

"Tell us."

Emma endured the embellished account of Dena sidling up to the uninterested Elmer, opening an intelligent conversation about the ongoing house cleanups and remodeling, followed by an account of her older sister's many professions and lack of ability at procuring a husband.

Mama shook her head, closed her eyes and put both hands over them. Ruth was shocked into a shriek of disbelief, and even the sweet tempered Esther gazed at her openmouthed.

"Sure I did. He's a nice guy. Sort of flat and boring, but I figure Emma will get a few sparks out of him. He likes me. He gets a kick out of me. I asked him if maybe he had something special going on over Christmas, something he could invite Emma to."

More shrieks from Ruth and Esther, followed by Mam's deadpan, "You did not."

"Why not? Emma obviously needs some help."

Emma groaned and then laughed. "Well, at any rate, he did show up at my door. He was very polite. I'm sure he's a very nice, decent man."

"You've had enough of the other kind and it didn't work out," Ruth said.

Why did that statement bring out such rebellion? She defended herself with quick words of denial that fell hard, destroying the gentle air of camaraderie between them, leaving everyone to turn to the children to divert attention from the urge to fight back.

But after a second round of coffee, the tension was soon forgotten and the hour spent around the kitchen table rolled on seamlessly, albeit leaving Emma in an unsettled state of self-doubt.

After the dishes were washed, mixing bowls and measuring cups and bags of flour appeared on the table, chilled cookie dough came out of the fridge, and each person was assigned their own duty as cookie baking began in earnest. Candles sputtered on the windowsills, but there was no snow, only the grayish brown hue of depleted vegetation and the stark outline of trees that appeared naked, shed themselves of all their leaves.

Emma was unwrapping Dove chocolates, ready to imprint them on the top of peanut butter cookies, the dough having been prepared and chilled the day before.

"Why Dove chocolates? They're expensive. Why not use Hershey's Kisses?"

"You can stack the cookies."

"Is that right?"

"Yup."

"They don't look Christmassy, though."

"Sure they do."

The conversation swirled around the kitchen, a good-humored flavoring of many different views and opinions, freely released, freely taken and regarded.

Whoever had heard of putting dried cranberries and vanilla chips in one cookie, asked Dena? Gross. Walnuts were just the clincher. No one was ever going to convince her that walnuts were made for human beings to consume.

Esther quietly spread the brown-butter frosting on the cranberry cookies and handed one over. Dena bit into it and pronounced it the best thing ever.

When talk circled around to Elmer Zook again, Emma spoke honestly about her misgivings, saying no one could blame her, she'd been through enough heartache.

"He's nice enough. It's just that part of me is afraid to try again. And part of me is still expecting that phone call from Matt."

"What? Don't you ever give up?" Dena exploded.

"Of course I do."

"I may be younger, but I'm wiser. It ain't gonna happen, Emma. Get over it. He's English now. Why would you ever give up your car for a horse and buggy? I certainly wouldn't."

Which of course brought the desired results, everyone laughing and shaking their heads at Dena's well-seasoned threats that seemed harmless enough at this stage.

"I think this Elmer is the one. I really do." Esther said.

Mam nodded in agreement, adding the fact that he seemed so conservative, so settled and steady in his beliefs.

"Someday, Emma, you will thank God for a husband who is dedicated to the church, strong in the support of our Amish traditions."

"My word. Mam, we haven't even gone on our first date, and it's not really a date. He simply needed a girl to take to the Christmas dinner."

"But it will work out. I just have a good feeling about it this time."

These were the words Emma remembered as she drifted into a dreamless sleep that night.

She sewed a new dress that week out of bright cranberry-red material that brought a humming to her throat as she worked. It was, after all, the Christmas season, her favorite time of the year, so perhaps that in itself was an omen.

Would Elmer Zook be God's gift to her? Oh, she hoped so. She hoped he would find her attractive, hoped she could fall in love with him. Misgivings fled as she worked, left in an aura of renewed hope and the energy and will for a new start.

She would bury the memory of Ben and Matt as efficiently as she would bury the self-blame and the self-pity. She would be cleaned by the blood of Jesus, forgiven, the slate wiped clean of any mistakes she had made, known or unknown. The faith in her heart sang along with the sound of her sewing machine, the dress turned out well, and the week flew by in a happy aura of newfound hope in her future. The brothers took notice and teased her about the new boyfriend, which made her smile. Somehow, it felt good to be teased about a man.

In her own sweet home, she made a hot cup of peppermint tea, took a long shower, and snuggled up against the dreary cold night with a fleece blanket, good book, and the now unfailing sense that all was well.

God was in His Heaven. He cared about her life, and she was about to embark on a long and blessed journey of discovery.

CHAPTER 23

WHEN THE FRIDAY NIGHT FINALLY ARRIVED, NOTHING STOOD IN THE WAY OF Emma's anticipation, or the happiness that followed. She felt beautiful in the red dress, pinned the black apron around her waist with confidence, slipped her feet into pretty black slippers and chose her best coat.

When the van pulled up to the small house, Elmer stepped up on the porch to walk her to the vehicle, and her heart was full. He was tall, she noticed, which was a good thing.

The van was filled with other Amish people, some who were good friends, others merely acquaintances from other church districts in Crawford County.

There were good-natured calls that bordered on teasing, which they both met with smiles or laughter, and all too soon were pulling into the parking lot of the banquet facility called "The Beacon."

Elmer stayed with her, following the group into the building.

"I often wondered about this place," Emma commented.

"So tonight you'll find out, right?" Elmer remarked.

"I guess."

She shrugged out of her coat without his assistance, then turned to hang it on a hanger alongside his. She smiled up at him, took a deep breath, and prepared to face the crowd.

He had nice eyes, and a nice smile. His shirt was an electric shade of green, but it didn't look bad on him. Anyway, all that was superficial, vain. This time she would get it right.

They were seated with his coworkers, some married Amish couples, some unmarried young men with bored or shy young women at their sides. Emma found it easy to make small talk with Elmer, liked the way he gave her his full attention.

The owner of Keystone construction spoke a few words, a prayer followed, and directions were given on where to fill their plates. The adjoining room had long rows of steaming tables with heavy ironstone plates stacked on either side, so many different foods all creating a delicious holiday aroma. Emma followed Elmer, pushing back the bit of annoyance that he hadn't allowed her to go first, and retained her sense of optimism, the feeling that all was going to be in her favor, now and forever.

She thought of Elmer and Emma, Two E's, like Eva and Elvin. Another good sign.

She lifted a large stainless steel spoon, dug into the vat of mashed potatoes, and felt a hand at her elbow, a voice in her ear.

"Hello, Emma."

She turned slowly, still gripping the spoon with mashed potatoes, to find none other than Matt Yoder's honey colored eyes much too close to her own.

She opened her mouth, but no sound came out of it. She was covered in chills, as if a wintry blast had kicked the door open. A tingling began in her arms, her hands went lifeless, which resulted in the clattering of spoon and mashed potatoes onto the ceramic floor, followed by the crash of the heavy ironstone plate that broke into dozens of pieces.

She felt the color leave her face, felt sick and weak and dizzy. She endured the gasps and stares, Elmer's concern and kindness, but could not take her eyes away from the gladness in the liquid warm gold of Matt's.

She finally managed to step away, whisper, "I'm sorry."

Elmer stepped in, asked if she was okay. She smiled weakly, nodded her head, apologized for being clumsy. He assured her she was fine, accidents happen, but she hardly heard him. Matt was here, in this same room. He was wearing black trousers with a forest green shirt with black suspenders, his face clean-shaven, the glistening black curls cut neatly.

As she stooped down to pick up the pieces, so did Matt, their heads nearly touching. "I need to talk to you," he whispered, and she nodded. But then Elmer seemed to realize he should be helping too, and effectively shooed Matt away as he grabbed the last pieces of broken plate.

Emma watched Matt move to the opposite side of the room, then filled her plate absentmindedly and returned to her table. "Are you sure you're okay?" Elmer asked again, and she nodded, fighting her emotion bravely, until it simply wasn't possible, then excused herself and fled to the safety of a restroom stall, where she bowed her head and wept silently into a scrunched-up wad of toilet paper. She sobbed sloppily a fresh supply until she shuddered, wiped her eyes, and stopped.

What was this? *What are you doing, Lord? Tormenting me with Matt when he is likely here with his new girl and I am still hopelessly, and yes, irretrievably in love with him?*

Why is he dressed in Amish clothes? Dear God, he told me the sacrifice was too much. I'll accept my past failures, Lord, I'll marry good level-headed Elmer, but please don't punish me with Matt's presence.

I can't take it. I can't take it. I love him even more than I ever have.

She patted her face with paper towels saturated with cold water, applied another light dusting of face powder, steadied herself with deep breathing, hoping no one in the adjoining stalls would hear, then made her way back to the table, feeling as if every pair of eyes were darts that found their way into her pride, effectively reducing it to a limp balloon. She tried to see where Matt had gone, but he seemed to have disappeared.

Somehow, she got through dinner. She ate enough to keep up her manners, made small talk with Elmer, managed to smile.

The owner rose to his feet. Announcements were made. The employee of the year was applauded. Bonuses were handed out. It was announced that Matt Yoder, an employee of fifteen years, would be stepping down from his position as truck driver due to his unusual return to his Amish people, a move highly respected by the company. He would head the new division of hardscaping and decks. Jeff Atkins would be his driver.

Emma sat like stone, her mouth gone dry, her pulse fluttering in her throat. She supposed one could die of shock, couldn't they? She felt an urge to get away, run from the room as fast as possible, but had no strength to carry it out.

The remainder of the evening passed in a painful haze of suppressed emotion, frightened, fluttering hope that was as uncertain and unsafe as a new hatchling. She wavered from joyful anticipation to life depleting despair.

She climbed into the van at the end of it, still searching for Matt. She made a good show of speaking to Elmer, but all the life had gone out of anything she said. When he asked if he could call her she said yes and thanked him for a wonderful evening, but she hardly knew what she was saying.

She made her way up the stone walkway through the bone chilling night, watched a few dead oak leaves skitter across the path of light from the motion lamp on the porch, and shivered. She unlocked the door and let herself in, closing it firmly before locking it again. She flicked on the battery lamp by her recliner and sat heavily in it, letting out a long shaky sigh and dissolving into tears.

Would Matt actually get in touch? He knew where her parents lived. He could find her if he wanted to.

Emma did not see the vehicle following the white van where she sat beside Elmer, neither did she notice anything amiss after she exited and made her way to the porch. She did not see the curly-haired man leave the vehicle that had been following them, or make his way slowly to her front door, raise his great fist to rap quietly.

Emma had just suppressed another ragged sob, wiped her nose and told herself to get a grip, in Dena's colorful language, when she thought she heard a sound.

There it was again.

Someone was knocking on her front door. It was eleven o'clock at night. Should she answer it? She breathed a prayer that God would protect her, turned the lock, and opened the door, her heart in her throat.

"Hello, Emma."

Those words were the sweetest ones, the most welcome ones she'd ever heard. She couldn't speak, merely stepped aside and allowed him to enter. His nearness was almost her undoing, but she gripped her arms to her waist, bent slightly with the weight of her endlessly demanding evening, the willpower and bravery she had brought into play just to get through it.

"Matt."

"Come here, Emma."

"No, no."

She could not raise her eyes to look at him.

"You're seeing someone?"

His voice was thick, desperate.

"No." She shook her head.

"You were with someone. Was he a friend, an acquaintance?"

"He . . ."

Up came her eyes that blazed into his.

"You know what, Matt? I can't do this, okay? You disappear for a year—over a year—you tell me it's too hard to be Amish, and there you are, like some . . . some jerk, expecting me to fall into your arms the minute you're ready for me. Really?"

The harsh words tumbled over each other like jagged pieces of glass as she turned and walked through the door and into the kitchen where she gripped the edge of the countertop with icy fingers, her body shaking like an injured animal. She stared unseeing out of the window, the cold gale battering the brown oak leaves against the panes. "Did you even think of me all that time, or did you suddenly remember me when I showed up at the party with another man? Oh, and then you follow me home like some creep?"

He was close to her now. She smelled the earthy undertones, the scent of moist wood and ferns on a forest floor.

She felt his sigh in her ear.

"It was a test, Emma."

She shrugged off his hands, whirled to face him, anger coursing through every vein in her body now.

"How dare you? What is that even supposed to mean? You didn't tell me anything. You just stopped calling, stopped answering my calls."

His eyes bore into hers now, no longer liquid gold, but a slow burning fire.

"Not a test for you, Emma. For me. I needed to be sure I could be Amish, even without the promise of you in my life."

She was breathing hard, denying the truth of his words. She swallowed, cleared her throat, straightened the edge of the rug with her toe.

"When I wrote and said I couldn't be Amish, I meant it. But then something happened. God started working on my heart. I started to feel the weight of my guilt, a deep desire to make things right with my parents, with God. But I needed to make sure I could really give up my life—the car, the cell phone, the cigarettes, all of it—before I drew you in again. I knew there was a risk that you would marry someone else, but I couldn't risk hurting you like that."

She stared at him a moment, taking it all in. "Don't you think it hurt that you just disappeared like that? How long were you planning to make me wait?"

"I'm sorry," he said, his eyes starting to fill with tears. Tentatively, he took her hand, and she didn't withdraw it. He led her to the sofa, where she sat a safe distance away, her hands folded in her lap, her eyes downcast.

"Emma, I knew you were right, that I couldn't put you in the place of God in my life. That if I was going to come back to my roots, it had to be because I believed it was right, not because I wanted you. I had to let go of you completely. Trust that if God wanted us to be together, that He would make it work."

She got up, away from him, too agitated to speak. She found her post at the kitchen window, her hands gripping her waist.

Then she felt his hands on her shoulders again, his nearness so comforting, yet still her feelings were a jumble of confusion.

Slowly, gently, he turned her, until she rested against him.

"I hate that I hurt you."

She raised her eyes to his. "You did hurt me. A lot. Do you even realize that you broke my heart, just like Ben? No, worse than Ben. You let me believe that I wasn't enough, that your lifestyle was more important than our . . . than our love."

He held her closer still.

"I am so sorry. I love you, Emma."

She stayed in his arms, melting against his chest, her anger slowly draining away. She had said her piece, and now all she wanted, desperately, was to be his forever, to never have to leave his embrace.

"I don't deserve you," he said, quietly now. "But I'll wait as long as it takes. Jacob worked seven years for Rachel, was given Leah, her sister, and went right back and worked seven more years for her again. So I figure fourteen years from now I'll be fifty or fifty-one, and that's not too bad."

Emma laughed outright.

"Seven years and you get Dena."

"Your sister?"

"Exactly."

"No, it's you I want."

She whispered, "You won't have to wait very long. Maybe about ten seconds."

And she drew his face tenderly to her own, the palm of her hand on his stubbled cheek, and found his lips with her own, conveying all her lost hopes and dreams into a blaze of joyful promise. With a groan he crushed her to him, until she felt his tears on her own face.

"I love you, Matt. Please promise me you won't disappear again."

"My dear sweet perfect girl," he whispered.

"I am your girl," she responded with a soft laugh.

He brought her to the sofa again, his eyes never leaving hers, then slowly got down on one knee, held both of her hands in his before he asked her in a voice choked with emotion.

"Emma, will you marry me?"

She lifted her face to the ceiling, her eyes closed as she steadied herself, then met his eyes with the truth of her love.

"I will, Matt. Yes, yes, yes, I will."

They talked almost all night, until he told her he was not going to bother a driver now, why would he? Not one soul knew he was spending the night, and he would return to Lancaster in the morning.

"God knows you're here."

"Do you think He minds?" Matt asked.

"Not if you sleep on the couch."

That was a bold statement, coming from her, and she became flustered, the blush spreading across her face.

Matt shook his head. "I can't believe this. It's almost as if I, you know, could wake up and it wouldn't be real."

"I know exactly how you feel. We've both been through a lot. But every cloud has a silver lining, which you definitely are."

"You didn't like me at all, remember? That trip with Elvin and Eva?"

"I liked you for yourself. I was simply not over Ben."

"He is one unlucky dude by now, I bet. Messing with someone's wife is a real fast ticket to misery."

"You have done that?"

"No. I never have. But I've seen it more than once."

"Matt, I love you so much. God sure had a strange way of bringing us together, but looking back, I can see how one thing led to another. Are you sure, Matt? You're sure you're not going to change your mind in the morning, disappear, decide to go English again?"

"Emma, my love, I am surer than sure. I have loved you for a long time—since that camping trip. But now I'm ready to be a good husband for you, a father even, if God allows. Nothing could change my mind."

When did the snow start?

Sometime during the night when the conversation was serious, soft flakes fell from leaden skies, turned the lonely landscape into one visited by fairies, the wonder of each flake incorporated into another to form a solid landscape washed spotlessly clean.

Matt loved the house, loved what she'd done with it. He was amazed at her story, the inheritance, the houses they renovated.

Yes, he would love to help as a side job, but his heart was with Keystone. And yes, he would move to Crawford County. Her home would be his home, and he'd be honored to live here.

The wedding would be in April they agreed.

She cooked a big breakfast, and he said he felt like the happiest man in the world at that specific moment, setting the table for two with a quiet reverence that gave away the sincerity of his gratitude.

Let people say what they may, she had faith in him. His heart was in the right place and their future stretched before them like a winding road glistening with the glow of God's love.

EPILOGUE

D ENA WAS NOT IMPRESSED WITH THE NEWS OF MATT'S RETURN, TELLING Emma that she was hopeless, that she didn't know what was good for her. And after all she did to set her up with the perfectly good Elmer, too. Ruth and Esther and Mam were equally shocked, but Dat reminded them that Emma was a grown woman and could make her own decisions. And after Matt visited a few times, they were all charmed by the way he respected Emma, listened to her opinions, supported her business flipping houses. Her brothers were impressed with how he handled a horse and buggy after all those years of driving a car. He told Dena that all the draws of the world didn't hold a candle to the love and security of a good relationship with your parents, which made Mam practically glow with respect for him.

Elmer took it hard at first, but soon after he asked Annie Riehl, and after that they never left each other's side.

The wedding was held on a warm spring day, with Eva and Elvin sitting at the table of honor with Emma and Matt. Eva was glowing, a third baby on the way, and couldn't have been more thrilled to see her dear friend marrying her favorite cousin.

Emma sat with Matt at her side, the sun on her shoulders, her friends and family all around. She thought of all the heartache, all the false starts, all the times she questioned what God was doing in her life. And here she was, her heart bursting with love, her beloved at her side. Matt seemed to read her thoughts and reached over to hold her hand beneath the table. She squeezed his strong fingers, a thrill of joy rushing through her whole being.

There would still be hard times, she knew. Life was never easy for long. But she had never been so sure of God's goodness, of His love, and that whatever trials she faced, she would have her faith, her family, and her beloved to see her through.

The End.

GLOSSARY

Allus schtruvvlich—all askew

Ach my, hesslich.—Oh my, that's too bad.

Botschaft—Amish newspaper

Dichly—bandana (plural is *dichlin*)

Fettadale—front part of the white head covering

Grosfeelich—proud, high-minded

Hesslich—way too

Maud—A single Amish woman hired by Amish couples to help around the house, often when they have just had a new baby.

Müde binn ich—prayer said at bedtime

nāva dale—neighboring district

nāva-hucka—best man

Net so govverich—Don't be unladylike.

Ordnung–Literally, "ordinary," or "discipline." The Amish community's agreed-upon rules for living, based on their understanding of the Bible, particularly the New Testament. The *ordnung* varies some from community to community, often reflecting the leaders' preferences and the local traditions and historical practices.

Rumschpringa–The period when teenagers begin dating. Literally, "running around." A time of relative freedom for adolescents, beginning at about age sixteen. The period ends when a youth is baptized and joins the church, after which the youth can marry.

Schmear kase–cheese spread

Schpeck–fat

Schtrale–a fine-toothed comb

Schrina truck–a construction vehicle

Unfadient gelt–unearned money

Verboten–forbidden

Visa tay–meadow tea

ABOUT THE AUTHOR

LINDA BYLER WAS RAISED IN AN AMISH FAMILY AND IS AN ACTIVE MEMBER OF the Amish church today. Growing up, Linda loved to read and write. In fact, she still does. Linda is well known within the Amish community as a columnist for a weekly Amish newspaper. She writes all her novels by hand in notebooks.

Linda is the author of several series of novels, all set among the Amish communities of North America: Lizzie Searches for Love, Sadie's Montana, Lancaster Burning, Hester's Hunt for Home, the Dakota Series, and the Buggy Spoke Series for younger readers. She also wrote *The Healing* and *A Second Chance*, as well as several Christmas romances set among the Amish: *Mary's Christmas Goodbye*, *The Christmas Visitor*, *The Little Amish Matchmaker*, *Becky Meets Her Match*, *A Dog for Christmas*, *A Horse for Elsie*, and *The More the Merrier*. Linda has coauthored *Lizzie's Amish Cookbook: Favorite Recipes from Three Generations of Amish Cooks!*

OTHER BOOKS BY
LINDA BYLER

LIZZIE SEARCHES FOR LOVE SERIES

BOOK ONE   BOOK TWO   BOOK THREE

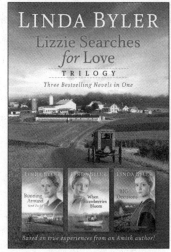

TRILOGY   COOKBOOK

SADIE'S MONTANA SERIES

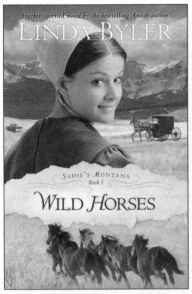

BOOK ONE

BOOK TWO

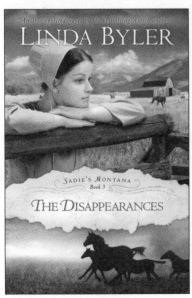

BOOK THREE

TRILOGY

LANCASTER BURNING SERIES

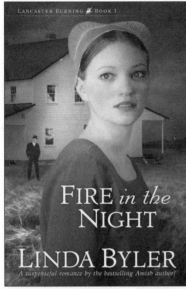

BOOK ONE

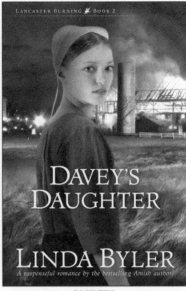

BOOK TWO

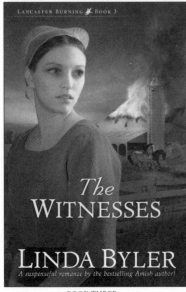

BOOK THREE

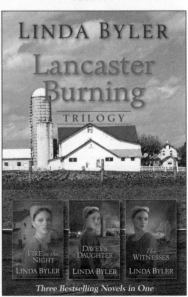

TRILOGY

HESTER'S HUNT FOR HOME SERIES

BOOK ONE

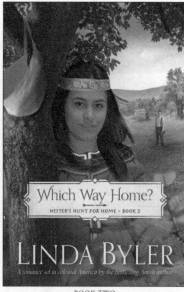

BOOK TWO

BOOK THREE

TRILOGY

THE DAKOTA SERIES

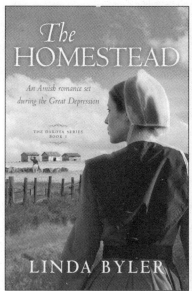

BOOK ONE

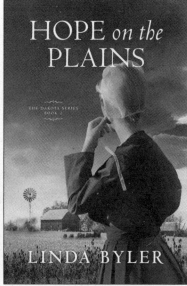

BOOK TWO

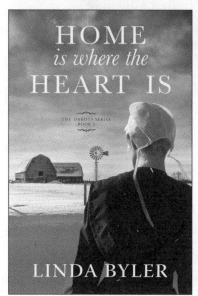

BOOK THREE

TRILOGY

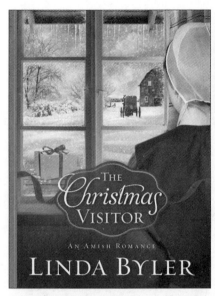

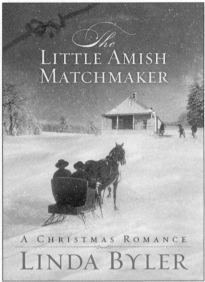

A Dog for
CHRISTMAS

An Amish Christmas Romance

LINDA BYLER

A Horse For
ELSIE

An Amish Christmas Romance

LINDA BYLER

LINDA BYLER

The More
the Merrier

An Amish Christmas Romance

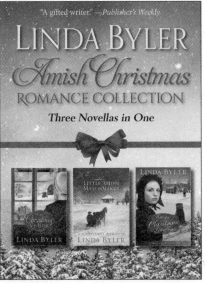

"A gifted writer." —Publisher's Weekly

LINDA BYLER
Amish Christmas
ROMANCE COLLECTION

Three Novellas in One

New Releases

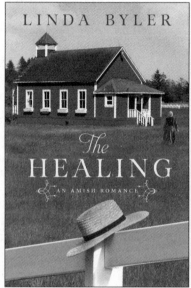

THE HEALING

A SECOND CHANCE

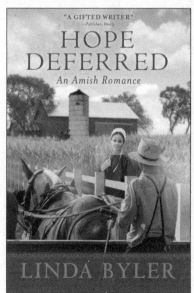

HOPE DEFERRED

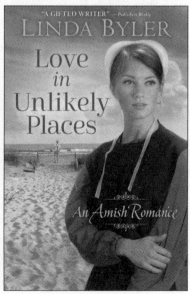

LOVE IN UNLIKELY PLACES